What the hell *was he doing?*

How could he even think of kissing Zoe Zagretti, and in the m̶i̶d̶d̶l̶e̶ ̶o̶f̶ ̶a̶n̶ ̶a̶c̶c̶ident site? No̶t̶h̶i̶n̶g̶ ̶w̶o̶u̶l̶d̶ ̶h̶a̶v̶e̶ ̶s̶t̶o̶pped him fro̶m̶ ̶d̶o̶i̶n̶g̶ ̶i̶t̶.̶ ̶H̶e̶ ̶n̶e̶e̶d̶e̶d̶ ̶a̶ long cold show̶e̶r̶ ̶a̶n̶d̶ ̶t̶o̶ ̶g̶e̶t̶ ̶h̶i̶s̶ ̶w̶ords stuck in h̶i̶s̶ ̶t̶h̶r̶o̶a̶t̶.̶

She nodde̶d̶,̶ ̶h̶e̶r̶ face thoughtful. "Because it was unprofessional conduct, or because you lost your nerve?"

He hadn't lost his nerve since he was fourteen. Until now. "It would be a conflict of interest."

She nodded. "I see. You're conflicted about your interest." She stepped away, putting much-needed distance between them. "I agree, this isn't the time or the place. But later, when you're ready, let me know, okay?"

He was sorely afraid he'd end up doing exactly that. He'd faced armed robbers, survived firefights, been trapped in a raging inferno. But this woman shook him to the core.

What other incurable cravings would he catch when he finally gave in and kissed her?

Available in March 2006 from Silhouette Sensation

Truth or Consequences

DIANA DUNCAN

*First published in Great Britain 2006
Silhouette Books, Eton House, 18-24 Paradise Road,
Richmond, Surrey TW9 1SR*

© Diana Ball 2005

ISBN 0 373 27443 2

18-0306

*Printed and bound in Spain
by Litografía Rosés S.A., Barcelona*

DIANA DUNCAN

Diana Duncan's fascination with books started before she could walk, when her librarian grandmother toted her to work. Diana crafted her first tale at age four, a riveting account of Perky the Kitten, printed in orange crayon. The discovery of her mum's Harlequin Romance novels at age fourteen sparked a lifelong affection for plucky heroines and dashing heroes. She loves writing about complex, conflicted men and strong, intelligent women with the courage to dive into the biggest adventure of all—falling in love.

When not writing stories brimming with heart, humour and sizzling passion, Diana spends her time with her husband, two daughters and two cats in their Portland, Oregon, home. Diana loves to hear from her readers. She can be reached via e-mail at writedianaduncan@msn.com or snail mail at PO Box 33193, Portland, OR 97292-3193, USA.

Char, you invited me into the condos and changed my life! Jubie, hon, thanks for your dedication and hard work. Without your gorgeous contributions, I wouldn't make it through some days with my sanity intact.

To our Beautiful Bad Boy, mere words don't do the job. If not for your constant inspiration, I wouldn't be where I am today. Many blessings, and wishes for success and happiness.

Thanks bunches to each and every one of my TAG Sisters for your encouragement, support and friendship over the years. You girls taught me the important basics of drool buckets and bibs.

Bundle up, girlfriends. This one's for you. ;)

Prologue

When you are pushed to the edge, you will either find something solid to stand on, or you will learn how to fly.
                                                                    —Old Adage

Riverside, Oregon, SWAT rear guard Aidan O'Rourke crushed the impatience nagging at his heels as he coordinated the tactical operation forming in Riverside Mall's parking lot. He was too busy to think. Too focused on the job to feel. At least, that's what he kept telling himself. Maybe, eventually, he'd believe it.

Hell, he shouldn't have any problem. Incarcerating his emotions in a steel cage was his MO for getting through life.

Sleet stung his face, but he ignored the rotten weather, just as he ignored dread's smothering weight on his chest. Normally, he guarded the team's back. But unless Captain Greene arrived, which didn't look promising, Aidan was high-ranking officer. Team leader and incident commander by default.

All the other members of Alpha Squad had answered the call-out, except his younger brother Conall, the team's door-kicker. Con was trapped inside the mall with a crew of bank robbers. Unarmed and defenseless.

Con's fiancée, Bailey, was trapped along with him. The robbers held three additional hostages—the bank manager, a pregnant woman and the O'Rourkes' eighty-year-old neighbor, Letty Jacobson.

Aidan had played with, worked with and fought shoulder-to-shoulder beside Con. He admired and respected his brother.

He also loved him—with bone-deep, fierce and abiding loyalty. Closest in age among the four siblings, he and Con had forged a nearly inseparable bond since birth. The O'Rourke brothers shared not only the calling to be SWAT cops, but also a connection of the heart that grew stronger by the day. No criminals would steal that from him. Nine years ago, Aidan had become head of the family when his father had been killed, a victim of senseless violence. One wrenching loss was enough. He'd vowed to protect his loved ones at any cost. He *would* get his brother out alive.

As he prepared to head across the street, his shoulders stiffened in rebellion, his warrior's instincts outraged at leaving the combat zone. He forced himself to move. He had to go. Had to establish the command post. Stick to procedure. Don't let emotions interfere. Bring everybody home breathing.

Blinding light stabbed his peripheral vision, and he pivoted. What the—?

A TV news crew had encamped in the rear of the parking lot, setting up cameras and floodlights around a white van. The lights illuminated Aidan, the team and the mall. A slick blond male reporter sporting a salon tan postured in front of the cameras, emoting dramatically into a cordless mike.

"Who the hell let civilians leak into the inner perimeter?" Aidan roared. "Tighten up that line! Not even a freaking gnat gets through unless he's packing a badge and a weapon!"

An abashed chorus of "Yes, sirs" swelled in the frosty air.

Swearing, Aidan stalked toward the van. "Kill those lights!"

A petite woman with short, wispy brunette hair stepped in front of him. Dressed for the turbulent weather in a well-worn purple parka, red scarf and matching gloves, she planted both palms on his Kevlar vest, jerking him to an abrupt stop. "That's Parker Dane, the award-winning anchorman."

Aidan glanced down into intelligent hazel eyes and deliciously feminine, almost feline features. The jolt to his senses, the kick of heat in his belly was anger, nothing more. "I don't care if he's the Pope, in town to bless the masses. Kill those damn lights, they're compromising my operation."

The exotic-looking brunette dropped her hands. Colorful beaded earrings swung as she waved at a stocky guy standing beside the van. "Douse the lights while Parker rehearses." She turned back to Aidan. "And you are?"

"Officer Aidan O'Rourke, acting SWAT Incident Commander."

Her gaze, a fascinating, changing combination of green, brown and gold, traveled the length of his body from tousled, wet hair to scuffed combat boots, then back. Unwelcome, uninvited warmth flooded his bloodstream, and he clenched his jaw. "You're in a secured area. Clear out."

She tilted her head. The icy wind tumbled shiny chestnut curls around her face like a halo. Talk about blatantly deceptive packaging. Her spicy tropical fragrance seemed incongruous in the dangerous winter night as she grinned up at him. "What does SWAT stand for? Sure, we are tempting?"

Like a numb limb with circulation suddenly restored, long-dead, disturbing feelings tingled painfully to life. A distraction he didn't need, and sure as hell didn't want. "I don't have time for games—"

"I'm Zoe." She interrupted him, a rare occurrence. His fierce concentration and alpha-wolf attitude intimidated most people. Apparently, it didn't impress the little gypsy, because she didn't budge an inch. "Zoe Zagretti, with KKEY, your key to breaking news. See it happen as it happens. I'm Parker's fact checker."

"I'll just bet you are." His libido was lusting after a *reporter,* for crying out loud. Perky harbingers of doom. Peddlers of destruction and death. Vultures, pimping people's anguish for the ratings god. Been there, done that, had bitter, painful scars on his soul. He'd rather suck face with a scorpion. He drilled her with a lethal stare that had made hardened felons cower. "You're endangering my officers and the hostages. Leave. Now."

Apparently also immune to the death stare, she whipped a notepad and pen from inside a battered canvas bag. "You can confirm there are hostages? How many? Who's holding them?"

Widening his stance, he stepped closer, aggressively invading her space. "I'm going to say this once. Pack your stuff, clamp a leash on your pet monkey and bug out."

She didn't so much as blink. "This is an opportunity to provide information to our viewers, and we have an obligation to take that opportunity. Any good news organization would do the same." She jutted her small pointed chin in a challenging angle. "The public has a right to know the truth."

Frustration burned in his gut. He was used to being obeyed without question. "The public has a right to safety. And protection from piranhas who rip personal tragedies apart on live satellite feed and feast on the bloody pieces. If one person, one item of equipment, is still on the premises in two minutes, I will personally place you all under arrest."

Her pretty red lips parted in a shocked gasp. "For what?"

"For starters, interfering with an officer in the line of duty."

"You wouldn't dare! The freedom of the press is a guaranteed constitutional—"

"Try me. You'll be on your way to jail before you can say 'yellow journalism.'" He flicked a glance at his watch. "One minute and forty seconds."

Not waiting for her reply, he swung around and strode away.

That's when everything went to hell.

Two four-wheel-drive SUVs careened around the corner of the mall, chained tires sparking on the ice. Gunshots exploded and bullets screamed overhead. Running, shouting police officers dove for cover and returned fire.

Adrenaline blasted through Aidan's veins, and his body moved before his brain fully registered the urgency. He whirled and lunged at Zoe, taking them both down in one leap. Cushioning her head in his hand, he rolled on the frozen pavement, absorbing most of the blow, and then rolled again, pinning her small body beneath him.

She didn't make a sound, didn't move as he snatched his Glock from his thigh holster and fired at the retreating SUVs. Dammit, the target was too far away, moving too fast. Sirens shrieked and lights flashed as police cars chased the SUVs into the storm.

Aidan sucked in a deep breath and holstered his weapon. He rolled to one side, and scooped the woman from underneath him. "Are you all right?"

Her small body limp, her face bleached by death, Zoe stared sightlessly up at the swirling sleet. Aidan's heart stopped, frozen with anguish. He'd let her down.

He'd let her die.

Chapter 1

"**Z**oe!" Aidan woke shouting her name. Panting, he sat up and blinked away the sweat stinging his eyes. He was no longer in that dark parking lot. He was in his bedroom. He glanced at the peaceful, sun-dappled mocha walls, and then studied the digital clock on the nightstand. It wasn't a cold December night, but a warm summer morning.

He exhaled a shaky breath. The mall incident had happened six months ago. When would the nightmares stop?

He scrubbed an unsteady hand over his bristly jaw. More importantly, why did his subconscious keep replaying it *wrong?*

He always dreamed everything exactly as it had happened, in sharply focused detail. The mall's bank had been robbed, his brother trapped inside for hours. The wheelmen outside had started a firefight and escaped. But nobody had died. Not his brother or his brother's fiancée, not the hostages, not even the bank robbers.

And especially not Zoe Zagretti. Since that fateful December night, Zoe and Aidan had continually crossed paths and crossed swords. Like a bad case of heartburn he couldn't relieve, the rabid reporter appeared at his crime scenes, poking her pert nose where it wasn't wanted and yammering questions he refused to answer. He'd swear she was tailing him.

Even worse, she turned up at least once a week in his bed—in his dreams. He climbed out from between navy-blue sheets and twitched the matching comforter into place.

Make that nightmares.

Naked, he strode into the bathroom. He cranked on the shower, and steam curled around him. The faint scent of plumeria lingered in the mist. Zoe's inquisitive, heart-shaped face instantly shimmered into his mind, and his body tightened on a surge of desire. Swearing, he snatched a purple candle off the counter, tempted to toss it in the garbage. Letty Jacobson, his family's irascible octogenarian neighbor, had given it to him for Christmas. While it seemed an odd choice for a bachelor's neutral-toned bathroom, he'd been touched by the gaily-wrapped gift, presented with generous delight, and put it on display.

He set the candle down, unable to bring himself to trash it. The smell appealed to him. The sultry, tropical fragrance reminded him of a trip to Hawaii—their last family vacation before Pop had been killed. The bright flower leis inherent to the islands were made from plumeria. Letty had mentioned fond memories when she'd bestowed the gift.

He scowled. The scent *used* to appeal to him, before it became associated with a certain sassy, pain-in-the-butt brunette. How could he be so exasperated and so attracted at the same time?

He stepped inside the shower enclosure. The shiny green/brown/gold stone tiles were the same shade as Zoe's eyes. Aidan groaned and banged his forehead quietly on the wet stone.

Exotic and sensual, with her bewitching, ever-changing eyes and lush red mouth, Zoe was not anywhere near his usual type. He preferred elegant, reserved blondes. Passionate, stubborn, rash women, on the other hand…no thanks. He shuddered and reached for the shampoo. Strong emotions were baffling. Crippling.

Caused way too much misery.

He'd never met a woman he wanted to risk everything for, or a woman who would risk everything for him. He liked amiable, level relationships maintained at a comfortable emotional distance. There might not be any mountaintops, but there was also no danger of hurtling over unexpected cliffs. As a career SWAT cop who dove into combat all too often, he had no desire to marry. In fact, several years ago when his grandmother's antique Claddagh wedding ring was bequeathed to him per O'Rourke tradition, he'd refused it.

His brothers still held out hope he'd change his mind and refused to usurp his bequest. So, the ring would remain safely with his mom until one of his brothers had a son. No way would Aidan put a woman through the hell his mother had suffered. No way would he subject a family to the anguish he and his brothers had experienced.

He stuck his sudsy hair under the hot spray. So, why couldn't he wash Zoe Zagretti out of his head? Out of his *life?*

Was she some sort of gypsy sorceress? After he'd refused to satisfy her chronic nosiness, had she cast a spell on him?

That idea was as batty as Letty's romantic notions about soul mates. Aidan snorted and reached for the soap. No freaking way. He didn't believe in woo-woo.

He grabbed a washcloth and vigorously scrubbed his chest. He knew what, or rather, who, was driving him around the bend, and his nemesis had a definite earthly origin. Things could not continue this way. So, what was he gonna do about it?

About *her?*

Dressed in her short yellow-and-orange paisley robe, Zoe opened the front door of her tiny studio apartment and a huge black-and-brown-striped tabby with one ragged ear streaked inside. "Morning Evander. How's tricks?"

The cat trotted toward what the landlord had optimistically called the kitchenette and grumbled the feline equivalent of "Where's breakfast?"

Zoe poured food into his dish and smiled as he scarfed it down. The fractious feline had appeared on her doorstep one morning, battered and bloody, and she'd adopted him. Her bond with Evander was her first relationship that had ever lasted more than a few weeks. Moving three to five times a year hadn't allowed for friendships, even if she'd dared. Loneliness and suspicion had been constant, uneasy companions as far back as she could remember. The one close person in her life, her mom, languished in a hospital in San Francisco, partially paralyzed and mentally disoriented by a stroke. Zoe diligently squeezed every nickel—twice—to maintain Rita Zagretti's physical therapy, while saving toward the huge sum needed to move her north. Add in tuition loans and her own moving expenses, and she barely made ends meet. So what if she had to skimp on groceries? Thanks to Hollywood, thin was in.

She strolled into the bathroom and turned on the water in the small stall shower. The apartment didn't boast a tub, something she missed terribly. But as long as she could scrape up the rent, the shabby studio in an aging neighborhood was all hers. No odd phone call, no chance sighting on the street would send her racing to pack and fleeing in terror to a new city. No matter what happened, she would stand her ground.

She would never run again.

Zoe stepped into the steamy stall. On a sunny Saturday morning, she could relax under the hot spray until the water went cold, a favorite indulgence. Someday, she would have a family and a cozy house with a luxurious whirlpool tub. Someday, she would have a husband to cherish, a man who would cherish her in return. And a passel of rowdy kids who would experience the secure, carefree childhood she'd lacked.

Someday, she would belong.

She wasn't quite sure how, since she'd never had the privilege. She'd been a child born of secrets and lies. Her past had imprisoned her in loathing, fear and isolation. Evander was her very first pet. Her very first friend.

She lathered her skin with body wash. She was a fast learner, though. You tended to learn fast when you were different. When you didn't dare bring a classmate home. She remembered watching giggling girls at various schools. Best friends, their arms around one another, planning sleepovers and sharing secrets. She'd longed to join in, but circumstances had forced her to remain at a distance. Though gregarious and outgoing, she'd always had to stifle her true nature. She never dared get close to anyone. Never dared invite anyone over.

Her secrets were too risky, too horrifying to confide.

With Evander, she could finally relax. Speak freely. No wariness about ulterior motives. No safeguarding every word. No worry about an accidental, terrifying slip of the tongue.

The fickle water supply suddenly went ice-cold. She barely had time to gasp before it surged back to hot. She and Evander were both wandering mongrels. He'd found someone to take him in. Would she? If she did, would she be able to set aside twenty-six years of conditioning and share herself with another person? She knew what it was like to be truly, completely on her own. A relationship would require an element of trust she'd never been allowed to explore.

After too many years alone, she craved the opportunity.

She leaned against the misty shower wall, closed her eyes and let the drumming water soothe her. As they had too often lately, her thoughts wandered to Officer Aidan O'Rourke. With his thick, wavy black hair, melted-caramel eyes and sinfully sensual lips, Mr. Tall-Dark-and-Bossy was the poster boy for bodacious hunks. Not to mention his ruggedly handsome face, hard-muscled physique and reflexes as fast and deadly as a timber wolf.

But what intrigued her most was his chivalry. Though he'd been livid with her that December night in the parking lot, her Dark Champion had unhesitatingly put his body between her and flying bullets. Then there was the emotional pain swirling in his wounded brown eyes, the quiet suffering bracketing his stubborn mouth. Reading back issues of the local paper—something she always did in a new town to learn the history—had revealed the reason. Several dates with Marvin, the geeky clerk in the Riverside PD records room, had filled in the gaps. And her heart had broken for Aidan.

Too soon, the water cooled. She stepped onto the turquoise-flowered bathmat and wrapped herself in a matching towel. Nine years ago, over half a million dollars had gone missing after an armored-car heist. Aidan's father was lead officer at the scene, and blame had fallen on him. The allegations were never proven, but his reputation had been soiled. He was taken off the streets and assigned permanent desk duty.

She blotted droplets from her skin. Before Brian O'Rourke could clear his name, he'd been murdered in a home-invasion robbery. They'd never found his body, but the blood at the site—his own study—was abundant enough for a judge to rule him dead by homicide.

Zoe wiped condensation from the mirror and fluffed her short, feathery curls with her fingers. A few of Brian's fellow police officers speculated that he'd faked the murder and was living it up in a private paradise. Zoe didn't believe the rumors for a second. She studied her somber reflection, and empathy for Aidan ached in her chest. Her intuition was screaming off the scale. Responsible cops and devoted family men didn't just turn. She *would* uncover the truth. It was more than just another intriguing story. Brian O'Rourke deserved to rest in peace. And his wife and sons should not have to live in torment.

When she emerged from the bathroom, Evander wove between her ankles. "You smell a rat too, don't ya, buddy?" Zoe bent to pet the cat, and his uneven purr rumbled. The rat in question was a vicious crook named Tony DiMarco. Tony owned a security company that trained and supplied armed guards…who then gave him inside information for bank and home-invasion robberies. He was responsible for the bank robbery that had brought her and Aidan together. He'd been badly burned and shot in the head during the confrontation, and had spent the past six months under armed guard in Mercy Hospital's rehab facility.

She had put her computer skills to work and painstakingly unraveled an intricate web of dummy corporations owned by his security company. Corporations that were being hastily liquidated. DiMarco had suffered brain damage and was incapacitated. So where was the money going? And why?

Secrets and lies bought trouble. Caused pain. She'd become a reporter so she'd have an open forum to educate and help people. Her outgoing personality, verbal acuity and unerring instincts were perfect for the job, as was a survival skill she'd picked up over the years…the ability to read people. She knew when someone wasn't quite what he or she seemed. Knew when someone was lying. Di-Marco was the key to the puzzle she was trying to unlock. She knew it clear to her bones. Proving it, however, was a ways off yet.

After donning a purple bra and bikini undies, Zoe chose low-rider jeans and a short-sleeved lavender peasant top from the lidded cardboard box parked at the foot of her mattress. Brian O'Rourke and Tony DiMarco had known each other years ago. The link couldn't be a coincidence. Proving DiMarco's guilt might clear Aidan's father's name.

Grinning, Zoe slipped bare feet into worn tan mules. Aidan O'Rourke thought he was a closed book, but he was easier to read than the *Riverside Daily*. He didn't detest her nearly as much as he pretended.

There was innate sensuality in the graceful way he moved. Compelling intensity hidden in the dark secrets in his eyes. Appealing assurance in his commanding presence. He made her heart beat faster, her knees weak and her stomach flip-flop. Just being near him was more exciting than riding the gigantic wooden roller coaster at Six Flags Magic Mountain. Every time they met, they sparred. And sparks flew.

Unlike him, she didn't try to disguise her interest. Not that it mattered. He didn't seem inclined to act on the attraction. She'd give up Lucky, her treasured green glass frog, to know why she didn't measure up. He wasn't seeing anyone on a regular basis. Attending the Seattle Star Trek convention with Marvin had left her fully informed in more ways than one, even if she did have to dress up like a Klingon. The three-hour drive each way was a treasure trove of conversation.

She fastened on faux amethyst hoop earrings. On second thought, maybe Aidan's standoffish attitude was for the best.

If her cop knew what she was up to, he'd blow a gasket.

She wasn't sure how or when she'd started thinking of him as "her cop," but she couldn't seem to break the habit. Each time they met, the more he warned her away, the more proprietary she felt. Under his bluster, she saw hurt. Isolation. She knew all about trying to hoe life's row all alone. She couldn't squelch the urge to hold him. Comfort him. She rolled her eyes. Yeah, the Big Bad Wolf would love the poor baby treatment. *Not.*

A light hand with blush, mascara and lip gloss gave her the in-genue look she wanted today. She tucked four boxes of Cracker Jack into the ancient, vinyl-lined canvas bag she called her survival kit. Not a traditional breakfast, but filling, energizing…and cheap when purchased at the dollar store.

She glanced down at Evander, trotting at her heels. "Caramel-covered popcorn and peanuts are as nutritious as sugar-coated cereal, right?" He chirped in agreement. She filled a water bottle at the tap, and then tucked it into her bag.

A light summer breeze drifted through the screened apartment windows, propped open several safe inches. She breathed in fresh morning air. Thank goodness she'd be out during the heat of the day, when the tiny room turned into an oven. Evander jumped onto a windowsill beside Lucky to snooze in the sun. She patted him. "Nap all day and prowl all night. You've got it rough, pal."

Shouldering her bag, she headed out to her ancient, but reliable red Corolla. Determination swung in her stride.

She had a bank robber to interview.

Chapter 2

11:00 a.m.

"I *am* his niece. I've been out of the country serving in the Peace Corps and only just discovered poor Uncle Tony had been hurt." Zoe innocently widened her eyes at the young, sandy-haired cop barring her way into Tony DiMarco's hospital room. This time, as opposed to her usual accuracy, her best guess was way off. When she'd seen Officer Richard Ryan's twinkling blue eyes and baby face, she'd figured he'd cave in five minutes. Instead, she'd been trying to talk her way past him for fifteen.

"Sorry, miss." Officer Ryan shook his head and planted himself more firmly in front of the door.

"He's probably terribly lonely. I'm sure he wants to see me. What harm could it do?"

The cop indicated the cell phone he'd used to call the station when she'd first arrived, and repeated his softly spoken but implacable litany. "No civilians allowed inside without permission from headquarters."

She wasn't getting anywhere. Desperation welled up. "I have permission." Shoot, she was gonna have to do this the hard way and take her lumps later. "From Aidan O'Rourke."

"Is that right?" Officer Ryan's lips quirked, and Zoe's hopes spun. The magic key! Open sesame! His friendly blue eyes crinkled at the corners. "That's different, then."

She nodded earnestly. "I understand you won't want my bag inside for security reasons." She plunked her survival kit on the rust-colored carpet at his feet. "I'll take my pad and pen, in case Uncle Tony needs to dictate any instructions."

A resonant male baritone drawled behind her. "Good old Uncle Tony could kill you six different ways with that pen."

Her heart flipped in a dizzying, tangled swoop of dread and exhilaration. Rats! She knew that caress-of-black-velvet voice.

Reluctantly, she turned around. Aidan stood directly behind her. If the scuffed brown boots, snug jeans faded in all the best places and white shirt rolled up on his muscled forearms were any indication, the Big Bad Wolf was off duty. Though she had a sneaking suspicion her cop never completely went off duty. He'd hooked a denim jacket over his shoulder with one finger. It was too warm for a jacket, so he'd probably stashed his gun in the pocket. A black pager rode at his waistband. He was on call. SWAT…slathered with awesome testosterone.

She sucked in a breath. "How long have you been standing there?"

A scowl creased his ruggedly handsome face. "Long enough."

Did the guy ever relax? Geez, did he ever crack a *smile?* She couldn't remember seeing one adorn his luscious, stubborn mouth. Then again, when they were together, he was usually steamed. She offered a smile brimming with cheery bravado. "Nice to see you again."

He flicked an enigmatic glance at Officer Ryan. "Thanks for calling me, Rich. Take five."

"Sure thing, O'Rourke. Figured you'd want to take care of your little fan girl personally." Grinning, Ryan sauntered down the hallway.

Fan girl, humph! She was *not* trailing after Aidan like the so-named swooning teens who followed around pretty-boy movie heartthrobs like Orlando Bloom and Elijah Wood. Zoe grimaced at Ryan's retreating back. Outfoxed by a guy barely old enough to shave. She must be slipping.

Aidan deftly inserted his big body between her and DiMarco's doorway. "What are you trying to pull now?"

"I need to speak to DiMarco."

His movements a symphony of masculine power and grace, he slung his jacket over an upholstered chair parked to the right of the door and crossed tanned, sinewy forearms over his wide chest. "He'd just as soon kill you as look at you."

"He's got no reason to hurt me." At least not unless he discovered she was trying to bring him down.

"DiMarco doesn't need a reason." His scowl deepened. "Besides, he hasn't said a word in six months. What makes you think he'd talk to you…if he were able?"

A male aide trundled down the corridor, pushing a large linen cart. "'Scuse me."

Zoe stepped aside. The aide wheeled the cart into the room, and then began to strip the bed.

Zoe glanced at DiMarco. The pale man slumped in a wheelchair, his head lolled to the side. He didn't appear aware of his surroundings. His room was butter-yellow, but the color didn't really matter. All hospitals looked the same, intersecting rows of doorstudded corridors. Behind each door was a person in pain. And all hospitals smelled the same…disinfectant and desperation.

She pushed the door with the toe of her shoe, nudging it closed enough to preserve the man's privacy. She probably wouldn't get any response from DiMarco, but a long shot bet that succeeded always paid off in spades. Her mom languished in a similar rehab facility in San Francisco. But within the stroke-paralyzed shell, sparks flickered in Rita's green eyes. Where there were sparks, there was life. And where there was life, hope. She wanted to see what was in DiMarco's eyes. "I thought he might respond to the press."

"Why bother?" Torment laced his bitter words. "You people make up whatever you want, anyway. Then you print it, regardless of who it hurts."

"Some do," she acknowledged quietly. "Not me. I want to hear DiMarco's side of the story." And if her news that someone was stealing his "hard-earned" money couldn't get a rise out of the guy, nothing could. Perhaps then the person rapidly accruing Tony's funds would hear that Tony knew, and tip his hand. She'd studied the crimes Tony was suspected of committing. Even cognitively impaired, DiMarco was a formidable enemy.

"He's a ruthless killer," Aidan growled. "'His side of the story' is bent beyond belief."

She gazed into Aidan's deep-brown eyes. Compelling. Seductive. Glittering with rich, dark heat far more addictive than her favorite espresso. "It's okay, Aidan. I know."

His eyes narrowed in suspicion. "Know *what?*"

"DiMarco and your dad were army buddies during the Vietnam War. They were stationed in Hawaii along with your mom, who was a civilian nurse. Your father mustered out injured, accompanied by your mom, while Tony went to war as a Black Ops assassin."

Startled surprise stamped his features before he shuttered his expression. "Yesterday's news, Ms. Zagretti."

"All pieces of the same puzzle." He didn't deny it, but then he couldn't deny the truth. "When DiMarco robbed the mall's bank, he was wearing your father's watch…a watch you and your brothers made and gave to your dad for Father's Day when you were young." She paused, loath to whammy him with a bad memory. "The watch Brian O'Rourke was wearing the day he died."

Lightning flashed in his eyes. He grasped her shoulders and spun her, trapping her between his body and the wall. He stepped close and lowered his face to hers, and his quiet voice thrummed with fury. "Aside from me, my brothers are the only ones who know that. How did you find out?"

For a big guy who was supremely ticked off, his grip on her shoulders was rigidly controlled. Her cop knew his strength and didn't abuse it. Heat radiated from him, enveloping her in the clean, appealing scent of soap and man. She put her hands on his forearms. His muscles jumped under her touch, and her breath caught. Touching him zapped her as strongly as the time she'd been sneaking around after a story and had grabbed a low-voltage electric fence. If his reaction was any indication, he felt the shock waves, too. "I observe. I listen. I see and hear things."

His jaw clenched. "You didn't leave when I threw you off the mall incident site," his deep voice rumbled ominously. "You hid and spied. What else did you hear?"

Gorgeous *and* smart. After he'd saved her life, he'd ordered her off the property. Instead, concealed by the storm and the chaos, she'd circled back. She'd climbed inside a huge Dumpster near where Aidan and his brothers were conducting a private powwow and had feverishly scribbled notes via penlight. "DiMarco's MO fits a series of home-invasion robberies that includes the robbery that killed your father." Perhaps if he understood her motives, her goal, they could work together. "I believe Tony DiMarco framed and killed your dad, and I think it was personal. All I need is enough proof to take him down."

His face was inches from hers, his breath warm on her lips. "Be warned." His body vibrated with rage, but his grip stayed gentle. "Don't screw with my family. I will do whatever it takes to protect them."

In spite of the trauma the O'Rourkes had experienced, she almost envied them. How wonderful it would feel to have someone who cared enough to put your welfare above all others. To have the ultimate protector watching your back. She and her mom had always been a distrustful, isolated island in a cold sea of humanity. With Mom working long hours at under-the-table jobs to support them, Zoe had often been alone, even at night. Always afraid. Especially at night.

She raised her chin. She refused to be afraid now. Not of the specter haunting her past, and certainly not of Aidan O'Rourke. "I don't intend to upset your family. I'm trying to help them."

He snorted. "DiMarco isn't the only one who knows how to assassinate with a pen. You journalists are champs. Making accusations my father can't defend. Mocking our faith in his innocence. Exposing our grief for the public to sneer at." His mouth twisted in pain. "'Mrs. O'Rourke, your husband is a dead dirty cop, how do you feel? Details at eleven.'"

Anguish squeezed her heart. Even after nine years, his wounds hadn't healed. How could they? He'd never had closure. She could give him what he craved. "I know you were hurt by biased reporting before, and I'm sorry." She surrendered to the compulsion to touch his cheek. "I'm not like that, I promise. I report the truth."

He jerked back like she'd burned him, and his smooth, hot skin and fine sandpaper whiskers brushed her palm. He snatched his hands from her shoulders. "Ms. Zagretti, you and your fellow reporters wouldn't recognize the truth if it bit you on the—"

"My friends call me Zoe." Well, if she had friends, they would. Sudden doubt assailed her. Did she even know how to make friends? Just because Aidan desired her didn't mean he liked her. Or wanted to. Perhaps her less-than-auspicious background would turn him off. Not everyone wanted to adopt stray mongrels.

"What kind of idiot do you take me for?"

She hesitated, then forged ahead. What did she have to lose, except her dubious dignity? "I'd like to be friends. Please, call me Zoe." He'd obviously expected a counterattack instead of an olive branch. "And I don't think you're an idiot at all. You're a very intelligent man."

He studied her face. "You're playing a very dangerous game, Ms. Zagretti. And I'm a very *dangerous* man."

Dangerous. To her peace of mind? Assuredly. To her libido? Definitely. But bodily harm? No way. Her instincts said he would never hurt her. Her self-preservation instincts were infallible. "It's not a game. It's my life's ambition."

Dark fury blazed, his brown irises smoldering. "Don't betray my family to further your ambition, or you will be one sorry lady."

"I told you, I want to *help*."

His brows snapped together. "You haven't seen the carnage that DiMarco is capable of. He's already hurt too many people, caused too much pain. You have to drop it."

"Don't you see? That's exactly why I *can't* drop it."

The door swung open, and the aide bumped out backwards, tugging the cart piled with bedding. Zoe waited, holding Aidan's gaze, willing him to believe her. The aide swung the cart around and entered the next room. Zoe infused her words with sincerity. "I'm good at my job. Give me a chance—"

The pager at Aidan's waist shrilled, snagging his attention. "Rich!" he roared.

Officer Ryan rounded the corner and jogged down the hallway toward them. "Heard it. Got a call-out?"

"Yeah." Aidan yanked his jacket off the chair. He skewered Ryan with his laser glare and pointed at Zoe. "If she gets anywhere near DiMarco, I'll have your guts for garters."

Ryan straightened. "I wasn't about to let her inside."

Aidan sprinted away, his gait the fluid, long-legged stride of a predator on the hunt.

Momentarily thwarted in her quest, Zoe shouldered her bag. A SWAT call-up, hmm? That was usually breaking news.

Thirty minutes later, dressed in black battle gear, Aidan stood with his hip propped against the white-tiled kitchen counter in a house the team had commandeered for the command post. They'd evacuated the entire block. At the north end of the tree-lined suburban street, Eric Kinkaid had gone ballistic and was holding his two young daughters at knifepoint.

Domestic disturbances counted among the worst situations police officers faced. Hazardous and unpredictable, often brutally violent, they simmered with explosive emotions that put the victims *and* the cops sent to help them in deadly peril. Aidan preferred a straightforward armed assault any day.

"Kinkaid lost his job a while back." Also wearing battle gear, Captain Lou Greene sat at the table scanning intel reports. Everything from blueprints of the hostage site to neighbors' observations of the suspect's moods and behavior were listed on the forms. "He's been moping around the house, drinking and talking trash. And we still can't locate the wife."

Captain Greene was filling in for Aidan's brother Con, Alpha Team's leader since Greene had "retired" to desk duty in February. Con was getting married that evening. Bailey, his fiancée, was fully supportive of his dangerous, unpredictable job. However, she'd put her foot down about him answering call-outs on their wedding day. Without Con by his side, Aidan felt as if he were missing a limb. He'd seen a lot less of his brother lately. He didn't begrudge Con one second of happiness, but his engagement had left Aidan somewhat adrift. At least they still worked together. Two months ago, Aidan had been offered leadership of Delta Team, but had declined. He liked working with his brothers, liked being the man who guarded their backs.

Their unsinkable mom called them her four "S" men. Not only because they stair-stepped in age from twenty-eight to thirty-one, or because they were all SWAT. She had a unique handle for each. Aidan, the strong. Con, the sensitive. Liam, the scamp. Grady, the searcher. As if Maureen O'Rourke had room to talk. The energetic redhead was as stubborn and capable as any of her sons. Maybe more than all four of them put together.

Speaking of stubborn, capable women, Aidan's recent encounter with Zoe had tied his insides into confused knots. As torqued as he'd been with her for snooping around his family, he hadn't been able to stomp out his attraction. He didn't even *like* her; why the hell did he want to take her to bed so badly his teeth ached?

He frowned at the ceiling. He had to divert Ms. Nosy off the DiMarco case. When things were settled here, he'd round up his brothers for a war council. Damn good thing Ryan had called him to the hospital. The exotically appealing Ms. Zagretti could talk a man off a ledge. Of course, she would have been the one who'd driven him out there in the first place.

"Yo, O'Rourke Senior!" Greene's hail jerked him out of the disastrous train of thought. "What's got your skivvies in a wad?" His CO's bushy brows slammed together. "You're normally a hundred percent focused."

Yeah, until Typhoon Zoe had blasted apart his common sense. "My skivvies are wrinkle-free. What's up, Cap'n?"

"See if the war wagon is on site. The suspect cut the phone lines, and we need a throw phone."

"Right away." Disgusted with himself, Aidan pushed off the counter and wove around the SWAT-team members milling through the house. The Kevlar-suited officers were prepared to stand by for hours awaiting a peaceful surrender, or scramble to execute an assault-and-rescue within seconds.

In the living room, he pushed aside dark-green drapes drawn

shut against prying eyes. The huge, black-armored SWAT truck idled at the curb, loaded with weapons, siege and breeching equipment and even a computer center.

A curious mob had gathered at the south end of the street behind the police barricade. Waiting the bad guys out was the one factor that civilians, and sometimes top brass, didn't comprehend. The public and upper echelons often demanded immediate results. He spotted a TV camera in the crowd, and scowled. Egged on by the press. Then the TV news programs trotted out Monday-morning quarterbacks to pick apart the team's decisions and performance.

"Ten-four on the war wagon." Waiting for a peaceful surrender was the best-case scenario. But if the incident dragged on for hours, the groomsmen and best man could be no-shows at the wedding. Aidan shook his head. Another hard reality check confirming his decision to avoid the matrimonial snare.

"*O'Rourke.*" Uh-oh. The snap in Greene's bass voice didn't bode well.

He strode into the kitchen and stopped short. Zoe Zagretti stood just inside the back door, along with a uniformed officer and a disheveled blonde whose haggard, tear-streaked face was stamped by hard living. The woman had two black eyes, and her baby-blue tank top revealed mottled bruises on her upper arms.

Aidan frowned at Zoe, then nodded at the uniformed cop. "Escort the reporter out."

Fresh tears welled in the blonde's eyes, and she clutched Zoe's arm. "No! She understands! She can help."

"Oh yeah, she's a regular Mother Teresa," Aidan growled, ignoring Greene's smirk. The entire team had been ragging him about Zoe's "devotion" since he'd saved her life during the mall incident. His brother Liam had informed him with great relish that in some cultures, if you saved a person's life, they belonged to you forever. Aidan shuddered. He needed Zoe Zagretti's devotion about as much as he needed thong underwear.

Zoe slid an arm across the blonde's shoulders and gave her a quick hug. "This is Shelly. She's Kylie and Emma's mom. You said you couldn't find her. So I did."

"How did you know—" Aidan exhaled roiling frustration. "You have a scanner that taps into police radio transmissions." He'd deal with that later. He gentled his voice and addressed the sobbing blonde. "Can you tell us why your husband is upset?"

"Eric's been on a four-day jag, drinking and smoking and snorting God knows what. He thinks I'm sleeping around on him."

"Are you?"

Shelly cried harder, and Zoe gave an indignant huff. "No, she is *not*. Even if she were, that's no excuse for her husband to use her as a punching bag and threaten the kids."

"Of course not." Aidan handed Shelly a paper towel to blot her tears. He pulled out the chair beside Greene and offered it to the shaken woman. "I didn't mean to upset you, but we have to know the truth going in. The more information we have, the easier it is to keep your little girls safe."

"Eric just went crazy." Wiping her eyes, Shelly dropped into the chair. "I'm so scared."

Greene introduced himself and grabbed a blank intel report. "Start from the beginning. What happened this morning?"

The CO was more than capable of obtaining the intel they needed. Aidan grasped Zoe by the arm, immediately regretting it when molten fire flooded his bloodstream. He should know better than to touch her by now. "A word with you, in private."

Shelly's face crumpled as if she were about to start crying again. "You'll be back? I need you."

Zoe nodded. "You bet. In the meantime, help the police prepare to rescue your daughters."

Zoe didn't resist as he towed her down the hallway and into the nearest room—the bathroom. He shoved the door shut with his booted foot. Her body was inches from his, and her tantalizing aura wove its spell around him. A sexy, appealing woman in a confined space…not one of his brighter ideas.

He let go of her, but aching need didn't release its hold on him. "I don't know what you said or did to worm your way into this command post, and I don't care. You're in the way, you're compromising the operation and you're leaving."

She jutted her chin in a gesture he couldn't help but admire.

"That woman is scared and hurting. I'm all she's got and I won't abandon her."

There she went again, whammying him with the unexpected. Being caught constantly off balance was a new and unsettling experience. "What?" He also despised sounding like a deranged parrot every time it happened.

"Shelly doesn't have family, and Eric's temper has driven off friends and neighbors. She doesn't know where to turn. She needs support. Not platitudes and judgment."

"I was doing my job, not judging her."

"I realize that, but some will judge her. You know the drill. 'What kind of woman stays with a man who smacks her around?' Besides, you're a tough guy. Not the best at handling feelings."

Zoe patted his arm, and his skin tingled beneath the protective barrier of his battle uniform. She seemed to be a natural toucher, and he was sure she didn't mean it as a come-on. If only he could convince his on-alert libido of that fact.

"Shelly was hysterical when she discovered what had happened. She's had a tough life, and I can relate. I'll keep her calm and encourage her to talk to you, without tying up an officer. Which benefits you *and* her."

He sighed, hating how his insides churned at the idea of Zoe suffering hard times. How his chest ached at the thought of anyone causing her pain. No matter how angry her meddling made him, he could never hurt her. In fact, he would annihilate anyone who tried. Chaos roiled inside him. "And KKEY's ratings."

Her fascinating, changeable eyes glowed green with empathy. "She's been abused enough, Aidan. I won't exploit her."

He didn't have one reason to believe a member of the press did anything for anyone without an ulterior motive. Nevertheless, he believed Zoe. *Chump.* "You are some piece of work, Zagretti." He'd been neutralized before he'd launched the first strike, and he knew it. Worse, *she* knew it.

She grinned. "I can stay." It wasn't a question.

"Three conditions. You stay in sight at all times. No eavesdropping. No access to classified tactical ops. And I preview your report for any intel that would compromise my team or the case."

"Sounds fair." Her dazzling smile did funky things to his blood pressure.

How did she breach his defenses and read him so easily? Why didn't his intimidation tactics—which worked on crack-heads, gangbangers and badass bad guys—faze her? Why did he long to kiss her full, red lips until she lost the power of speech?

He scrubbed a hand over his jaw. Maybe he should just yield to the insane compulsion. Kiss her and get it over with. Exorcise her from his head. Banish her from his dreams. Purge her from his system once and for all. His gaze played longingly over her lips. Soft. Red. Moist, and partially open.

Her eyes widened, and golden highlights swirled in the green-and-brown depths. Her breath hitched. His own breathing was none too steady.

He had a gut-wrenching suspicion one kiss wouldn't be nearly enough.

Her warm gaze caressed his, and her exotic scent beckoned him nearer. His senses were acutely attuned to her. Under the lavender blouse, her breasts rose and fell rapidly, and each soft breath whispered an intimate invitation. Though his brain screamed a warning, his body swayed closer. A tantalizing brush of clothing. An erotic sizzle of heat.

He lowered his head, already anticipating her sweet taste. Her long lashes drifted down. He was an ancient explorer teetering on the edge of the map. About to plunge into uncharted territory. Take a step into total darkness.

Hurtle willingly over the edge of the cliff.

A millimeter from devouring the tempting, forbidden fruit, he checked. Jerked back. What the *hell* was he doing? In the middle of an incident site, for crying out loud. Nobody, *nothing,* ever distracted him from the job. "Are you a witch?"

Her eyes popped open. She blinked. Was that disappointment clouding her gaze? She arched a bewildered mahogany brow. "Umm…yeah. Want to see my astral projections?"

Had he said that out loud? "I don't know what—never—uh… Never mind." His heart was pounding like a virgin's on prom night. He hadn't stammered since he was four. Maybe he needed to work out more. Add on an extra Kata session. Take a long, cold shower—or six. "I…ah…" The words stuck in his throat like a roadway spike strip, but had to be said. "I apologize."

She nodded, her elfin face thoughtful. "Because it was unprofessional conduct, or because you lost your nerve?"

He hadn't lost his nerve since he was fourteen. Until now. "Uh…it would be a conflict of interest."

"I see." She nodded again. "You're conflicted about your interest." She stepped away, putting much-needed distance between them. "I agree, this isn't the time or the place, and I also apologize for getting carried away. But later, when you figure it out, let me know, okay?"

He was sorely afraid he'd end up doing exactly that.

A fist pounded on the outside of the door. "O'Rourke, Greene needs you in the kitchen."

Thank God. He'd faced vicious armed robbers, dodged rapid-fire rounds in firefights and been trapped by a raging inferno in a meth lab without getting rattled. Yet this one small woman shook him to the core. He glanced at his reflection in the medicine cabinet, and resisted the urge to hammer his own face. He was losing his freaking mind. Zoe Zagretti might not be crazy, but she sure as hell was a carrier.

What other incurable cravings would he catch when he finally gave in and kissed her?

Chapter 3

12:00 p.m.

Disappointment weighted Zoe's limbs. Wrong situation, wrong place and horrendously inappropriate. But every instinct she possessed mourned the loss of something much more significant than a mere kiss. Which was pretty crazy if she stopped to analyze the feeling. A kiss was just a kiss, right?

Then again, how would she know? Kisses had been as scarce in her life as friends. When she couldn't even trust people enough to engage in meaningful conversation, intimacy was out of the question. If not for the romance novels she devoured, she wouldn't know the first thing about relationships.

She followed Aidan as he prowled down the hallway. The view from behind was every bit as delicious. He moved with the loose-limbed, confident rhythm of a trained dancer. Since she couldn't imagine her reticent cop prancing around in a unitard at a ballet class, he probably practiced martial arts.

She brushed his arm to snag his attention, and warm, rock-hard biceps bunched under his black uniform. "Tai Kwon Do?"

He jolted, stumbled and half turned. "What?"

She should probably stop touching him. Every time she did, he practically leapt out of his skin. Yet, she'd seen him hug Con the night of the mall incident, and all four O'Rourke men generously bestowed guy-type contact. Only *her* touch startled Aidan. "Do you practice Tai Kwon Do?"

"No. Kendo." He turned and strode on.

Ah. Obviously, Officer SWAT—sexy, wicked and taciturn— was allotted only so many words per day, and had used up his quota speaking to her earlier. She was intrigued, and direct questions were the fastest route to information. "What's Kendo?"

"Ancient Japanese samurai martial art. Literally means Way of the Sword."

She pictured him wielding a sword in his big, capable hands, the embodiment of lethal elegance and power. Primitive desire streaked through her veins and her stomach somersaulted, something it did often in his imposing presence. Geez, Zagretti, chill out. After their close encounter of the lip-lock kind, her hormones were dancing the lineup from *Chicago*. "An ancient Japanese martial art would be unusual and fascinating material for a story. Would you show me sometime?"

"I don't think so."

All righty then. The man needed to learn how to play. To laugh. She would work on warming him up. Though a few minutes ago, he'd been plenty hot. He smelled delicious. Warm, clean and potently male. She'd never before noticed a man's scent, but now possessed new respect for pheromone theory. SWAT was packing major sensory ammo. Her neurons had surrendered without a shot being fired.

They entered the cozy yellow kitchen. Shelly sat at the table, a wooden bowl piled with shiny scarlet apples at her elbow lending both color and a crisp, fruity aroma. The homeowner had decorated the small house in bright colors and homey accents. Zoe had felt welcome the second she'd walked in. Unexpected longing spiraled through her. She yearned to put down roots. To have a place that belonged to her, that no one could snatch away. She made a mental note of the cheerful red-and-yellow color scheme for someday when she had a house of her own.

Liam, O'Rourke brother number three, sauntered in the back door with his K-9 partner, Murphy, alert at his heels. She knew better than to try to pet the big German Shepherd. Murphy was working, his posture all business. His intelligent brown eyes watched Liam, awaiting a hand signal or verbal order. "No explosives or booby traps, at least outside the home."

Aidan's youngest brother, Grady, who was a paramedic as well as a SWAT officer, spoke a low, rapid-fire tattoo of medical jargon over the landline.

Each time she watched Aidan and his brothers in action, her admiration grew. She'd love to dip her toes in the incredible gene pool that had produced four handsome, courageous, selfless men. The boys resembled the pictures she'd seen of their dad. In contrast to her murky background, the O'Rourkes had inherited awesome DNA.

Liam flashed her a five-hundred-watt smile. His sunny grin was dazzling, yet her previously dancing hormones had taken five. Funny, she'd always preferred bright, sunlit days. But lately, she'd grown partial to storm clouds. Liam tweaked her with their running joke. "Hey, Geraldo. Find Al Capone's vault yet?" The opposite of Officer Scowly, easygoing Liam was rarely without a grin, and accepted her as one of the gang. He offered no-strings affability, a rare and valuable commodity in her experience, and she wasn't about to shun it.

"Hey yourself, Deputy Dog. Want to give me breaking details?"

Aidan and Con had rich, warm brown eyes like their dad. Grady's eyes were clear gray-green, but Liam's were the true, deep green of the Emerald Isle, and now they twinkled at her. "And risk getting pounded by the A-man? Pass."

Zoe offered Shelly a wave and an encouraging smile, glad to see the previously wan woman looking hopeful. Sitting in a room pulsating with testosterone could do that to a gal. If these guys couldn't save her children, nobody could.

Aidan turned to Zoe, his face stony. Their near-miss kiss might never have been. "As long as you're quiet, you can stay. The minute you let out a peep, you're gone. Is that clear?"

Zoe nodded. She didn't expect his attention on her in the midst of a hostage crisis, nor would she respect him had it been. Yet, deep down, his cold dismissal stung. A smile wouldn't kill him. "As ice."

Greene drew the men aside to show them several diagrams. Aidan's laser gaze focused on Greene, and he seemed to have forgotten Zoe existed. She caught a peek of the emergency dynamic entry plan, formed in case the team had to storm in and rescue the kids. She stayed still, barely breathing, not drawing attention to herself as Greene continued to brief Aidan.

"Our negotiator, Wyatt Cain, is stuck on the other side of the city, with the river between him and us, and the bridges are up. You'll have to negotiate."

Aidan didn't bat one long, gorgeous eyelash. "Fill me in."

"Since Eric got fired, he's spiraled downhill. Another potential job flatlined yesterday, and it sent him over the edge."

Aidan scrubbed a hand over his strong jaw. "We've seen suspects crash and burn over less."

"True. He's been on a four-day bender…beer, pot and cocaine, which reached critical mass last night. He accused Shelly of cheating on him and beat the hell out of her." Greene's words were even, but his expression was fierce. "When he finally fell asleep early this morning, she left the kids with a neighbor and went to the pharmacy for a prescription. He woke up and discovered her gone, saw the kids playing outside in the neighbor's yard and snatched them, then barricaded everyone inside the house. The neighbor called dispatch and said she saw him brandishing a hunting knife."

"In other words, he's totally unpredictable." Aidan frowned. "A freaking time bomb."

"It gets worse. The medication Shelly went to refill was for the four-year-old, Emma. She has asthma. There's an inhaler inside the house, but we don't know if Kincaid has allowed her access."

Anger crackled inside Zoe. How could a husband and father do such horrible things to his family? Sick regret drowned the anger, and nausea churned in her stomach. She knew better than to ask. She and her mom had spent their lives on the run from her own father. The fact that she didn't know who he was, or anything about him only intensified the terror. She took a deep breath and forced her focus back to the situation at hand. The past was over. She was done running from the bogeyman.

"Doc Holliday is briefed and prepared for that?" Aidan glanced at Grady, who nodded. All SWAT team members had code names. Aidan was Alpha Eight, because he was the last of the eight Alpha team members inside, last to take cover. He was the rear guard, the man who protected everyone's backs.

Zoe had researched the teams. The more she learned, the more she was in awe. SWAT officers were amazing in their bravery and dedication. Unflinching in the face of death, they performed the most dangerous jobs, took the hairiest risks. When other cops called 911, SWAT answered. True-blue warriors, they did their jobs and left. No accolades, no thanks. Riverside SWAT officers made a whopping dollar more an hour for life-threatening duty, and donated hundreds of hours of their own time to train. Unless a situation escalated, like today's, nobody even knew the officers' lives had been on the line.

Soon, she'd have enough material to propose a week-long feature to her boss. She burned to inform the public about the sacrifices these men made to protect them. She'd lived in more than a dozen cities and never paid any attention to SWAT teams until recently. They deserved admiration and respect.

She reported the truth, but these selfless men lived it.

At Greene's nod, Aidan continued. "Has Kincaid beaten his wife before?"

"Yeah. He has a history of domestic violence."

Aidan's jaw clenched, and a muscle ticked in his cheek. "What about the kids, he hit them, too?"

"The wife says no."

"One thing going for them." His voice was tight. "Let's hope he doesn't cross the line today."

"We tossed in the throw phone. Attempt to establish contact."

Zoe glided to the table and sat beside Shelly. The woman reached for her hand, and Zoe gave it a squeeze.

Aidan turned away to access the throw phone. "Hello, Eric?" Concentration hummed in every controlled movement. "This is Officer Aidan O'Rourke with Riverside PD. What's going on?"

The throw phone had a speaker, so everyone in the room could hear Eric Kincaid's slurred answer. "The ball-and-chain called 5-0, huh? Figures."

"I'm here to help." Aidan kept his tone low and soothing. "But I have to know what's happening."

"The bitch has been sleepin' around on me." Kincaid adopted a self-pitying whine. "Nobody gives a shit."

"I care." Sincerity rang true in Aidan's words. "I want everybody to walk out of your house safe and sound, including you. How are Kylie and Emma?"

Shelly's grip on Zoe's hand tightened, but she didn't make a sound.

"I can't get a damn job anywhere, man. They won't even hire me to sling fries."

"That's frustrating, and must make you feel angry and powerless."

"Yeah." Kincaid's unsteady voice rose and fell randomly. "I got no money, and my wife don't want me no more."

"Your wife is very worried about you. You want to talk about your problems, Eric, and I want to listen. But, first, I need to know how your daughters are. Are they all right?"

"Can't you hear the brats? *Shut up!*" His shriek was muffled, as if he'd moved the receiver away from his mouth.

"They're scared. They don't understand that you're not angry at *them*." Aidan paused, presumably to let the statement sink in. "If you hurt Kylie and Emma, there won't be anything I can do for you. The police officers surrounding your house will take you to jail."

Zoe pursed her lips. For a man who ruthlessly restrained his own feelings, Aidan excelled at pinpointing Eric's.

"Aw, they're okay. The little one's whining about not breathing too good, but she always snaps out of it."

Shelly clutched Zoe's hand. Zoe slid an arm across her shoulders and hugged her. "It'll be all right," she whispered in Shelly's ear. "Aidan will help her." Zoe knew that Aidan would find a way to save the little girls.

An hour later, she wasn't so sure. Aidan had tried everything to get Eric to let the children go, or at least allow Grady to treat

Emma. Aidan was walking a fine line, both sympathizing with Eric and controlling him, and doing an incredible job. But Kincaid wouldn't budge. "Work with me, Eric. Send out Emma and Kylie, and I'll give you something you want."

"Hey, man, you got any scramble?"

Aidan frowned. "You know I can't give you drugs."

"Why the hell not? Everybody knows cops got the quality candy."

Aidan ignored the jibe. "How about some smokes? Or maybe you're hungry? Let's order out for burgers, or a pizza."

"You're starting to piss me off, pig!" Eric shouted like a sulky, spoiled child.

Obeying Aidan's earlier command, Shelly had remained quiet. As Eric's anger escalated, her desperation grew. Pale and visibly shaken, she leaned over and whispered in Zoe's ear, a mere thread of sound. "When Eric is stoned, he loves to play his electric guitar and perform for his sleazy buddies. Maybe the cops can use that to get him to come out."

Zoe grabbed a pen, scribbled a note on the back of a blank intel report, and then jumped up and passed it to Aidan.

He arched a brow, nodded. "I understand you play the guitar. Send out the girls, and you can play and sing for us. There are fifty cops out here. Lots of rock fans in this crowd."

Not only tempting, but a subtle way to let Kincaid know he was totally outnumbered. Her cop was good!

"Rad idea, man! Are there reporters? I can wail on live TV!"

"I might be able to arrange that, if you release Kylie and Emma."

"I wanna be on TV first. Then I might let 'em go."

Aidan scrubbed a hand over his jaw. "All right. Can you hold on while I try to arrange it?"

"Sure." Eric giggled drunkenly. Obscenely. "Don't got nowhere to go."

Aidan pressed a hold button and turned to Greene. "No way. Lord knows what he'd do on live TV. Besides, every lunatic in the city would be clamoring for their turn on the tube."

Zoe tiptoed back and whispered to Shelly, "Do you have cable TV?" Shelly nodded, and Zoe strode up behind Aidan. "Aidan," she ventured. "I think I can help."

He swiveled, his face etched with anger. "I told you to butt out."

"I have an idea."

"Yeah, you have plenty of those, but I'm not interested in good ratings." He dismissed her with a brusque wave.

"Uh, bro?" Liam shifted his stance, and Murphy's ears twitched. "Chill out, and at least listen to what she has to say. You're sure as hell not getting anywhere."

Aidan shot Liam a look that would melt steel, but turned back to Zoe. He crossed his arms over his chest. "Okay, let's hear it, Brenda Starr. What's the million dollar brainstorm?"

Zoe tamped down her own anger. They both had the same goal—to save those children. Personal grievances could wait.

"With a couple of hundred feet of coaxial cable, connectors and a splitter, you can hook a camera into the house's cable jack from outside, and also to a TV inside the SWAT armored truck. The closed circuit will 'broadcast' Eric's performance to both. He'll *think* he's on live TV."

Aidan studied her. Was that admiration burning in his gaze? "And Command can monitor the officer who goes inside with the camera." He gave a nod of respect. "Smart, Zagretti." Warm fuzzies swirled inside Zoe at his rare compliment.

Greene turned to Liam. "Procure the equipment, set up the war wagon." The CO yelled into the living room. "Send a uniform to get Aidan's civvies out of his car!"

Zoe swallowed hard. That meant Aidan would be the man going inside with the camera. The man facing the threat.

Liam jogged out with Murphy trotting at his side, and Aidan told Eric he'd soon be on "live TV." Again, he tried to convince him to set the girls free, with no luck.

In less than fifteen minutes, a camera was connected to the Kincaids' cable jack and also to a TV inside the huge armored truck the guys referred to as the war wagon. It had taken a remarkably short time to pull everything together. Zoe's throat tightened. To a tiny girl trapped with a raging junkie and struggling for breath, it probably seemed an eternity.

Shelly waited in the command center house with several uniformed officers, while the SWAT team and Zoe reconvened inside the war wagon. The driver parked in front of the neighbor's driveway, so the team could storm in if they had to perform an assault-and-rescue.

Zoe had imagined the vehicle's interior as dark and cramped, with Uzis and battering rams hanging on the walls. Instead, it was clean and airy. White cabinets lined the walls, and the dove-gray ceiling sported a bright fluorescent light. If she didn't know that the cabinets bristled with weaponry, she'd think she was in a cozy office.

The team, including Grady and Liam, with Murphy alert at his feet, waited on padded gray benches beside the back doors. In the front, Zoe assisted Aidan and Captain Greene with the equipment hookup. A narrow counter supported a computer and the portable TV where Greene would monitor Aidan's progress.

Dressed in his jeans and white shirt, with a Kevlar vest hidden underneath, Aidan stood next to Zoe as she showed him how to operate the camera. Her palms sweated with the effort to appear unaffected. This was the first occasion they'd spent any time in close proximity, and even under the tense circumstances it was an exercise in sensual torture. The man smelled scrumptious.

She pressed a button, and the team swam into view. Captured in the viewfinder, Liam gave them a thumbs-up. "This model is a little focus-challenged, so you have to keep adjusting."

"No problem." Aidan's big, warm hand brushed hers as he rotated the dial, and her insides jittered. "Kincaid is a little focus-challenged himself. He'll never notice."

Whoa, a joke? She grinned at him in pleased surprise, and he arched a brow. What do you know? Her cop had a sly sense of humor lurking under his perpetual scowl.

For a man about to confront a volatile, knife-wielding druggie, he was amazingly calm. Not that she expected otherwise. Even last winter when his brother was trapped with armed bank robbers, Aidan had orchestrated the rescue as coolly as a Fudgesicle in Antarctica. He never showed fear. Did he *feel* afraid? She didn't have enough experience with men to know. Especially tough guys. News anchors didn't count. They freaked if their hairstyle looked bad or ratings dropped two-tenths of a point.

Aidan passed her the camera, and then secured a gun to his ankle. He already wore an earpiece and hidden throat mike that would keep him in verbal contact with Greene if he had to abort the visual transmission. He tugged his pant leg into place, and shrugged on his denim jacket. An inhaler for Emma was in the pocket. Grady stood by to treat Emma the instant Eric was neutralized.

Aidan took the camera from Zoe. "Ready to roll."

She gave his hand a brief squeeze. "Be careful."

His inscrutable gaze didn't divulge any of his secrets. "Always am."

He strode toward the doors. As one, the team stood. The men offered smart-ass comments and slaps on the back underscored by genuine concern.

Grady, Liam and Aidan slapped palms and said in unison, "Fortune favors the brave." From the looks of it, a familiar pre-battle ritual. Their gazes locked and a silent, heartfelt exchange passed between them. For one poignant moment, they were brothers instead of cops.

Liam smiled. "Don't do anything I wouldn't."

Aidan snorted. "Short list, bro."

Grady shook his head. "If you end up wounded, *I'm* not notifying the wedding party that the best man is AWOL."

Aidan rolled his eyes. "Con would understand."

Liam's smile widened into a wicked grin. "On the other hand, the mothers, bridesmaids and the bride-to-be…yikes! Facing a mob of furious females in formal wear? Uh-uh."

Grady chuckled, displaying his dimples. "I'd rather go *mano a mano* with crashing meth heads. Naked."

Zoe's heart lurched. Nobody'd mentioned that Aidan could *die.* Cops probably couldn't afford to think that way, or they wouldn't be able to do their jobs.

Aidan's lips quirked. His second hit-and-run with a near smile in an hour. "See you later, girls."

"Big brother, you are so full of crap, your eyes are brown." Grinning, Liam saluted as Aidan propped the camera on his shoulder and exited the vehicle.

Zoe stayed glued to the television screen. Via the camera lens, she saw through Aidan's eyes as he approached the front door and knocked. "Mr. Kinkaid, I'm here to put you on TV."

Zoe held her breath as the door swung open and Eric appeared. His pale eyes were red-rimmed, and a scraggly beard darkened his gaunt face. His brown hair was rumpled, his clothing disheveled. He brandished a huge, notched knife in his right hand, and sun glinted off the blade. He peered at Aidan, then the camera and grinned drunkenly. "Great, man."

He stood to one side and Aidan stepped into the living room. Drawn blinds cast the room into sinister shadow. Beer bottles and cigarette butts littered the coffee table, sprinkled with grainy powder residue where Eric had snorted lines of coke. Two little blond girls huddled on the couch, the smallest as white as death and wheezing audibly. They stared wide-eyed at the stranger, but remained mute, terrorized beyond crying out.

Zoe's throat closed up. Their fear became her fear, as sharp and cold as splinters of ice. Freezing. Hurting. Terrified and alone in the dark, she struggled to breathe.

Grady patted her shoulder. "Zoe? You okay?"

Jerked back to reality, she gasped in a shaky breath. "Y-yes." She shook her head. *Get a grip, Zagretti.* She'd covered many heartrending stories, and while she always sympathized with the victims, she'd never *become* one. Her overreaction must stem from her connection with Aidan. Watching the scene unfold through his eyes as it happened made the horror all too real.

Aidan backed slowly toward the window. "Mind if we open the blinds? We need more light to get a good picture of you."

"Okay," Kincaid assented, and Aidan tugged the cord, exposing the room to the street.

"Way to go, bro," Liam murmured.

From previous observations, Zoe knew that Hunter Garrett, the team's steely-eyed sniper, was positioned somewhere outside. The big leonine man now had a clear shot into the house.

Aidan glided slowly, non-threateningly away from the window again, positioning himself between Eric and the children. Emma's pitiful wheezing rasped in the background. Aidan swung the camera back to Eric. "See yourself on TV?"

Eric faced the screen in the living room. "Yeah! Iced!" He slashed his knife through the air, and Zoe's stomach roiled.

Aidan focused the camera on Eric's face, eliminating the knife from the picture. "So, you ready to sing?"

Eric swayed, his face suddenly uncertain. "Uh. I guess."

"We definitely want to showcase your talent on camera. Where's your guitar?"

Eric's forehead wrinkled in thought. "Bedroom."

"Well, go get it, dude."

Eric wavered. His narrow features crumpled in indecision, clearly torn between his desire for fame and fortune and a blurry suspicion that he shouldn't leave the room.

Aidan gave him an ego-boosting close-up on the TV screen that would do Steven Spielberg proud. "C'mon, this is your big break, buddy. What are you waiting for? You're gonna be a star."

"Doors," Greene ordered, and war wagon's big double doors swung wide. Greene didn't take his eyes from the screen as the SWAT team surged forward. Modern-day knights in black body armor and helmets, their weapons held steadily in large, capable hands. Awe-inspiring. Any bad guy with an ounce of brains should surrender at the mere sight of them charging in. "Ready…"

Every muscle in Zoe's body went rigid, every nerve on edge. The critical moment. Emma couldn't hold out much longer. If Aidan couldn't talk Eric down, he would have to take him down and risk injury, not only to himself, but the children. The fact that Kincaid was both stoned and stupid made him unpredictable, and even more dangerous.

"Okay." Toying with the knife, Eric staggered out of sight.

"Go!" Greene barked, and the team charged outside.

Aidan dropped the camera on the coffee table. Zoe had a panoramic view of the living room as he scooped the children into his arms and sprinted out the back door.

At the same time, the team burst through the front door just as Kincaid shuffled back into the living room. His mouth fell open, and the guitar dropped from his hands with a discordant clang.

"Police! Get down! Down!" The team members shouted. Three MP-5 rifles pointed unerringly at Kincaid's head, and a snarling

K-9 backed him into a corner. Two other team members split off and swept the house. "On the floor!"

Even stoned and stupid, Kincaid knew the jig was up. Whimpering, "Don't hurt me," he flopped on the carpet and buried his head in his hands.

Forty minutes after the door breach, Aidan strode toward his car. The standoff had ended the best possible way. Quickly, with no shots fired, and no injuries. Grady had successfully treated Emma at the site, and she and her sister were safe with Shelly. Kincaid would be a guest of the state for a while. Barring further emergencies, the groomsmen and best man would make it to the wedding on time.

Zoe had stayed with Shelly until Emma was stabilized, and the police barricades came down. Then Aidan had seen her speaking in front of a KKEY news camera. Disgust had twisted inside him at the thought of her using Shelly and those scared, defenseless little girls for five o'clock fodder. Until he'd moved near enough to hear what she was saying.

Her heart-shaped face solemn, her earnest voice had declared, "No woman or child ever deserves to be victimized. If you, or someone you know is trapped in an abusive situation, help *is* available. Please, call the National Domestic Violence Hotline at 1-800-799-SAFE. You don't have to live in fear. There is no shame in asking for help. Call today. Your life, or the lives of your loved ones may depend on it."

Aidan stalked down the tree-lined sidewalk. In direct contrast to the sunny day, a storm of confusion thundered inside him. He'd thought he had Zoe Zagretti pegged, but she had surprised him at every turn. She had consistently done the unexpected. Today, he'd admired her smarts. He had actually enjoyed her teasing. Hell, he'd damn near kissed her.

He rolled his taut shoulders. Maybe he'd jumped to unwarranted conclusions where she was concerned. However, he'd reserve judgment until he had more evidence. Keep his guard up. No way would he give her any information, much less his trust.

About to cross Elm Street, he faltered in mid stride. Zoe was slumped in the driver's seat of a battered red Corolla. Her eyes were closed, her face ashen. She wasn't moving. Was she breathing? His heart lurched, then tried to pound its way out of his chest. Her body looked limp, lifeless.

She looked far too much like his worst nightmare come true.

Chapter 4

"Zoe!" Aidan's shout emerged a mere croak as he sprinted across the street. He wrenched open the car door and knelt on the pavement. Zoe lurched sideways, nearly falling into his lap, and his arms instinctively closed around her. She *was* breathing, thank God. "What happened? Are you hurt?"

She blinked dazedly at him. "Aidan? What the heck…?"

Grady had once brought home a bedraggled, starving black kitten. The boys had taken turns feeding the tiny animal around the clock with a doll's bottle. Alone in the dark kitchen in the middle of the night, Aidan had held the kitten in his hands, and it had stared at him with wide, trusting green eyes. Zoe looked at him the same way, her eyes huge in her white face. Her slender body felt fragile and insubstantial against him. Fierce protectiveness surged through him and caught him off guard…rattled him to the core.

He battled the urge to sweep her up, carry her to his house and take care of her. "Are you hurt?"

She shook her head and winced. "No. I started feeling squicky inside the war wagon a while ago. I thought if I rested for a few minutes, the nausea and headache would fade enough so I could drive home. Maybe I'm coming down with a twenty-four-hour bug or something."

He touched his palm to her forehead. Her skin was as soft and cool as the plumeria petals whose scent she favored. "No fever." He studied her wan face, a shade too thin for his liking. "When did you last eat?"

"I had some Cracker Jack about three hours ago."

"For breakfast?" He grimaced. "No wonder you're sick. Can you stand?"

"I think so."

He moved back, but supported her around the waist as she swung her legs over the seat and eased shakily to her feet. She swayed into him, and his hand accidentally slipped under the loose hem of her blouse and slid across the silken skin of her stomach. His body leapt to awareness.

She inhaled sharply, and her abdominal muscles quivered under his palm. "*Hello!* Hand check."

He snatched his burning palm away. "Sorry. Accidental contact…ten minutes in the penalty box."

She chuckled. "I know, it's okay. If I'd thought you'd done it on purpose, I would have stomped your enthusiasm."

His "enthusiasm" was at DEFCON One, maximum-force readiness. He clenched his jaw, mentally counting backwards from ten. *Stand down, officer*. He was supposed to be rescuing the woman, not ravishing her.

Still fighting the urge to scoop her into his arms, he assessed her wobbly stance. "You're in no shape to drive." He glanced down the tree-lined street. "My car is around the corner. Can you walk that far?"

"Yes. The fresh air is helping. Would you hand me my survival bag, please? There's ibuprofen and water inside."

He retrieved a tattered frog-printed canvas bag from behind the front seat. She leaned against the fender and sipped from a water bottle while he locked up the Corolla.

He detached the car key, pocketed it and handed her the rest. "I'll have an officer bring your car home later and leave the key in your mail slot." He'd be returning the car himself, but she wouldn't see him.

She dropped the other keys in her bag. "Have you always been this take-charge, or is it a recent affliction?"

He bit back a grin. The more time he spent with the intrepid reporter, the tougher it was to keep his distance, to act unaffected and remote. To remember he disliked her. Which is why he intended to avoid temptation and stay far away. "My mother claims I was assertive from the moment I made my entrance two weeks early."

"Ah, to paraphrase Steppenwolf, 'Born to be Bossy.'"

He couldn't stop the grin this time. "You like classic rock?"

"Love it. You?"

"Yeah." Something they had in common. Other than the desire to bring down DiMarco. For her, that meant a byline. For him, it was a personal crusade.

He propped his hand against the small of her back, and they strolled down the sidewalk at a snail's pace. She stumbled, and he moved closer. "Whoa, careful." He slid his arm around her waist and tucked her close to his side. She fit perfectly, as if she'd been created to be his companion.

As if she belonged to him, and he to her.

As though reading his dangerous thoughts, a squirrel scolded from a nearby branch, and Aidan nearly tripped this time. *Careful* is right!

He had no intention of detouring off his determinedly mapped-out life. He wasn't going anywhere near the cliff's edge. Especially not with Zoe Zagretti. The woman was TNT—tenacious, nosy and nothing but trouble.

A far-too-appealing package. Far too passionate. Far too likely to detonate and leave them both walking wounded.

They rounded the corner. A lawn mower droned at the end of the block, and happily shrieking children played a raucous game of kickball. He'd never have kids of his own…his one regret about his boycott on marriage. He breathed in the scent of fresh-cut grass, trying to ignore the clutch in his chest. He'd fill the empty space in his heart by spoiling future nieces and nephews. Knowing Con and Bailey, there would be plenty.

Parked beneath a maple tree, his black '64 T-Bird convertible glinted like polished obsidian in the dappled sunlight. "That's my car."

Zoe's luscious lips tilted in an unsteady grin. "Ohmigosh! You drive the Batmobile!"

Stunned, he lurched to a stop. As a kid, he'd possessed undying admiration for the Dark Knight. He still had several boxes of Batman comic books, purchased eons ago with hoarded allowance and lawn-mowing money. He told himself he kept them because they were highly collectible, but in truth, a lingering sentiment remained. He'd loved the T-Bird on sight. Why had he never noticed what Zoe saw at first glance? The vintage car's long, lean lines *did* resemble the Batmobile. Her perceptiveness impressed him. Intrigued him.

Terrified him.

If he slipped up and let Zoe Zagretti get under his skin, get into his heart, he would never be able to hide anything from her. She would never allow him to step back, to keep his emotional distance.

His secure, comfortable existence would be blown to hell.

He must have appeared as confounded as he felt, because she shot him an abashed look from under her lashes. "Sorry. I didn't mean to insult your ride. I think it's gorgeous."

He opened the passenger door for her. "No offense taken. I was…" *Freaked out!* "…surprised by your insight."

She slid inside, and he strode around the front of the car and climbed into the driver's seat. She chuckled softly. "I'll bet you had Batman pajamas and Con had Robin ones, and you pinned pillowcases around your necks and catapulted off your bunk beds pretending you could fly."

Her speculation was so near dead-on accurate, amusement bubbled in his chest. He couldn't stop the laughter that burst out of him. "Close. We wore Underoos and bath-towel capes, and jumped off the garage roof. Robin jammed his big toe and hobbled for a month."

Her breath hitched, and color flooded her cheeks. She stared at him in soft-eyed appreciation, her expression as awed as if he'd just rescued a stray puppy from a rampaging river. "Hey, you *laughed*."

Was he so tight-assed that a mere laugh would throw her for a loop? He fastened his seat belt. Yeah, he was. His self-preservation radar spiked on high alert around her, raising his defenses. He offered her a wry smile. "I do that occasionally, when something strikes me funny."

Her eyes gleamed with warm approval. "Remind me to work on my stand-up comedy routine."

The engine growled to life, and Aidan steered the T-Bird to the intersection. With the top down, the summer breeze caressed his face like a lover's soft touch. So, she appreciated his laugh, huh? That shouldn't matter so much. It definitely should *not* make him hot.

Maybe she wasn't the only one coming down with a twenty-four-hour virus. He shook his head. "Where to?"

She gave him an address in an older, rundown area of town. He wasn't crazy about her living in a neighborhood where she could get shot for wearing the wrong color. However, he didn't have a say in the matter. Nor did he want any. What was it about this woman? How did merely being in her presence twist his insides into complicated knots?

"Aidan? Don't feel weird about the superhero thing. I liked Wonder Woman. Oh, and the guy in the blue tights, too, but I always rooted for Lois."

Another grin surfaced as he took Ash Street, heading toward the inner city through heavy Saturday-afternoon traffic. "Big surprise there." All he had to do was endure several minutes of safe, polite conversation, drop her off, and never again get within five miles of her. Evade and escape. A simple, easy tactical plan any moron could follow. "Did you have any 'super' adventures with brothers or sisters?"

"No, I'm an only child." She glanced at him, and her wistful expression made her loneliness painfully apparent. Made his throat ache. "I'll bet having three brothers was a blast."

"For us. I'm not so sure about Mom and Pop." In truth, his parents had adored each other and their rowdy brood. His childhood had been abundantly full of laughter and love. "Are your parents close by?"

"I'm…on my own. My mom had a stroke when I was a senior in high school, and she's in a care facility in San Francisco. I'm saving up to move her here. My father—" She cleared her throat, but he caught the slight hitch in her voice. "Has never really been in the picture."

His heart fisted. Without his family's support, he wouldn't have survived. He couldn't imagine going it alone, especially so young. He steered the car into the turn lane. Understanding dawned as he idled at the red light. No wonder she was so zealous about her job. She had no family or history of her own, so she invested herself in the stories of others.

"That must be tough." He despised the thought of Zoe struggling all by herself. Then chastised himself for letting it hurt. Emotional distance was the first survival skill his training officer had taught him. Compassion was fine. Empathy was dangerous. Cops who invested emotionally in their work burned out. Fast and hard.

"I do okay." She shrugged. "A lot of people have it way worse."

No trace of self pity, no whining. Admiration snaked through him. The girl had guts and a winning attitude. Dammit, he didn't want to care about her. Didn't want to respect her. Didn't want to crave her sexy smile and admire her agile mind.

He turned right and navigated the potholed side street, and then pulled up in front of a ramshackle, one-story apartment complex. No trees blocked the relentless sun. The shabby apartments squatted in a half-square around a patchy brown lawn choked with weeds and strewn with rusted appliances.

"Home sweet rented home." Zoe unbuckled her seat belt. Wariness edged her expression, as if she feared he might judge her by her living conditions. "I'm working my way up the food chain at the station, and right now, I'm plankton."

How many people had she trusted enough to bring home? How many *had* judged her? He quickly exited the car and had her door open when she was ready to step out.

She smiled and placed her hand in his offered palm to steady herself. Her entire hand fit in his palm. "Your mother sure raised you right."

Her balance was still uncertain, and he slid his arm around her waist as they navigated the cracked sidewalk. His brain insisted he was helping. His body, on an independent circuit, voted for scoring. He again mentally counted backward from ten. In Gaelic. "She tried."

"I read in a back issue of the paper that her women's rowing team won the Pacific Northwest championship last year." She fished the keys out of her bag and after two tries, unlocked the apartment door. "Great hobby."

She was genuinely interested, and so easy to talk to, the words tumbled out of their own accord. "My whole family loves the water."

"Really? Me, too. Lake, pool or bathtub, there's almost no place else I'd rather be."

Something else they had in common. "Mom took up rowing after Pop died." Only he knew how long and tormented the journey had been. His mother was the strongest woman he knew, yet she'd been devastated. After the first few shocked days, she'd pulled herself together for her sons. But he'd seen the unrelenting anguish she'd tried so hard to hide. As the oldest, he'd attempted to shield his brothers from their mom's worst grief. "She says the physical activity helps her work off stress."

"The same way Kendo does for you."

There she went again with the startling insight. The back of his neck itched with the freaky feeling that she could read his mind. Which was whacked. But he felt exposed and vulnerable. His private fears and weaknesses were not up for grabs.

They stepped inside, and he closed the door behind them. The apartment was a one-room studio, the inside as cramped and careworn as the outside. She'd propped the windows open a few inches, not wise in the crime-riddled neighborhood, but heat permeated the room. Worn green shag carpet was scrubbed scrupulously clean, as were the dingy walls.

Zoe had draped colorful scarves above stained vinyl shades at the windows. Tropical-island prints from a calendar were artfully arranged on the walls. Leafy plants in hand-painted pots added freshness. With a few inexpensive, imaginative touches, she'd transformed the claustrophobic, dreary place into a bright, cozy and welcoming cocoon.

Obviously, she didn't have many visitors. The one seat was a red canvas director's chair perched in front of a desk made from a door propped on filing cabinets. A small portable TV and an up-to-the-minute computer system sat on the desktop. She needed a good unit for research, of course, but he'd bet his trusty Glock pistol she'd somehow finagled it for a bargain price. A twin mattress encased in bright yellow linens and topped by a turquoise throw was tucked into the corner on the floor. Aidan glanced around, unsure where to put the shaky woman.

"The bed is fine," she murmured, again reading his mind.

He led her to the mattress, and gently lowered her.

She sighed and rubbed her forehead. "Thanks."

The ugliest cat he'd ever seen lounged in the windowsill above her. The mud-colored, battle-scarred feline with one ragged ear stretched, yawned and then jumped down. Purring, he kneaded Zoe's lap. She patted the animal. "Aidan, meet Evander. Evander, Aidan."

Aidan laughed. A dangerous habit he seemed to be unable to control in her presence. He squatted and scratched the cat under the chin. "You named your cat after the guy who got his ear chomped by Mike Tyson?"

"Well, if the gnawed appendage fits…"

Their eyes met in mutual amusement. A connection sparked. A moment of shared understanding that felt eerily as if they'd forged a tentative bond. Warmth curled around his heart, and heat coiled in his belly. As if she instinctively recognized his response, Zoe's eyes widened and her breathing accelerated.

Aidan surged to his feet, severing the link. The temperature was much too hot. He switched on a small fan near the head of the bed, the whir overly loud in the sudden silence. He needed to feed Zoe and get the hell out of Dodge. Stay the hell out of Dodge. Dodge was a damn scary place.

Next stop, Over-the-Cliff City.

"What can I fix you to eat?" He strode to the mini fridge across the room. Four cupboards, a sink, and an inexpensive microwave, toaster and double hotplate completed the "kitchen."

"Peanut butter on crackers and a glass of milk, please."

Her tiny fridge held half a dozen eggs, a quart of milk, a package of hotdogs and several seasonal fruits. She'd mentioned that her father wasn't in the picture, so her mother would have had it hard. Poverty had probably been status quo all Zoe's life. That was another reason he wasn't about to leave a woman behind to raise his children. The emotional strain was traumatic enough, but the additional financial burden made it untenable. He would not be doing Zoe any favors by getting involved with her.

He opened a cupboard door. The meager contents made Mother Hubbard's pantry look like Ivana Trump's penthouse kitchen. Zoe had two plates, two glasses, two coffee cups and two sets of flatware. Another indication she never had company. She was alone too much.

He found a box of crackers and arranged some on a plate. Zoe had said she was saving to have her mother moved from a San Francisco care center to Riverside. Long-term care was exorbitant enough without incurring extra moving expenses. Zoe obviously got by on very little.

Hot, prickling shame crept over his skin. He'd thought her vain. He'd thought she stayed thin purposely, because TV cameras added ten pounds. The horrible truth was she didn't have enough to eat. His hands shook as he spread peanut butter on crackers and then poured milk. Rage scoured his insides like acid. He'd been on enough domestic calls to know that in the wealthiest country in the world people went to bed hungry every night.

The fact that he gave a generous monthly donation to the Riverside Food Bank didn't take away the sting of knowing *Zoe* went to bed hungry.

She needed someone to look after her. But it couldn't be him. He couldn't give her the stability she needed. Couldn't make long-term promises. The battle raging inside him made his stomach cramp. He'd read about an ancient form of torture where a man's arms and legs were bound to four horses and then the horses were

driven in opposite directions, tearing the man apart. He could relate. He carried the plate of crackers over and handed it and the
glass of milk to her.

"Thanks." She patted the mattress beside her. "Please, sit.
Have some."

He had to give her credit, you'd never know she had it rough.
She might feel rocky on the inside, but she presented an upbeat,
smiling face to the world. He knew from personal experience it
required a buttload of courage to stay positive and fight your way
back to your feet when life repeatedly slammed you to the mat.

Even if he could bring himself to take her food, the lump in his
throat would choke him if he tried to eat. "No thanks. If you're
okay now, I have to go."

Her lashes didn't lower quite fast enough to hide the hurt swimming in her eyes. Obviously, she thought he found either the company or the environment distasteful. "I'll be fine. I'm feeling
better already, and I'm sure eating will help." Her voice wavered,
and she cleared her throat. "Thank you for the ride home and the
room service."

Pain punched into his chest. Dammit, he hadn't meant to hurt
her feelings. "No problem. I'd stay, but I've got family stuff to do."
Even if he didn't, he'd be out of here, PDQ. The environment
didn't bother him. The company did. He'd suddenly discovered he
liked it—far too much. "Sure you're all right?"

"Yup. See you around the incident sites, SWAT."

"Is that a promise or a threat, Brenda Starr?" Though he managed to tease her, his aching heart turned to lead and sank in his
chest as he strode outside.

A little over an hour later, Zoe was sorting through a stack of
cracked dinner plates inside a huge Dumpster parked behind an office complex. The contents came from a liquidated restaurant supply company. Until very recently—like last week—the company
had been owned by another corporation headed by Tony DiMarco.

After Aidan had departed and she'd eaten, she'd shaken off the
lingering taint of melancholy. Of course he hadn't been able to stay.
His brother was getting married tonight. He hadn't run out like his

Jockeys were on fire because of the oppressive heat and cramped dinginess of her ramshackle apartment. Or because he couldn't stand to be around her. *Probably*.

She'd determinedly put him out of her mind, parked herself in front of her computer and continued the DiMarco investigation. A short time later, she hit the jackpot with a real estate sale. The office building's name had struck a chord. Sure enough, it was on her compiled inventory of DiMarco's suspected properties.

Now, she wiped a bead of perspiration from her forehead and dug deeper. As far as Dumpsters went, this one wasn't horrendous. Mostly damaged restaurant supplies and office furniture. She'd waded in much more fragrant and colorful garbage for evidence. No stale Chinese takeout or greasy pizza crusts this time. Or holey undergarments. And since she'd propped up one of the Dumpster's massively heavy lids against the building's wall, it wasn't dark. She'd brought a penlight, just in case, but hadn't needed it. She shuddered. Thank heaven for small favors.

Zoe examined an unopened package of coffee stirrers. Seemed like the person who had cleaned out the building had tossed stuff willy-nilly. She envied anyone financially secure enough to throw away brand-new merchandise. Who was covertly liquidating DiMarco's assets? More importantly, where was the money going? She was on the right track, could feel it in her bones. The restaurant supply house was near the top of the list—many of DiMarco's other suspected corporations branched out from it. She didn't have much time left before all his holdings were converted to cash and the trail went cold.

Proving DiMarco's security company owned all the others was the first and most difficult step. She was attempting to unravel the tangled web. If purchase dates and amounts corresponded even remotely with the robberies, she might figure out the path taken to launder the stolen money. Not to mention DiMarco would have a hard time explaining how he'd paid cash for more than two dozen businesses.

She relocated a stack of brand-new linen tablecloths. Throw it out and write it off seemed to be the ongoing philosophy. Maybe she'd salvage a few; it would be a shame to waste them. Speaking of administrative waste, the "official" DiMarco investigation would be hampered by legal channels and red tape. Zoe was under no such restrictions. A step at a time, she would link DiMarco to the corporations, and the corporations to the robberies…the likeliest motive for Brian O'Rourke's murder. Perhaps the cop had gotten too close to uncovering DiMarco's operation while attempting to clear his name. She simply had to find the connection. Then she would break her story and turn over her evidence to the police.

To Aidan.

She discovered a phone receiver without a cord and tossed it over her shoulder. Aidan had certainly been solicitous this afternoon. He'd treated her with care and consideration, and hadn't shown a flicker of distaste about her living conditions. At least not outwardly. Who knew what the enigmatic man thought privately?

The more she interacted with her cop, the more she liked him. She'd finally made him laugh. Memory of that sweet victory curled warmly around her heart, and she smiled. She'd pierced a layer of his defenses. They'd connected in a basic, elemental way. He'd momentarily dropped his "cop face" and let her see the man behind the mask. Then he'd freaked out. Run away.

He might be reluctant to get involved while he still had unresolved issues in his past. She knew all about that. Maybe once he had closure, he'd be less skittish. After years of futile attempts to achieve closure for herself, she was trying to wedge the door to her past firmly shut. Would her murky lineage keep a man from becoming serious about her? What about when her someday soul mate wanted children? She had no paternal information. No medical history. No gene-pool statistics besides the fact that her mom had declared her father "really bad news."

Hardly a statement that would thrill a future husband.

Fighting not to feel as worthless as the garbage trampled under her feet, Zoe uncovered a dented file cabinet containing a big bag of shredded documents. Good, she'd finally reached the managerial stuff. Too bad the files were destroyed. She'd take them home anyway. If the gang on *CSI* could piece shredded documents together, so could she. She wrestled aside a cracked computer monitor. Down at the bottom of the pile, she spotted two battered, broken central processing units, otherwise known as CPUs. Aha! That was more like it. She straddled one and attempted to pry it apart. Even if the hard drive inside was damaged or erased, special programs could retrieve the data. Most people didn't know that.

"You, in the Dumpster," a commanding male baritone ordered. "Put your hands where I can see them and slowly climb out."

"Ack!" Zoe started, and nearly banged her head on the filing cabinet. She couldn't see the man from inside the metal container, and he couldn't see her. Still, she'd know her cop's deep, sensual voice anywhere. What were the odds? Of all the Dumpsters in all the towns in all the world, Aidan O'Rourke had to walk up to hers. "Sorry, no can do," she yelled.

What could be called a heavily pregnant pause ensued. Then she heard Aidan groan. "I should have known. It couldn't possibly have been anyone else. Fate has a twisted sense of humor." The sound of his gun sliding into a leather holster was reassuring. At least he wasn't going to shoot her. "Evacuate the Dumpster, Zagretti."

"Can't." She shook the CPU. She had to wrench the hard drive loose before he thwarted her. "I'm not done yet."

"Yes, you are. The psychiatrist's office across the street called in a complaint. You're scaring their patients."

"And they sent the SWAT team? Overkill, don't you think?"

"I was in the neighborhood, and answered the call."

"I'm just looking around." She grabbed a nail file out of her bag and pried at the casing edges. "I'm not bothering anyone, and garbage is fair game."

"Why can't you shop for bargains at the discount stores, like a normal person?"

Her cop sounded so flummoxed, she giggled. If she let him assume she was Dumpster-diving, he wouldn't interfere with her investigation. "Free is a very good price."

He sighed heavily. "I'll give you to the count of three."

"Is that one, two, three, then do it?" she shouted, her question echoing off the metal walls. She continued prying, and the casing loosened. "Or one, two and do it *on* three?"

"I don't have time for this, Riggs."

She grinned. He'd caught the reference from *Lethal Weapon 2*.

"You like action movies, too?" The casing broke apart. She unscrewed the brackets with her nail file and tugged out the book-sized hard drive and stuffed it in her survival bag, then started jimmying the second CPU. "You know, we have an awful lot of the same likes and dislikes."

"You're giving me a headache, Brenda Starr."

"I have ibuprofen in my bag." *And, I hope, evidence that's going to put away DiMarco for good.*

Another long pause ticked past. "Come out, or I'm coming in after you."

She wasn't leaving without the evidence. Which gave her one option. Great. She shoved the CPU behind her. Somehow, she'd have to distract him long enough to remove the hard drive. "Welcome to my world, SWAT."

His big hands gripped the edge of the Dumpster and then his thick, wavy hair appeared over the top. He stared down at her, half buried in rubble. His gorgeous mouth slanted. "Now who would want to throw away a perfectly good reporter?"

"You'd be surprised how many people have a jones for journalists."

He jumped inside, landing gracefully on the debris beside her. The Dumpster was so large, his head didn't reach the top. "Can't imagine why."

He was wearing his denim jacket, presumably to cover his gun. A black flashlight shoved handle-first into the front pocket of his jeans made a bulge that caught her attention. Of its own accord, her gaze wandered to the bulge slightly to the right of the flashlight.

He cleared his throat, and she jumped, realizing exactly where she was staring. Cheeks burning, her gaze darted to the strong planes and angles of his handsome features. He arched a brow, and her blush burned hotter.

She struggled to form words with a mouth suddenly gone dry. "I'll bet a month's rent you were a Boy Scout."

A dumbfounded expression creased his forehead. "Eagle Scout. How did you…?"

She flicked a hit-and-run glance at the protruding flashlight. "You carry that in your T-Bird? Always prepared."

Something strangely like relief flickered across his face. "Oh. Right."

"What?" She grinned at him. "Did you think I could read your mind?"

He grimaced as though that's exactly what he'd thought. "Of course not. Not possible."

She read him a lot more easily than he'd ever guess. His snarly attitude might keep everyone else at arm's length, but she wasn't fooled for a second. Intimidate her? No way. He intrigued her. "There are more things in heaven and earth, Horatio—"

He finished the quote from Hamlet in tandem with her. "Than are dreamt of in your philosophy."

Not just another pretty face. But she already knew that. "I like a guy in a bulletproof vest who knows his Shakespeare."

Aidan snorted. He spread his hands, indicating their surroundings. "Exactly how I wanted to spend Saturday afternoon. Doing the backstroke in trash."

He stood near enough for her to smell his warm, masculine scent. She'd never tingled all over while standing thigh-deep in a Dumpster before. "It's not bad, as far as trash goes."

"And you're the resident expert?"

"You betcha." She retrieved an object near his left foot. "Look at this lovely napkin holder. Only slightly dented."

His lips twitched. "I was wondering what to get my mother for her birthday."

She laughed. "You're all set. Hey, why don't you help me?" She'd send him to the opposite end, and scavenge the hard drive. "Then we can both leave, and everybody's happy."

"The courts call that 'aiding and abetting.'"

"That's garbage."

"No, it's the law."

She laughed. "I meant it's only junk that someone else threw away. Free for the taking. Therefore, I am not breaking any laws."

"You have the most convoluted sense of logic of anyone I've ever met." He moved closer, and she sidestepped him. He frowned. "C'mon, Zoe, work with me here. I'm a police officer. I'm legally obligated to settle a valid complaint." Resolve glinted in his eyes. "If necessary, I will sling you over my shoulder and bodily remove you."

She sat on the CPU and raised her chin, silently daring him. She wasn't going anywhere without the second piece of possibly valuable evidence. "I'm not done yet, and I am morally obligated to make said removal as difficult as possible."

His eyes narrowed and he echoed her earlier question. "Have you always been this hardheaded, or is it a recent affliction?"

"I prefer *tenacious*. A trait you see every time you look in the mirror." His determined gaze captured hers, and the jolt of heat weakened her knees. What would it be like to have his focused intensity concentrated solely on her in the bedroom? Aidan the cop was a formidable presence. Aidan the lover would be an irresistible force. Her cop never left any job half-finished. He meticulously completed every task. Personally checked each detail. SWAT…seduction with attentive thoroughness.

It took two tries before she could speak. "Even cops scour trash for evidence. In the case of the State of North Dakota versus Herrick in 1997, the court ruled that 'once something is discarded, it no longer affords the previous owner any expectations of privacy.'"

"Evidence?" Suspicion stamped his chiseled features. He crossed his arms over his wide chest. "Whose garbage is this?"

Rats! Distracted by dancing hormones, she'd slipped. "Haven't you been listening? Garbage doesn't belong to anyone."

He advanced on her. "Zoe…" Her name was a growled warning.

She backpedaled to the farthest corner, under the lidded half of the container. "On second thought, you probably have better things to do—"

Without warning, a loud rumble shook the ground beneath her feet. Then the Dumpster's lid slammed down, trapping them in darkness.

Chapter 5

3:00 p.m.

Zoe shrieked. Outside, an ear-splitting grinding noise was followed by shrill beeping. Panic screamed along her nerve endings, and a surge of adrenaline spiked her pulse. The Dumpster tilted, and she was thrown into Aidan.

He lost his footing and lurched backward into the wall. His arms closed around her, held her against him. "Hang on!"

He didn't have to tell her twice. Stuck to him like Velcro, she flung her arms around his neck. "It's dark!"

The Dumpster rose, an out-of-control express elevator. "That's the least of our problems." His muscles tensed as he braced, struggling to keep them upright.

"I hate the dark! Get me out of here!"

His arms embraced her, strong and reassuring. "Okay, don't panic."

Shaking, she clung to him, her anchor in the dark, whirling chaos and buried her face in his neck. "Too late!"

"Zoe," his deep, velvet voice brushed her ear. "I've got you. You're all right."

His unique scent—warm essence of man—penetrated her fear. The strength of his powerful, solid body pressed to hers calmed her. She wasn't alone. Aidan wouldn't let anything bad reach out of the darkness and snatch her away. The Dumpster rocked wildly, and she clutched him tighter. "What's happening?"

"We won't be in the dark for long. The beeping, chugging monster outside is the garbage truck."

"Oh, no!"

"This could only happen to you, Brenda Starr." He shook his head. "This is the first time I've ever been recycled."

The Dumpster jerked to a halt and began to tip. The contents slid, banging into them. Aidan shielded her between his body and the metal wall. "Keep your head down."

"Aidan, you'll get hurt."

"At least trash doesn't return fire." He grunted as the file cabinet slammed into his back. "Maybe."

"I'm sorry."

"It's no rougher than playing football with my brothers."

The Dumpster angled downward, and his weight combined with an avalanche of trash squashed her. "I can't breathe."

Rock-hard biceps bunched as he levered up, affording her an inch of space. "Better?"

"Y—" The Dumpster tipped, the lid swung open and they were freefalling.

She landed flat on her back on lumpy plastic bags. Seconds later, Aidan crashed on top of her, face down. He flung his arms over his head and covered her, taking the brunt of the blows as the Dumpster's contents bombarded them.

More grinding. A thunk echoed as the metal container hit the pavement. The beeping stopped, the truck's gears screeched, and then the vehicle chugged into motion.

She'd always loved thrill rides, but this was nuts. She lay buried in debris, sheltered by Aidan's big body. Her nose pressed into the soft cotton covering his broad chest, which rose and fell rapidly as he struggled to breathe.

She writhed up the length of his body until her face was free and she could see the truck's interior. Open panels in the roof gave her a mercifully clear view of cerulean summer sky passing overhead. A not-so-daisy-fresh smell permeated the cramped space, but the breeze helped. Aidan's face rested in her shoulder, and his breathing evened out. For some crazy reason, his heavy weight on top of her felt reassuring. "Are you hurt?"

He lifted his head and held her gaze. "No. You?"

His full, sensual lips were inches from hers. His warm breath feathered over her mouth. Long lashes as thick and intricate as black lace surrounded enigmatic eyes alive with warm highlights. She could plunge into those golden-shimmered pools and live forever.

"Zoe." Large, steady hands cradled her face. "Are you okay?"

She surfaced slowly from the glowing brown depths. Blinked. Falling into the truck was nothing compared to the fall into his eyes. She drew a deep, shuddering breath. "Yes, but…ouch." She squirmed. "Your gun is killing my ribs."

"Sorry." Propped on his elbows, he raised his upper body a few inches.

"And your flashlight is riding my hipbone. I think it's very glad to see me." She slid her hand between them. "It's one of those big Everreadys, huh?"

He jumped. "The flashlight got knocked out of my pocket on the way down."

"Oh!" Face flaming, she jerked her hand away so fast, the movement nearly gave her whiplash. Was it possible to spontaneously combust from embarrassment? Nevertheless, happiness curled through her. She turned him on. A lot. A whole lot. Or maybe being snuggled up this close and personal with any woman would turn him on. She wished she had the nerve to ask. "Accidental contact. Ten minutes in the penalty box?"

His unexpected laughter sent tingles spiraling up her spine. He didn't seem embarrassed. Maybe women groped him every day. Considering his rampant good looks, the idea wasn't terribly farfetched. "That one's gotta cost you at least twenty minutes, Zagretti."

The grumbling and grinding started again, and the trash bags beneath them heaved. She stared at Aidan. "What now?"

"Compactor." He shoved himself off her, scattering debris, then reached down and helped her up. "Stay on top."

Clutching hands, stumbling in place, they scrambled up the roiling mountain beneath their feet. Stairmaster as envisioned by the Marquis de Sade. Fighting mass and momentum, Zoe floundered as the riptide tried to force her backward and suck her under. If she slipped, she'd be crushed. She clung to Aidan's hand. "Don't let go of me."

Fierce determination glinted in his gaze. His hand gripped hers, and resolve hummed in every straining muscle. "Never."

He wouldn't. Not even if he went under with her. Reassuring thought. She gasped for breath. "'Two local residents compacted.' There's a unique story, if I'm around to report it."

He wasn't even breathing hard. He probably jogged. Not to mention he was almost a foot taller, most of it legs. "Hang in there. It can't last much longer."

Sure enough, without warning, the awful noise stopped. The contents lurched and settled, and she stumbled into him. Once again, he caught her. Panting, she looked up at him. "Does this remind you of anything?"

"Yeah." His white, wicked grin flashed. "The fitness center from hell."

His crack mirrored her own thoughts so closely, she chuckled. "Remember the rescue scene in the original Star Wars?" She paused to breathe. "Luke, Leia, Han and Chewie were in the trash masher, and C3PO thought they were dying."

"'A little short for a Storm Trooper, aren't you?'" he quoted. "Unfortunately, this isn't the movies." His grin faded. "Look what your mule-headedness got us into."

She grimaced. It couldn't be helped. She couldn't just walk away from the CPUs and shredded files. "Well, if I'm stuck in refuse, at least I'm glad it's with a capable guy like you. Otherwise, I would have been crushed."

"A guy worth the garbage." He eased back, but kept his hands around her waist, balancing her as the truck rumbled unsteadily along. Chivalry at its best. "Maybe I can use that as a toast at Con's wedding tonight." His dark brows slammed together. "Aw, hell!"

"What?"

"I was on my way to pick up my tux when dispatch called about the wacko in the Dumpster. I was a block away. I figured it would take five minutes, and save sending out a patrol car."

"You have a police radio in your car, and listen to it off duty? I'll take *workaholic* for five hundred, Alex."

"I like to know what's going down in my precinct." He released her and glanced at his watch. "The shop closes at five today. I'll never make it in time."

Mourning the loss of his touch, she clutched a protruding metal bar on the lurching vehicle's side. "Nothing like waiting till the last minute to pick up your tux."

He shot her a sardonic glance. "Yeah, too bad an inconvenient hostage crisis mucked up my schedule."

"Okay, point to you. I suppose you can blame me."

"No, I put the blame directly where it belongs. On myself."

What did that cryptic remark mean? "Do you have a cell phone? Can you call dispatch and have them send a patrol car to rescue us?"

"The guys would razz my ass off." He groaned. "I can see it now. Toy garbage trucks parked on my desk. Dozens of trash bags stuffed in my locker. Specially brewed *L'eau de Trash* cologne for Christmas. No way. I'd rather perform my best-man duties wearing pink tights and a tutu."

"You definitely have the legs for it, but purple is a better color for you." He snorted, and she sent him a teasing grin. "All righty then. How about one of your brothers?"

"Same results, worse razzing. Till the day I died." He shuddered. "Mom might be able to do it, though."

He tugged a cell phone out of his jacket pocket, propped a hand on the wall for balance, and hit a button. Zoe smiled. Extra points for a man who had his mother on speed dial.

"Mom, it's Aidan." He had to nearly shout over the truck's grumbling progress. "I'm a little tied up. Could you do me a favor and get my tux?" He paused to listen. "I know I should have picked it up sooner, but I worked double shifts all week." Another pause. "No, ma'am, I am not on a SWAT call-out four hours before my brother's wedding. The noise? Uh...I'm helping a…friend…relocate." He grimaced. "Yes, it's a woman." He looked at Zoe, his eyes widening in near panic. "Uh-uh." He shook his head vehemently. "No, ma'am. Gotta go. See you later."

Zoe waited until he pocketed the phone. "What did she want?"

For the first time since they'd met, he evaded her gaze. "Nothing."

Hmm. Interesting. Curiosity burned inside her. She'd have sacrificed the rent money to know what his mom had asked that had him so flustered. "We should try to attract the driver's attention."

"You happen to have an air horn on you?"

"Not today. No harm in trying, though."

He shrugged. "Nope."

Together, they banged on the truck and shouted.

Aidan shook his head, "This is insane. He'll never hear us over the racket."

"I don't suppose we could shoot our way out?" She was only half-kidding.

"Sure…if the ricochet didn't kill us. We'll wait till he stops, and then get his attention."

Good plan. Too bad the truck didn't stop again.

She stayed in one spot until she picked up the trick to balancing on the bulky mass, and then rummaged for her canvas bag. With most of the trash contained, nothing was too messy. Thank heaven for small favors. "Finally! My survival kit."

Aidan leaned against the wall, his swaying body easily accommodating the truck's jerky movements. "What kind of survival kit?"

Rats! A huge rip in the seam clear through the vinyl lining revealed the hard drive hidden inside. She rotated the bag, turning the tear away from him. "Among other things, Cracker Jack, water bottle, ibuprofen, pen, pad, penlight, makeup, safety pins and a romance novel. All the necessities."

"If you're marooned at a pajama party."

The second CPU wasn't far away. The impact had cracked it open. Turning her back on Aidan, she used her body to hide her movements as she unscrewed and removed the hard drive and crammed it in her bag beside the other one. Safety pins from her stash fastened the ripped edges together. The hard drives were still visible if you looked closely. She'd have to keep him from looking too closely. She zipped the top. "What's in your survival kit?"

"Butane lighter, flares, flashlight, Swiss Army knife, ammo, first aid supplies, water and dehydrated food packets."

"What about a needle and thread to sew up your own wounds, Rambo?"

He chuckled, the husky timbre sending delicious shivers over her. "Mine will keep you alive longer than lipstick and love novels."

"Depends on where you're stranded. And who you're stranded with." Her survival kit might now include new, major pieces to the DiMarco puzzle. That topped dehydrated stroganoff any day.

She stepped to one side and spotted his flashlight at her feet. "Here's your flashlight." She couldn't stop the flush that crept up her neck when she passed it to him.

His gorgeous features projected studied innocence. "You seem to be fond of my Everready."

She glanced down. Her fingers were still involuntarily clenched around the thick handle. She let go as if it had burned her. "There's a crack in the end." Her blush flared hotter.

He flicked the switch, and light gleamed. He flicked it off and nonchalantly jammed the handle in his jeans pocket. "The old Everready can take quite a beating and still perform."

Hoo boy, was it hot in here? "Gives the phrase 'you light up my life' a whole new meaning."

"You have quite a way with words, Zagretti."

"That's why I'm a journ—" The truck angled around a sharp corner, knocking her down. It bumped and rocked over uneven ground before jerking to a stop. The beeping and grinding commenced and the back of the floor began to rise. "Now what?"

Aidan dove at her and scooped her into his embrace. "We're about to get dumped. Hang on."

She struggled to hook the canvas bag over one arm and accidentally banged him in the ribs.

"Ouch. Must be a buttload of makeup in there. You plan on being stranded with Tammy Faye Baker?"

"Sorry." How would he react if he knew he'd just been clobbered with possible evidence that might put his father's killer in jail? She clung to him as her feet were swept out from beneath her, and the world slid away.

The back flap banged open. Surrounded by a sea of trash bags, they tumbled out the rear of the truck, and landed on a pile of refuse. He protected her from the trash raining on top of them. In seconds, they were buried.

They dug out just in time to see the truck chugging off in the distance.

Zoe stood, splotched with gunk she didn't dare identify. She looked at Aidan and then at the mountains of debris. Flies droned, circling in the bright sunshine like jumbo jets stacked up over LAX. "You can't say I never take you anywhere."

Aidan chuckled again, warming her heart. "You sure know how to show a guy a good time."

She unzipped her bag, fished out a package of sanitizing hand wipes and handed him half. "Dis my survival kit now, SWAT."

He scrubbed his face. "Okay, point to you."

Zoe cleaned her face and tossed the wipes. She turned back to paw through the rubble.

"Looking for our dignity? Too late. It's trashed."

She laughed. His intelligence and wry wit were the biggest turn-ons of all. "I saw some shredded paper, and I want it."

"What for?"

"It makes terrific plant mulch." One hundred percent true. She simply didn't specify that she wasn't in the market for mulch.

"Right." He glanced at his watch. "Three minutes. Then we're leaving, with or without it." He crossed his arms and waited. Not helping, but not hindering, either.

"After all this, I am *not* walking away empty-handed." Okay, she had the hard drives, but he was on a need-to-know basis regarding those. And she couldn't think of an urgent reason to tell him. Determined to ignore the smell, she pawed at the pile.

"This place probably has hot- and cold-running rats."

"Ack!" She jumped back, and her nervous glance skittered over the rubble. Nothing moved except the horrified goose bumps crawling over her skin. She turned and glared at him. "You're trying to scare me into quitting."

"Would I do that?" He shrugged, an innocent picture of male solicitousness. "Just looking out for you." He consulted his watch. "Two minutes."

"I spot a rat, all right," she muttered, resuming her search. "Six foot one, with dark wavy hair and a tendency to spout ultimatums."

Seconds before time ran out, she hit pay dirt. Make that pay garbage. She cleaned her grimy fingers, slung her survival kit over one shoulder and grabbed the bag of shredded documents.

He sighed and took it from her. "Let's move." His long strides ate up the ground, and she had to hustle to keep up. "We have a long walk ahead, and if I'm late for the wedding, Mom will kick my ass."

She hadn't met Maureen O'Rourke yet, but liked her already. Any woman who could inspire fear in a man who unflinchingly faced knife-wielding lunatics was top-notch in her book. "I had to bus it until I saved up to register and license my car in this state. The twenty-two bus line comes out this way. All we have to do is find a stop." She patted her survival kit. "I carry several tickets, in case my car breaks down."

"Resourceful, aren't you?"

"Eagle Scouts aren't the only ones who can be prepared."

He indicated his stained, rumpled clothing. "Even with tickets, I doubt they'll let us on the bus looking like a couple of winos after a hard day's night."

"I've sat next to worse, believe me. They'll let us on."

He studied her, his expression intrigued. "You always see the glass half-full, Zagretti?"

"The woe-is-me gig is a real bummer. Been there, done that, sniveled into the T-shirt. Occasionally, I get down in the dumps." She glanced around, giggled. "Present circumstances not withstanding. Keeping a positive attitude takes practice—and sometimes grim determination—but it beats the alternative all to heck."

His sideways glance brushed her with admiration, and her insides glowed with warmth. "Refreshing."

He fell silent as they walked through rows of garbage, his expression growing pensive. Heading toward the landfill's entrance, they passed a tweed upholstered loveseat and rocking chair that had minor wear and tear.

Zoe frowned. She would gladly have used the still-nice pieces in her apartment. "Amazing what people toss out."

Aidan walked a few more steps. Suddenly, he stumbled, and the bag fell to the ground. Startled, she turned and glanced up at him. Frozen, he gazed blankly into the distance, his stricken face bleached of color.

"Aidan?"

He swayed. Then his mouth wrenched in pain, and he dropped to his knees.

Sharp fear arrowed into her. She cupped his face in her hands. His blind gaze stared through her as if she wasn't there and instead, he saw something too horrible to bear. "Aidan, are you hurt? Are you sick?"

"Chair." A fragile thread of sound. A whispered breath.

Had he been hit in the head by falling debris and just now manifested concussion symptoms? She stroked his hair, carefully checking for injuries. He was shivering. "Aidan, look at me." He did, and the raw anguish in his eyes slammed into her heart, stole her breath. His distress wasn't physical, but emotional. "What's wrong?"

"Pop's chair."

Understanding hit, bringing more pain. He must be having a flashback. "That furniture reminds you of your father's chair?" She kept her voice soft, her tone gentle. "But it can't possibly be. Not after all this time."

"No." His voice sounded oddly detached. "There's no blood."

Tight and aching inside, she knelt in front of him and gripped his shoulders. "Do you want to talk about it?"

"Never have." She saw his internal battle to recover, to distance himself from the hurt. But he was losing the fight. "Not to anyone."

"Maybe you should. It's not good to keep hurt trapped inside for so long." She should know. She'd longed for another person to connect with, someone to halve her sorrows and double her joys. Instead, she'd been forced into solitude. Aidan didn't have to go it alone, but he'd chosen to. Why? "All those feelings fester and then explode when you least expect it."

He swallowed hard, struggling for control. "I had to be strong. For the others."

Her heart splintered. He'd protected his family, at his own expense. "You don't have to be strong for me. Let it out. Pain shared is pain halved. You'll feel better."

His shadowed gaze finally settled on her, but there was no recognition. His wary expression looked like that of a little boy who'd been told the antiseptic wouldn't sting, but didn't quite believe it. "Will I?"

"Yes, you will. Let me help you, Aidan." Kneeling face-to-face, she briskly rubbed her hands up and down his arms, hoping the warmth would soothe him. "Tell me."

He sucked in a shuddering breath. The story emerged slowly. Reluctantly. As though he didn't want to speak, but couldn't stop the words from leaking out. "We went to a soccer game that day. Grady was a senior in high school—state championships."

He faltered, and she touched his cheek. "I'm listening."

"It was supposed to be a family event, but Dad had the flu. He didn't want to miss the game. He insisted on going. Mom wouldn't let him."

"Your mom sounds like a very sensible woman."

"They were great parents. Both attended games and school events, and Pop did all the Boy Scout stuff. Work was the only thing that ever kept him away."

"That's nice, they were so supportive." She'd never had that. Her mom had worked two, sometimes three jobs, and even if Rita could have afforded the time, she couldn't afford extras for Zoe. Zoe was fiercely glad Aidan had grown up with both family support and confidence-boosting activities.

"Grady's team won, and he got MVP. Liam, Con and I carried him into the house on our shoulders. Mom brought up the rear with his trophy. We were yelling a cheer. Halfway across the living room, we noticed the house was wrecked. Stuff missing."

Zoe bit her lip so hard she tasted blood. She'd had no idea the family had walked in on the carnage. Could only imagine their shock and horror.

"We instinctively split up to search. Mom ran upstairs to the master bedroom. Grady and Con rushed to the kitchen. Liam and I tore into the family room." He covered his face with his hands. His voice was no longer detached, but raw with torment. "It was…the murder had happened in there. I'll never forget the way that room looked. Even sick and weak, Pop had fought like hell. There was blood all over. Everywhere. So much blood."

"Oh, Aidan. Oh, no." She hugged his trembling body, and tears welled in her eyes. She blinked them away by sheer force of will. She'd be no use to him if she fell apart.

"Con and Grady ran in, and we didn't want Mom to see the carnage. Con and I had to hold her back at the doorway…it took both of us to keep her out. She was screaming. The sound didn't even seem…" He swallowed again and it sounded as though it hurt. "Human."

She heard screaming echoes in her head. Felt confusion and roiling terror, as if she shared the awful memory. Disoriented, she pushed the frightening déjà vu aside. Aidan needed her. "That had to be so hard. I'm so sorry." She hugged him tighter.

He let her hold him. "We had to take her forcibly to our neighbor Letty's house. Grady was the most shook up, so I told him to stay with her. While the CSI team worked, I kept Con and Liam from falling apart. After the investigators removed the evidence they wanted, Grady came back. I went to the store and bought cleaning supplies. Told my brothers what we had to do. The four of us cleaned up the mess. Scrubbed away the gore."

"That was incredibly brave."

"No. We just couldn't let Mom come home to that."

Her heart breaking, she rubbed his back. Even caught in the grip of shock and grief, he'd thought of others first. Taken charge and done what had to be done.

His body rigid in her arms, he shook harder. "It took us the entire night. We ripped out the remaining carpet and took it and Pop's ruined chair to the dump. None of us said a word. None of us showed any emotion. Until we threw that torn, lumpy, recliner away. We stood in the back of Con's truck and looked at our father's chair sitting in the garbage, bloody and battered. Then we broke. Wrapped our arms around each other and cried."

A sob stuck painfully in Zoe's throat, and she swallowed it. Silent tears leaked from her eyes as she stroked his hair. "I'm sorry. I know it's not nearly enough, but I'm so sorry."

"That was the only time I cried. Not even at the memorial service." He drew a ragged breath. "They never found his body."

"I know," she murmured.

"We couldn't have a funeral. There was no coffin to drape the flag over. After the honor guard played 'Taps,' they just handed the folded flag to mom. I was so proud of her. She stood tall and straight and accepted the flag with quiet dignity. But the devastation in her eyes killed me. I would have done anything, given everything to make it better."

"There's nothing you could have done."

"You don't have to tell me that." His voice caught. Still shaking violently, he wrapped his arms around her and buried his face in her shoulder.

She held him, rocked him. "You're safe with me. Let go. It's okay to cry if you need to."

"I don't cry. Tears are useless." His anguished words wrenched out through clenched teeth. "And that bastard DiMarco isn't worth it. He's going down."

Had DiMarco not only murdered Aidan's father, but also crippled Aidan emotionally? Hot anger surged, burning away her sorrow. "You bet he is. Big-time. I'll do everything I can to help you put him away."

He raised his anguished gaze to hers. He gripped her shoulders. "You stay away from him, do you hear me? He's an animal. He tortured Bailey, was going to torture Letty. He tried to kill Con, and he'll kill you too…with less thought than squashing a bug."

"I won't give him the opportunity."

He shook her. Even devastated and angry, he still tempered his strength. "Promise me you'll stay away from him—away from the case."

"I can't do that." Not even to relieve the torment in his eyes.

"Then I will have to make you." His breath caught. "If it's the last thing I do."

She appreciated his compulsion to protect her, but could not let his fear stop her from doing her duty. She would never ask him to hold back on his job. "Aidan, I know how much he hurt you and your family. I can help. I have lots of connections at the station and with several newspapers."

He blinked. Blinked again. Shook his head. Like fog blasted away by a strong wind, the haze cleared from his eyes, the dazed look faded from his face. He surged to his feet, and dark fury flared. "What did you do?"

Startled at the abrupt switch, in both topic and tone, she slowly stood to face him. "What?" Did he mean taking the hard drives and documents? She furtively checked her bag. The tear was still facing away from him. He couldn't possibly know about the evidence. "I don't—"

"Nobody has ever— How did you get me to spill my guts like that?" he ground out. "Some reporter's trick?"

Taken aback, she stuttered. "N-no. I didn't do anything. You needed to talk, I listened."

"Everything I said is off the record. Not for quoting."

Hurt spiraled inside her, and she tamped it down. His anger was not personal. He had good reason to lash out. Reporters had exploited his family, caused them undue anguish. And he was scared after opening up to her. Shaken by exposing private grief he hadn't even shared with his loved ones. He didn't understand she would never take advantage of his pain. "Of course it is."

He snatched up the bag of shredded files, turned and strode out the gates. "Let's go. I'll see you safely home. But after that, don't follow me. Don't hound me. If you show up at an incident site, I will arrest you for endangering an ongoing investigation."

Deep down, she knew he wasn't mad at her. His raw, exposed emotions had caught him off-guard and upset him. And being a big, strong, he-man, the perception of weakness probably embarrassed him. He didn't mean to be insulting. Nevertheless, she couldn't help feeling bruised inside.

It was gonna be a long bus ride home.

Chapter 6

4:00 p.m.

After a strained, silent twenty minutes, Zoe and Aidan stepped off the bus. The number twenty-two line ended across town from her place and miles from where she'd left her car by the Dumpster. She'd used all her tickets procuring them a ride from the landfill. No biggie. Exercise might calm her turmoil.

She took the bag of shredded files from him. "Bye, Aidan. Hope the wedding goes well." She pivoted and walked away.

"Hey." In three long strides, he caught up to her and grasped her arm. "Where are you going?"

She turned around, and he released her. "To get my car."

"It's a long way."

She shrugged. "It's okay." She wasn't holding a grudge. After the difficult confrontation, she suspected they would both benefit from time to regroup and gain perspective. Or would time and space widen the rift? She had too little experience to dance this complicated tango. One misstep could easily land her flat on her face. "I like to walk."

Regret stamped his handsome features. "Look, I was a complete jerk. It's not your fault being at the landfill motivated a meltdown." He exhaled a slow, controlled breath. "I'm sorry. I had no right to take out my angst on you."

Relief trickled through her, dissolving the tight knot in her chest. She hated being at odds with him. Worse, the tentative bond they'd forged—first with shared humor, then shared pain—had been broken. She'd received a compelling glimpse of the sensitive, compassionate man behind the mask before he'd again walled off his heart. "Was that your first time at the landfill since your dad was killed?"

Shadows lingered in his eyes. "Yeah."

"It was clearly traumatic for you. Apology accepted."

It was his turn to express relief. "Thanks." He spread his hands, a fluid, masculine gesture. "I live a few blocks from here. Let me give you a ride home."

He got super-size brownie points with chocolate sprinkles for admitting to utter jerkiness with unabashed sincerity. "I doubt you want me in your beautiful car all grody and smelling like last week's trash." She smiled. "I can walk."

He gave her a cool, polite smile in return, and her heart clenched, longing for the return of his teasing grin and deep laughter. "You can clean up at my apartment. I have a washer and dryer, and it won't take long."

Guilt or chivalry? His hospitable offer didn't appear overly eager. The easy, comfortable choice was to refuse. To leave, and allow him to retreat into his emotional fortress. To feign casual chitchat next time they met and pretend as if he'd never spilled out his private agony while trembling in her arms.

No way. Coy games were not her style. She valued open, honest expression and always laid her cards on the table. She wasn't about to throw away an opportunity to spend more time with him. Surely, his reticence wasn't personal. He was withdrawing out of fear, using aloofness as a shield. If he got to know her better and still gave her the big brush-off, *then* she'd have a reason to be hurt. If she didn't risk the pain, she'd never have the opportunity to know him better.

Besides, she despised being filthy. Hated the thought of con taminating her car and the resulting cleaning chore. Washing her clothes at his place would save bucks at the Laundromat, and every penny counted. Rationalization? Maybe. Oh well, who was keeping score? "All right. Lead on."

After a careful, innocuous conversation about the nice weather cooperating with the wedding, they arrived at Aidan's condomin ium complex. His spacious high-rise with a breathtaking river view was as different from her studio as Trump Plaza from the pro jects. The apartment told her a lot about her cop. Not into showy expense, he appreciated good quality. No single director's chair for him. A polished cherry dining table was surrounded by enough chairs to seat his entire family, whose framed pictures lined the fireplace mantel. The muted sand, sapphire and dark-green palette drawn from forested seascapes on his walls indicated a love for nature. The chocolate-brown leather furniture and plush rug re vealed his sensual side.

She pictured him lounging beside a crackling fire on rainy evenings. He'd wear black silk pajamas and sip wine while read ing one of the many books aligned in glass-fronted bookcases. She just as easily pictured herself snuggling beside him, or maybe challenging him to a game of chess on the exquisitely carved teak set by the window.

"You can clean up first." Shattering her silly daydream, he pointed down a long hallway with gleaming oak floors. "Set your clothes outside the bathroom, and I'll toss them in the washer while you shower. You can use my robe hanging on the back of the door." His manner remained courteous and distant, as if she were a stranger he'd accidentally jostled in a crowd.

Zoe nodded. The mirror over the mantel caught the movement, snagging her attention. A smudge streaked her nose and right cheek. Her hair stuck out in stiff spikes, and her blouse was splotched with heaven only knew what. She self-consciously smoothed her sticky hair and stared down at her stained cloth ing…a grubby urchin spoiling the beauty of Aidan's serene, classy living room.

She didn't belong here. Solitaire, not chess, was her game.

Dejection dogged her footsteps as she trudged down the hall, careful not to touch anything. Putting out her soiled clothing for Aidan to wash felt awkwardly personal. Nobody else had washed her undergarments since before she'd started doing her own laundry at age seven. She'd ridden the highs and lows of an emotional roller coaster since early this morning, and was now suffering the disorienting effects.

She spared a longing glance at the huge whirlpool tub before hurrying through a shower in the luxurious bathroom. Hot water was probably plentiful in a place like this, but she didn't want to chance shorting Aidan.

Bundled in his thick white terry robe, which smelled enticingly like its owner, Zoe exited the bathroom. She didn't find Aidan in the living room or kitchen.

The door to his bedroom gaped open, and she glanced inside. He wasn't in there, either. She studied the big four-poster cherry bed neatly made with royal blue linens. Classic, traditional furniture for a classic, traditional guy. Like her, he preferred extra pillows. Though she doubted he had the same reason. She never felt secure unless pillows surrounded her body. Hugging one to her chest eased her fear of the dark and nighttime loneliness.

Another door at the end of the hallway was slightly ajar. Through the narrow opening, she saw that the room was bare of furniture, the walls painted warm gold. Swords hung in brackets on the far wall. Aidan balanced in a half-crouch, facing away from her. Stripped to the waist and barefoot, he wore only black drawstring pants tied low on his lean hips. Perspiration glistened on his tanned skin. Hard muscles bunched as he circled in controlled movements, and light danced off the sword gripped in his right hand. Not a wimpy fencing sword, a long, lethal weapon. In slow motion, he advanced, then retreated, the blade whirling in a shining arc as he fought an invisible opponent.

She watched, mesmerized as the fluid attack flowed from one graceful maneuver to the next. The man was a living, breathing weapon. All rippling muscles and coiled strength—a stalking wolf, cornering his prey. His sheer animal power and beauty stole her breath, and she gasped.

He spun. Spotting her, he racked the sword, then strode to the door and flung it wide. His smoky glance studied her tousled wet hair and the ample robe hugging her body before slowly moving down to her neon-pink toenails, and then back up again. When he finally spoke, his voice was husky. "That was fast. I didn't expect you to finish so quickly."

His accelerated breathing expanded his wide, sculpted chest looming directly in her line of sight. She tried not to stare, but failed. Dark hair dusted his bronzed pecs and formed an enticing path, luring her gaze downward over taut abs to his washboard stomach, where the trail disappeared into his waistband. Everything inside her tightened in yearning. "I was afraid I'd use up the hot water." *Waste not, want not.* And she *wanted* so badly she ached. She hadn't even known the meaning of the word until now.

She raised her gaze to his. *Mistake.* His eyes were more dangerously compelling than his magnificent body. His attitude might be cool, but his irises blazed with sensual golden fire. Hunger leapt between them like a starved tiger escaping from a cage. He quickly dropped his lashes, shuttering his expression. The tiger had razor-sharp claws; Aidan's desire for her bothered him. Why?

She gulped, attempting to swallow her confusion. "What were you doing?"

"A Kata." His full lips curved in a reluctant smile, and she understood how junkies felt, craving a taste of the ultimate high so badly it hurt. "Before you ask, it's a sequence of specific movements of a martial art. It helps me stay grounded. Centered."

He stepped into the hall and closed the door, barring her from his sanctuary as firmly as he'd locked her out of his heart. Combined with his emotional withdrawal, he might as well have shouted that he didn't want her involved in any personal aspects of his life. The loss hurt far more than she expected.

Standing so close, his powerful aura was nearly visible. Nearly palpable. Awareness hummed in the air. Though he'd shut her out emotionally, their bodies still recognized each other on a basic, elemental level. The pull was more than desire.

It felt like fate.

Scared, shocked, Zoe gasped and lurched back a step. Whoa!

Way too intense, way too fast! How could Aidan be her future? His world fit as uneasily on her narrow shoulders as his bulky robe. And though he wanted her—against his will—she wasn't sure he even liked her.

She fought to rein in her rioting senses. He probably needed centering after reliving his father's murder. He *didn't* need unwelcome advances. "It's beautiful, as intricate and graceful as a ballet." *You're beautiful.*

"It's a great workout, both physical and mental."

"I'd like to learn." *You could teach me so many things.*

"Most community centers give low-cost classes. Some even offer free sample courses."

He meant to be considerate, but the reminder stung. He'd seen how she lived, and knew she couldn't afford even a community class. Just as he'd furnished his apartment with high-class items all the way, Aidan would want to decorate his arm with an elegant, refined woman. Zoe was so far out of his league she wasn't even in the ballpark.

Floundering in deep, unknown waters, she turned away. She was used to window-shopping and not buying. Used to going without. She always managed to convince herself that what little she had satisfied her. This wasn't any different. But for the first time in years, tears of longing burned behind her eyes.

He cleared his throat. "After I shower and we're waiting for your clothes to dry, I'd like to debrief you about the DiMarco situation."

"All right." Maybe he had the right idea. Stick to business, and sort out all the crazy emotional stuff later…when she was alone. With great difficulty, she readjusted her focus. Perhaps if she shared select pieces of information about the case, he'd return the favor.

He strode toward the bathroom. "Make yourself at home. Help yourself to a snack or whatever you'd like."

"Thanks." Would he be surprised if she blurted out what she'd *really* like to help herself to? Or horrified? Mr. Large and in Charge probably wouldn't appreciate a woman who made advances. Zoe wouldn't appreciate him pulling a Casanova on such short acquaintance, either, but why did he go to such extremes to hide his interest? Maybe her enigmatic cop was leery of the powerful feelings simmering between them, too. Did he like her or hate her? What the heck was she supposed to do? Bewildered and frustrated, she headed for the kitchen.

She had her head stuck in the fridge perusing the delectable choices when a brisk knock sounded at the front door. She glanced hesitantly down the hallway and heard the shower. Aidan couldn't answer. Should she?

The knock sounded again, more insistent.

"Okay," she muttered. "I'm coming." She hurried to the door and flung it open. And came face-to-face with Aidan's mother.

Maureen O'Rourke had a plastic-bagged tux slung over one shoulder of her crisp, dark-green pantsuit. A much older woman wearing a jaunty yellow feathered hat and a black-and-yellow polka-dot dress stood beside her, bearing a covered casserole.

Maureen's striking, intelligent emerald eyes were an exact copy of Liam's, and the same shade as her pantsuit. Her surprised gaze traveled the path her son's had earlier, from Zoe's damp, rumpled hair to her pink toenails. "I don't believe we've met. I'm Maureen O'Rourke, Aidan's mom."

"Um, hi, I recognize you from Aidan's pictures. I'm Zoe Zagretti."

"Hello, Zoe." Maureen indicated the woman beside her. "This is Letty Jacobson, our longtime neighbor and dear friend. She's an honorary grandma to my clan."

"Nice to meet you." Letty's lively blue eyes twinkled merrily. "I would shake your hand, but I have a hot dish for Aidan. Though I suspect it's redundant."

Maureen pressed her lips together. Stifling a smile, or abject disapproval? Zoe couldn't tell, and her stomach pitched in unease. When Maureen spoke, her voice was carefully neutral. "Is Aidan home?"

"He's in the shower." Maureen's perfectly groomed brows arched a fraction, and a flaming blush inched up Zoe's neck. *Whoops*. Aidan's mom could only jump to the conclusion that Zoe had spent a lusty afternoon frolicking in her son's bed, followed by round two in the shower. Zoe *wished*. "Uh, I'm only here so he can debrief me."

Letty chuckled. "I'm happy to see our boy did the job with his usual single-minded efficiency."

Zoe choked. Was it too much to hope the glossy oak floor under her feet would open up and swallow her?

Fighting roiling shame, she sucked in a deep breath. "Let's start over. Aidan and I aren't dating or anything. We had a minor mishap at the city landfill, and being the gentleman he is, Aidan offered to let me clean up at his place."

Maureen murmured a noncommittal "I see."

Belatedly, Zoe realized she was blocking the doorway and moved aside. "Come in, please."

Standing under the pounding spray, Aidan scrubbed rigorously. He never brought women to his apartment. Instead, he went to their places, so he could leave when he wanted. And he never spent the night. Waking up with a woman was too uncomfortable. Too vulnerable. Way too intimate. Yet, he'd brought Zoe here. Worse, he wanted to *keep* her here.

He worked up more suds on the washcloth. If only he could wash away his attraction to the sexy little gypsy traipsing around his apartment wearing nothing but his robe. At the thought, his aching arousal tightened further. Zoe shouldn't have bothered to save him any hot water. He was taking a badly needed cold shower.

Dammit, what was wrong with him? His past relationships had been easygoing and casual. No angst, no conflict, no snapping and growling like a grizzly with a sore tooth. In fact, ladies normally complimented him on his sense of humor. He'd never had trouble with runaway desire. Never lost his temper. He'd certainly never dropped to his knees and spilled his guts, barely staunching the urge to *cry* in their arms. He shuddered in self-loathing.

He grabbed the shampoo and lathered his hair. Zoe *hadn't* used subterfuge to make him confide about Pop. She had a way of listening not merely with her ears, but with her heart, a deeply rooted compassion that showed how much she cared. Her genuine interest combined with abundant, unashamed empathy made her ominously easy to talk to.

Around Zoe, his imagination taunted him with erotic, heart-shaking scenarios he wouldn't normally think. He did ridiculous, irrational things he wouldn't normally do. He blurted out stupid, angry words he didn't mean.

With a soft smile, a mere glance, she triggered his most frightening, primitive emotions. Emotions he'd battled all his life to keep the safety on. She made him want things he'd never thought he could have, feel things he'd never thought he could feel. She made him laugh. Made him yearn.

Worst of all…she made him hope.

Zoe Zagretti scared the everloving crap out of him.

She was a dangerous, confusing woman. And he wanted to throw her down on his bed and make love to her until she cried out in his arms with completion. He burned with the temptation. Ached with the need.

He stuck his head under the freezing water, welcoming the sting. He didn't know what to do, where to turn for answers. Hell, he didn't even know which way was up any more.

He hadn't been this disoriented and afraid since Pop died.

Aidan cranked off the water and reached for a towel. Best not to leave the persistent journalist alone in his apartment too long. Anyway, he was probably getting all torqued out of shape over nothing. After what he was about to do, she'd probably never speak to him again. If he was lucky.

Reason had failed. Taking what he wanted using ruthless force was a last resort, but Zoe had left him no choice. No matter how distasteful. In this case, the end definitely justified the means.

A man had to do what a man had to do.

In the midst of toweling his hair, he paused. Were those female voices? Ringing feminine laughter? He cocked his head, listening intently. Recognition dawned, and he blanched. Holy freaking hell. Zoe was on the loose in his kitchen with his mother. And Letty. He bolted for the door, then froze. He was naked. He and his family were close, but not that close.

Panic screamed through him as he stumbled into his clean jeans. Who knew what kind of damage Ms. Zagretti could wreak, had already wreaked? At this very moment, she might be deftly eliciting information—prying every family secret—from both women. He had to get out there. *Now.*

He needed to send his mother and Letty packing in enough time to accomplish his objective and finally achieve some peace.

Three hours later, Zoe slammed her car door and stomped up the sidewalk toward St. Matthew's church. *Stupid.* She was a flaming idiot. After his mother and Letty had left, Aidan had flashed his charming smile and strutted his magnificent bod, and Zoe had swallowed the bait, hook, line and sinker. Over hearty club sandwiches and home fries he'd prepared with his own hands, he'd dazzled her with solicitous conversation and intense concern for her wellbeing.

And she'd *fallen* for it. He'd completely breached her defenses. In the end, she'd done exactly what he'd wanted. *Her* of all people, the woman who possessed an infallible BS radar. Only after she'd gone home and the sensual cloud had dissipated, had she realized how badly he'd betrayed her.

She marched up the church steps. If looks could kill, she was gonna fry Aidan O'Rourke's gorgeous butt into a charcoal briquette. She didn't lose her temper often, but right now, it sizzled through her veins as hot and explosive as a lit fuse in a firecracker factory.

SWAT…sneaky, weasely, amoral traitor.

A good-looking guy wearing a tux approached her as she stalked into the flower-laden sanctuary. "Hello, and welcome." She didn't recognize the man, but he had cop's eyes. "Friend of the bride or groom?"

Neither. "Groom." She self-consciously smoothed her red beaded gown, the only semi-suitable formal dress she'd found in her size during her last-minute dash to the thrift store. The matching three-inch sandals for two dollars were a bonus. She didn't belong here, either. But wild horses weren't about to keep her away. "In the back, please."

The usher escorted her to a seat in the last pew, and she forced herself to take slow, even breaths. She would not cause trouble at Con's wedding. But afterward would come the mother of all showdowns. Aidan would not get away with this. She wasn't letting the cheating, lying Benedict Arnold out of her sight, until he handed over the evidence he'd stolen. *Her* evidence.

She glanced around the packed sanctuary. Classical music drifted above the murmuring crowd. Sweet-scented pink roses spilled from every nook and cranny. Dozens of white candles twinkled like miniature stars. She gritted her teeth. Hanging on to her mad in the magical, romantic atmosphere grew tougher by the moment.

A lush melody floated out, Vivaldi's "Summer: Adagio." Four tuxedo-clad men strolled out a side door, and the murmurs went silent. Aidan, Con, Liam and Grady took their positions in front of the altar and then turned around.

A collective feminine sigh rippled through the room. Zoe lost her breath, as if all the oxygen had suddenly been sucked from the stratosphere. Dear Lord in heaven. Talk about weapons of mass distraction. The O'Rourke men en masse, their potent masculinity showcased in formalwear, were enough to bring the entire female population to their knees. She clenched her fists. *Get a grip, girl.* No matter how magnificent, she was still going to wring Aidan's neck.

Following three bridesmaids in sleek, pink satin gowns, a tiny flower girl scattered pink rose petals on the pale blue carpet. The "Wedding March" rang out, and everyone stood as the radiant bride glided down the aisle on the arm of a beaming African-American man. The awed, tender love on Con's face as he watched Bailey approach jammed a lump in Zoe's throat and sent hot tears trickling down her cheeks. She'd give everything she owned to have a man look at her with such yearning expectation. Such unfailing hope. Such immeasurable joy.

She cried silently through the entire, beautiful ceremony, attacked by an unsettling cocktail of sentiment, frustrated regret and empty, aching longing.

She had time to rebuild her fury as she furtively followed Aidan's car to the reception at the Ambassador Hotel. His generous offer to clean up at his place had been a sham. A clever fraud, designed to lure her to his apartment so he could get her alone and defenseless, use her and then dump her.

The rat was a terrific actor. His performance this afternoon merited an Oscar. And she was in terrible trouble. Her inborn lie detector had failed where he was concerned. Which meant she couldn't believe anything he said or did.

A horrifying fact she'd discovered too late.

She lost track of him in the parking lot while removing the wedding gift from beside her now-mended survival bag in the trunk. Carrying the wrapped Atlantis crystal wineglasses she'd also found at the thrift store, she marched inside. The dress, shoes and gift had blown a week's grocery money in ten minutes.

After a fruitless search for the object of her ire, Zoe accepted a flute of champagne from a passing waiter and surveyed the crowded dance floor. Letty bustled over to say hi, resplendent in purple organza set off by a hat piled with faux sugared grapes.

Zoe sipped the dry, bubbly champagne, a rare treat. She couldn't afford Kool-Aid, much less wine. "Liam's had three partners since I've been standing here. Does he ever dance with the same girl twice?"

Letty heaved a sad sigh. "Unfortunately, dearie, poor, heart-broken love-'em-and-leave-'em Liam never does anything with the same girl twice."

Heartbroken? Liam, the charmer? Not likely. Zoe's tongue burned with the urge to ask about Aidan's girlfriends, but she quenched the urge with the remaining champagne.

Thirty aggravating minutes later, she finally spotted Aidan's tall, handsome form leaning against the wall at the back of the huge ballroom. Alone. *All the better to make mincemeat out of your mangy, spurious hide, my dear.*

She wove through the throng, and stormed up to him.

He frowned. "This is a private celebration for friends and family. The press is not invited."

From the remote look on his face, she might have been a complete stranger instead of a woman with whom he'd spent an extraordinary afternoon. Obviously, their time together had only been meaningful to *her.* Their unique link one-sided. She'd thought him unable to hurt her any worse, but her heart twisted in pain. "I'm not here in an official capacity. Reserve a slot in your busy, scheming schedule for a chat after the reception."

"We have nothing more to say to one another." His frown deepened. "I warned you to leave my family alone. Go home."

Like a magical faerie queen from a Celtic myth, Aidan's mother materialized from the open doorway beside him. "For shame, Aidan James O'Rourke. I taught you better than to speak to a lady that way."

Red streaks slashed his cheekbones. "She's not a lady. She's a reporter, Mom."

"The two aren't mutually exclusive, boyo." Maureen smiled warmly at Zoe. "When I was in San Francisco with the rowing team last fall, I saw her on TV with a touching report about hard-to-place children awaiting adoption. Thanks to her insightful story, I imagine some of those children got loving homes."

Aidan's gaze flicked to Zoe. The painful uncertainty shadowing the mahogany depths slammed her with a startling, hit-and-run revelation. He wasn't unaffected by her. The exact opposite, in fact. Perhaps her cop wasn't going to such lengths to protect only his family. Perhaps he was also protecting himself. He scowled. "She barged in uninvited."

"She did no such thing." Maureen planted her hands on her hips. "I invited her, back at your apartment."

"Great." Aidan's expression turned thunderous. "Enjoy the party. But stay the hell away from my family."

It was time someone called him on his self-delusions. Past time someone pointed out a few hard, cold truths. Zoe was just the girl for the job. She angled her chin and murmured sotto voice, "When this is over, you and me are gonna rumble, SWAT."

Maureen must have possessed a faerie queen's hearing, because she developed a sudden coughing fit. A masculine snicker sounded from behind Zoe, and she turned to see Con, his arm around an amused, but trying to hide it, Bailey. When had the bride and groom arrived? Zoe glanced to her left, and realized she and Aidan were surrounded by his entire family. Grady studied Zoe, his gray-green eyes lit with speculation, and Liam chuckled.

Aidan narrowed his eyes. "This is no joke."

Zoe shook her head. "Absolutely not. And if you'd stop being so…" *Pigheaded* probably wouldn't win her any points. Then again, she was clinging to the last dregs of patience with her cop. "So…"

"Uptight?" Liam supplied helpfully.

"Headstrong?" Con chimed in.

"Intense?" Grady added.

"Defensive," Zoe amended. "And just listen—"

"Very helpful, little brothers." She could hear Aidan's back teeth grinding from where she stood. "Nothing like ganging up on a guy."

Zoe exhaled a sharp breath. "I am not the enemy. Well, I wasn't before you…before this afternoon. Now, I'm not so sure." She gazed around at the curious faces fixed on them, and turned to leave. "Um…later."

Aidan stopped her with a hand on her arm, and glared at his brothers. "Does the peanut gallery mind if I have a private conversation here?"

Con smirked. "Not at all. Go right ahead." Bailey surreptitiously elbowed her new husband's ribs, and he grunted.

Maureen shot Aidan the disobey-me-and-die look perfected by mothers around the globe. "Perhaps you should dance with our guest. And mind your manners, boyo."

"Yes, ma'am," Aidan growled. "Good idea. Probably the only way we can have a conversation without an audience." He took possession of Zoe's hand and towed her toward the dance floor.

"None of the A-man's ladies ever talk back to him," Liam muttered as Aidan whisked Zoe past. "If you ask me, he needs an irreverent woman."

"I'm not his woman," she hissed over her shoulder. The last thing she wanted was an emotionally constipated male. That would be no different from living alone. Worse, in fact.

Over by the DJ's station, Letty waved at Zoe, and as if on cue, a new song began. "When a Man Loves a Woman." Sexy, romantic music to fight by.

Aidan pulled Zoe into his arms. "All right. What do you have to say that is all-fired important enough to disrupt my brother's wedding?"

"As if you didn't know, Mr. Artful Dodger." Held closely in his strong embrace, his clean, masculine scent washed over her, muddling her resolve. She shook her head in a futile attempt to clear the sensual haze. "I didn't mean to start anything here. I only wanted to make sure I caught you immediately afterward. Before there are consequences, and it's too late."

One big, capable hand swallowed hers and snuggled it to his shoulder, while the other slid around her. Her dress bared the small of her back to his broad palm that intimately cradled her body. The erotic friction of warm skin against skin sent shivers racing over her. His deep voice rumbled in her ear. "The damage is done. Let's have at it."

He held her gaze as they swayed. The seductive music wrapped them in a cocoon, wove a captivating spell. Her breasts pressed into his unyielding chest, where his heartbeat pounded beneath the tux. His rock-hard thighs brushed hers in a sensual caress. His warm breath feathered through her hair, sending tingles over her scalp and down her spine.

With his body joined so intimately to hers, there was no mistaking the fact that he was aroused. Very, very aroused. And she was drowning in the deep, mysterious pools of his incredible eyes.

"Zoe." Her name rolled off his tongue. Meant as a warning, it sounded more like he was savoring rich, intoxicating wine.

She inhaled shakily. Battling to gather her splintered concentration, she attempted to pull away. "Um…I'd better wait in the car. I'll meet you outside when the reception is over."

"Oh, no, you don't." He held her tightly, thwarting her escape. "You came spoiling for a confrontation," he murmured in her ear. "And I'm going to indulge you. Right here, right now."

Chapter 7

9:00 p.m.

"I don't want to make a scene here." Zoe's frantic gaze darted over Aidan's broad shoulder. As capable at taking the lead on the dance floor as everywhere else, he'd discreetly maneuvered to a side door.

"We're not." He glided them outside, and into the parking lot.

"Oh, you—" Fury surged back with a vengeance. He'd done it again. Muddled her mind with blatant sex appeal and caught her off-balance. It was all just a ruse to gain strategic advantage. His erection pressed into her stomach, and she jerked out of his arms. Okay, *that* he couldn't fake. But sexual attraction was nothing more than basic chemistry.

A dozen insults battled for freedom behind clenched teeth, but she believed in fighting fair. Stick to facts and no dirty tactics. "You seduced me this afternoon, against my will."

"What?" He looked and sounded as shocked as if she'd suggested that he run back through the reception naked.

She hadn't meant to bring up the subject of seduction. Silently counting to a hundred, she marched deeper into the parking lot, brightly illuminated by the full moon overhead and rows of domed light poles. She found herself standing beside her Corolla. Good. If she needed to make a run for it, her trusty wheels would be handy.

Aidan followed, and she dragged in a deep breath. "You stole something very important from me."

"Ah. Came to that conclusion so soon?" He pursed his gorgeous lips. "As you judiciously pointed out, if something is free for the taking, technically, it isn't stealing."

"You used me."

He stepped closer. "I did not seduce or use you. Like you, I took advantage of an opportunity to gain what I needed."

Confusion battled to the top of her warring emotions. "Are you trying to tell me the sizzle between us was…is unintentional?"

"As the Chernobyl disaster, honey." Clearly frustrated, he thrust a hand through his hair. "If it helps any, I don't like it any better than you do."

Confusion retreated under dismay. She'd been right. He despised his attraction to her. She'd been furious with him for seducing her, yet finding out he hadn't done it on purpose made her even more upset. He'd steamed her veggies without even turning up the heat. He had *way* too much power over her. "So you didn't deliberately get me…uh…hot and bothered to distract me?"

"No. In fact, I thought I'd hidden my feelings better." He again stepped closer. Ha! She was wise by now to his favorite intimidation maneuver and didn't give an inch. He frowned. "While we're slinging accusations, you want to tell me your motives are totally altruistic?"

Zoe opened her mouth to retort, then hesitated. Honesty was her creed. The Greek word for truth literally translated to "unforgetting." She could never forget that she didn't know who she was or where she came from. Therefore, truth was much more important in every other aspect of her life. Even furious, she wouldn't lie to herself or him. "I admit, I *am* hoping that nailing the DiMarco investigation will bump me up at the station. I need money to move my mom here. But I also sincerely want to help your family."

"We don't want your help. Don't need your help."

"Really?" She keyed open her trunk and sardonically waved her survival bag, now much lighter because it held only her usual supplies. "Without me, you wouldn't have the hard drives you swiped while I was in the shower." She looped the bag over her shoulder, an automatic gesture. "Replacing them with similar-sized books so I didn't notice until I got home was vilely brilliant, by the way."

"They're evidence."

"Don't cops have rules about stealing evidence?"

"They didn't actually belong to you, either. Besides, as long as evidence is in plain sight—and due to the rip in your bag it was— it's considered legally obtained and admissible in court." He crossed his arms, and his biceps bunched under the tailored jacket. "Which might not be the case if you tamper with it. You have plenty to keep you busy trying to piece those shredded documents together."

She should have known he was too smart to buy the plant-mulch ploy. *She* stepped closer this time, practically nose-to-nose. Two could play space invaders. "You haven't had time to give the hard drives to the FBI." *She hoped.*

"Maybe, maybe not."

"I want them back."

He shrugged, and tension crackled in the air. "Isn't gonna happen."

"They're mine. *I* did the research. *I* found the link. *I* dug them out of the garbage." Anger rode her hard, and she poked him in the chest with her index finger. "Until I get them back, I'm going to stick closer than your shadow. You won't be able to sneeze without me saying gesundheit."

He wrapped his hand around hers and held it to his chest. Under her palm, his heart pounded like a war drum. His eyes flashed fire, but his grip was gentle, his voice brushed velvet. "You don't want to go one-on-one with me, Zoe. You can't win."

"Hide and watch. I would have shared what I found with you. But why should I play fair when you don't?"

Without warning, the truth slapped her in the face. She was more upset over his betrayal—over the fact that he'd only pretended to care—than at losing hard-won evidence.

Disillusionment sliced her anger into sharp little pieces that hurt, and scalding tears pressed behind her eyelids. "You washed my clothes and fed me and showered me with charm and concern…and it was all a *lie*."

He swallowed hard, his eyes hot and intense. "I didn't lie to you. With words *or* actions."

She choked on a valiant struggle not to cry. In spite of her efforts, a single tear leaked out. "I'm left with nothing. While you got what you really wanted."

"No, sweetheart." His voice had gone husky. His smoky gaze locked on hers, then followed the tear trailing down her cheek. "If I'd gone after what I really wanted, I'd have done this." He tugged her to him and covered her mouth with his.

His soft, full lips tasted her, tantalized her. Stunned shock quickly fled, leaving only desire. His hand cupped the back of her head, urging her to the perfect angle for his plundering mouth.

She relaxed in his embrace and opened to the searing intimacy. His tongue thrust inside, silky hot. The world shuddered to a halt as his mouth devoured hers. Pleasure, as pure and brilliant as the moonlight, raced through her veins. She couldn't think, could barely breathe and didn't care. She kissed him in return, the sensual rhythm as instinctive and natural as the dance they'd shared.

Heat and energy arced between them, and he groaned, a low, ragged sound. His need tasted dark and dangerous in her mouth. His heartbeat raged against hers, evidence of his tenuous hold on control. He took, yet gave back so much more, and raw, elemental passion inside her blazed to life.

Trembling from the onslaught of desire, she slid her arms around his neck. Burrowing closer to his hardness and heat, she both took and gave in return.

Aching to devour him, she nipped his lower lip, and a primitive growl rumbled from his throat. He deepened the kiss, fiercely, arousingly feasting on her as if only she could sate his hunger. Fevered madness broke over them with the awesome power and glorious heat of a summer storm.

He possessed her, claimed her. He was everything she'd ever wanted, everything she'd dreamed. She didn't have the words, and told him the only way she could. With her kiss. She felt his defenses crumble, and he responded by revealing his hidden world. Opening his heart. For a brief, shining moment, she discovered a place where she fit.

Triumphant joy sang inside her as she savored their shared emotions. Reveled in their unparalleled connection. There was no one before Aidan, would be no one after.

With one kiss, he'd won her…body and soul.

Her knees weakened at the revelation. Then a thunderbolt exploded inside her brain, and everything went black.

Aidan crawled out of unconsciousness to muddled awareness. The last thing he remembered was kissing Zoe. He'd teetered on the edge of the map, and then plunged right over the edge. But instead of falling into darkness, he'd found light.

Found life.

Found the part of himself he'd thought lost forever.

His wary instincts had been right on the money regarding the sexy reporter. She wasn't a threat to his family.

She was a threat to his heart.

He shook off a surge of fear. In a combat situation, knowing every detail about your destination, opponent and ultimate mission goal was three-fourths of the battle. Now that he was fully briefed, he'd manage this fatal attraction the same way he did everything else. With unfailing logic, stubborn Irish determination and steely self-control. All he had to do was develop a viable tactical plan and stick to it.

He blinked, attempting to clear his vision. Where was he? Nothing was visible in the inky blackness. He'd been slammed with a stunning revelation, to be sure, and their kiss had crackled with electric heat. But he'd never passed out from a kiss before. He'd never passed out, *period*.

He *had* been blitzed a time or two, but this was far worse than any hangover. He felt like roadkill. His weakened muscles ached, his dry, gritty mouth rivaled the Sahara, and his head pounded as though an escaped prisoner was drilling an exit hole out the back of his skull. He'd only felt this rotten once before—in SWAT training when he was required to take a hit from a Taser. He hadn't lost consciousness then, but whoever had attacked him must have ramped up the voltage.

He tried to stretch and found himself pinned in a fetal position in the tight, dark space. His right wrist snagged on something, and he yanked. Metal rattled, and his arm moved heavily…handcuffed to…what? Using his free hand, he gingerly explored his surroundings. He was cuffed to another person. Judging by the soft tangle of limp extremities, his companion was an unconscious female. His fingertips brushed a lush mouth, pert nose, closed eyelids and short, silky curls.

Recognition slammed home, and horror sank sharp talons into him. *Zoe!* The shape of her features was engraved on his heart. If his alertness hadn't been compromised, he'd have instantly recognized her by scent alone.

He couldn't feel any breaths whispering from her parted lips, and his chest tightened. Praying as he never had before, he pressed two fingers to her throat. His own pulse stopped until he felt hers beating slowly but steadily under his fingertips. A sigh of relief burst out of him.

"Zoe." He patted her cheek. "Can you hear me?"

She whimpered, and his guts cramped. How long had he been out? Had the assailants hurt her?

"Zoe, wake up."

She stirred slightly, and moaned something incoherent, but didn't regain consciousness.

His heartbeat hammered in his ears. So help him, if they'd hurt her, he would kick asses and ask questions later. "C'mon, honey," he murmured. "Wake up."

She moaned again, stiffened, and then cried out.

"Hey, now. It's okay." He gathered her carefully into his embrace. "It's Aidan. Are you hurt?"

"Aidan?" She flailed, her panic palpable in the heavy darkness. "It's pitch dark! Get me out of here!"

"Shh. We need to be quiet." She was his to protect, now. He didn't question it. Didn't balk. Simply accepted the heart-shaking responsibility. "Zoe, listen to me." His voice low, he held her close, trying to still her thrashing. "You have to stay calm. Take slow, deep breaths."

"Help me!" Vibrating with terror, she clutched his jacket lapels and buried her face in his shirt.

"I won't let anything happen to you, sweetheart." He curved his body in a shield around hers and hugged her tighter. "Did they hurt you? Tell me."

She inhaled a deep, shuddering breath. "I feel terrible." Another faltering breath, as he held his own. "But not injured. What happened? Were we hit by lightning? Are we dead?"

"We're very much alive." Relief filtered through him, more strongly this time. If Zoe was asking questions, she was okay. "You're not far off the mark with the lightning, though. I think someone Tasered us while we were kissing."

"What? You mean like a stun gun?"

"Yeah. It short-circuits the central nervous system and causes temporary paralysis. Higher voltages can render a person unconscious." He stroked her soft wrist, bound in cold steel. "Apparently, they handcuffed us together and stuffed us in the trunk of a car." Or a large metal coffin. Wisdom precluded mentioning that grisly theory.

"Oh." She hesitated. "Wow. I wonder how much of the jolt was from the kiss and how much from the Taser?" He'd debated the same question.

Every jerky movement of her tight, quivering muscles divulged her valiant struggle for control. "Why would anyone want to kidnap us?"

"Who have you ticked off lately?" he asked wryly, and again kept his suspicions to himself. No sense in upsetting her more. "Besides me?"

"Nobody."

"That must be a first."

"Nobody I know of, anyway." She burrowed nearer. Any closer, and she'd be inside his jacket. "Maybe they're after you, SWAT."

"And brought you along for the ride? I doubt it." His enemies were liable to just blow him away. He gently rubbed the satiny skin of her back, pleased when her trembling eased a fraction. She'd constantly annoyed him over the past six months with her daring, but now he thanked heaven for her dauntless courage. If they were gonna get out of here in one piece, he needed her firing on all cylinders and not immobilized by fear.

"Nobody will know I'm gone until I don't show up at work on Monday. Except Evander. I hope he's okay all alone." She sounded so forlorn, Aidan was tempted to kiss her again. Merely to comfort her. *Yeah, right.*

"Evander is probably lounging on your bed with a cold drink in one paw and the remote in the other." He settled for a brush of lips to her forehead. "Don't worry. Before long, my brothers will notice me missing from the reception and call out the cavalry." *If* they didn't assume he'd swept Zoe off to bed. Which, after that knock-his-combat-boots-off kiss, is where they might be spending the weekend if not for the fateful intervention.

"It must be great to have family." An edge of longing quavered in her reply. "To know you have people you can count on, no matter what."

"Sometimes they're a pain in the butt, but yeah. It is." He again stroked her hair. "First the garbage rodeo, now this. Anybody ever tell you that you're one hell of an exciting date?"

"I don't date. Uh, much."

Now, that was interesting. And strange. Didn't she have *anyone* to lean on? He'd figured men would swarm around smart, upbeat, outgoing Zoe like bees to a lemon blossom. She sure kissed like she knew what she was doing. His aggressive hunger would have frightened some women. Hell, the searing intensity had scared *him*. But Zoe's response had flared instantly. Without hesitation, her desire had met and matched his. Bright and explosive, TNT to his flame.

"Aidan?" Growing more agitated, she shifted in his embrace, and her voice rose in pitch. "We have to get out of here. I *hate* the dark. I can't hold on much longer before I completely lose it and start screaming in panic."

"Absolutely no panicking. Hang in there, honey. I'll get you out." His ingrained training had already assessed the scenario and tossed around ideas. He just hoped one of them worked. Timing, as always, was everything. "I've been formulating a plan since I came to."

Damn, he wished they'd cuffed his left hand instead of his right. However, keeping Zoe busy might stave off her panic. "Feel behind you where I can't reach. Is there anything useful?"

"Just a sec." Rustling noises ensued. "My bag! My bag is here." More rustling. "I have a penlight in it!"

"Wait. Probably not a good idea."

"Aidan, I *need* light." Desperation spiked her words. "I would rather have the kidnappers open the trunk and shoot me dead this minute than be helplessly trapped in the dark!"

"Personally, that wouldn't be my first choice." Great. She was about to implode on him. The last thing they needed was to alert the kidnappers that their victims were conscious. One more round with a Taser tonight, and he could be his own night-light. "All right. Cup your hands around it and shield the tip."

Her fumbling movements brushed his chest, and then a small glow vanquished the dark void. Stark terror etched every tense line of her face. He smiled reassuringly at her. With both their lives at stake, he had to keep her calm until they could make their move. He resorted to humor's defusing effect, and leered at her in his best big-bad-wolf imitation. "What a tiny flashlight you have, my dear."

Her lips wobbled dubiously, but she managed to retort, "Hey, buster, beggars can't be choosers."

"I'd be happy to share mine, but I seem to be without my Everready at the moment."

"Really?" Her lush mouth curled at one corner. Then a shaky smile finally broke free. "Could've fooled me."

There was the girl he knew and…whoa! Uh…okay, she was growing on him. Eliciting her one small, trembling smile felt like a bigger victory than when he'd pitched his high-school baseball team to the state championship.

She glanced around. "Are you sure we're in a car? I don't feel it running."

"Listen." He engaged her observational skills to help sublimate her fear. "What do you hear? What do you feel?"

She cocked her head. "A deep, vibrating hum, like a huge outboard motor, and…sloshing water. And we're rocking. Why?"

"I think we're on a ferry. Probably headed for one of the islands off the coast." He hoped. The alternative destination was the middle of the ocean, where the car would be shoved off and sunk. With them pinned in the trunk like rats on the *Titanic*.

She gulped. "So…what's the holdup, SWAT? Let's bail."

"I have to disable the interior light and spring the lock. Then we need to wait until the car drives off the ferry and onto a road." *Unless we're sinking to the bottom of the Pacific.* "*Then* we can jump out, run like hell, and pray there's cover and that nobody notices we're gone until it's too late."

Her wide, scared eyes studied his face. "Can you spring the lock?"

"Sure. No problem." If he couldn't, they were in trouble. He was bluffing more than during poker night with the guys. He kneaded his pockets. "Damn, they took my keys, phone and knife." Pop had given each O'Rourke son a Swiss Army knife on his thirteenth birthday. Aidan grieved over the loss for sentimental as well as practical reasons. "What else do you have handy?"

She rummaged in her bag. "They took my phone, too. But I'm glad men think girly stuff is useless. Little do they know. They left the bag. How about manicure scissors and a nail file?"

He gave her a reassuring grin and parroted her words. "Beggars can't be choosers."

His movements were slow and awkward in the cramped quarters. Severely hindered with his right wrist chained to Zoe's, he located the wires to the interior light and sawed through them with the minuscule scissors. Then he worked at prying the lock with the nail file.

He'd begun to make progress, when, without warning, the file snapped in half. At the same moment, the penlight winked out. Zoe yelped in distress, and he swore under his breath. "Shh, honey. We can't let them hear us."

"I can't turn it back on." Her frantic struggle jostled him, physically and emotionally. Seeing self-assured Zoe so vulnerable, so afraid, twisted his insides into knots. "The batteries must have run out. Oh, God, Aidan, *hurry!*"

"I'm close," he lied. The only thing harder than jimmying a lock in murky light with a nail file while handcuffed to a semi-hysterical woman, was doing it in pitch blackness with *half* a nail file. Sweat beaded his upper lip and trickled down his spine as he switched to the manicure scissors. "Hang on, sweetheart. I'm right here with you."

Outside, the chugging ferry motor sputtered, slowed. Chains rattled. Adrenaline streaked through him, and he viciously wrenched the scissors. At any second they could be shoved to a watery grave. Could he loosen the lock before seawater flooded inside and they drowned? "Can you swim?"

"Very well." Suspicion painted her reply. "Why?"

"Just passing time." Can you swim miles in fifty-degree water in a beaded gown while cresting six-foot breakers and handcuffed to another person? *Don't think about that. Work the lock.*

Outside, metal scraped, and the ferry bumped something. A dock? Footsteps clattered, three or four men, judging by the weight and cadence. Car doors slammed, and the motor rumbled.

His painfully clenched muscles eased. They wouldn't start the car if they planned to shove it overboard. "Here we go."

He continued to pry the stubborn lock as the car rocketed down a paved road. When his scraped, bleeding fingers could barely function, it finally gave. "Success!"

Zoe clutched at his hand, joined to hers. "Thank goodness! Let's blow this gig!"

He peered out. Black highway zoomed beneath them, a flesh-grinding washboard of asphalt. He held the trunk closed, so it wouldn't give them away. "We're going too fast to jump and survive. We'll have to wait." Jumping out handcuffed together was a calculated risk. If they didn't stay in sync, either or both could be badly hurt. Then they'd be easy pickings. But waiting until they arrived at their destination and the bad guys took him out was not an option. He could hold his own in hand-to-hand combat, but even he couldn't fight one-handed and protect Zoe at the same time.

She was his responsibility. At all costs, he had to keep her alive.

After too many agonizing minutes that carried them closer and closer to who-knew-what fate, the car slowed and made a turn.

Jouncing and bumping along, Aidan did another fast peek outside. "Dirt road. Heads up, honey. After we jump, tuck and roll. Stay low, and run off the road to our left. We don't want to cross in front of oncoming traffic."

"I'll try, but I'm not sure I can run very fast." Her voice hitched. "I'll be a liability to you. My muscles are weak from the Taser, and stiff from being curled up so long."

He had the same worries about himself, but the alternative was unthinkable. "You're gonna do great. I have faith in you."

"You do?" A trembling pause ticked past. "Th-thanks."

"Ready?" He again glanced out. The rocky road beneath them still zipped by at a fast clip. They needed a buttload of luck.

"On the count of three." His fingertips brushed her cheek, felt vibrating tension in every molecule of her slender body. He grinned at her. Though she couldn't see it, she would hear it in his voice. "That would be one, two, and go *on* three, Riggs."

"I appreciate the clarification, Murtaugh." She chuckled weakly. "And if you say, 'I'm getting too old for this crap,' I'll bop you one."

He wasn't too old. But with each passing minute, he grew way too attached to a certain spunky, persistent, too-smart-for-her-own-good reporter. "One." Aidan sucked in a deep breath. "Two."

He paused long enough for a hurried, silent prayer. "Three!" He shoved open the trunk lid.

Clinging to one another, they jumped.

Chapter 8

11:00 p.m.

Zoe would do *anything,* including bail out of a speeding automobile, to escape the dark trunk. She slung her bag over her right shoulder and clutched Aidan's big, warm hand, her anchor in the swirling tumult. Starry sky wheeled overhead as they hurtled into space. The world spun in a dizzying arc, and she lost all sense of time and place.

Suddenly, she crashed to her hands and knees. Stunned by the bone-jarring thud, she tried to tuck and roll, but her cramped limbs would not cooperate. As Aidan landed gracefully beside her and completed his roll, the wrench on her wrist sent pain screaming up her arm. His momentum jerked her sideways, and she sprawled on the gravel like a rag doll.

He pulled her to him, wrapped his arms around her and rolled toward the side of the road. Locked together, they tumbled over the embankment. She instinctively tucked her face into his shoulder, and his wide palm cradled and protected the back of her head.

Rocks jabbed her spine, and sticks and coarse weeds tore at her bare skin.

Finally, blessedly, they stopped moving.

Breathing rapidly, Aidan rose on his elbow above her, his face etched with concern. "Are you all right?"

Her body shrieked in pain. She must have scraped off ninety percent of her skin, and her muscles throbbed like someone had beaten the holy heck out of her with a baseball bat. He probably felt twice as bad. Nobody had sheltered his body, and he'd taken the brunt of the blows. "Yes. You?"

"Locked and loaded." He surged to his feet, yanking her upright. "Let's move."

Dizzy, she swayed, blinked. A formidable expanse of open field loomed in the stark moonlight. But densely grouped trees at the far end promised cover for the hunted. She gulped. First, they had to make it across the wide expanse of no-man's land.

She glanced to her left, relieved to see red taillights streaking away from them. "The kidnappers didn't notice."

"Let's make tracks before they do." He broke into a sprint.

She barely had time to hike up her dress. Staggering, she scrambled through the hillocky pasture spiked with potholes.

Twice, she fell to her knees, and Aidan hauled her to her feet. "C'mon, Zoe. Move!"

Her breath sawed in her lungs, hot and jagged. "I jog every morning, but not in three-inch-heels and a fitted gown, SWAT."

"I know it's tough." He jerked his thumb backward. "But consider the alternative."

She dug her fingers into his tux sleeve for a better grip as they ran. "Who *are* they, and what do they want?"

"Think about it, Brenda Starr." He tossed her a wry glance. "Whose cage have you rattled recently?"

Appalling realization dawned. "Someone connected to Di-Marco's operation." Probably the mysterious someone ruthlessly liquidating the crippled man's assets.

"Bingo. Give the lady an exclusive byline." He leapt over a log, dragging her with him. "And they're likely to shoot first and find reasons later."

Halfway across the field, she looked over her shoulder and her stomach pitched in terror. "The taillights have stopped! They're backing up!"

"I saw." He cursed under his breath and towed her faster. "Run like your life depends on it."

His long legs raced through the knee-high grass. No way could she keep up. He thrust an arm around her waist, half carrying her over the rugged terrain.

Approaching the shadowed tree line, her feet involuntarily slowed. In spite of her mental command to move, her body dragged against Aidan's momentum. The unrelenting darkness ahead spiked her terror as high as the pursuers behind.

He tightened his hold on her. "There's nowhere else to go."

"I know." She risked another glance over her shoulder. The car had stopped close to where she and Aidan had escaped. Five swearing men plunged over the embankment. Moonlight glinted off the pistols gripped in their hands.

"Trust me, Zoe." Aidan propelled her between heavy branches and into the gloom. "I'll take care of you."

"I trust you." With everything she had and everything she was. Nevertheless, fear squeezed her heart, stealing her breath. Now was not the time or place, but as soon as possible, she was going to indulge in a panic attack. A girl could only have her phobia shoved in her face for so long before she broke.

The woods forced a slower pace. Spiked pine boughs slapped their faces. Evergreens towered in the black void, angry sentinels protecting the forest. As Zoe and Aidan wove and dodged, tangled undergrowth tripped their fleeing footsteps. Was the landscape on the bad guys' side?

The shouts behind them grew louder, and Zoe's burning muscles trembled. "They're gaining on us."

Without warning, two gunshots blew apart the quiet night, and a tree limb exploded inches from Aidan's head.

Horror made her clumsy, and she stumbled. "That shot nearly hit you!"

Aidan kept her on her feet. His stride didn't falter as he casually shook bark out of his hair. "Ya think?"

A surprised, strangled laugh choked out of her, pushing back the worst fear. The close call hadn't rattled him one iota. His unshakable confidence was inspiring. "I guess that cool head under fire keeps you alive," she panted.

He glanced at her. Fierce determination stamped his handsome features. "It's gonna keep you alive, too."

Her cop had a protective streak a mile wide. Probably from being the oldest son. If they made it out sans bullet holes, she owed him one. Or six. "I'm sorry you got dragged into this because of me."

He veered to the right, towing her in his wake. "Be glad I'm here. Those guys got more than they bargained for."

"My guardian angel." She was only half kidding. Without him, who knew what tortures she would have faced?

He slanted her a roguish grin. "Just call me St. Aidan." His grin fled. "Duck!"

She dove under a low branch, and couldn't help but return the smile. "Ha! That'll be the day."

"Bad form to malign the man who saves your hide."

"You never know." She pressed her hand to her ribs, attempting to ease a stabbing pain. "Maybe I'll save yours."

He snorted and swerved around a huge, menacing boulder. "The phrase 'ice festival in hell' springs to mind." He lurched to a stop, teetering on the edge of a steep ravine. His gaze ricocheted right, then left.

Less than a hundred yards behind, their pursuers crashed through the bushes. Another volley of shots exploded. Aidan tugged her forward. "Follow me."

Like she had a choice? He strode over the edge, and she clambered to keep up. Gravity hurtled them down the incline, and her feet only intermittently touched ground as she skidded and bumped down the steep hill. Her wrist smarted like the devil from being dragged in Aidan's unstoppable wake. If the handcuffs were longer, he'd be flying her behind him like a kite.

At the bottom, she nearly collided with a broad tree trunk. He jerked her out of the way in the nick of time. Who was she kidding? Every molecule in her body hurt like the devil. She'd be head-to-toe bruises tomorrow. If she lived to count them. "Whoa!" She dug in her heels. I can't…breathe!"

He urged her onward. "If we stop now, you won't have to worry about breathing."

She groaned and valiantly tried to keep up. Didn't Mr. Invincible ever run out of steam?

She stumbled along behind him on the banks of a chattering creek. The rocky obstacle course stubbed her toes and wrenched her ankles in the high heels. Better step carefully. Wouldn't do to sprain an ankle like a dimwit heroine in a horror movie. A sprained ankle could mean their deaths. The thought had barely registered when she tripped and fell hard, yanking Aidan down.

He pushed to his knees. "You okay?"

"Yes," she wheezed. "But…I need…a minute."

Gunshots whistled over the ravine, pinged on rocks overhead. Could their pursuers see them, or were they firing at random? A shower of gravel rained down. "No time." He grimaced. "We have a three-, maybe four-minute lead."

She struggled to her knees and repositioned her bag on one shoulder. Tangled vines and bushes trailed over the ravine, cupping the embankment in front of her like giant, lanky fingers. A thick, earthy smell wafted out.

Aidan sniffed. "Hmm." He edged the vine-laden branches aside. "Perfect."

Slowly, she raised her gaze and saw a crack in the hillside. Perfect for what? *Oh no.* He couldn't mean what she thought. Cold trepidation prickled along her skin.

He gestured at the black, yawning mouth. "Inside."

Her limbs froze. "I can't go in there."

"You can." He cupped her face in his hands and encouraged her with his steadfast gaze. "With me."

Splashing echoed in the deathly quiet night. Their pursuers were closing in. "Uh-uh." She couldn't go into that black void if her life depended on it. Unfortunately, it did.

"Sorry, honey. We're out of options." He bulldozed her inside and crawled in behind her.

Impenetrable darkness surrounded her. The overpowering smell of cold, damp earth pressed in from every side. She touched the wall to steady herself, and damp soil crumbled beneath her palm. She was trapped in a dank grave. A sob stuck in her throat. "D-did I mention how m-much I hate this p-plan?"

He rearranged the branches over the opening, and then turned to face her, both of them kneeling in the tight space. He positioned his body as a shield in front of hers and wrapped his arms around her. His voice dropped to a whisper. "Relax." His sandpapery cheek curved in a smile against hers. "Try picturing me in my underwear."

She burrowed into his chest, and a faint chuckle edged past the sob. She whispered back, "That's to help ease the fear of public speaking."

Outside their hiding place, angry swearing and stalking footsteps grew louder, closer. A graveled voice spat out a vile curse. "Where'd they go?"

Trembling, she clung to Aidan, and his hand stroked her hair.

"They probably followed the creek upstream, Rico," a second, younger man replied. His tone turned whiney. "The boss is gonna tear a strip off our hides if she gets away."

"Manny, go back to the car and get the flashlight. Somebody should have thought to grab it in the first place, dammit," Rico snarled. His voice grew less distinct, as if he'd moved away. "Meet us downstream. We'll hunt them down if it takes all night. There's nowhere for them to go on this island. She won't escape.

She. Aidan was right, they were after *her.* Icy fingers of déjà vu crawled up Zoe's spine, and wild shaking overpowered her. The desperate flight toward freedom, the determined hunters closing in on her trail felt all too familiar.

Her worst childhood nightmare come to life.

"You're all right, sweetheart," Aidan breathed a whisper of sound in her ear. His encircling arms pressed her tightly to his solid body. "I won't let anyone hurt you."

Zoe huddled in the dark, the past and present tangling into a murky web of fear. How was he going to stop them? Nobody, nothing could stop them. Violent shudders wracked her. Smothering blackness swallowed her hopes for a bright new future. The hunt would never end. The terror would never fade.

She would never be free.

She clenched her teeth, but couldn't prevent a whimper from escaping.

"Shh. I'm here," Aidan murmured, his breath hot in her ear. "Darkness can't harm you. The night is working for us. It's hiding us. Protecting us." He tipped up her chin, and his mouth possessed hers. His silky tongue slid slowly inside, stroking, soothing. Exerting exquisite control, his soft lips coaxed her response. So different from the untamed hunger that had erupted between them before, his gentleness vanquished fear and despair.

Poignantly sweet, his kiss comforted and aroused. Sheltered and cherished. Pledged steadfast loyalty and protection. She clutched the lapels of his jacket and drank in his strength, courage and absolute confidence. Warmth flooded her icy limbs, filling the dark void inside her with hope.

Aidan stroked her back, his callused fingertips trailing delight along her bare skin. His tender kiss and sure touch pulled her out of the desolate shadows of the past. She was still trembling, but irrational fear had fled, conquered by desire. In the parking lot, they'd connected body to body. Now, they bonded heart to heart. The first time, they'd shared passion. Now, they shared compassion. Passion had brought them together. But compassion would forge a lasting bond.

Zoe eased back from Aidan. How long had the night been utterly silent? "Did they leave?" Breathlessness fluttered in her question. Arousal, not fear.

"Yeah." His low reply was husky. "Let's get you out of here." He lifted the bushes, and they emerged from hiding.

Cool night air washed over her, and a giddy cocktail of relief and desire sang along her nerve endings. She turned, and for a lingering moment, Aidan held her gaze. A shaft of moonlight reflected on the fierce tenderness glittering in his beautiful, compelling eyes. He stroked a featherlight caress down her cheek. "All right?"

A rush of wonderment jammed the answer in her throat, and she nodded. He might be emotionally guarded, but his expression and body language clearly revealed his true feelings. The connection they shared wasn't just sexual.

Though he wasn't ready to admit it, he *cared*.

And she cared in return. The feelings growing between them went even deeper than she'd realized. She didn't have any first-hand knowledge, but she was a keen observer of the human condition. The bond they shared was rare...and very special. They'd crossed an irrevocable line. They could never go back to feigning casual rivalry.

The revelation thrilled and scared her. Everything she'd yearned for all her life finally dangled within reach. But the tiny, bright flicker could be snuffed out in a heartbeat. By the bad guys. By a thoughtless word or deed on her part. By Aidan's fear of involvement.

She of all people knew how quickly and easily everything could be snatched away. How badly it hurt when you were left holding the empty dregs of your dreams. She was more than willing to take the risk. However, she wasn't willing to let a rash, premature move on her part spoil everything. "Which way?"

He surveyed their surroundings. "Up and over."

They clambered up the bank with him bearing a lot more of her weight than she liked. She attempted to shake off the enervating effects of their kiss and subsequent startling discovery and get with the program. "Where are we going?"

"East, to that big bluff over there."

She glanced toward the tree-covered hill lurking in the distance like a sleeping giant. "How can you tell it's east?"

He grinned and pointed up. "God's compass."

Countless stars sparkled overhead, diamond-bright beacons of encouragement in the vast night-time sky. "I guess I should thank those lucky stars I'm stranded with an Eagle Scout, huh?" She trailed him around a tree trunk the size of a compact automobile. "Are we gonna get these handcuffs off now?"

"The bad guys took off in the opposite direction, but I want more distance between us and them before we stop again."

Though it was July, year-round Pacific Northwest rainfall kept the woods well-watered and cool. Aidan set a challenging pace, but their footsteps fell silently on the verdant undergrowth.

After they'd jogged in eerie quiet for fifteen minutes, Aidan's steps slowed. His glance brushed her. "It's okay to talk now. Is there a reason you're terrified of the dark?"

Lifelong conditioning never to speak the unspeakable made her automatically hesitate. Then she threw off the ingrained caution like a stained, ragged coat that no longer fit. This was Aidan. She trusted him without reservation. She took a deep breath of pine-scented air. Thanks to her daily jogging routine, she could still power walk and carry on a conversation. He'd kept his question pitched soft and low, and she followed his lead. "My mom had to get what work she could, mostly night shifts. I was alone a lot, starting at a very young age."

"How young?"

"Six."

He swore softly. "Too damn young."

"She couldn't help it, Aidan." Just as Zoe couldn't help leaving her mom in a distant care center. But she would reunite with her as soon as humanly possible. "Mom didn't like it, either, but she couldn't afford sitters. She couldn't afford the money or the risk."

"Risk?"

Nerves jittered in her stomach. She trusted Aidan, but telling him the truth about herself was harder than she'd expected. How would a cop from a long, proud lineage of dedicated cops feel about her dubious background? She swallowed hard. "My—my parents never married, and mom kept her own place. Their relationship was volatile, and they often needed time apart. Mom said a few months after my third birthday, they had a huge fight over a large amount of cash she'd found." She swallowed again, and her voice dropped. "I don't remember, but apparently, she threatened to take me and leave and he tried to kill her. Mom tossed the money out the window. While he was retrieving it, she grabbed me and ran."

Zoe's confession slammed into Aidan like a steel battering ram, destroying his defenses. He'd guessed she'd had a tough childhood, but had never imagined that kind of horror. His life's work was to put people like her father behind bars. Yet, he couldn't do anything to ease her pain.

He couldn't protect her from her past.

His hands clenched into fists. Helplessness sat uneasily on his shoulders. He'd rather face unending pain and torture than be powerless to keep someone else from being hurt. The inability to protect his loved ones was his worst nightmare. He didn't want to examine the reasons why protecting Zoe had zoomed to the top of his list.

Even involved in their conversation, he continually assessed their surroundings, kept his ears attuned to background noises. No sounds of pursuit followed them. "I'm sorry, sweetheart. Fathers are supposed to keep their little girls safe. Not hurt them."

She tentatively touched his clenched fist with her fingertips, and he forced his fingers to relax and curve around hers. Joined to her at the wrist, he couldn't hide his reaction, and didn't want her to mistake anger for revulsion.

She inhaled shakily, and he moderated his stride to let her catch her breath. "The worst thing was just when I'd settle in to a new place, mom would glimpse a face on a crowded street, receive an anonymous hang-up, or get "a bad feeling," and we'd pull up stakes and run again. Sometimes on a moment's notice."

So she'd never even had a real home. At least when his world had imploded, he'd had his family. He steered her around a rocky outcropping, and peered through the imposing treetops to ensure they were traveling in the right direction. Zoe rubbed her arm and shivered. He glanced at her. "Are you chilly? The temperature drops in these woods at night."

"No, the exercise is keeping me warm. The goose bumps are from my past coming back to haunt me. When I moved to Riverside, I vowed I'd never run again." The sorrow in her eyes wrenched his heart. "And here I am in the dark woods, being hunted."

Savage resolve churned inside him. "I meant what I said, Zoe. I won't let anyone hurt you." Even if he had to die in order to prevent it. Again, he didn't question the compulsion, but simply accepted it.

"Even though this is really scary, I feel a lot safer with you here."

He swept the area in a visual scan, listening intently. As they hiked, the undergrowth rustled with small animals settling down for the night, and crickets creaked from the bushes. The normal night-time noises assured him that their pursuers were nowhere in the vicinity. "You're doing great."

"I used to be okay about being alone at night. I mean, I wasn't crazy about it, but I wasn't scared. I watched a lot of TV to keep me company. Still do." She slanted a wry smile at him. "Thus, the abundant movie trivia."

He gently squeezed her fingers, still entwined in his. The feeling of being intimately linked to this woman—and not just physically—was eerie. But nice. Sometimes he felt alone even in the midst of his family. Startled, he realized that he hadn't felt that way since Zoe had blasted into his life. "Mine is because Letty's niece worked at a theater and got more free tickets than she could use. Mom had four growing boys to entertain through a lot of rainy Northwest winters on a cop's salary. Free movie tickets were a Godsend." He hated to ask, but had to know. "What happened to make you so afraid?"

She bent her head and fiddled with her bag. The pause lasted so long he opened his mouth to tell her it was okay, to forget it. They clambered over an upended log, and before he could speak, she began. "The year I turned seven, we found an abandoned travel trailer parked in a remote campground somewhere in Oklahoma. It was winter, and the campground was deserted. We had the rest rooms and showers all to ourselves. A luxury compared to the closet-size bathroom in the trailer."

And he'd thought roughing it was six people using two bathrooms. He encouraged her with another press of his fingers, and lifted a low-hanging branch for her to step under.

"An hour after mom left for her shift at a truck stop, a windstorm hit, knocking out the power. It was pitch black so far away from the city, and there were no other people around. Even if we could have afforded a phone, there was nowhere to hook it up." The tiny hitch in her voice damn near killed him. He'd vowed to keep her safe, but he had no way to protect her from her past. "Anyway, who could I have called?"

"The police."

"Even nowadays, with the stalking laws in place, women have

trouble getting help. Besides, my father had 'connections,' and Mom didn't know what kind. He could have been involved with the mob, or had cops on his payroll. He didn't allow anyone to take pictures of him, and often used an alias. He was a nameless, faceless evil. Always behind us, always lurking in the shadows ready to snatch me away." She was trembling, and he slid an arm around her waist and drew her close. "Alone in that dark trailer, I heard loud bangs and thumps from outside and thought for sure he was breaking in."

"Ah, sweetheart, I'm sorry. You must have been so afraid."

She moved closer to him, until their shoulders nearly touched. "Of course, I know now it was just the storm, but at the time, I was terrified. I had my own personal bogeyman."

He hesitated. He'd unwittingly spilled his guts to her once before. This time, he made a deliberate decision to confide in her. "In a way, I know how you felt." Though it was hard, opening his own wounds might provide her some comfort. If nothing else, she'd understand his empathy. Know he wasn't merely spouting platitudes. "When Pop was murdered, I felt like a nameless, faceless evil had snatched him away."

She nodded. "Now the evil has a name. Tony DiMarco."

Yeah, and when all the evidence was accumulated, DiMarco would finally get what had been coming to him. "Pop's loss trapped me inside a dark, empty hole. I was afraid it would never be light again. But at least I had family to help me."

She squeezed his hand this time. "I'm really glad you did."

Her generosity in the face of her own pain was nearly overwhelming. He forced himself to continue. "The loss was much harder for Mom. Mom and Pop were crazy about one another. Sometimes, they'd share this look that didn't include us boys. A private look, just for the two of them. She was the center of his world, and he, hers."

She smiled. "That's wonderful. Love like that is beautiful and priceless. Everyone yearns for that kind of love."

Maybe, but he'd seen the destructive power of love. "Not me. I don't want to leave a grieving woman behind to fend for herself. I don't want to be the center of anyone's world. Because when the center is destroyed, the world crumbles."

She considered that for a few moments. "Your mom seems to be doing okay."

Sure, now. It had taken years for the anguish to fade from her face, leaving behind lines etched by grief. Years for the dullness in her green eyes to dissipate. For the bad dreams to stop making her pace her bedroom floor until dawn. He didn't want to go there. "I didn't mean to make this about me. I wanted to let you know I understood."

"Thank you. I know how hard it is to talk about such personal pain."

Such a small act of kindness, yet she was so grateful. She needed more kindness in her life.

"Aidan?" She hesitated. "You know, it's possible for someone to be the center of your world without being your whole reason for living. I wonder what your mom would have done if given the choice of never loving your dad? You and your brothers wouldn't exist."

Startled, he stumbled. She'd thrown him a curveball he'd never considered. He didn't know what to think. What to say.

He was spared an incoherent reply when the crickets suddenly fell silent. Aidan froze, every sense screaming to red alert. On his right, twigs snapped as small, night-time creatures fled in terror.

"Get down!" He grabbed Zoe and shoved her to the ground. Then he threw himself on top of her, shielding her with his body.

Chapter 9

Twelve midnight

Aidan strained to see into the woods. Stealthy, padded footsteps made him swivel his gaze to a nearby thicket. Glowing amber eyes glared back at him.

"Oh, crap."

Zoe stirred beneath him. "What is it?" she murmured.

"Cougar."

"A *cougar?*" she gasped. "As in, giant carnivore?"

"I didn't mean John Mellencamp."

She huddled in the ferns. "If we're quiet, he'll go away, right?"

"Wrong." Bringing her with him, he cautiously rose to his feet and got a good look at the crouching cat. A big one, over six feet long and weighing at least one-sixty. Cougars always attacked the smallest in the group, and would target Zoe. "We have to make ourselves look as large and threatening as possible, and as unlike prey as we can. Stare it in the eyes. Raise your arms over your head and spread them out. Wave your bag around."

"A-are you s-sure we won't draw unnecessary attention to ourselves?"

"Cougars like to sneak up on their prey. We want it to know we see it." He deliberately spoke louder to intimidate the cougar. "And smile. Show your teeth. He thinks they're weapons."

"You've g-got to be k-kidding. Not even on my worst PMS day could I take a bite out of *that*."

Ears flattened, the cougar crept forward, fixated on Zoe. Aidan's stomach clenched. The animal wasn't backing off. There had to be a reason for its overt aggression. It either had no fear of humans, or was extremely hungry. Maybe it had a den nearby and was protecting cubs. Either scenario could be lethal. "Stay upright. Keep waving." He crouched, feeling for a weapon.

"He's coming closer!" She retreated several wary steps.

"Move toward it! Don't give ground!"

"Are y-you insane? A two-hundred-pound kitty can have any patch of ground he wants."

Aidan rose, gripping a branch and a handful of rocks. He forcefully strode toward the cougar, tugging a reluctant Zoe in his wake. "He doesn't want your patch of dirt. He wants *you*. Don't make it seem easy." He pitched the rocks, striking the cougar's flank. "Go on! Get out of here!"

The wild animal snarled, baring sharp fangs, and backed up a few steps. Aidan again moved forward, lunging with the branch.

"The bad guys want me, the cougar wants me," Zoe's voice cracked. From behind him, she waved her bag at the big cat. "Really, I never cared for popularity."

"Go on!" Aidan was almost close enough to whack the cougar with the branch. "Get!"

Growling, the animal swiped at the branch with razored claws, but backed away. Aidan lunged a second time, and the cat retreated farther. After a long, nerve-wracking duel, the cougar finally melted into the brush.

Every muscle taut, Aidan watched and listened. The cougar could spring out at them, or circle and attack from behind.

Unaware they were still in danger, Zoe sagged against him. "I have a new topic for a feature. 'Close wildlife encounters of the potentially deadly kind.' I thought you weren't supposed to look predators directly in the eye."

The crickets began to chirp their singsong chorus once more. Satisfied that the cougar wasn't coming back, Aidan turned. "Let's move. We have a long way to go." He kept his grip on the branch, the only weapon he had, and supported Zoe with his other hand. "You don't look a dog or wolf in the eye. Or a bear. To those animals, a direct stare is a challenge." He pitched his voice low and continued to listen. The men hunting them were far away in the opposite direction, but he couldn't afford to let down his guard. He picked up speed again. "With cats, it shows dominance. And as I said, we wanted the cougar to know we'd seen it."

Zoe uncomplainingly kept up with the brisk pace he set, though her feet had to be killing her in those sexy heels. Especially as the challenging terrain steepened. "Yikes! Wolves and bears?"

He surveyed the landscape. They'd nearly reached the base of the bluff. "Watch those protruding tree roots." He guided her around the obstacle. "Don't worry. We probably won't run into either."

Aside from the threat of hungry wild animals, Zoe worried about a more basic problem as she and Aidan trekked through the woods. The strain of the last few hours combined with the cougar scare had only made her growing need worse. "Can we spring these handcuffs now?"

He halted at the edge of a small clearing, and his vigilant glance probed every murky nook and cranny. "A brief stop before we climb probably won't do any harm. Do you have a pair of sunglasses in your bag? I need something long and thin, but sturdy. The earpiece would be perfect for picking the lock."

"No sunglasses." She unzipped her bag. "I suppose the broken nail file is too wide?" At his affirmative nod, she riffled the contents. "The ink cartridge from a pen?"

"Not strong enough."

"Eyelash curler…too bulky. Mascara wand…too flimsy." She continued the search with increasing desperation. "I have a wire-bound spiral notebook. The wire is fairly sturdy."

He nodded. "Twisted double, it could work."

She hurriedly unwound the wire and passed it to him. "Have you done this before?"

"There's a first time for everything." He lifted their bound wrists up to a patch of moonlight and inserted the wire.

She willed him to succeed. Quickly. When her hand went numb from lack of circulation, she shifted from foot to foot. "Can you hurry?"

"I'm doing my best. This would be easier if you'd stop jigging."

"The thing is…well…" Shoot. He'd seen her fibbing to Officer Ryan, wallowing in garbage and cringing in fear of the dark. How much worse could it be? Ha. A *lot*. "I had several glasses of champagne at the reception. Between that and hours of abject terror, I…uh…need to use the facilities. Badly."

He glanced at her in concern. "This is gonna take awhile. On a scale of one to ten, how urgent is it?"

"Forty-three." She couldn't help fidgeting again. "What's wrong? Picking handcuffs looks dead easy in the movies."

He snorted. "It's not so easy in semidarkness, using my left hand. And these are police-issue steel cuffs, not a pair of fakes tricked out so Harrison Ford can pop 'em with a paperclip. It's purposely difficult, so every Tom, Dick and armed robber can't do it on a whim."

"I'm gonna have a problem." She gnawed the inside of her cheek in agitation. "Soon."

"How desperate are you?"

"More desperate than Madonna when she kissed Britney Spears on international TV for the publicity."

"That bad, huh?" He pointed to his left. "I can stand on one side of those thick bushes, and you on the other. With our arms stretched across the top, you can take care of business in relative privacy."

A very *distant* relative to privacy, but need conquered modesty.

It turned out that fleeing through the woods in a fitted gown and three inch heels was a snap compared to taking care of business in the woods in said gown and heels while handcuffed to Aidan like escapees from a bondage festival.

She located tissue from her stash and refused to think about bugs. And possible approaching armed bad guys. Not to mention wolves and cougars and bears. "Sing."

"Huh?" Aidan's puzzled question floated from the other side of the hedge.

"I can't do this with you listening. Sing something to keep yourself busy."

"Yes, ma'am." Strangled humor bubbled in his reply, but luckily for him, he didn't laugh. "Do you have a request?"

"I don't know. Pick something. Anything."

After a short pause, he began to sing softly, his voice as deep and rich as embossed velvet.

Done, and much relieved, she followed him back to the patch of moonlight. She feared he might tease her, but he studiously resumed lock duty.

Zoe studied his handsome face bent intently to his work. "We've definitely established that beggars can't be choosers. But your idea of an appropriate song for the occasion is 'You Really Got a Hold On Me?'"

He shrugged. "I'm no Smoky Robinson, but it's the first song that sprang to mind."

Was there a subliminal message in the song? It definitely had possibilities. "Your mind is bent, SWAT."

He laughed, the husky vibrations dancing through her. He should laugh more often. "Tell me something I don't know."

"You have a beautiful singing voice."

He made a low wolf growl in his throat that melted her into chocolate fondue. "All the better to accompany you on business trips, my dear."

"Thanks, but I prefer traveling solo on those jaunts."

She held perfectly still while he worked the lock. He slipped several times, and the wire popped out. If he didn't succeed, their chances of survival decreased exponentially. His effectiveness in a fight would be zilch. And it grew harder and harder to navigate the gloomy, obstacle-strewn forest while shackled together. Slow minutes ticked past. Aidan seemed to possess endless patient persistence, but for Zoe, not fidgeting became a major victory.

Finally, the handcuffs dropped to the ground, and she sighed and rubbed her sore wrist. "Free at last! What now?"

He stuck the cuffs into his trouser pocket and indicated the mountain hulking in front of them. "We scale the hill and establish an SOS signal."

"I think we'd have a better chance of rescue if we hike down to the shoreline. Maybe we can flag down an outgoing boat."

He frowned. "Where did you take wilderness survival training?"

"Hey, I watched *Survivor*."

"Great. When we need to vote someone off the island, you're in charge. Until then, we do things my way."

After the past hours of easy camaraderie, his brusque dismissal stung. He'd instantly demoted her from equal to lackey. Hurt wrenched inside, and she stacked her arms and bobbed, like the blonde on *I Dream of Jeannie*. "Yes, Master."

His frown morphed into a scowl. "The grand prize on this island isn't money. Our lives are at stake, Zoe."

"I know." Her cop had gone above and beyond the call of duty to keep her alive tonight. Ashamed of her defensive overreaction, she shuffled her feet. "I'm sorry. But darn it, your bossy-boots attitude tweaks my inner imp."

His full, sensual lips twitched and then he grinned. "I believe there's a twelve-step program for that."

"Oh, yes. SAA. Smart Alecks Anonymous. I have their number."

He snickered. "I'll bet you do."

She held his gaze, her own earnest. "Aidan, you need to realize that I can contribute to our survival. Because I'm a terrified civilian doesn't make me incompetent, or my ideas less valid." Her lips wobbled, and she pressed them firmly together. "I thought we were a team. After all, the contents of my bag got us out of that locked trunk and opened the cuffs."

He sighed. "I don't have an objection to teamwork, honey. However, you need to understand that on this operation, I am team leader. I'm trained to handle these scenarios. My sole objective is to keep you safe. Keep you alive."

"*Our* objective is to keep *each other* alive."

"Don't worry about me, I can take care of myself." He rolled his shoulders, tension evident in every hard line of his body as he glanced around. She'd noticed that the banter during their trek hadn't distracted him from constantly scanning their surroundings for danger. "If I have to stop and explain every decision, the delay could be fatal."

"I wholeheartedly appreciate your devout protection." However, the lone-wolf attitude had to go. Hopefully she could show him the advantages of having her as an ally. "And I see where you're coming from. We can't be fighting over every little thing if we're going to survive. But I've done a decent job of looking out for my own welfare for a long time now." She paused to let that sink in. "Underestimating me and protecting me are two entirely different animals. Please don't bark orders at me like I'm a brainless twit."

He nodded. "I apologize." His full lips quirked in a wry smile. "Which I seem to do a lot around you. You're an intelligent, capable woman, and I didn't mean to insult you." He cupped her face in a large, warm hand. "My single-minded focus comes across, as my brothers so aptly stated at the reception, as 'uptight, headstrong and intense.'" His thumb brushed her cheek, sending delightful shivers down her spine. "The shoreline is downstream. The bad guys went that way. What would happen if we flagged down one of them by mistake?"

His tender gaze dissolved the hard knot in her chest. "I didn't know the shoreline was downstream. I thought getting there would be easier and boating off the island would be faster than tromping through the woods. The bad guys are combing the island, so we might run into them anyway."

"A chance we have to take. I have a plan..." He grinned at her eager expression. "Which I will explain when we reach the top of the bluff."

"All righty then." The uncomfortable misunderstanding had served its purpose. Forced to talk out their differences in operating styles, they finally understood one another. She squared her shoulders and marshaled her rapidly dwindling resources. "What are we waiting for?" She determinedly marched up the hill.

His long stride easily kept pace with her. He flashed another grin. "You're game for anything, Zagretti, and one hell of a good sport."

"Glad to be of some use." She giggled. "Master."

He reached out and tweaked a curl. "Impertinence alert."

"You haven't seen anything, yet, SWAT."

He laughed softly. "Is that a promise or a threat?"

She slanted an arched look in his direction. "Depends on how easily you spook."

"Ask my brothers, it's tough to scare me."

"No worries, then."

The hill soon turned into a nearly vertical track, and Zoe lost the ability to talk as she toiled up the steep incline. Merely breathing became an impressive feat. Even gripping Aidan's hand, she struggled to reach the top.

Aidan's wary gaze continually canvassed the area, and each rustle, every flutter from the underbrush jerked him to attention. Neither needed to remind the other that a snarling cougar lurked in the deep woods behind them. Or that gun-toting bad guys could eventually find them.

Finally, the ground evened out and they reached the top. Good thing she wasn't afraid of heights, because they were a long way up. Aidan stopped beneath an old-growth pine, and propped the branch he'd used to drive off the cougar against the broad trunk. Far below, the roar of the Pacific Ocean echoed through the forest to her left, and a brisk sea breeze tugged at her hair, making her shiver.

Aidan studied the huge, ancient pine. The lower limbs were thicker than his waist. "The perfect spot for what I have planned. Take off your dress."

She blinked, goggled at him. "SWAT...seriously without any tact."

His wicked wolf grin flashed. "Now whose mind is bent?" He chuckled. "When our abandoned cars are discovered in the parking lot, my brothers will call out a ground and air search. The seagoing SOS flag is red with a black circle and square. After sunrise, your dress will be visible for miles from the treetop, and the beads will reflect light like a lighthouse beacon. Once we find a place to hole up, we'll lay out a directional signal visible from the air to pinpoint our location."

Torn, she shifted uneasily from foot to foot. "Look, SWAT, I'm not opposed to giving my all for the cause, especially our survival. But the only thing I'm wearing under this dress is a pair of red satin panties and a navel ring."

She watched her words burn into his imagination. Heat flared in his eyes, and lightning arced between them. His thoughts were an open book. *The Kama Sutra.* He swallowed hard, visibly reining in control. "I'll give you my shirt and jacket."

Whew. At least she wasn't chilly anymore. Okay, she could handle wearing his shirt and jacket. In fact, it was a lot more than she had on right now. "Turn around."

He slowly complied. "I've seen a woman's body before." His deep voice was husky.

"Not this woman's body." Another time and place, in a more secure environment, she wouldn't mind.

He shrugged off his jacket and shirt while she wriggled out of her dress. With the gown clutched to her breasts, she turned. And froze. No woman with a pulse could help but admire his wide, bronzed back, rippling with hard muscles. It was her turn to swallow hard and rein in a rioting libido.

"Point to you." A nervous giggle slipped out. She didn't doubt he'd behave honorably. However, the situation was awkward. "You're the first guy who's ever talked me out of my clothes." She dangled the gown over his bare shoulder. Standing so close, both naked to the waist, his body heat shimmered over her skin and every nerve ending tingled in response. Another inch, and the tips of her breasts would brush his back. Her nipples tightened, and she hastily took a step away from temptation.

"It's the silver-tongued Irish blarney." Without turning around, he took the dress from her hand and held up his shirt and jacket. His low chuckle torched her simmering hormones. "It couldn't possibly just be the lesser of two evils at the moment."

She moved back to button on the soft cotton garment, warm and redolent with his wonderful scent. Wearing his still-warm shirt seemed shockingly intimate, an affectionate, familiar act shared between lovers. Her hands unsteady, she rolled up the sleeves and then donned the jacket, leaving the front open. "I'm decent."

He pivoted, hands on lean hips, his muscled thighs braced wide in an imposing masculine stance. The breeze trailed playful fingers through his thick hair. Moonlight caressed his broad chest and ridged abs, and defined the strong, chiseled beauty of his face. Though Michelangelo had signed only one of his pieces, he would have proudly put his signature on such a magnificent work.

Aidan's smoky gaze stroked her from tousled hair down the long expanse of thigh left bare under his shirttail, to her red heels. Then just as slowly, just as thoroughly, his intent gaze repeated the journey. A rugged, savage pirate, surveying his plunder. Need glinted in his warm caramel eyes. "You mean you're dressed." Desire thrummed in every hoarse word. "*Decent* is an entirely different game."

She'd play games with him any day. Her stomach tumbled, and the lack of oxygen made it hard to breathe. "Guess you better sign me up for *What Not To Wear*."

"Honey, that shirt looks better on you than it ever did on me. You can borrow my clothes anytime."

She indicated her dress clutched in his strong hands. "And you, mine."

Aidan stared down at it. "A one-way ticket to the apocalypse," he muttered so low she barely heard. He shook his head as if to clear away the sensual haze, and ripped her dress down the side seam. The fabric parted with a rending tear, and she winced. The thrift-store gown was the most lovely, expensive garment she'd owned in a decade. He grimaced. "Sorry. I'll replace it."

"Don't worry, it's not your concern."

"Everything about you concerns me." The flash of intense possessiveness in his eyes made her stomach flip-flop again. "You mentioned a water bottle?"

Hours ago, in the garbage truck. "Good memory." She dug the bottle out of her bag, and he squatted and poured a meager amount into the dirt at his feet. He mixed a thick mud paste, and then painted a black circle and square on the red gown.

"You're a talented guy."

He wiggled his eyebrows at her. "So I've been told."

"Don't get braggarly. It's not becoming in a saint."

He gave her an innocent stare. "I was merely agreeing with

you." He cleaned his hands with the wet wipe she passed him, and rose. With the makeshift flag draped over a brawny bare shoulder, he hoisted himself into the tree and began to climb.

She returned the water bottle to her bag and apprehensively watched his upward progress. Scaling a hundred-foot tree in formal slacks and slick dress shoes in the dark couldn't be easy. "Won't the bad guys spot the flag and track us?"

His quiet reply floated down from far above. "I'm hanging it on the ocean side. Anyone on the island won't see it because of the trees. It will only be visible from the air or water. We'll hole up in a separate location."

"You *are* talented." Zoe balled her hands into fists and shoved them into the jacket pockets. Her right knuckles brushed soft silk. So that's where he'd stashed his cummerbund and bow tie. She quit talking, for fear she'd distract him and make him fall. Instead, she watched silently for long, heart-shaking minutes until she could no longer see his movements, and then lowered her gaze.

Her breath froze in her lungs as a husky blond man slunk out of the shadowed forest and pointed a pistol at her. "My hunch paid off. Look what I found. A babe in the woods." He bared his teeth in a parody of a smile. She preferred the cougar's toothy snarl. He looked up, and she held her breath. "What were you eyeballing in that tree?"

What indeed? "A-a-an owl."

"A bird watching a bird." He laughed heartily at his own bad joke. "Where's the dude?"

The acid taste of fear leached the moisture from her mouth. The guy was several inches shorter than Aidan, but had at least twenty pounds on him. Not fat…bulky. Solid muscle, like he spent all his time at the gym. Terror iced her veins, but she feigned nonchalance. "What dude?"

"The one who obviously scored big in the last hour." Muscle Man's leering gaze oozed down her body, making her long for hot water and a gallon jug of antibacterial soap. "I liked the 'do-me' dress better, but this has possibilities."

"He—he's in there somewhere," she lied, gesturing vaguely at the forest. "Gathering wood for a fire. He told me to wait."

"And no wonder." He moved closer, and she took a step back. I bet he wants another taste. You're a juicy little trick."

She strained to hear Aidan, but sensed no movement, no sound. "Yeah. Bite me. I'll give you heartburn."

The man tightened his grip on the gun and waved the pistol at her. "The boss said you were brainy. He admires that."

"Really? I wonder what he sees in you?" He stepped forward and she again stepped back. Unlike the cougar, invading this predator's space wouldn't intimidate him.

"He hired me for my brawn, not my brains." He moved closer, continuing the obscene dance.

"Ya think?" Her hands brushed bark and closed over the tree limb Aidan had carried up the hill. Uh-oh. She'd backed into the pine where Aidan was trapped, a sitting target. If Mr. Muscle spotted him and started shooting, Aidan had nowhere to go. Her heart galloped. *No*. Aidan would not get hurt or…worse. She gulped. Not if she had anything to say about it.

Gripping the branch, she surreptitiously edged around the immense trunk. "So, where are your pals?"

Muscle-bound jerked his head toward the woods. "I told them we should check up here. They're probably rappin' with your man. We're real friendly, once you get to know us."

She was so not getting friendly with him. Or sticking around long enough to get to know him, or his boss. Zoe's fingers tensed on the branch as she prepared mentally and physically for what she had to do.

Mr. Muscle would follow her without a doubt. Whether he'd shoot her in the back was another question, one she refused to worry about. She'd either survive the next few minutes, or not. Either way, Aidan would have a fighting chance. She couldn't run very fast in these danged heels, but all she had to do was lead the bad guy far enough away for Aidan to get his feet on the ground.

She sucked in a deep breath. "It's been a thrill-a-minute chatting with you…" She swung the branch out from behind her and threw it at his head. "But I have to run."

He instinctively flung up his hands to ward off the limb, and Zoe sprinted toward the forest.

Chapter 10

July 27, 1:00 a.m.

Zoe tore into the underbrush and zigzagged as quickly as she dared through the treacherous woods. Muscle Man was faster than he looked. A lot faster. She'd barely covered fifty feet before he tackled her and knocked her to the ground.

He rolled, flipped her onto her back and pinned her down in the ferns. His body pressed full-length on hers, and the air punched out of Zoe's lungs. Oh, God, that better be a gun at his waistband and not…

She tried to suck in enough air to fight. Better a fast, clean death than rape. Kicking, clawing, she struggled beneath him. Never let them see your fear. She infused every ounce of toughness she could muster into her order. "Get off me, creep."

His coarse laughter scraped away her thin veneer of bravado. "Don't get your thong in a twist. The boss doesn't like used merchandise." He snagged the front of her jacket and jerked her upright. He dragged her back to the clearing like a Rottweiler with a rag doll.

He restrained her with one hand and tugged the pistol from his waistband with the other. "We have orders to bring you in undamaged. The cop, on the other hand, is fair game."

Panic screamed through her. Had he spotted Aidan? Her covert glance darted around the area. Aidan wasn't on the ground. Relief made her weak when she needed strength. He hadn't had time to climb completely down. Panic surged back. What if he was low enough to be seen?

She squared her chin. Get a grip, girl. You can't help Aidan if you freak. She could at least create a distraction to keep Muscles from looking around. "You would have been disappointed if I hadn't at least tried to escape."

Her captor yanked her against him, and his hand slid beneath the tuxedo jacket. He grabbed her breast and squeezed hard. "Makes me want to keep you close, babe."

Her stomach lurched in revulsion. Apparently, it was okay to feel up the merchandise. She clasped her palms together and clubbed his wrist, and he abruptly released her. "Take your hands off me while you still have enough fingers to count to ten."

She lurched backward, and once more found herself standing in front of the ancient pine.

He laughed again, and she clamped her knees together to hide their shaking. His amusement scared her more than rage would have. Psychos like him laughed while they tortured people to death. "I totally get why the boss is eager to meet you. He's a big fan of your work."

Her verbal acuity was her biggest asset. Her only weapon. Keep talking, divert his interest. "I'm ecstatic. Always great to have fans." Her pulse thundered in her ears as she sidled outward, circled around. Would he guess her plan?

He followed her movements, which put his back toward the tree. Exactly where she wanted him. Watching her, not Aidan's hiding place. She licked dry, trembling lips and tried to slow her breathing as she gathered her reserves for another escape attempt. "Have his people call my people. We'll do lunch."

Mr. Muscle nodded. "Yeah, he's gonna love you. And I'll get the reward for hauling you in." His square face split in a smile that made the back of her neck crawl. "Maybe he'll even let me have *you*. If there's anything left when he's done. I'm okay with seconds."

She'd throw herself off the cliff first.

"You have a date to keep. Let's go." He lunged at her.

She dodged beneath his arm and ran.

He grabbed her by the jacket tail and swung her around. His arm flew up, and he backhanded her across the face with his gun hand. Stars exploded in her vision, and the sharp sting brought a rush of involuntary tears. The metallic taste of blood leached into her mouth. "No more games, babe."

An ear-splitting crash rang out from above, followed by a savage, hair-raising growl. Aidan hurtled out of the tree like an avenging angel and dropped onto her captor.

Muscle-bound grunted, and the two men went down in a tangle of vicious curses. They rolled, fought, swore. Fists pummeled flesh. Bones crunched.

Horrified, Zoe stumbled back to make room. The last thing Aidan needed was for her to get in his way. She tripped and fell hard. Still watching the men, she felt along her scraped calf, and found the tree branch she'd flung earlier.

Bolstered by the branch, she struggled upright. The grappling men surged to their feet. Mr. Muscles's hands wrapped around Aidan's throat, and Aidan struggled, his face mottled. Muscles's arms tensed and his fingers whitened.

Aidan thrust his left arm up between Mr. Muscles's wrists and broke his hold. He rammed his forehead into Mr. Muscles's Neanderthal brow. Zoe cringed as Muscles reeled backward. Weaving unsteadily, Aidan kicked his opponent's feet out from under him, and Muscles went down, groping for his gun. Zoe's heart bucked as he raised the weapon and fired.

Aidan flung himself aside, smashing into a huge limb, and the bullet gashed bark. Aidan staggered. Terror roared in Zoe's head. Had he been shot? Before Aidan could recover his balance, Muscles lunged at his legs, tackling him to the ground. Then Muscles clambered upright and aimed the pistol at Aidan's head. "Die, you sonofabitch!"

"No!" Zoe screamed. Clutching her makeshift weapon, she

charged. Muscles half-turned, and the gun moved off Aidan. Zoe raised the branch and slammed his gun arm downward. Two quick shots tore into the ground. Dirt and pine needles sprayed. The gun dropped out of his hand. Powered by momentum, she whirled and swung. The branch thudded into the side of his head. He dropped faster than the temperature at the top of the bluff.

Panting, she squatted and raised one of his eyelids. He was out for the count. She'd seen plenty of cop shows and kicked the gun out of his reach before picking it up. She stashed the weapon in her bag, and her gaze spun to Aidan. He knelt in the dirt, weaving from side to side. His right arm hung useless. His face was stark white in the moonlight, and sheened with perspiration. His breath sawed in ragged gasps.

She scrambled over to him, went to her knees and gently held his shoulders to support him. "Were you shot?" Her frantic gaze whirled over him.

He groaned. His eyes rolled back in his head, and he slipped out of her grip and crumpled onto the forest floor.

"Aidan!" Trembling, she brought her face close to his and listened intently. He was breathing. Her own breath hurtled out in a relieved rush. Starting at the top of his head, she examined him for wounds, felt for blood. None anywhere. Thank goodness! She blinked back tears.

She patted his bristly cheek, cool beneath her trembling palm. "Aidan! Wake up!"

He stirred, moaned.

"Come on, SWAT. I need you." She patted more briskly. "Open those gorgeous brown eyes."

Too many long, agonizing heartbeats dragged past. Then his dark lashes fluttered, and his eyelids floated up. He frowned at her, his expression bewildered. "Zoe? What…the hell?"

"Where are you hurt?"

He grimaced, and blinked pain-clouded eyes. "Dislocated shoulder. When I hit the limb." That explained why he'd passed out when she'd gripped his shoulders. He jerked upright, groaned, and fell back.

"Whoa." She tugged off the tux jacket and covered him. "Easy there. Stay down for a few minutes."

"Where's the…other guy?"

"Perfecting his hockey puck imitation. He's not going anywhere."

"Got to," he gritted out. "Make sure. Restrain him."

"Now that I know you're okay, I'll take care of it."

"No! Stay away. Too dangerous. I'll…do it." Aidan struggled, sat up quickly. Another groan escaped his too-pale lips, and he lost consciousness again.

She knelt beside him, and pressed shaky fingers to his wrist. "Not this time, SWAT." His skin was cooler than she'd like. But his breathing was even, and a strong pulse throbbed beneath her fingertips. As long as he didn't go into shock, he was better off oblivious than suffering. For the moment. They'd have to move, soon. The gunshots could bring the other bad guys on the run.

"Everything will be fine," she insisted. "I've got your back." Okay, he couldn't hear her, but *she* needed the reassurance.

Nerves fluttering, Zoe crept toward the unconscious bad guy. She checked Muscles's vitals. His breathing and pulse were also strong. Two for two.

After wrestling him out of his shirt and tying his hands behind him with his belt, she cleaned the bloody lump on the side of his head with a wet wipe. Blood trickled steadily, but it didn't look serious. Didn't head wounds bleed a lot? She tore off a shirt cuff and folded into a pad. She used the sleeve to fasten the makeshift bandage.

Grimacing in distaste, she searched his jeans pockets and hit pay dirt with Aidan's wallet and confiscated knife. She recognized the Celtic design key chain that held his apartment and car keys. Continuing the search, she discovered Mr. Muscles's heavy silver lighter and cigarettes. He didn't have any ID. Big surprise.

Puffing and sweating, she wrestled him to a smaller tree and propped him against the trunk. The guy weighed as much as an SUV. She bound his feet and tied him to the tree with his shoe-strings and the rest of his shirt. His sneakers and socks had to go. If he escaped, being barefoot would slow him down.

Should she gag him with a sock? She wrinkled her nose. The guy had plainly never heard of Odor-Eaters. Talk about cruel and unusual punishment. The other shirtsleeve did the job. She considered confiscating his shoes and pants for herself, but bulky clothing would only slow her down. She hurried to the cliff's edge and tossed over his shoes and sweaty socks.

She ran back to Aidan. He'd come around while she was tying up Muscles, but hadn't tried to sit up. He was learning. "The bad guy?"

"I tied him up with his belt and shoelaces."

Pain pinched his colorless face and equally white lips. "Why didn't you use the cuffs in my pocket?"

"I forgot about them in all the confusion. Anyway, he's secure." She knelt beside him, smoothed his forehead. "How are you feeling?"

"You're bleeding." He reached up and gently touched the corner of her mouth.

"I am?" She swiped at her chin. In the melee, she'd also forgotten about her split lip. The moment she was reminded, she noticed the throbbing. The scrape on her calf also chose that time to make itself known. "No biggie."

Dark anger smoldered in his gaze. "Bastard hit you. I hope I get another chance to rip him a new one."

Though it was the middle of the night, sunlight warmed her inside. For so long, she'd had no one but herself to rely on. Aidan's staunch loyalty and anger on her behalf filled her with happiness…and hope. "I'm all right. How are you doing?"

"Okay." His low declaration sounded anything but. "We have to move. The gunshots will lead the others to us."

She fished in her bag and found ibuprofen and her water bottle. "These might help some."

She expected him to argue, but he let her support his head and silently swallowed the tablets. Her cop was nothing if not practical. He wiped his mouth with the back of his uninjured hand. "I'm no good to you like this. You have to put my shoulder back in."

In the midst of what had to be agony, he was thinking of her. She gulped. "How?"

"Plant one foot on my chest, raise my arm and pull."

She smothered the shocked retort that sprang to mind. In no way did he appear to be joking. She had no medical training. What if she hurt him worse? "Are you sure that's a good idea?"

His calm, confident gaze held hers. "You can do it."

"Aidan, I don't—"

"Zoe, you have to. I can't keep passing out every time I try to stand. C'mon. No time to waste."

Hands fisted, she gathered her courage. She had no choice. Aidan needed her.

Apprehension jittered inside as she removed her right sandal. She wouldn't get any leverage wearing one shoe, and took the other off as well. She planted her right foot on his chest and gripped his hand. "Ready?" He nodded, and her nerves shrieked. Maybe *he* was, but she wasn't sure she'd ever be. Bracing herself, she pulled.

Aidan's tendons strained, and joints popped. He hissed in a breath and clenched his teeth. Suffering etched every line of his face. "Harder, honey. Use all your body weight. You can't hurt me any more than I already am."

"I'm sorry. I'm so sorry." *It hurts me as much as you.* Cringing inside and sick to her stomach, she pulled with all her strength against his taut, pain-wracked muscles. More grinding, popping sounds echoed from his joints. He groaned, and she winced. *Please, let it have worked.* "How's that?"

"Better than it was, but not completely in. My arm still isn't functional." He shook his head. "You're not strong enough. That's as good as we're gonna get."

"I'm sorry." Failing him hurt more than causing him physical pain.

"Not your fault. I've seen it take two guys in the field. We need to move." He tried to shove upright, and his face blanched impossibly paler.

"Slowly this time." She helped him sit up, and the tux jacket crumpled into his lap. "Would a sling ease the pain?"

"Probably. Carry one of those around, too?"

"No, but you do." She dug the cummerbund and bow tie out of the tux pocket. As she rigged the sling, his warm, smooth skin jerked under her careful ministrations, and he bit back a grunt. She winced. "I'm sorry. I'm trying not to hurt you."

"I know. Stop apologizing, sweetheart. Just do what you have to."

The cummerbund cradled his useless arm, and the bow tie

stretched across the opposite shoulder and fastened the ends. "Perfect. Maybe when we get out of here, I'll do a story demonstrating the survival applications of formal wear." If they made it out alive. She shook her head. None of that. Together, they were a formidable team. They would make it.

She studied his drawn features. "I hate to rush you, but can you stand?"

At his nod, she helped him to his feet and draped the jacket over his shoulders.

He wove in place, trying to gain his bearings. "You're pretty talented, yourself. Nice distraction while I was up the tree. You maneuvered the gym rat under me like a pro. And ten points for the direct hit."

She scooped up her sandals and bag. She'd have to help him, and would have steadier balance barefoot. "I was once told by a ticked-off anchorman that I'm a master of distraction. Or would that be mistress?" She chuckled and picked up the fallen limb. The branch had come in handy. "Since you're the master."

A smile eased his set mouth. "Either way, I'm glad you're on my side." He slung his good arm across her shoulders. With her supporting him, they wobbled toward the forest.

He stumbled, and she caught him, nearly collapsing under his weight. He swore. "The pain is making me loopy. I can't protect you like this."

"Don't be so hard on yourself. You're only human, Aidan. You've been through a fall, a fight and in and out of consciousness in the past half hour. I wish we could let you rest and recoup longer, but we need a place to hide."

"You're preaching to the choir, sweetheart."

She led him farther into the woods, the ferns damp and cool beneath her sore feet. The forest smelled lush and green, with a musty undercurrent of danger. He stumbled again, and she stopped to let him regroup. Her instincts prickled. The urgent need to flee crawled up her spine, and she shivered. Her nervous glance assessed their surroundings. They couldn't go far until Aidan was strong enough. "So you jumped out of the tree, not fell? I wondered when I heard the crash."

"Do you think I could sit there and watch that bastard hit you?" He cupped her cheek. "Grab you? March you into the woods at gunpoint before I could climb down, and do whatever he wanted—" He clenched his teeth, and a muscle ticked in his jaw. "Hell, yes, I jumped."

Suddenly, he stiffened. *"Wait."*

She nervously glanced around. "What is it?"

"Where's the gun?" He scowled. "That should have been the first thing I thought of."

"It's in my bag."

"At least one of us is firing on all cylinders." Though approval gleamed in his eyes, frustration roughened his voice. Depending on her had to abrade his do-or-die tough-guy nerves. He inclined his head. "Before we get too far, you have to cover our tracks. And hide the gym rat from sight. Use the boughs that broke off the pine. Try to make it look like natural windfall."

"All right." Her instincts screamed with tension. She did not want to leave him and walk back to the clearing alone. She'd been stalked all her life, and knew the cold, smothering feeling when the enemy got close. She scanned the area, but saw nothing. Heard nothing. Had the cougar returned? She eased Aidan down beside a huge fallen log, then dug in her bag and handed him the gun. "At least we have a weapon now."

He popped the clip. "Moron. Blasting up the woods, and he's only got three bullets left." He scowled and slammed the clip back into place. "You'll have to search him for an extra clip."

"He didn't have one." She stooped to slip into her shoes, and got an unpleasant surprise. "My sandals don't fit. My feet must have swollen after I took them off. They're not used to three-inch heels."

"Your poor feet have taken a beating tonight."

She stroked his cheek. "Not compared to you."

Zoe started to leave, but he tugged her back. "Clean your face first. The scent of blood will attract predators."

Not reassuring. Was the cougar tracking her? Was that why her senses drummed with unease? Ignoring the sting, she swabbed her mouth and chin, and then her calf. She buried the wipe at Aidan's direction. Barefoot, she hurried to the clearing.

Muscles had regained consciousness. He glared at her and muttered angry, muffled sounds as she tented him with pine boughs. She didn't stop to chat.

She finished clearing away signs of the fight, and ran back to Aidan. "Done."

With her help, he struggled to his feet. "You're doing a phenomenal job, Zoe. No whining, no hysterics, clear thinking in spite of the fact that you're scared." He smiled, his teeth white in the gloom. "You're one hell of a gutsy woman."

His admiration delighted her more than a Pulitzer. And she *had* whined a little, in the trunk and in the dark cleft under the creek bank. "Um…thanks. But you haven't seen my best work, SWAT."

"Uh-oh." He grinned. "*Now,* I'm worried."

"You can depend on me."

His steadfast gaze held hers in a warm embrace. "And you on me. I won't let you down."

Her breath caught in her throat. When her Dark Champion looked at her like that…fierce, determined, strong…all man… he melted her bones. Stole her heart. Owned her, body and soul. "A-all r-right. Since that's settled, let's go."

They turned, and he froze. "Do you hear that?" he murmured.

"What?" She listened, every instinct on alert. Faint rustling, now easily audible over the abrupt silence of the night insects. Goose bumps marched up her arms. "The cougar?" she whispered.

"Four feet, but they're human. Coming toward us."

She'd almost rather face the cougar. At least the four-legged animal acted logically, and for a good reason. Panic once more reared its ugly head. "We can't run. I don't have shoes on, and you can barely walk." She studied him. "Can you shoot them?"

"In near darkness with my left hand and only three bullets?" He paused. "Maybe. But I don't like the odds."

"Never tell me the odds." She tossed the Han Solo quote at him. He flashed her a grin, and she reined in her panic. Aidan trusted her. Counted on her. They could handle two armed men. *Yeah, right.* "We're stuck between the cliff and the bad guys. What do we do?"

"Use the environment as a weapon."

"Exactly how do…?" She gasped. "Hold on! That gives me an idea. When I ran the first time, Muscles told me that the big boss is hot to see me. Apparently, he wants to deliver his message in person. The goons have a reward for me 'undamaged.' They won't shoot me. I can be bait."

He scowled. "No."

"Why not?"

His scowl deepened. *"No."*

She planted her hands on her hips. "It makes sense. There's no time for anything complicated, and you're not up to another slug-fest." And she could live another eighty years without seeing him face the business end of a bullet again.

He scrubbed his hand over his jaw. Studied her for a long, tense moment. "Dammit, Zoe. I don't like putting you at risk."

She gave him a scowl of her own, hiding her underlying anxiety. "Well, I'm not so keen on the fact that they're allowed to kill *you* on sight. Who would protect me then?" Which wasn't what worried her, but *was* the type of logic he responded to.

He glanced around, listened intently. Their pursuers were closing in. "All right. Pay attention, because we barely have time to lay this out. And we'll get one shot. *One.* If we FUBAR, we're dead."

Zoe hunkered in the bushes. Her heart hammered so loudly she could barely hear the approaching hunters. Now she knew how Bambi must have felt. The men wouldn't shoot her. But if they caught her, the plan was FUBAR, as Aidan had declared. She'd heard the SWAT team use the term before. Fouled up beyond all repair, to phrase it nicely.

And Aidan would pay the ultimate price.

She couldn't see or hear him. A wide expanse of dark, empty space separated them. Yet her instincts felt him. Could sense him also watching and listening. Could almost count his breaths. She felt as if they were two halves of one person. A sensation both spooky and comforting. She shivered. Did he feel it, too?

The men shuffled closer, and she caught a strong whiff of cheap aftershave on the night breeze.

Lights. Camera.

Action.

She stood. Blinked guilelessly at the approaching men. "Oh, no. Bad guys." She turned and ran.

As expected, they followed.

Heedless of bruising rocks and sharp splinters, she sprinted full out. Toward Aidan. Toward the cliff.

Brush and branches crashed behind her, and she sped up. Prayed she wouldn't miscalculate. Right before she hit the cliff's edge, she hooked left and dropped to the ground.

The guy on her heels kept coming. Too late, he saw the drop-off and skidded, tried to stop. Hidden behind the old-growth pine, Aidan thrust the limb in front of his shins. The man tripped, fought for balance, and then plunged over the edge. A terrified scream trailed off, followed shortly by a huge splash.

The second man either was warned by the first's scream, or had been here before. He jerked to a shaky halt several feet from the cliff's edge. Aidan leapt from behind the tree and swung the branch at his back. Even hurt and one-handed, he landed a massive blow. The second man followed his friend over the bluff. Another scream. Another splash.

Dead silence.

Zoe clambered to her feet, and limped to Aidan's side. His expression worried, he stroked her face with his good hand. "You okay?"

She nestled her cheek into his palm, loving the warm, secure feeling that washed over her at his touch. "Sure. You?"

"Yeah." His hand rested on her shoulder, and they both stared the long distance down into the restless Pacific. In the moonlight, white-capped waves lashed like silver-tipped blades. The men had both fallen over with enough momentum to clear the sharp, lethal rock formations directly below the bluff, and were swimming toward shore.

She smiled at Aidan. "Well, that takes care of Thelma and Louise."

He started to laugh. Then a startled look creased his face as the earth rumbled under her feet.

She shook her head. How could that be?

The ground tilted. She staggered, and her arms flailed trying to keep her balance.

"Get back!" Aidan shoved her, hard.

Propelled backward, she sprawled in the dirt.

The ground crumbled away in front of her, and Aidan hurtled over the cliff.

Chapter 11

2:00 a.m.

There was no outcry. No splash. No sound except horrifying thuds from below. And her own scream. "Aidan!"

Oh, God, oh, God, oh, God. He hadn't gone over the side with any momentum. He'd be crushed, shattered on the rocks.

Sobs tore from her throat as she crawled forward. Her desperate gaze scanned the water, saw nothing but whitecaps. Her fingernails clawed furrows in the dirt. "Aidan!" Her broken whisper echoed into empty space.

"Zoe, stay back!" Aidan's shout ripped apart her grief.

He was alive! Her breath staggered, and she inched the upper half of her torso over the edge. Earth crumbled beneath her and trickled down the bluff. "Aidan?"

Gripping a protruding tree root with his good hand, he hung less than four feet below the steep drop. So near, yet it might as well be miles. "The ground isn't stable near the edge! Stay back!"

She inched farther out, reached down. Stretched. She couldn't quite touch him. "Let me help you."

He looked up at her. The calm resignation in his gaze made her chest ache. "You're not strong enough to pull me up. There are no toeholds. Even if there was something to grab on to…with only one good arm, I can't let go of this root."

She stared down at the jagged rocks far below him. He couldn't hold on forever. When he tired, when his grip loosened, he'd fall to his death.

No! She wouldn't let that happen. "I'll think of something."

"No, sweetheart." The strain of trying to hold on gave his quiet voice a ragged edge of desperation. Chopped his breaths. "Get the gun from beside the pine tree. Head downstream to the shoreline. Stay in the creek. Hide near the dock. Wait for a rescue plane or the Coast Guard. Or sneak onto the ferry."

"What about you?"

"Don't worry about me. I'll work my way down. Meet you at the dock. If I'm not there by the next ferry…leave without me."

Tears gathered in her eyes. "I don't want to leave without you."

"You have to. It's the only way." His voice turned gruff. "Get going. So I can start climbing."

Zoe stared at him for several long, silent moments. She frowned, and worried her lower lip with her teeth. "Don't you dare die on me. Do you hear me, SWAT? I won't stand for it."

"I'll do my best, honey. Go on, now. I'll see you soon."

"That's a promise. Don't fall," she choked out.

Then her sweet face disappeared from Aidan's sight.

Aidan breathed a sigh of both relief and sorrow. He didn't want to die. But if his number was up, he sure as hell didn't want to take Zoe with him.

There were worse ways to go. His death would be quick, if not so clean. He studied the stars, bright pinpoints of fire in the sooty sky. The hard, white moon spotlighted the ocean with an incandescent glow. As a boy, he'd loved family campouts. Clear summer nights. Campfires and singing. Meteor showers. Mom with warm, gooey s'mores. Pop telling ghost stories. Was Pop watching him from beyond the stars? Maybe that's why he didn't feel afraid. "Air out the guest room, Pop," he muttered. "I think you're about to have company."

His hand slipped on the root, and he tightened his grip. He'd fight to stay alive, but there was no enemy to engage. He'd tried every way possible to hoist himself up. Nothing had worked. Dangling in space by one hand without any leverage, he was screwed. His fingers were already growing numb. Struggling only made it harder to hang on. He'd cling until the last second. But before too much longer, he'd be forced to let go.

Plenty of time for last prayers. Final goodbyes.

Painful regrets.

In the absolute clarity only experienced during the moment before death, he realized he'd denied himself all the good things in life. After Pop's memorial service, he'd slammed the door to his heart and boarded it up against life's storms. Over the years, cobwebs of fear and anger had collected in the darkness until they'd choked off his emotions. Coasting along, never too sad, never too happy, he'd been satisfied. Mundane was neat and tidy.

Boring was safe.

Then Typhoon Zoe whirled into his life. Her spirit had danced right through his barricades and thrown open the doors. Her zest for living flooded his self-imposed dungeon with light. Her sparkling laughter swept away the cobwebs. For the first time in years, he felt truly alive.

His heart wrenched in sorrow. And wasn't that an ironic twist of fate? Dangling from a cliff with nowhere to go but down, his emotions were finally at full throttle.

He was about to die, without ever having really lived.

What a waste.

Zoe would make it. He had to believe that. She'd survive. Marry. Have mischievous, inquisitive kids who would drive everyone crazy, but make the world a better place.

She'd go on without him.

Anguish stabbed his chest with a red-hot poker. That's what he wanted. So why did it hurt so damn much?

His fingers slipped again. Not much longer now.

Goodbye, sweetheart. Learn from my mistakes. Be happy.

"Aidan!" Zoe's voice overhead made him jerk his head up.

Disbelief. Relief. Fear. Anger. Disparate emotions swamped him. "Zoe? Why aren't you gone?"

"I wasn't born yesterday, SWAT. If I leave, you die." Headfirst, she slithered over the cliff's face on her stomach.

Icy fear clogged his veins. If she joined him, she would die, too. "Don't!"

She kept coming, and cold sweat drenched his entire body. "Dammit, go back!"

"Don't shout." She slid in the loose dirt, and his heart leapt into his throat until she regained control. "You're distracting me, Master."

"Zoe." He fought for a reasonable tone. Damn hard with terror choking off his breath. "Go back, before you fall."

"I won't fall. My ankle is tied to a tree." She stretched down and fastened a rope around his waist. "Now, so are you."

Incredulity rendered him temporarily speechless. He tried again. "Where'd you get rope?"

"Made it out of strips of your tux jacket braided with strips of Muscles's jeans. Denim is strong stuff, and luckily, you're not down that far, so it didn't have to be too long."

"You're risking your life for a stop-gap measure." He strove to keep the desperation from his voice. "You still don't have any way to pull me up. A clothing rope will support your weight, but it's not gonna hold me for long. Not when you start wrenching on it."

"Oh, ye of little faith. I have a plan."

Oh, Lord. He echoed her earlier words. "Did I mention how much I hate this plan?"

Zoe's nerves jittered, and she concentrated on cinching the knot. He didn't hate it half as much as she did. She wasn't deluded enough to think she possessed the upper-body strength to pull Aidan to safety. She couldn't even put his shoulder back in. Even if she were Xena, Warrior Princess, herself, the rope *wasn't* strong enough. However, it would hold him until she could carry out her plan. She would not stand by and watch him fall to his death. No matter what terrible things she had to do.

She finished securing Aidan, and then crawled hand-over-hand back to the top of the cliff. She sprawled in the dirt for a few seconds and regained her wind before shoving to her feet.

Muscles's watchful stare fixed on her as she approached with her hand behind her back. She'd cut off the guy's pants a while ago with Aidan's knife, and he was left in a bloody head bandage and black and white-checkered NASCAR boxer shorts. Zoe didn't blame him for looking wary. She took a deep, shaky breath. Things were about to get worse.

Much worse.

She sucked in another breath. Gathered her courage. Aidan's life was at stake. Bluffing would not get the job done. She had to be willing to follow through on her threat.

Mr. Muscles had to see his death in her eyes.

She planted her feet and stared at him. Didn't speak. Didn't blink. She held his gaze until he blinked first. Aidan had called the intimidating stare a dominance issue. Bending, she tugged out his gag. "Did you see us shove your cohorts off the cliff?"

His pale eyes widened. He nodded.

She forced her voice to sound hard and cold. "Then you know I'm not averse to killing." The other men weren't dead, but he didn't know that. He hadn't seen them swimming in the Pacific.

His Adam's apple bobbed. He gave another careful nod.

Sweat soaked Zoe's palms, and trickled in a thin line down her spine. Slowly, she pulled her hand from behind her and pressed the gun to his temple. The fact that her hand was shaking as badly as a junkie craving a fix could only heighten his terror. "How much do you want to live?"

His eyes opened wide and startled. He gulped. "Don't waste me. I was just having a little fun with you, babe."

The acrid smell of his fear curled in her nostrils. She swallowed a surge of nausea. Threatening to take the life of another human being was the hardest thing she'd ever done.

No. *Meaning* the threat was the hardest thing she'd ever done.

She swallowed again. She couldn't throw up. He'd never buy her act if she yakked on his shoes. "You don't want to die tonight?"

"No!" The whites of his eyes gleamed in the moonlight. "Don't shoot!"

"That's up to you." She narrowed her eyes, and tried to control her trembling. "The cop is trapped over the bluff. I need him to survive on this godforsaken island. I don't need you for anything." She paused to let that sink in. Let him think she was as cold-hearted as she sounded. "You get my meaning?"

"Yeah." He bobbed his head. "You say it, I do it."

"He's less than four feet down, but can't climb with a dislocated shoulder. You're tall enough to reach and strong enough to pull him up."

"You're the boss."

She untied his ankles, then moved behind him to loosen the belt binding his hands. "Don't try anything. Even with both kneecaps shot out, you can still pull him up. I won't hesitate."

"I believe you, babe."

The nausea grew overwhelming, and she retched behind his back. Good thing her stomach was empty. If she weren't telling the truth about her intentions, why would a hardened criminal believe she'd kill him? Where had all this sudden ruthlessness come from? What kind of person *was* she?

She stayed behind him and kept the pistol at his back as they walked toward the bluff. *A person who was trying to save the man she loved.* Zoe staggered and nearly dropped the gun.

Whoa! *Love?* When had that happened? Probably the moment they'd met. She'd looked up into determined brown eyes shadowed with unspoken pain and claimed him as her cop.

When had it become a reality?

Agony stopped her heart. The moment he'd disappeared over the cliff, and she thought she'd lost him forever.

Muscles had reached the cliff's edge. Her pulse jolted into triple time as he dropped to his stomach and slid toward the edge.

Zoe moved to one side, spread her legs and trained the gun on his head. "If the cop dies, you die."

"Now, don't get trigger-happy, babe. Nobody has to die."

She prayed not. She was taking a huge gamble. However, she had no choice. Aidan *would* die if she didn't get him off the cliff. She'd learned long ago that sometimes you have to risk everything in order to gain anything. "Aidan?" she called.

"Yeah?"

"The bad guy is coming to rescue you. Let him pull you up."

"What?" He sounded as shocked as if she'd informed him his mother and Letty had just robbed Oregon Pacific Bank. "If this is your plan…"

"Don't look a gift SUV in the mouth, SWAT."

"Uh…Zoe? Are you okay? This has been a stressful night, and watching me fall was traumatic—"

"I'm fine. Go with the flow, Aidan." *Stressful* was putting it mildly. She was exhausted, filthy, scared and holding Muscles at gunpoint made her sick to death inside.

Muscles scooted farther over and leaned, stretched out his hand. Zoe's stomach heaved again. Muscles strained and Aidan grunted. Zoe's fingers tightened on the gun. She prayed harder than she ever had in her life.

A thousand agonizing heartbeats later, Aidan's dark, tousled hair appeared over the rise. His face came into view, dust-streaked and sharpened by pain. His shoulders appeared, scratched and bruised. Then he was stretched full-length on solid ground.

Alive. Safe.

The breath she didn't realize she'd been holding exploded in a rush, and Zoe reeled in relief. She'd saved him!

She fought down tears and the burning lump in her throat. No time to get emotional. Stay focused until Aidan was truly safe. She shuffled sideways, putting herself between him and Muscles, who sat watching her. She wiggled the gun. She'd never realized before how incredibly heavy a weapon could be. Both physically and mentally. "Scoot back. Don't get up until I say."

"No arguments from me, babe." His cautious movements put ten feet between them.

Aidan struggled to his feet behind her, his breaths harsh. He had to be in killer pain by now, but headstrong Irish grit kept him going. And she loved him for it. Elation sang inside her. She loved everything about him.

He rested an unsteady hand on her shoulder. She suspected she was supporting more of his weight than he realized. "Dammit, Zoe! Of all the stubborn, rash…" His voice was hoarse with strain. *"You risked your life—"* He inhaled shakily. "I told you to *leave*."

Okay, maybe she didn't love his bossy side so much. "And if I had, you'd be a jigsaw puzzle right now. Did you really believe I would walk away and let you *die?*"

"You should have put your own safety first."

"Right." Anger and lingering terror made her shake. "Show up at your mother's house with pieces of you in a box? Sorry, Mrs. O'Rourke, but I was too worried about my own hide. Guess it will have to be a c-closed-casket s-service," she choked out.

He whispered a curse and pressed against her back, body to body. As close as they could get to a hug under the circumstances. He was trembling violently. His fingers squeezed her shoulder. "Thank you for saving my life," he murmured into her ear. "But you scared the ever-loving crap out of me."

"And you didn't scare *me?*" she muttered. "I'll have to add hair dye to my budget to cover all the gray." She glanced at Muscles. The wound on his head had soaked through the pad. She'd have to fix that before they left. "We don't have time for this."

"No. We don't." Aidan inhaled again, and she felt him struggling for control. "Hell, Brenda Starr, you've turned me upside down, inside out and every which way but loose."

"Ditto, SWAT." She cast a quick glance over her shoulder, and her heart stuttered. He was battered, weary and patient suffering clouded his eyes. "Will you be okay? You look terrible."

His sensual mouth slanted in a crooked grin. "And they claim appearances are deceiving."

"Can you hold the gun on Muscles while I cuff him?"

"I think I can manage." His tone was wry. "Even with my left hand, at this range, I could hardly miss."

She moved to his left and passed him the pistol.

He gestured at Muscles. "Up." In spite of his condition, or maybe because of it, he looked and sounded dangerously lethal.

Muscles slowly rose, and Zoe studied the big man. "I'm sorry about…bullying you into helping the cop." He was a criminal who had tried to kidnap her and kill Aidan. Apologizing to him probably seemed ridiculous. But he was a human being and she had threatened his life. She couldn't do anything but apologize. "I didn't have a choice."

He shrugged. "Business is business, babe." Aidan gestured with the pistol again, and they all walked toward the tree line. Muscles barked out a nervous laugh. "At first, I thought you were gonna whack me for copping a feel. A pissed-off chick packing heat is freaking scary."

"I'm not ecstatic about it, either, punk." Aidan scowled. "And unless you want to meet a lot more 'pissed-off chicks' in your questionable future, keep your hands to yourself."

Muscles spread his hands, palms out. "Chill out, 5-0. You took a taste. You gotta admit, she has a nice rack under that sexy shirt. Small, but perky."

A low, savage growl rumbled in Aidan's throat, and Zoe glanced at him in alarm. Rage vibrated off him in almost visible waves. "Shut the hell up."

Zoe's instincts prickled, and the hair rose on the back of her neck. Not at Aidan's anger. At the familiar, eerie sense of being stalked. Just like before, every nerve screamed, every muscle went taut. She peered into the gloom. Was the underbrush moving? "Aidan! I think someone is—"

The ferns parted, and the cougar prowled into the clearing.

Muscles rapidly backed up. "Holy crap! Rico didn't say anything about wild animals!"

Aidan pointed the gun at the big cat. "He smells the blood on you. Don't move."

The cougar snarled, and stalked toward Muscles, who again backpedaled.

"Freeze! Every time you move, he moves." The sinews in Aidan's arm roped as he aimed, prepared to shoot. "I'm working left-handed, and don't want to hit you by mistake."

Muscles yelled, "Freeze? Hit me by mistake? Screw this!"

Then everything happened at once. Muscles panicked and bolted for the woods. The cougar leapt. The gun roared.

The cat flinched away from the noise and scrambled aside. It regained its balance, turned and followed the fleeing man into the trees. Aidan spun, shooting twice more. The cougar veered off track, but didn't falter. "I missed, dammit!"

Horrified, Zoe strained to see through the gloom. "Will he make it?"

"I don't know. *Damn*." Aidan leaned against a wide trunk. "At least the gunshots slowed the cougar down. The gym rat got a head start. If it helps any, he has better odds now than tied to a tree."

It was the proverbial last straw. Zoe dropped to her knees and burst into tears.

"Hey!" Aidan crouched at her side, his voice deep with concern. "Sweetheart? What is it?" His hand skimmed over her. "Are you hurt?"

"I was so m-mean to him."

"What?" Incredulity rang in his question. "He's a criminal, Zoe. He kidnapped us. He molested you and tried to kill me."

"I—I know. But he's still a p-person. He *did* save your life. I p-pointed a gun at his head and told him I would shoot him, and I meant every word," she sobbed. "I hit him and tied him up and ordered him around and was such a b-bitch to him and now he'll probably die a horrible, grisly death. No matter what, he doesn't deserve that."

"Come here." He urged her up, his one-handed movements awkward. His good arm hugged her close to his warm, hard body. "You've had a rough day, and you're suffering post-traumatic stress. Everything will be all right."

Rough day? The master of understatement. "Look around, SWAT. How can you s-say everything will b-be all right?"

"I just fell over a cliff and survived, thanks to you." He tipped up her chin, and wiped away her tears with a gentle thumb. "You have to get it together, honey."

"Have to find it, first."

He chuckled and briskly rubbed her back. "Where's my glass-always-half-full girl? I need her in order for both of us to make it through this. And we have to go, sweetheart."

"Right." With difficulty, Zoe squelched her tears along with the out-of-control emotions threatening to tear her apart. *Suck it up,*

Zagretti. He's right, things have to get better. "I'm just slightly frazzled around the edges."

"No wonder." He brushed his lips over hers, a quick, soft caress that filled her with warm resolve. "C'mon. The gunshots will alert the rest of the bad guys." He tucked the pistol in his waistband and urged her toward the tree line. "And I'm out of bullets."

Ashamed, she wiped her face with her shirtsleeve. "I'm sorry. I didn't mean to fall apart and endanger us."

"You're doing damn good," he murmured. "You can fall apart after this is over, for as long as you want."

"I'll hold you to that, SWAT."

After a fast adjustment to his sling, which had held up well, considering, he rapidly covered their tracks while she snatched up their things.

They slogged into deep shadow. Shades of gray splotched the choking blackness, along with occasional slices of silver moonlight. She groped for the steady warmth of Aidan's callused palm, and his strong fingers entwined with hers. Insects chittered and small bodies scurried out of their path. She'd never realized how many predators prowled at night. Leaves rustled overhead, and she tensed. An eerie cry echoed in the damp air. An owl. She stared up uneasily at the huge, winged silhouette wheeling into the sky, and stepped on a prickly bush. "Ow!"

He stopped and glanced down. "I forgot you were barefoot."

She smiled. "You had one or two things on your mind."

"We're hidden here, and you can move faster if your feet are protected. Have a seat." He steered her to a fallen log. "Pass me the cardboard from your notebook." He folded it into crude insoles. She held them in place while he wrapped the homemade braided rope in spirals around her foot. She tied the ends at the ankle, and he extended his hand. "I need the manicure scissors. I can't believe you made rope with them."

"I used something much more efficient." She retrieved the Swiss Army knife from her bag. "I assume this is yours?"

"Yeah." Her heart ached at the tenderness in his eyes. "Nice to have it back. Pop gave it to me on my thirteenth birthday." The blade bit through the rope. Aidan bound her other foot. She fastened the rope, and he gave her his socks to pull on and hold everything together. He patted her foot. "There. Not exactly Nikes, but better than nothing."

"He had these in his pockets, too." She returned his keys and wallet, and then helped him retie his dress shoes, minus socks. "I've never bought designer labels. Silly to spend good money for someone else's name, if you ask me." At least that's what she'd convinced herself.

She stood and turned her foot from side to side, impressed with his ingenuity. The impromptu slipper-shoes were surprisingly comfortable. "What now?"

"Find a place to barricade ourselves until daybreak. Rest and gather our strength. Then reassess."

The knife snapped shut. In the midst of thrusting it into his pocket, he froze. In the distance, faint sounds echoed through the forest. His eyes narrowed. "Or not."

She frowned. "Do I hear barking?"

His mouth compressed in a grim line. "They're hunting us with dogs." He grabbed her hand. "C'mon, sweetheart. We can't hide from dogs. Kick it into high gear."

Running flat out, she clutched his hand and trusted his lead. She couldn't see a thing except menacing shadows and distorted shapes. Behind them, the barking became more strident. Had the dogs caught their scent?

Aidan dragged her down a bank, and her feet plopped in ice-cold liquid. She gasped at the shock. "It'll be harder to run in the creek."

"Also harder for them to track our scent." The barking grew louder. "Hustle!"

Though the makeshift slippers grew heavy and sodden in the calf-deep stream, she appreciated some protection between her feet and the rocky creek bottom. No time to remove them, anyway.

They stumbled and slipped in their headlong flight. The sideways current dragged against them, making every step an effort.

After slogging what seemed like miles, her calf muscles burned, and her thighs wobbled like cooked spaghetti.

Beside her, Aidan staggered. How could he keep up this pace after being wounded and falling over a cliff? He had to be running on sheer stubbornness. She dropped to her knees in the icy stream and gasped for breath. "I can't take…another step. Go on…without me."

He hauled her up. "No way. All for one and one for all."

If he could do it in his battered condition, come hell or high water, so could she. Zoe stubbornly lifted one leaden foot at a time. She could barely breathe, but set her body on auto pilot and strove to distance fear and pain. She sucked in oxygen. "The Musketeers…really fits."

He squeezed her hand. "Breathe, don't talk."

"Yeah. Tell you…later."

They pushed ahead. Farther downstream, she cocked her head. The barking sounded fainter, and off to their right. "Did we lose them?"

He slipped, splashing chilly water to his waist, and up her right side. "I doubt it."

She clung to him, keeping him upright. Would this nightmare never end? "Naturally. Wouldn't do…to let us get complacent."

They slogged around a bend. He dodged an overhanging tree limb and laughed raggedly. "There's my snarky, feisty girl."

A cramp shot through Zoe's side, doubling her over. She hugged her ribs. "Lungs don't…work," she wheezed. She again fell to her knees, and this time Aidan dropped beside her. Shivering, she planted her hands on the stony creek-bed and hung her head. "Leg muscles…don't work, either."

A moment of silence ticked past, broken only by the sounds of their pursuers closing in. "Okay." Aidan inhaled, catching his breath. His tone was deathly calm. "Hide under the tree roots over there. I'll lead them away from you."

Behind them, the barking again became louder.

Fierce determination exploded inside, and she shoved to her feet and yanked him up beside her. "In the immortal words of Mr. 'Gym Rat' Muscles, 'screw that.'"

He uttered another low, ragged laugh. "Or not."

Helped by the brief respite and energized with resolve, her second wind kicked in, and she jogged downstream beside him. Though she was soaked, frozen, sore and exhausted, it no longer mattered. "You sure know how to push my buttons, SWAT."

His velvet voice rumbled out as rich and tempting as imported chocolate. "In the immortal words of Zoe middle-name-unknown Zagretti, 'you haven't seen anything yet.'"

She shivered again as the sensual burn shimmered over her, warmed her from the inside out. Her nipples tightened against the wet cotton. How did he *do* that? How the heck could he turn her on in the middle of an ice-cold creek while running for her life? Maybe terror had unhinged her mind. "It's Francesca."

He rammed his shin into a boulder, swore and flailed, but kept his balance. Barely.

She tried not to focus on the yelping dogs chasing them. Had terror sharpened her senses, or did she hear crashing underbrush and men's voices more clearly?

The hunters were closing in, yet she and Aidan slowed, both running out of steam. Out of time. Fear coiled tightly in her chest. "I think they're gaining on us!"

He urged her to a painfully faster pace. Soon, her legs would give out altogether. "Don't look back. Keep going."

The creek widened and grew more shallow with each step, aiding their flight. They splashed around another bend, down a hill, and then staggered onto a beach.

The sand bunched and shifted under their feet and made running harder than ever. Zoe swayed against the sharp slap of ocean breeze as they staggered toward the shoreline.

They'd sprinted halfway down the beach when a pack of leashed dogs broke through the trees. Four yelling men followed.

Zoe glanced back at their pursuers. Then ahead, at the roaring Pacific Ocean. Her heart slammed against her ribs.

They were trapped.

Chapter 12

3:00 a.m.

Aidan's harsh breathing rasped over the crashing breakers. He pointed. Fifty yards ahead, a long, thin shadow thrust onto the ocean's surface. Bobbing objects floated alongside. "Head for the dock."

Gunshots roared, kicking up sand beside him. He dodged, and they both ran. Renewed terror hit Zoe with a burst of adrenaline-laced speed. Gasping breaths slashed in her throat, and her sodden rope shoes squished against sand. A sharp breeze whipped her face and wet body with icy tendrils of fear.

Barely holding their lead, they sprinted hand-in-hand down the beach. They clambered onto the uneven wooden dock. Aidan flung her forward. "Run to the far end," he panted. "Find a boat with an outboard motor and power up. No key; it starts like a lawn mower. Yank the handle."

Her footsteps pounded along worn boards. She risked a quick look over her shoulder before climbing into a rocking boat. Aidan's knife blade glinted in the moonlight as he zigzagged down the dock, cutting boats adrift. Bullets exploded, and he ducked. Wood pilings splintered beside his head.

Zoe yanked the handle in a half-dozen frantic pulls, and the motor blasted to life. "Aidan! Come on!"

He stumbled toward her. "Get in the bow! Get down!"

She scrambled to the front, and he leapt into the boat. He grunted with pain when he landed, but his blade again gleamed, sawing the rope holding them to the piling. He fumbled for the steering mechanism, and the boat plowed toward open sea.

Dogs barked, footsteps thundered and gunshots blasted behind them. Miniature geysers sprayed as bullets pockmarked the sea. While she huddled in the bow, the bad guys blazed away at Aidan. A sharp crack jerked her upright, heart in her throat. "Are you hit?"

His face gray and drawn with strain, he crouched over the motor. "No. Stay down!"

Other motors burst into roars far behind them, and he snarled in frustration. "Damn! I cut loose as many as I could."

Zoe hunkered on the bottom as choppy waves lifted the small craft and then slammed it down, again and again.

Inexplicably, the boat began to slow. She glanced back at Aidan. "What's happening?"

Grim fury set his handsome face in stone. "A round hit the hull. We're taking on water."

She looked down. Her hands were so cold, she hadn't realized she was wrist-deep in seawater. Her stomach fluttered. "Who said things can't get any worse?"

She unzipped her bag, dumped out her makeup case and frantically scooped water with the vinyl pouch. "Even if I had a gallon bucket, it's flooding faster than I can bail."

Growling motors cut through the night behind them. With every passing second, merciless headlights loomed larger.

Aidan spat a word she'd never heard from him before and steered the floundering boat around a massive rock outcropping. The pursuing lights disappeared from view. Sheltered on the other side, he idled the motor, and the hull scraped rocks. He tossed her the stern rope. "Knot the end. Lasso a boulder."

Feet spread, she rode the pitching boat. Two swings later, she caught the crest of a boulder. His grin flashed, white and wicked in his dark-stubbled face. "Damn, you're good."

The grin disappeared, and he scooped three flares, a folded tarp and fishing lures from a plastic bin under the wooden seat. "Put these in your bag." After she stashed them, he snatched the gun from his waistband, and she zipped it into her bag. He threw her the lone battered life vest. "Put it on. Jump."

Her heart crashed painfully against her ribs. Was he going to take the boat on alone? Use himself as bait? "You don't stand a chance in this leaky death trap! They'll capture and kill you!"

"I'll join you in a minute. Go!"

Balanced precariously in the heaving vessel, she hitched her survival kit over her shoulder. Her numb fingers fumbled with the vest's unfamiliar buckles. "If you're lying, I will follow you into the afterlife and make Heaven a living hell."

"A vow you're more than capable of keeping." His chuckle was labored. "I'll warn St. Peter."

A hard shove in the small of her back plunged her into the freezing water. The Pacific Ocean never got much warmer than fifty degrees at this latitude, and the icy shock made her gasp. She spat out salty water, battling desperation and despair. Aidan was one-handed, exhausted and beat-up. With no one to help him. If he took off in the boat, he was doomed.

She clung to a rock and struggled out of the sodden slipper-shoes as relentless waves slapped her against the outcropping. Anxious seconds that felt like hours crawled past. Finally, he splashed into the water beside her.

He moaned in pain and went under as the boat zoomed out to sea. Zoe's hand instinctively shot out and caught him by the hair. She yanked hard, and his head surfaced.

Barely conscious, he coughed and gagged. His face was bleached white in the moonlight.

"Aidan?" With effort, she tugged him closer and managed to wedge her arm under his. Unfortunately, it was his injured arm, and he groaned. "Sorry." She cringed. "What's wrong?"

He bit out the words through pinched, colorless lips. "Hit shoulder. Friggin' rock."

She clung to the outcropping with one hand and him with the other and fought to keep hold of him in the turbulent waves. "Hang in there. I won't let you drown."

"I'm. Endangering. You." He coughed again. "Let go."

"Not in this lifetime, SWAT. You protected me, now I'll protect you."

"*No.* You have…a life vest…a good…chance." He ground his teeth. "I'm strong. I'll manage. Save yourself."

She glanced apprehensively at the dark, cresting waves. They could be miles from shore. No way could he make it. If they were gonna die, they would die together. However, she would do everything in her power to ensure their survival. "Don't even go there. Because it is so not happening." She pressed a kiss to his wet, salty brow. "All for one and one for all, savvy?"

"Damn. Stubborn. Woman."

"Ah, now you're catching on." She wrestled off the flotation device and put it on him. Looping the handle of her survival bag over his head, she tucked it against his chest. He had a length of coiled nylon rope from the boat draped over his good shoulder. She tied one end to the vest and the other to her waist, going under twice and swallowing a gallon of seawater in the process.

Aidan seemed too stunned to do anything but mutter incoherent protests through chattering teeth. Her stomach lurched. The lethal combination of pain and frigid water would send him into shock. If they didn't drown, shock would kill him. How would she warm him up? She shoved aside growing fear. One problem at a time. First, she had to get them both to shore.

"Aidan," she spoke softly into his ear. "I'm going to turn you over. The life vest will support your head. I need you to float on your back and kick your feet, okay?"

"Don't. Risk. Your life. For me. Again."

"I'm heartily tired of that song." She sighed. "I much prefer 'You Really Got A Hold On Me.'"

He growled faintly, which she counted as progress. Frustration would help keep him warm inside. And the kicking would not only aid her, but warm him on the outside.

Zoe had always been at home in the water. Everywhere they'd

lived, she'd sought out community pools, lakes or rivers. Swimming had fit her youthful needs to a *T*. It was solitary, didn't cost anything and satisfied her craving for freedom. She and her mom had spent over a year in Florida when Zoe was a freshman in high school. She'd hit the beach every day after classes, and after her job at a fast-food franchise during the long, hot summer. She could do this.

She took a deep breath and pushed off the rocks. Towing Aidan, she swam parallel to the outcropping.

He helped by kicking, but his movements soon grew sporadic. Her pulse thrummed in her ears. The cold water was taking its toll. She had to keep him awake and aware. If he lost consciousness, he could die before she got him to shore.

"How'd you make the boat go off by itself?"

A long pause dragged by. She arched one arm over another in a steady crawl. Her nerves wound tighter with each stroke. "Aidan?" She tipped her mouth out of the water and shouted to make sure he'd heard her. "How'd you rig the boat?"

"Jammed the throttle. Tied down steering mechanism."

"Great idea. Won't it sink, though?"

"No. Even leaking…she'll streak without passengers. When bad guys finally catch up…find her empty. Won't know…where to start looking."

Her cop was incredibly resourceful, even under extreme duress. "Brilliant."

She was a strong swimmer, but before long, weariness and numbing cold weighted her arms and legs. She didn't have the energy to speak, and they both fell silent. She could only swim. Only pray.

On and on. Until she could barely lift one arm over the other. Her strength, energy and optimism faltered. Were they doomed to die together, after all?

Just as she feared she would sink under the relentless waves and not have the strength to surface, Aidan coughed. "Zoe. Don't. Surrender," he croaked. "No matter…how long and dark the night. The sun…always triumphs…in the morning."

Not only her own life, but Aidan's was at stake. No way could she give up. The encouragement spurred her onward. Finally, just ahead, a jagged outline loomed high above her. Cliffs! *Please, let there be a beach, and not merely piles of rocks.*

One last burst of energy carried her forward, and her toes brushed sand. Fatigue overwhelmed relief.

Dragging Aidan behind her, she crawled onto the beach. Gasping, shivering, she lay facedown and collected her reserves.

Long before she was ready, she pushed up on all fours. Her trembling muscles felt like jelly. Aidan's legs were still in the raging surf. She grabbed the life vest. Inch by agonizing inch, she dragged him onto dry sand. Gusty wind plastered her wet shirt to her goose-bumpy skin. Shaking uncontrollably from cold and exhaustion, she bent over his head, tried to shelter him. His closed eyes and slack face made her heart lurch. She brought her ear close to his face. He was breathing, thank goodness. "Aidan?" She patted his icy cheek.

He didn't answer.

She had to get him warm. How? She had Muscles's lighter, but finding wood and building a fire would take too long. Anyway, a campfire wouldn't do much good when they were soaking wet and exposed to the brisk ocean breeze. Plus, an open fire would draw the bad guys like a beacon.

The cold, grueling swim conspired with extreme thirst and hunger to make her slow and weak. She lifted her bag from around Aidan's neck and removed the life vest. Her bag's contents were damp but not waterlogged, thanks to the vinyl lining and nylon zipper. He'd passed her flares, fish hooks and a folded tarp before pushing her out of the boat. The thick, tightly-woven canvas tarp was waterproof. She spread the heavy material over him. "Aidan, can you hear me?"

No response.

The only heat available was body heat. Teeth chattering, she struggled out of her sodden shirt. She didn't have the energy to wrestle him out of his pants. She crawled under the tarp and loosened his sling, arranged his injured arm beside him. She carefully lay on top of him, then twitched up the tarp to cover them like a tent. Sliding her arms around Aidan's neck, she nestled her face into his throat and tried to ignore the darkness. Tried to stop trembling. Tried not to dwell on how close she'd come to losing him. Twice.

Think warm thoughts.

Her breasts rested against solid muscle, hard and reassuring beneath her. His chest rose and fell with each even breath, and crisp hair gently abraded her nipples. His heartbeat thudded steadily against hers. His cool, firm skin smelled like an intriguing combination of tangy seawater and his own unique scent. Snuggling close to him comforted her. Restored her.

Sheltered from the wind and pressed body to body, the bone-chilling cold slowly receded.

She didn't know how much time passed before Aidan stirred beneath her and mumbled incoherently.

"Aidan," she said softly. "Wake up."

He shifted again. Muttered. "What—?"

She smoothed thick, damp hair off his forehead. "Aidan, it's Zoe. Talk to me."

His sharply indrawn breath lifted his chest, and her with it. Skin intimately brushed skin. "Zoe?" His voice grew stronger by the second. "What the hell?"

Sparkling relief bubbled through her veins, as sweet and intoxicating as the champagne she'd savored at the wedding. She raised her head, but couldn't see his face. "Welcome back, SWAT."

His fingers curled around the nape of her neck, then stroked down her spine. Her body quivered in response, and his hand hesitated north of the damp scrap of satin. "Zoe?" He sounded pole-axed. Poor guy probably felt like he had been. "You're naked."

Weary joy swirled giddily. She couldn't hold back a giggle. Leave it to her cop to cut to the chase. "Well, there's nothing wrong with your observational skills."

His heartbeat kicked into double-time, and she cupped his face and twitched up the corner of the tent in an attempt to assess his condition. "How do you feel?"

"Like I have a naked woman on top of me," he growled.

That explained the bump in heart rate. Oh well, a fast pulse would increase his body heat. She dropped the canvas back into place. "I'm warming you up."

"Yeah?" His deep voice vibrated in her ear. "It's working."

It was impossible to be this intimate with him and remain unaffected. Tingles glittered down her spine. She shivered under the delicious onslaught, and her nipples tightened. He made a primitive, male sound low in his throat, and heat washed over her. Clearly, he wasn't unaffected, either. "Ah…don't get any ideas."

He laughed raggedly. "Too late."

"You seem to be feeling a lot better." Judging by his response, he wasn't debilitated.

"You don't feel so bad yourself."

She adjusted her position to accommodate the big, hard bulge pressing into her stomach. Holy smokes. His wet slacks left nothing to the imagination. Supposedly, when men were cold, body parts shrunk. Apparently, her cop was growing warmer by the second. "I saw a hot-water heater in an ad that promised 'quick recovery.' A major appliance has nothing on you."

He chuckled again. "You're effective medicine, sweetheart."

As far as cures went, he was darn effective himself. A spark of vitality flickered inside her, restoring some of her strength. Her hope. "Am I too heavy? How's your shoulder?"

"You're fine. Shoulder's not as bad. The cold water reduced the swelling and pain." His fingertips lovingly traced the small of her back as if he were learning the landscape and liked what he found. "How did we end up on dry land? The last thing I remember is diving out of the boat."

"You hit your shoulder again and were disoriented. I swam us to shore."

His body went taut. A short, sharp silence ensued. "In other words, you took another huge risk with your own life. You should have let me make it to shore myself."

"You would have died." Frustration thrummed inside her. Instead of James, his middle name should be *Bullheaded.* "Would you leave *me* to save yourself?"

"That's not the same scenario."

In a different century, her Dark Champion would have been a noble warrior, wielding a sword in protection of his lady. "Why? Because you have a…ah…big flashlight, and I don't?"

Though she couldn't see it, she felt his scowl all the way to her toes. "Because I'm trained in survival."

"Training doesn't help when you're incapacitated and shocky. We're a team, savvy?"

"One member of this team," he gritted, "does not comprehend rank and discipline."

Losing her temper wouldn't benefit anyone. "Discipline, huh? I had no idea you were into kinky."

He muttered something about spanking under his breath that she doubted had anything to do with discipline. The imp inside her longed to hear it. He sighed. "I'm going to buy you a T-shirt that says, Doesn't Play Well with Others."

"I play just fine…when the game makes sense." She sobered. "If anyone understands this, it should be you, SWAT. I will only learn my capabilities by facing and overcoming challenges. Don't try to take that away from me."

Clearly startled, he didn't speak for several long minutes. "I don't want to deny you anything, sweetheart." He sounded shaken. "I'm trying to keep you safe."

"I know." She softened her voice. "But life happens, Aidan. You can't protect me from it. And I don't want you to." She gave him a gentle hug. "In the end, nobody gets out alive. I'd rather experience every moment to the fullest, make the most of every opportunity for a brief time, than grow stagnant."

He went absolutely still. In the shocked silence, she couldn't even hear him breathing. Finally, he inhaled sharply. "Dammit," he whispered. He was trembling. "You don't have to throw me over a cliff twice. Okay, I get it."

She frowned. Her sixth sense told her he wasn't ready to explain why her statement had rattled him so badly. Sometimes, it was better to quit while you were ahead. "I'll scout around, see if I can find shelter." Before he could protest, she slipped out from under the tarp and struggled back into her wet shirt.

Aidan lay in darkness and mustered his strength. He had to help Zoe, yet couldn't make his body obey the order. His thoughts raced in his head like the lead car at the Daytona 500. He'd nearly made the same mistake again. He'd not only locked up his own emotions, he'd tried to arrest and incarcerate Zoe's joie de vivre.

Not intentionally. Her zest for life was one of the things he appreciated most about her. Along with her bravery, creativity, smarts and sound moral compass. But his overprotective instincts wanted to lock her in a gilded cage. Which was no way to live.

No matter how good the intentions, a cell was still a cell.

He blew out a frustrated breath and scrubbed his hand over his face. He had to learn to let go. To live in the moment. Zoe could teach him a thing or two about that.

He swept the tarp off his face, eased to a sitting position and woozily glanced around. He caught a flash of white near the cliff's base. Zoe had survived a horrendous childhood to become a light in the darkness. Not like the harsh glare that would be cast by the flares he'd liberated from the boat. She shone with a soft glow that illuminated every shadowed corner in his soul. A pure brightness that unflinchingly revealed the truth. Forced him to face facts.

She baffled him, dazzled him and frustrated the hell out of him. And he reveled in the challenge. She'd saved his life…twice. At considerable risk to her own. The realization made him tremble. If anything happened to her, it would rip out his heart.

Because he loved her.

He reeled from the nuclear blast, but didn't duck the fallout. Merely accepted it. He'd spent the past six months denying the reality slowly being hammered into his thick skull. But he couldn't deny the truth when it slapped him in the face.

Holy crap! He *loved* her. With a consuming, heart-shaking fierceness he'd vowed never to feel. Fear and exultation tangled inside him. He'd never wanted to leave a woman behind. Zoe refused to be left behind. He'd never wanted grief to devastate his soul mate. Zoe would grieve as deeply as she loved, but she hadn't let pain stop her from living before and wouldn't in the future. He'd never wanted a woman to be dependent on him. An unsteady chuckle slipped out. He'd received his wish. His intrepid reporter was about as independent as they came. Zoe didn't *need* him. But if she *chose* to share her life with him, she'd be loyal forever.

They had incredibly hot sexual chemistry. Meshed emotionally and intellectually. She carried the same aching loneliness within her that shadowed his own soul. In some ways, she was as strong as he. In other ways, stronger. Together, two halves made a whole. Could they have a future?

The possibility staggered him. Thrilled him. Terrified him. So much was at stake. He'd have to risk everything.

He clenched his fists and made a silent vow. He would get them both out of here alive. Neither would die just when he'd discovered how much they had to live for.

"Zoe," he called. "I need your help." There, that wasn't so tough to admit, was it?

"Coming!" She hurried to his side, a pale angel of mercy in the murky gloom. Shivering, she knelt in front of him. "What do you need?"

You. He rubbed her shoulders. Her skin was chilled under the damp tuxedo shirt. "You're freezing in this wind. You shouldn't have put that wet shirt back on."

She fussed with the tarp, wrapped it around him. "I can't run around in nothing but panties."

"No objections from the rear guard." He understood her preference to be cold over the vulnerability of being naked. While he was comfortable with his body, he wasn't yet comfortable with his naked, vulnerable emotions. "Rig the sling again so I can help you search."

"You should stay put and rest." He shot her an exasperated look, and she sighed. "Okay, fine." She scooped up the waterlogged cummerbund and bow tie. "Tough guys," she muttered. "Can't live with them, can't strangle them in their sleep."

He chuckled. "Don't blame you there. I've been a pain in the ass since the day we met." He sobered, cradled her chin in his hand. "I haven't been fair to you."

She tilted her head. "What makes you say that?"

"I made assumptions based on your occupation. About your M.O., morals and motives. I was wrong. Dead wrong. I'm sorry, sweetheart."

She froze in the act of fastening the sling. Blinked. "Uh…wow," she whispered. "Apology accepted." Her full, sexy lips trembled, and she pressed them together. "Um…does this mean you're unpacking the baggage?"

"Honey, the baggage fell over the cliff when I did. It's shattered into a million pieces."

Tears sparkled in her eyes, and she shuddered. "Like you almost were."

"A super-size wake-up call." He stroked a fingertip down her nose. "We need to find shelter." He struggled to his feet, and the world swam in a dizzying arc.

Her arm slid around his waist. "I found an opening that might be a cave." She hesitated. "I couldn't…didn't go inside."

"Lead on."

With Zoe shivering beside him, he trudged up the beach. Weak and woozy, he took twice as long as he should have, and aggravation tightened his jaw. He hated being a liability to her.

He glanced around the small crescent of pale sand carved out of towering cliffs. The ocean roared at their backs, trapping them in the cove. At daybreak, they'd be completely exposed. Easy pickings for the bad guys.

They reached the rock wall, and she stopped. "Here."

"Maybe." He studied the narrow fissure. "I'll check it out. Pass me a flare." He strode forward, but a wave of dizziness assaulted him. He staggered, missed the cleft and rammed into the wall. Pain drove him to his knees, gasping in the sand.

She wrapped the tarp around him. "I'll d-do it." Her shaky tone belied her brave words.

He ground his teeth and struggled to rise. Dammit, she was terrified to go in there. He was failing her.

She patted his good shoulder. "Aidan, just sit and rest. You'll hurt yourself again, and then where will we be? I can't carry you."

She hesitated at the cleft, counting softly. Blew out a quivering breath. "H-how d-do I light the flare?"

"You can't, not until you get far enough inside so the light won't reflect out." He reached out to her. "Help me up. I can't make it alone and neither can you. We'll conquer it together."

"You finally admitted it." She smiled broadly. "We make a great team."

Following his instructions, she erased their tracks from the beach, and then returned to where he leaned against the cold rocks.

Her wide, fearful gaze met his. "How long before we can have light?"

"I don't have any way to gauge, honey. I'll be with you every step of the way."

"All right." She gulped, nodded. "Will you hold my hand?"

"You bet." He didn't figure he'd get her inside without doing so. He'd probably have to pull her most of the way. "Ready?"

She nodded again, and he squeezed inside. Following the dark, twisting, claustrophobic passage, he turned down several blind alleys and almost got stuck twice. He was far enough inside to fire up the flare, but didn't have room. He'd set his hair on fire.

When he slowed to wind around a low ledge, Zoe stopped, frozen. He tugged on her hand. "C'mon, sweetheart. Keep moving."

"O-okay." Her rapid, panicked breaths sounded far too close to hyperventilating. And in spite of the fact that they were out of the wind, her shaking had increased.

Entombed in cold, hard granite, he slithered forward as quickly as possible. "We're getting close. Smell that?"

She sniffed, lurched to a halt. "Is that odd smell bats? Wait. I hear rustling!" Her voice rose three octaves, and she broke contact. "There's a horde of bats in here!"

"Zoe…no! Don't let go!" If he lost her in the dark maze, he might never find her again. He grabbed for her hand, but missed.

"I can't!" She skittered backward, away from him. "I have to get out!"

Chapter 13

4:00 a.m.

"Zoe, stop!" Aidan turned to follow, but bumped his shoulder. He groaned and clutched the wall. *"No. Bats!"*

"No bats?" Her terrified question floated back. "Spiders? Snakes? Creepy-crawlies of any variety?"

"No." At least he hoped not. "The Cascade Range is made up of volcanoes. That sulfur smell means there are hot springs ahead. Which indicates a cave. Soon, we can light a flare."

"What's that rustling noise? C-can't we light a flare now?"

"It's the simmering water. There's not enough room for a flare yet." He kept his tone low and soothing. "Come back to me, Zoe. You don't want to get lost in here all alone."

Her gulp was audible. "I'm…paralyzed."

"Come on, sweetheart. Walk toward my voice." Her footsteps shuffled on the sandy floor, and he kept talking. "Keep moving, Zoe. My hand is right here. Reach out and take it."

When her ice-cold fingers finally grasped his, he sighed in re-lief. "I've got you."

She shook so hard her teeth chattered. "I—I panicked."

"It's okay. Everything will be okay. Hold on to me and don't let go again." He squeezed her hand. "It might help if you close your eyes, so you can't 'see' the dark."

"M-maybe. All right. I c-can d-do this." A long pause made him hold his breath before she finally declared, "I *can*."

"Yes, you can." Her breathing had reached critical mass. He needed to calm her down before she passed out and they were lit-erally stuck between a rock and a hard place. "Just a little farther. Remember, you wanted to tell me something about the Muske-teers? When we were in the creek."

"M-Musketeers?" She paused. "Oh, yes. You said one for all, and all for one. Which made me think. You're like Athos…wise and sad, and a strong, excellent leader." The distraction worked, and her inhalations slowed. "Con has the bravado of D'Artagnan. Liam has Porthos's humor." Another breath. "Grady is like Aramis…an interesting combo of smarts and swashbuckler."

"You have the O'Rourke brothers pegged." His chuckle re-bounded eerily in the winding passage. "Does that make you Mi-lady D'Winter?"

Zoe snorted. "She was…nuts."

He pressed onward, following the ever-stronger sulfur smell. "You're making my case for me, Brenda Starr."

"Thanks bunches. I never slug wounded men," she panted from behind him. "Consider yourself owed."

"I look forward to payment in full." He squeezed around the final bend and into an airy, echoing cavern. "We made it. Hang tight for three more seconds before you open your eyes."

He scratched a flare into life and grinned at the sight in front of him. "Open sesame."

Zoe gasped, her astonished gaze traveling around the golden, glittering chamber. "It's beautiful! Gold?"

"Pyrite. Fool's gold." He swallowed hard. Her wet shirt had turned sheer, her dusky nipples clearly visible in the shimmering light. She was far more beautiful than the cave.

He led her behind a short rock wall. "Right on target."

Shivering, she plopped her survival bag on the sand beside the steaming pool. "Now that we're closer, it smells kind of like hard-boiled eggs. I'm so cold, I can't wait to jump in."

He knelt, jammed the flare into the sandy floor and dipped a cautious fingertip into the bubbles. Natural hot springs could exceed boiling temperature. "Perfect. Climb in."

"I'll help you start a fire first."

Driftwood liberally scattered the sand—evidence that seawater had once flooded the cave. The wood was bone-dry, so he dismissed that concern. He had enough worries. They both needed food, and more importantly, water. How would he get them out of here? He bent to grasp a log, swayed and nearly fell. He clenched his jaw. How was he supposed to protect Zoe when he was staggering around like a frat boy on pledge night?

She took the log from him. "Let me."

"Here." He handed her his knife. "Slice small slivers of wood." Using Muscles's lighter, torn pages from her spiral notebook and kindling, they soon built a crackling fire.

He propped his back against the wall, closed his eyes and let the heat radiate into his aching muscles.

"Aidan?" Zoe's soft palm nestled above his heart. "Shall I help you undress?"

He looked down at her hand, small and fragile against his tanned chest. Looked up at her weary, trusting eyes, shimmering golden-green in the firelight. Looked at the scrapes and bruises marring her creamy skin. Every protective instinct inside him surged to the surface. "I'll manage. Hop in."

She stuck out her lower lip in an exaggerated pout. "Aw, I've been wanting to get you out of your pants since the night we met. SWAT...some women adore trouble."

He chuckled. "How can I say no?"

Her impish grin flashed. "You can't." She knelt, untied his shoes and removed them, and then stood. Her smiling gaze held his as her nimble fingers unfastened and unzipped his fly. It wasn't so tough to give her what she wanted, after all.

She drew his pants toward his hips. Tugged. "I can't seem

to…they're caught on…" She glanced down and a blush stained her cheeks. "Oh. My. Gosh. No wonder."

He'd been sporting a raging erection since he'd awakened with her naked breasts pressed to his chest. "I'll do it."

Her blush flared hotter. She snatched away her hands. "I don't want to uh…damage anything important." She choked and spun, putting her back to him.

"Zoe," he said, his voice soft and low. "Don't be embarrassed because you turn me on. I'm not."

"I know you're attracted to me." Her uncertain murmur was barely audible. "I'm just not sure you want to be."

"I wasn't sure at first, either." He reached out and wrapped a silky curl around his forefinger. "I am now."

"You—" Her shoulders hitched. "You're all right with it? You actually like me?"

Her tremulous question punched him in the gut. She'd had so little in her bleak life. He wanted nothing more than to reassure her. He knew she desired him. Enjoyed being with him. He didn't know if her feelings were as intense as his. A grubby cave in the middle of a life-or-death chase was hardly the place to blurt out a declaration of love. She'd never had anyone or anything. He would not cheat her out of a courtship. He wanted to shower her with flowers. Candy. Jewelry. Laugh with her over favorite movies. Cook her hearty meals. Stroll with her hand-in-hand and talk about her hopes and dreams.

He wanted to *show* her how much he cared.

He stepped closer, and put his hand on her shoulder. "Oh, yeah. I like you, sweetheart." He rested his head against hers. "I like you a lot."

"I…" Her voice caught. She was trembling. "L-like you a lot, too."

"Good to hear." He rubbed his thumb along the side of her smooth neck, and she trembled harder. He kissed her hair. "Let's get into that nice warm water."

"You first."

She kept her back to him while he laboriously stripped off his damp slacks and jockeys and stepped into the pool. He sat on a protruding ledge and sank chest-high into steaming water. A contented sigh slipped out as heat soaked his injured shoulder.

She picked up his pants. "Don't want these to dry stiff."

He flicked her a wry glance. "Stiff is damned inconvenient."

"Not always." At his chuckle, she blushed again, but grinned as she rinsed salt water out of his clothes and draped them over a log beside the fire. "Your turn to shut your eyes."

He tipped his head back and let his eyelids drift closed. He heard her wet shirt slither down. Seductive whispers of satin as she stepped out of her panties. Rippling water caressing her skin. She'd be leaning over the pool, rinsing her clothes.

Naked.

Erotic mental images blasted his system, and his entire body clenched. He gritted his teeth against the urge to raise his lashes just enough to watch her. She'd never know. He balled his good hand into a fist. No. He would not invade her privacy and violate her trust. But temptation danced an enticing tango against his closed eyelids.

More splashes. Her forearm teased his, and then her silken calf brushed his thigh beneath the warm water. His muscles tightened painfully, and he hissed under his breath.

"Sorry." She sounded breathless. "Did I jar you?"

Clear to my toes. "No." He opened his eyes to see her anxious, elfin face close to his. There was no way to sit in the small pool without touching. Thank the Lord the bubbles reached her collarbone. A man could only resist so much temptation.

She passed him the water bottle. He sipped and handed it back. She frowned. "Drink it all. You need to stay hydrated."

"So do you."

"I've had mine. Go ahead."

He examined the nearly full bottle. "Really."

She jutted her chin in the endearingly stubborn gesture he'd come to know and love. "I'm not thirsty."

He held out the bottle and drilled her with an implacable stare. "We both drink or nobody drinks."

She sighed. "Yes, Master."

"Much better." He grinned as she took a swig. "I like my women naked and obedient."

She choked, coughed and sputtered water. "Funny, that's how I prefer my men."

He chuckled. "I'm yours to command, sweetheart."

She again passed the bottle. "Don't make promises you're not up to keeping."

Cool, refreshing water slid down his dry throat. "I'm more than up for it," he muttered under his breath.

Her eyes widened. "Hungry? For food," she hastily added. "I have Cracker Jack. Thanks to the foil pouch, they're not even soggy." She tore open a red-and-white box.

He set aside the water bottle and tried to figure out how to eat one-handed. Since they had to share, dumping the snack into his mouth from the pouch seemed a little crass.

"Allow me, Master." She giggled, and fed him the crunchy, candy-coated popcorn and peanuts.

In the quiet, isolated cavern, the outside world ceased to exist. He quickly grew accustomed to the mineral smell, and the heated water lapped sensually against his weary muscles. As they lay cocooned in warm steam, talking quietly and sharing the makeshift meal, the threats and stress of the past hours faded.

She opened a tiny envelope. "Wonder what we got for the prize?" A miniature plastic monkey tumbled onto her palm, and she smiled. "How cute! I have a fondness for monkeys."

He arched a brow. "Too many Tarzan movies?"

"No." She chuckled. "When I was young, I was enamored with Curious George."

"Easy to understand. You and George are kindred spirits." He grinned at her. "Babar the Elephant books were my favorites."

"The elephant who grew up to be king of the jungle." Her answering grin brimmed with mischief. "I get your fascination with him, too."

"I liked him because he always found a silver lining in every cloud." A lot like Zoe. "I got a stuffed elephant for my sixth birthday that I named Babar."

Her finger gently traced the monkey's plastic grin. "When I was six, I wanted a Curious George doll so badly. Mom couldn't afford the official version, but she found one of those so-ugly-they're-cute sock monkeys at a rummage sale. George slept with me every night to keep away the loneliness." She glanced at him from under her lashes. "That probably seems silly to you."

"Not at all. I kept Babar until I started fifth grade. I made a big show of tossing him in the trash, but I suspect Mom has him stashed in the attic with our baby clothes and other sentimental stuff. Do you still have George?"

"No." Her voice grew quiet as she set the plastic trinket on a rock beside them. Too quiet. "We had to run on a moment's notice. He…got left behind."

He covered her hand with his. "I didn't mean to stir up another bad memory."

"It's stupid to get upset about such a minor thing after all these years." Her nonchalant shrug belied the haunted longing in her words, the sorrow pooling in her eyes. "It was just a toy."

Were all her childhood memories painful? He sternly cleared the thickness from his throat. Cops did not cry. "You're not a help-less little girl, Zoe. You don't have to be afraid." He wrapped his arm around her waist, hugged her. "And you're not alone anymore."

"You're quite a guy, SWAT." She swiped at her cheeks. "Thank you for not judging or condemning me because of my past."

He massaged the back of her neck. "The past is over. Dead and buried. I know that all too well."

"Now is all we ever really have." She gave him a wobbly smile. "I'm a pro at living in the moment."

She would be. For too many years, that's all she'd known. Her past was a menacing shadow. Her future uncertain. He studied her guileless, heart-shaped face, inches from his. Did she ever dare plan the future? Did any of those thoughts include him?

Their gazes met and held. The firelight reflected dancing golden lights in her beautiful, expressive eyes. Her feminine scent min-gled with the rich smell of caramel, tantalizing his senses. Water droplets sparkled on her delicate throat and slim shoulders. He ached to lean forward and sweep his tongue over her damp, creamy skin. To kiss every lovely inch. To devour her.

As if she'd read his mind, her pupils dilated, and the pulse at her throat throbbed faster. "Last bite." She sounded breathless again. She fed him, and his tongue swirled the sugary crumbs from her skin. She gasped as he drew her finger into his mouth and laved the tip.

Cradling her hand in his, he lavished attention on each finger in turn. "You taste sweeter than the candy."

She trembled in his grasp. "Oh, my. What talented lips you have, Mr. Wolf."

He savored her palm. Lingered over the rapid pulse at her wrist. Nibbled the baby-fine skin of her inner arm to the bend of her elbow. "All the better to eat you up," he growled.

"Are you going to devour me?" she whispered.

He slowly kissed up her inner arm to her shoulder, and then nibbled her neck. "Do you want me to?"

She moaned. "Very much."

He nuzzled her throat. Slammed with the primitive desire to make her his, he suckled her damp skin, drinking in her essence. He gently kneaded her breast, and her nipple puckered in his palm. He teased it between his thumb and forefinger, and she moaned again and rubbed her other breast against his arm.

His head spinning, Aidan slid his hand through the bubbles fizzing over her belly. He hesitated before cupping her downy curls. He'd better be less clumsy at hitting the target here than he was at firing a weapon left-handed. His fingertip glided over her small, delicate nub, and she gasped, jerked back.

He froze, concern churning in his gut. "Did I hurt you?"

"No," she breathed. "I—I didn't expect it to feel so…intense."

Her awed denial drenched him in ice water. What the hell was he doing? His libido was running amok with no interference from his common sense. He withdrew his hand and softly kissed her mouth. "We have to stop."

Her eyes darkened in distress. "Did I do something wrong?"

"Not at all." *But I did.* He could kick his own ass. He had no business pushing her so far, so fast.

She worried her lower lip with even, white teeth. "You're not enjoying yourself?"

"Too much." He laughed raggedly. "We're moving way too fast."

"It's just kissing. Just touching."

His little innocent had no clue how soon he would have lifted her on top of him and thrust into her. "We're naked. Isolated. There's nothing to stop us from going too far." He scrubbed his hand over his face and battled back overwhelming desire. *Get a grip, man.* "And we have no protection."

She frowned. "Who says we'd go too far?"

Cold fear iced his veins at how close he'd come to aggressively shattering her innocence. "You're so tempting. You feel so good in my arms." He touched the small mark of possession branding her throat. He wasn't normally a barbarian in the bedroom. He'd never even left a whisker burn on a lover. "I might get carried away without meaning to."

Her arms slid around his neck and she pressed close, rocketing his pulse into triple-time. "This might be our only chance to be together. Let's live in the moment."

"Sweetheart." He brushed tousled curls off her forehead. "I can't risk it. I can't risk *you*."

"Everything always gets snatched away." Her voice quavered, and his chest tightened. She sucked in a ragged breath. "This is consensual. Why is it a problem?"

"I will not make love to you for the first time under extreme circumstances." He inhaled slowly. Exhaled. It was tough to reason with no blood circulating in his brain. "Plus, I'm not entirely in control and I don't want to hurt you. And I won't do something you might regret when you're thinking more clearly."

"You would never hurt me. I trust you."

Her faith floored and humbled him. Too bad he didn't trust himself. "I can't take a chance with you, sweetheart."

Her lips trembled, and she pressed them together. "All right. I didn't mean to force myself on you." She turned her face away. Her body quivered, and she swallowed hard.

His heart shattered. "Please don't cry."

"I'm not crying." Clearly, she was. "I'm fine." Obviously, she wasn't.

He struggled to alleviate her distress. Talk about a situation going FUBAR—and fast. "Zoe, it's not you."

"It's okay, Aidan. Really." Keeping her back to him, she clambered out of the pool. "I know I'm not in your league."

Still facing away, she stood between him and the fire and wrapped her arms defensively around her middle. Gleaming with moisture, her petite body trembled in the firelight. Water droplets trailed from her slender shoulders down her spine and nestled in the small of her back. He groaned under his breath. He'd always loved the small of a woman's back, where it curved into her buttocks. So delicate. So vulnerable. You didn't turn your back on someone unless you trusted them fully.

He surged to his feet, strode to her and pressed full length against her. "Can you feel how much I want you?"

"Y-yes."

"Believe it. I've never wanted anyone more." But he wouldn't betray her trust. He had to protect her, at all costs. Even from himself. He dropped a kiss on her shoulder, and she quivered. "No, you're not my usual type. You're special. Unique. I've never met anyone like you. After this is all over, I want to keep seeing you. You are too important to me to screw this up by doing something rash and irresponsible. Do you understand?"

She sniffled, laughed shakily. "Sort of." She hesitated. "We're so different. I'm not sure I'll ever totally understand you. I'm all about seizing the moment before it disappears forever, while you're big on planning ahead. But I respect your decision."

Yeah, they were different. It didn't mean they couldn't connect, did it? Holy crap. He might have already screwed things up. He was damned if he did, and damned if he didn't. "Living in the moment is great. Living dangerously is foolish."

She turned in his arms. Warm, wet skin pressed to warm, wet skin. Her nipples grazed his pecs, her soft belly cradled his arousal. He gritted his teeth. He'd damn well better qualify for sainthood after this. Her long, dark lashes were dewed, her beautiful eyes heartbreakingly sad. "Nobody has ever wanted me before. It was wonderful while it lasted."

Oh, *hell*. He lowered himself to the canvas tarp, tugging her down to sit on his lap, facing him. It brought them into extremely intimate contact. He cupped her bottom, and her satiny stomach rubbed against his sensitized flesh, making him groan with pleasure. "I want you every minute we're together. So much, I'm crazy with it." He captured her mouth and kissed her, his tongue thrusting in rhythm with his hips.

She purred deep in her throat and leaned into the kiss. With his good arm around her, he couldn't balance and she toppled them onto the tarp. Gasping, she lifted her mouth from his. "Did I bump your arm?"

There wasn't enough pain in the universe to squelch his desire for her. "No." He claimed her mouth again.

Her fingers threaded into his hair, and she cradled his face as if he were her most cherished possession. Their breaths mingled. Her hot, silky tongue mated with his. "Aidan. My cop. I want you so much," she murmured against his lips. "I need you more than I've ever needed anything."

She sparkled with life. Filled him with hope. She smelled like caramel and warm, willing woman.

She tasted like his radiant, shimmering future.

And he lost his mind.

He ached to give her what she wanted, needed. But he would not hurt her. Refused to gamble with her future. He slid his knee high between hers and flexed his thigh against her soft, moist center. She moaned into his mouth and arched into him.

He'd never had a woman respond with such fervor. Zoe was a lit firecracker, all bright sizzle and hot sparks, and he reveled in her glow. Her questing hands and eager mouth explored, tasted. She stroked and tickled and licked and kissed. Her rapid, heated breaths rasped erotically in his ear.

Exhilarated by the electric storm, he increased the pace. Slick, damp skin glided sensually over slick, damp skin. "You feel so good, sweetheart."

"Mmm. So do you." She wriggled against him. "And you smell delicious." She rained kisses on his face. I love the way you kiss me. The way you touch me."

Until now, his lovers had been quiet and restrained. But Zoe sighed when he kissed her, moaned when he caressed her and purred when he stroked her. She whispered secret thoughts and intimate feelings in his ear, and he loved it. Her husky voice, her breathless praise was fiercely arousing. What she lacked in experience, she more than made up for with passionate enthusiasm. It was like being ridden by a sensual tornado. He wasn't even inside her, and he had never been more turned on. Never been more aware of, more in tune with his partner, both physically and emotionally. Her pebbled nipples teased his chest, and he groaned. "I've never been this hot."

"Me…either." She rocked against him, quivering in his embrace. Her spine arched, her body drew taut. "I think…oh!"

He slid his tongue into her ear. He breathed in, washing her with cool air, and then out, following with warmth. "That's it, honey. Go over for me."

She shuddered, a tight bowstring vibrating on the edge of release. "Yes, Aidan," she panted. "If you will…for me."

Planning on satisfying only her, he clung to his slipping control as the fiery friction of their bodies hurtled him towards ecstasy. He clenched his jaw as his climax gathered, hovered on the brink. He was rapidly approaching the breaking point. Zoe was about to push him over the edge of the world. And he didn't care. "Now!" he growled. "Now, Zoe!"

Shaking uncontrollably, she cried out his name. Her teeth nipped his shoulder, and hot, sparkling pleasure exploded inside him, poured out of him. He let go and fell willingly, joyfully into the void.

Love surged up to meet him. It buoyed him, filled the emptiness, surrounded him in warmth and light. He held Zoe tight and gloried in the head rush.

She went limp on top of him, and he rubbed her back as their breathing slowed. She lived inside his heart now, and he would never let her go. "All right, sweetheart?"

"Mmm. You are amazing." She sighed and raised up to look at him. Her eyes glowed with happiness, her cheeks were rosy pink, her shapely, red lips lush from his kisses. "New research topic. How many ways can we do this without actually doing it?"

Deep, heart-felt laughter rumbled out of him. His Brenda Starr was one in a billion. He was the luckiest man alive. "I can't wait to help advance your research." He trailed a fingertip down her pert nose. "Right now, we need to rest. Morning is close." And a guy could only push his tattered self-control so far.

"Rats." She snuggled into him, planting kisses over his chest. "I suppose you're right." Suddenly, she gasped, and her horrified gaze met his. "Oh no!"

His stomach lurched. Even consumed by passion, he'd struggled to ensure she was protected, that he didn't go too far. He did a fast, mental scan. Nothing seemed out of place, but then again, he had abandoned all self-restraint at the end. "What's wrong?"

"Here." She gently touched his good shoulder and gulped, perilously close to tears once more. "I'm so sorry."

He glanced down at the faint, even teeth marks, and chuckled. "You didn't even break the skin."

"But it's…I'm…I'm not *that* uncivilized."

Yeah, in bed, she was a wildcat. And he loved it. Before Zoe, sex had been as tame and bland as the rest of his life. Merely scratching an itch. He hadn't known what he was missing. "That sexy little nip hurtled me into Paradise." He stroked her tousled curls. "You are exactly what I want. Exactly what I need."

Her breath caught. "You mean that?"

"Every word."

After rinsing off in the warm pool, they snuggled on the tarp. Aidan put her nearest the fire, spooning her from behind. Listening to her slow, even breaths, he fell asleep.

In his dreams, the night whirled with cold terror. He heard rapid-fire gunshots. Saw Zoe's sightless death stare.

"Zoe!" Shouting her name, Aidan startled awake from the familiar, horrifying nightmare.

She turned in his arms and opened sleepy hazel eyes, smudged with concern. "Shh. It's okay. I'm right here."

He remembered the soul-deep agony of losing Pop. The bleak, empty hole in his heart that wouldn't heal. The icy pain that never quite disappeared. Sweating, trembling, he gathered Zoe close and kissed her forehead. Her warmth surrounded him. Her inner light shone behind her mesmerizing hazel eyes and banished the aching emptiness. She was his. He would not let anyone or anything take her from him.

"Aidan?" She stroked his cheek. "Are you all right?"

"Yeah." He glanced at his watch. The sun would be up. Dawn brought hopes for rescue.

As they rose and prepared to leave the cave, he prayed harder than he ever had in his life.

Chapter 14

6:00 a.m.

Zoe had slept less than two hours, but vitality sparkled inside her as she followed Aidan through the narrow rock passage. They didn't even need the flare he used to light their way—she glowed from the inside out.

Physically and emotionally bonding with Aidan had given her the connection she'd craved all her life. She mentally hugged his words to her heart. He'd said she was unique. Very important to him. He wanted to continue their relationship! Aidan was a man of his word. He didn't offer his loyalty easily or lightly. Once given, nothing short of death would make him rescind it.

For the first time ever, she had a future to anticipate. For the first time ever, she was genuinely happy.

For the first time ever, she belonged.

She fit with Aidan, as she had never fit with anyone. Many torturous paths over long, lonely years had led her to the one man who would safely hold her heart in his hands. All this time, she'd searched for a home. Home wasn't a place, but a person.

At the height of their pleasure, she'd bitten back a dangerous declaration of love that would have killed their fledgling bond before it had a chance to grow. She shuddered. Aidan wasn't ready to hear "I love you" yet. Strong emotions strained his comfort zone. A smart woman would give him time to adjust before putting the big whammy on him. The last thing she wanted was to scare him into backing off. But her feelings shone inside her, as glittery and warm as a newly-minted coin.

She loved him…body, heart and soul. Though he hadn't committed in words, his actions spoke loud and clear. He might not realize it yet, but she was pretty sure he loved her, too.

For the first time ever, the future beckoned with possibilities.

They were again dressed in dry clothing. She in the tux shirt and high-heeled sandals, Aidan in dress slacks and shoes. After a breakfast of her next-to-last box of Cracker Jack and hideous hot mineral water, Aidan had discovered a second passage at the rear of the cave. They had nothing to lose by exploring.

Zoe stubbed her toe on a protruding rock. "Ow! See daylight yet?"

"No, but the sand is compacted, like this path has been used before. Good sign." He squeezed her hand. "Doing okay?"

"Better than okay." She no longer cared about the claustrophobic darkness threatening their small, brave flare. She would follow him into the bowels of hell.

As it turned out, she didn't have to. Right before the last flare sputtered out, the passage opened onto a wide beach. Sunrise gilded the horizon pink and gold, and foamy green waves kissed the shoreline. She smiled at Aidan. "No matter how long or dark the night, the sun always triumphs in the morning."

He jerked, his face startled. "Where did you hear that?"

"You said it when I was swimming us to shore. I was so cold and tired and I started to wonder if we would make it. Your words gave me the strength to keep going."

"Pop," he whispered. "After the armored car robbery money went missing and he was forced into desk duty, he used to say that all the time." He hesitated as if unsure whether to continue. "I've felt him close by since I fell over the cliff. I was so whacked, I didn't realize I'd spoken out loud."

Joy resonated inside her. Her cop had risked confiding something deeply personal, a belief some might ridicule. He would never share anything so private if he didn't trust his heart with her. Near tears, she touched his cheek. "That tenacious Celtic warrior's blood is his legacy. Passed from father to son, part of him will always live on in you."

He swallowed hard. "I never thought of it that way. It's comforting." He pressed a tender kiss to her palm. "Have I mentioned how much I love the way you think?"

Zoe shivered, impacted by both the warm emotion thrumming in his deep voice and the cool morning air. "Not lately."

"I love the way your mind works, Zoe." He slid his arm around her and drew her close to his bare chest. "Summer mornings out here are chilly."

He loved her mind. It was a good start. She shivered again. "Yeah, a hot cup or six of espresso would be great." Careful not to bump the sling, she snuggled into his reassuring heat. "Why aren't you cold?"

He pulled back slightly, and his smoky glance drifted down her body, warming her from head to toe. "With you dressed like that? I'm not anywhere near cool."

His arousal nudged her stomach, and she grinned. "I noticed. Hard to keep a good man down, huh?"

His forefinger tilted her chin up, and his intense gaze caressed her face. "I'm not turned on 24/7 with every woman. Only you, Zoe."

Her heart stuttered. The world disappeared as she gazed into his compelling brown eyes. He lowered his head, and his soft lips enticed hers into a deep, sensual kiss.

He pulled back, and her eyelids drifted up. Her pulse tripped through her veins double-time. "Who needs espresso, when I have you?" She brushed a tousled lock of hair from his forehead. He was even more appealingly male, more ruggedly handsome, sporting dark morning stubble. He looked like a beautiful bad boy who had tumbled directly out of bed after a carnal night of sin. She probably looked like his partner in crime, only not nearly as gorgeous. "Ooh! Smoke!"

He grinned. "I admit, it was hot, but…"

She pointed. "No! Behind you! Through the trees…smoke! Several columns of it!"

He spun. "I'll be damned. Civilization!"

They approached cautiously. Hidden in the woods, they peered at a dozen log homes hunkered inside a clearing chiseled from the forest. A wide dirt road bisected the encampment. Tangy smoke drifted from chimneys, and a dog barked. Nearly every house sported a pickup, several with trailered boats. Most doors stood ajar. A middle-aged woman watered pink petunias. A man in overalls retrieved a bucket from a red truck. Zoe pursed her lips. "It's awfully early to be up and around."

She watched Aidan's cautious gaze assess the situation. The weathered wooden building at the far end looked like a set from *High Noon*. A sign reading General Store and Post Office hung over the doorway. Three carved totem poles stood sentinel in a turnaround out front. The wide front porch sported a bench where several gray-whiskered men sat chugging from steaming mugs. "A fishing community has to get going before sunrise."

A curvaceous redhead in khaki slacks and a yellow cardigan stepped out of the largest house and strolled toward the store. She chatted with the grizzled seniors on the porch and tossed her head in laughter. Aidan nodded. "We're good to go. The perps won't pursue us in front of so many witnesses."

Zoe breathed a sigh of relief. She couldn't wait to escape this godforsaken island and start her future. The sooner the better. "What are we waiting for?"

He kept her slightly behind him and his left arm free as they walked down the dirt road. The only time he stopped being a cop was in the bedroom.

The men and woman on the porch fell silent and turned to gawk. Unseen, wary stares burned into Zoe's spine from every window they passed. Even the totem poles glared malevolently. She edged closer to Aidan and murmured, "If someone starts plunking on a banjo, I am so out of here."

He choked back a laugh. "Don't diss the natives."

She studied the solemn faces riveted on them. "They're not exactly rolling out the Welcome Wagon."

"We're half-dressed strangers who look like *Survivor* rejects. They probably think we're shipwrecked druggies."

They reached the porch, and he nodded at the group, which had been joined by a slim blond woman and a short, balding man. "Good morning, folks. I'm Officer Aidan O'Rourke with Riverside PD." He flashed his badge. Thank goodness she'd rescued his wallet from Muscles. "We had an accident with our boat, and need to use your phone."

The balding man smiled and stepped forward. "Sure thing. I'm Dave. Own the store. C'mon in."

The store's interior was scrupulously clean, the well-organized shelves fully stocked. The yeasty scent of freshly baked bread made Zoe's stomach grumble. Though she'd learned to subsist on very little, her stomach wasn't always a team player.

Dave turned and waved at a partially open doorway. "The phone is in the back office." He studied Aidan's sling. "I hope nobody was hurt too badly. Should I call Doc Adams?"

Aidan slid his arm around Zoe's waist. "Don't wake him. We're anxious to get back to the mainland. Our people will have the entire Riverside PD out on search and rescue. Where are we, by the way?"

"Satisfaction, on Five Mile Island off the Washington Coast. While you're making your phone call, I'll rustle up something to eat." Dave slanted Zoe an appreciative male grin. "And maybe warmer clothes for the little lady?"

Her cheeks heated, and she tugged down the hem of the tux shirt. "That would be very nice, thank you."

She and Aidan headed into the tidy office, and Dave disappeared. Zoe spotted someone lurking in the corner and jumped. The other person jumped, too. It was the ghost of her reflection in a large mirror on the side wall. She touched the imprint of Aidan's kiss at her throat and smiled as the wonderful memories rushed back.

Aidan picked up the cordless handset from the desk and stabbed the on button. With the receiver at his ear, he frowned.

"What's wrong?"

Puzzled, he punched another button. "No dial tone."

She peeked over his shoulder. "Is it charged?"

He checked the battery light. "Yeah."

"Weird. Maybe the base is unplugged or something." She glanced around. "I don't see it. We should let Dave know—"

As if on cue, Dave poked his head in the doorway. "Problem?"

Aidan indicated the receiver. "Phone isn't working."

"Yeah, I took it off the hook out front." The storekeeper strode inside, his hands clenched around a shotgun.

Screaming terror froze Zoe's insides as Aidan stepped between her and the gun, shielding her with his body. He snapped, "What the hell is this?"

Dave's pleasant expression didn't change. "I figure you know. Put the phone down, nice and slow."

Aidan carefully set the phone on the desktop. "You're making a huge mistake, pal." A lethal threat vibrated beneath his quiet, even tone. "I'm a police officer."

"I know who you are. And I'm racking me up a nice bonus." Trembling, Zoe watched in the mirror as he waggled the gun at Aidan. "Boss wants to talk to the little lady. But I get money for *you* dead or alive. So don't be trying anything stupid."

The muscles in Aidan's back knotted. "If you shoot me with a shotgun at such close range, there is no way you can avoid hitting her."

Dave shrugged. "She might get hurt, but you'll still be dead. And I guarantee, nobody will find your body." There was nothing charming about his smile this time. "Nobody ever does."

Aidan held the storekeeper's gaze. His taut readiness said he was waiting for the chance to lunge. Zoe grasped his arm, willing him not to. He shook her off. "I'll stay as a hostage. Let her go, and I'll double the reward."

Zoe opened her mouth to protest, and Dave snorted. "On a cop's salary?"

"My family has money. We can afford it."

"They can pony up a million bucks?"

Zoe inhaled sharply. Who wanted her so badly they'd pay half a million dollars? And why? What hornets' nest had she stirred up with her investigation? She hadn't discovered anything important. Or had she?

"Sure." Though the lie flowed easily from Aidan's lips, Zoe knew darn well his family couldn't scrounge up that amount.

"Don't think so." Dave motioned with the gun. "Outside."

Aidan tugged Zoe in front of him and stayed between her and the gun as they walked through the store. His valiant protection both warmed *and* terrified her. "I have three brothers, all cops. They won't rest until they find us. No amount of money is worth the price they'll make you pay."

"We ain't never been found out. I'll take my chances."

They stepped onto the porch, and Zoe's frantic gaze spun over the watching men and women. "Please, help us. Call nine-one-one."

Four dispassionate gazes slid away. Not one citizen of Satisfaction moved. The moisture evaporated from her mouth. What kind of place had they stumbled into? She tried again. "The man with me is a cop. You're aiding and abetting a kidnapping that crossed state lines. The Feds will stomp you hard."

Dave chuckled. "Folks around here like breathing too much to doublecross the Boss." He inclined his head toward a large log building looming behind the store. "Move it or lose it."

As Dave marched them inside, his right hand shot out. She heard an electric crackle, saw a blue flash of Taser fire, and Aidan convulsed and crumpled at her feet. Dave left, and slammed and bolted the heavy steel door behind him.

"Aidan!" Heart pounding, she fell to her knees and gently lifted his head into her lap. His eyes were closed, his body limp. His breathing and pulse were slow, but even. "Aidan?"

He didn't respond, and she glanced anxiously around. Their prison appeared to be a large warehouse. Casement windows opened outward at the top, near the beamed ceiling. Big ceiling fans circled in slow motion, and plants in various stages of drying hung from the rafters. Wired bundles of the same plant were stacked on wooden pallets scattered around the room. The stuff didn't look like oregano.

She sniffed, analyzing the sickly sweet odor. They'd found a marijuana farm of gargantuan proportions. KKEY had done a feature on wilderness pot farmers. They viciously defended their territory, regularly shooting hikers unlucky enough to stumble into their midst. She glanced down at Aidan, and her stomach cramped. They also shot law-enforcement officers on sight.

She retrieved a towelette from her survival bag and wiped Aidan's face. "C'mon, SWAT, wake up."

He stirred, moaned.

She patted his cheek. "Aidan. Open your eyes."

His eyelids drifted up. His glazed eyes studied the ceiling and he slurred one pithy word.

"Yeah, I think that about sums it up. Apparently, 'the Boss' manages a big-time pot farm. I bet they use that cave for smuggling."

He blinked. Groaned again. "One more SOB zaps me…I'm gonna shove the Taser up his—" He struggled. "Can't move yet."

She stroked his hair. "Take it easy for a few minutes."

The door creaked open, and the attractive redhead in the yellow sweater slipped inside carrying a plastic grocery bag. She was older than Zoe had first thought, probably in her midforties. "I brought food and water." The woman halted when she saw Aidan. "I didn't think he'd come around yet. Either of you moves, I leave."

Aidan stiffened, and Zoe could tell he was surreptitiously gathering his resources for an attempt to gain his feet. "We need your help, ma'am."

The woman edged back. "I don't talk to cops."

Zoe rested her hand protectively on Aidan's shoulder. He needed sustenance to restore his strength. Even if he managed to gain his feet and disable the woman *and* they made it out without being spotted, he couldn't run. "We'll stay put." She held the woman's gaze, attempted to connect. "This is Aidan O'Rourke and I'm Zoe Zagretti. What's your name?"

"I know who you are. I saw you on TV yesterday with that lady whose husband took her kids hostage. I'm Dorothy." The redhead sidled closer, but stayed out of reach. She squatted, set out paper plates and napkins and then withdrew bottled water, wrapped sandwiches and two red apples from the bag. Her sharp green eyes lingered on Zoe's throat, and then skimmed over her scraped and bruised limbs. She flicked a glance at Aidan, cradled in Zoe's lap, and her eyes blazed with reproach.

Aidan tensed, and shock rippled through Zoe. Clearly, Dorothy held Aidan responsible for her injuries. "Aidan would *never* hurt me. I'm bruised from running through the woods." Zoe's gaze entreated her. "Dorothy, we haven't done anything wrong. We don't deserve to die. Please help us."

"I wish...I can't." Tears glistened in her eyes. "I can't." Her glance skittered past Zoe, to the wall. "What you said on TV, is it true? Are there safe places a woman can go?"

Realization dawned, and with it, empathy. This woman was as much a victim as they were. "Yes," she said softly. "It's the absolute truth. You can call 1-800-799-SAFE any time, and they'll help you."

Dorothy stood. "I have to leave, before..."

Zoe tried again. "Please, Dorothy. Phone nine-one-one and tell them we're here. You don't have to give your name. Make an anonymous report. Aidan won't let anyone retaliate against you."

Dorothy shook her head, edged back. "I did all I could. I'm sorry." Her voice caught. "I'm so sorry." She crept out.

Battling despair, Zoe helped Aidan sit up. Side by side, they wolfed the food.

He crumpled his napkin and tossed it on his plate. "Life with you is never boring, Zoe."

Weariness weighed her down. She'd thought they were on their way home. She'd barely blinked, and their lives were back in jeopardy. She couldn't take much more. "Right now, boring sounds very appealing. Please, give me a few hours of boring." He cuddled her against his bare chest. Beneath smooth, hot skin and hard muscles, his heart beat steady and sure. She smiled up at him. "Well, okay, maybe not totally boring."

He kissed the tip of her nose. "I need you gone. Need you safe." She started to protest, and he put his finger on her lips. "Hear me out."

"What do you want me to do?"

His intent gaze catalogued the room. "If you stood on my shoulders, you might be able to reach a window."

She cringed. "Your pain would be excruciating."

He snorted. "What's a little pain between friends?"

"There you go, getting kinky on me again." She trailed her fingertip over the fine, dark hairs on his forearm, and his heartbeat accelerated. "I can't purposely hurt you."

"Our captors have no such qualms." His mouth twisted in a sardonic smile. "Honey, if we don't get out of here, a little ding in my shoulder will be the least of our problems."

"Seriously, Aidan, there has to be another way. I don't want to leave you."

"I can't fight my way out of here one-handed *and* protect you. You have to go, or we're both screwed."

No way would she be a liability to him. "What's the game plan?"

"Leave me the fishing lures." She dug them out of her bag, and he continued. "When you make it outside, head for deep cover. The dock is west of here; follow the sun. Find a boat and head out to sea, toward the mainland. It's east, away from the sun. I'll catch up with you at the Riverside PD."

"All right."

He positioned himself beneath a back window toward the woods. Zoe removed her sandals, stuck them in her survival bag and slung it across her chest. Aidan crouched facing the wall, and she stepped onto his shoulders. He gripped her hand and rose to his full height, hissing out a slow breath.

She winced. "I'm sorry."

"Don't worry about me, sweetheart."

"Someone has to." Sometimes, his tough-guy attitude exasperated her, but in reality, she deeply admired him. This intelligent, brave, resourceful man had endured incredible pain all night with nary a complaint.

"No need. I'm gonna kick butt and take names." He let go of her hand and she slowly stood. He locked the fingers of his good hand around her ankle to help her balance. "You still have my knife from last night. Stab it into the wall for a handhold."

Using the rough, stacked log walls for hand and toeholds, Zoe climbed up to the window. Straddling the sill, she tied the rope from her bag around the heavy casement handle. "Behave yourself." She blew him a kiss. "No smoking the wacky tobbacky."

His face stern, he stared up at her. "Don't come back for me this time, Zoe. I mean it! Get out while you can." His thick brows drew together in a scowl. "I want your word."

And leave her cop to face the enemy one-armed and empty-handed? Yeah, like that would happen. "Word. Master." The coast was clear, and she shinnied down the rope.

Zoe disappeared from Aidan's sight, and he sank to the floor. Gritting his teeth against the pain in his shoulder, he slammed his good fist on the wooden boards. Infuriating woman! What were the odds she would listen to him this time? He grimaced. About the same as him donning a sparkly tiara and becoming the tooth fairy.

He strained to hear shouts or sounds of pursuit. Nothing. Five minutes ticked by, and he slumped in relief. She'd made it!

Aidan rose and scavenged supplies. He needed to set booby traps, build weapons and a barricade. He'd neutralize anyone who came for him and gain time to escape.

At ten minutes and counting, he prayed Zoe had obeyed him for once and saved herself.

After fifteen minutes, he cautiously began to believe it.

Stop thinking about her. Focus on evade and escape. He bent his concentration to one-handedly constructing vicious booby traps from broken pallets, nails, wire and fishing lures.

More time passed. His thoughts drifted to the night before, and his body tightened. Hell, he had to live through this. He wanted the chance to make love to Zoe…all night long. He grinned. He'd give her a whole new meaning for the term *Master*. A challenge he was definitely up for.

"Psst! SWAT!" Zoe's whisper floated down to him.

Real, or conjured from his fantasies? He jerked his gaze up to see her balanced in the window. His heart leapt at the sight of her determined face. At the same time, his stomach clenched in fear. His contrary, stubborn, courageous gypsy would be the death of him. "I told you not to come back," he growled.

"One for all and all that jazz." She tossed in a rope, and it dangled down the wall. "Grab hold."

He sighed. Argument was futile, but he tried anyway. "*Go,* before you get caught. You're not strong enough to pull me up."

"I have the other end tied to a pickup. I'll tow you up." Her impish smile gleamed. "And before you ask, I did a story about teenagers and the dangers of joyriding. One of the little angels taught me to hot wire. Nobody around here locks their vehicles. Trusting bunch of crooks, aren't they?"

He shook his head. She'd stolen a truck from under a posse of drug runners! Brenda Starr was gonna scare twenty years off his life before she was through. His mouth slanted in a reluctant grin of admiration. Being with her was a free lifetime pass to an amusement park—up, down and lots of screaming. Hair-raising, heart-thundering exhilaration. But, damn, if he survived, the ride would be worth it. "You've got more guts than sense, sweetheart."

"You're welcome." Her smile widened. "See you on the other side." She again disappeared from sight.

A daring plan took shape. He had nothing to lose and everything to gain. He quickly unbound his injured arm, stuffed the sling in his pocket, then wrapped the rope around his wrist. As the rope grew taut, instead of bracing his feet on the wall and climbing, he let his arm support his weight. He groaned and fought not to pass out as he was winched up. Talk about the mother of all pain. He groaned again. But by the time he reached the window, his shoulder joint had popped back into place.

Just as he swung a wobbly leg over the sill, the door burst open and Dave rushed inside. "What the—" He triggered the tripwire on Aidan's booby trap and screamed as the tangle of jagged wood, metal, hooks and wires swung from the wall and nailed him. The shotgun flew out of his hands, and he bellowed.

Aidan didn't stick around to admire the results of his handiwork. Panting, sweating, with black spots dancing in front of his eyes from the agony in his shoulder, he rappelled left-handed to the ground.

He staggered, and Zoe caught him. She planted a quick kiss on his cheek. "Somebody here call a cab?"

Aidan laughed. He would never change her. Never control her. Never own her. Nor did he want to. Her unquenchable spirit made Zoe her own, unequaled woman. The woman he loved. He had let her into his heart, and he would never be alone again. She helped him stumble to the truck and shoved him inside. Since he still couldn't see straight, he slid over so she could drive. "Don't expect a tip, lady. I'm a little short."

"Not so I've noticed." She grinned. "But I accept barters." Shouting men tore around the corner, and she scrambled into the driver's seat and gunned the engine. "Gotta give my fan club points for persistence."

The truck bumped across uneven ground toward the one road leading out of the settlement. The posse chased them on foot.

"Oh, yeah, they're rabid." He flexed his fingers and shook his tingling right arm as blood rushed back into circulation. "Not an asset in this case."

She glanced over at him. "Hey! How'd you fix your arm?"

"Wound the rope around it. When you towed me up, my weight put it back in. The advantage of a dislocation over a break."

"Do-it-yourself orthopedics." She cringed. "Ouch."

"Better than the alternative." His shoulder ached like a bitch, but his arm was quickly regaining mobility. If he had to fight, at least he had two working hands. He tore apart the glove compartment, and then groped under the seat. "Weapons?"

"Don't think so. Ahhh!" Gunshots roared behind them, and at the same time, a tall, slim man jumped into the road ahead and stood directly in their path. Zoe let up on the gas.

"Keep your head down!" He shoved her down and grabbed the wheel. "Don't stop!"

"I can't run him over!"

"I can." He grimly stomped his foot on top of hers, forcing the gas pedal to the floor.

"Oh, my God!" She screamed again and closed her eyes as the truck hurtled toward the man.

At the very last second, he leapt out of the way. Another round of gunfire exploded, and the truck swerved wildly. Crap, someone had shot out a tire!

He fought the bucking steering wheel, but couldn't control the pickup. It skidded sideways and slammed into a tree. Pellets of safety glass scattered over them like hail. Jarred by the abrupt stop, Aidan ricocheted to the floorboards, and Zoe tumbled on top of him.

Aidan untangled himself from her slender limbs. If she was hurt, he would rip out these guys' eyeballs. And feed 'em to them for a midday snack. Sheltering her from the men outside, his hands quickly skimmed her body. "You okay?"

She nodded shakily. "Yeah. You?"

The passenger door was flung open. "Out," a graveled baritone barked from behind the door. "Keep your hands in sight."

"No matter what happens, stay behind me," he whispered in her ear. "If they take me out, run like hell." Blocking Zoe with his body, his hands up, Aidan climbed out of the pickup.

A stocky, tough-looking guy stepped into view and pointed a Beretta M-9 at his face. "Now you've gone and seriously pissed me off, O'Rourke."

Icy shock tore through Aidan's gut as he stared at the man holding them at gunpoint. The man who was supposed to be incapacitated in Mercy Hospital's rehab facility. The man who had tortured his brother.

The man who had murdered his father.

Tony DiMarco.

Chapter 15

7:00 a.m.

Blockaded behind Aidan, Zoe couldn't see. Malignant malice thickened the air, and her instincts froze with dread. How did their captor know him? She'd been scared during the past ten hours, but the fear now icing her blood went far beyond terror.

The Boss had arrived.

The man snarled, "Move."

Aidan scooped Zoe in front of him, and the Boss herded them through town with a gun at Aidan's back. She clung to his big, warm hand, and fear for him chilled her bone marrow. Everyone had said the Boss wanted to talk to her…and kill him.

When they reached the center totem pole, their captor barked, "Secure him."

Two men lunged forward, and she turned. One yanked Aidan's hands behind his back. The sharp wrench had to hurt his sore shoulder, but his face remained stoic. A second man reached into a nearby boat and grabbed a length of rope. They bound Aidan's hands to a metal ring embedded in the totem pole.

Zoe pivoted and faced their captor, and fear exploded into shock. "Tony DiMarco!"

The burly man dressed in camouflage fatigues and combat boots inclined his head. "In the flesh."

"You're supposed to be…how did you get here?"

"Curiosity and the cat." An odd gleam burned in his obsidian eyes. "You want the satisfaction of knowing, don't you?" He gave her the sharp, lethal smile of a predator. "Lesson one, little girl. Money is power. I can buy anything I want. I've had men working at Mercy Hospital since shortly after I was admitted, including one as my physical therapist." He tapped a large, firm bicep. "I've been exercising on the sly, and taking muscle relaxants so I look soft and flabby. Another of my men smuggled me out in a linen cart so you and I could keep our appointment. They'll ensure nobody misses me for hours."

She took a deep, shuddering breath. Hold it together. Keep a clear head. Maybe she could talk their way out alive. Words were her greatest weapon. The more DiMarco rambled, the more time she had to think. She'd watched Aidan talk Eric down at the hostage site; maybe she could use some of his negotiating tactics. She wasn't about to let him die. "You seem darned anxious to speak to me."

"Yeah, especially after I overheard your conversation outside my hospital room yesterday. You need to hear *my* side of the story, untainted by an O'Rourke."

Had she said anything to set him on the warpath? She struggled to remember. More importantly, had Aidan? She assessed the man she'd researched and tailed for six months. A smothering cloud of evil emanated from him, sending chills up her spine. He was shorter than Aidan, but bulkier. Twenty or so years older, but strong and fit, solid muscle. A former army Black Ops assassin and security expert.

In comparison, Aidan had been on the run, beaten up, thrown over a cliff and injured. He'd be hard-pressed to subdue DiMarco in hand-to-hand combat. She glanced at her cop tied helplessly to the totem pole. If he even got the chance. DiMarco and his men were also armed to the teeth. Fear threatened to swamp her again, and she forcefully shoved it down. "So, let's talk. But be warned. You won't get a thing from me if you harm Aidan."

"Let me show you lesson number two, little girl. It came to my attention some time ago, but I saved it especially for you." He nodded, and the thin man who'd jumped into the road sidled behind Zoe. The hair on the back of her neck prickled. The man grasped her upper arms, and she flinched.

Aidan growled. "Touch her, and you're gonna wish my brother had killed you quick and clean, DiMarco."

"Merely a preemptive strike. Our eager reporter is soft-hearted and impulsive. Immaturities she'll outgrow."

He nodded a second time, and two men emerged from a nearby house with Muscles between them. So, he'd outrun the cougar and avoided a grisly death.

Muscles saw them and wailed, "I didn't do nothin', Boss, I swear." He tried to break free, but the men dragged him over to the totem poles.

She bit her lip. Perhaps her relief was premature.

When Muscles was bound to the pole to Aidan's left, DiMarco walked up to him and smiled, making Zoe shiver. "Don't make it worse by lying, Kent. You know how much I hate liars."

Kent gulped. "Okay, okay, I borrowed some cash off the last shipment." He gulped again. "I ran a little short, but I was gonna pay it back. I wouldn't steal from you, Boss."

"No, Kent." DiMarco patted the man's cheek. "You won't."

Kent's face blanched. He screamed and lunged, trying to escape. "No! No! Please, Boss!"

His terror was a living, breathing entity. Nausea churned inside Zoe, and her palms grew damp. Her gaze sought Aidan for reassurance. The helpless fury smoldering in his eyes made her queasy stomach cramp.

Ignoring Kent's sobbing pleas, DiMarco withdrew a covered syringe from his shirt pocket.

Zoe flushed hot and then cold, and goose bumps erupted on her skin. He couldn't torture a man right in front of them. She fought to break free, but the man's grip on her arms tightened. "You can't do this!"

"This is my town, little girl. My laws. A leader commands respect. Watch, and learn."

He was insane! The egomaniac had obviously brought her here to put on a show for the press. Did he think she'd do a feature about his twisted dictatorship? Did he think to win her respect with his sick power trip? "DiMarco, that's enough! I believe you're a powerful man. You don't have to prove anything to me."

"It's important for you to witness this. So you'll truly understand what respect is all about."

"I understand! I do! Don't hurt him on my behalf, please." Her panicked gaze again flew to Aidan. His jaw was so tightly clenched, a muscle ticked in his cheek and the cords in his neck stood out. His eyes tender with compassion, he shook his head.

Caught in a backlash of helpless fury, she sagged against the hands holding her captive. Aidan had tracked DiMarco for years. He'd read all the case files. Knew what the man was capable of. Knew begging for mercy was futile.

He'd seen DiMarco's MO written in his own father's blood.

"Make no mistake. I'm going to hurt him on *my* behalf. On behalf of Satisfaction." DiMarco popped the cap, and Zoe's mouth went dry. What kind of drug was he going to shoot into Kent?

Kent sobbed hysterically. "Please, Mr. DiMarco, don't kill me! I'll pay you back with interest."

"You already have." DiMarco's voice was slick, hard ice. "You can either be a good example, Kent. Or a terrible warning." His black eyes glittered. "You've served your purpose in life."

Zoe's head spun, and spots whirled in front of her eyes. DiMarco wasn't going to torture Kent. He was going to kill him!

And she couldn't stop it. No one could.

Kent's pathetic whimpers tore through her as the men held his arm still and DiMarco administered the injection. At first nothing happened. Then Kent shrieked and writhed. He convulsed. Foam bubbled on his lips. Blood streamed from his nose, and he gasped for breath.

She couldn't bear it. She slammed her eyes shut. *This can't be happening. Please, this can't be happening.*

Kent's horrible choking, gurgling noises seemed to go on forever. Finally, thick silence descended.

Weak and trembling, Zoe instinctively sought Aidan. She caught a glimpse of what had been Kent hanging from the pole beside him and retched. She stared at DiMarco, numb with shock. "How could you?" she whispered. "You're a monster!"

"I'm a *king*. And *nobody* interferes with my empire. Not even the almighty O'Rourkes. Which brings us to lesson three."

Staring into his soulless eyes, she saw Aidan's death. She staggered under the brutal blow, and her heart pounded in her throat, choking her. DiMarco was going to kill Aidan. The same torturous way he had Kent.

And she couldn't stop him.

No one could.

Her panicked gaze shot to Aidan, and she saw the same realization etched on his stoic face.

Oh, dear God!

She stomped her captor's instep, and he howled and released her. Shaking uncontrollably, she edged away from DiMarco until her back was pressed to Aidan's warm, solid body. "I'll give you anything. Do anything you want. *Anything.* Just don't hurt him."

"Sweetheart, no!" Aidan hissed.

"Would you?" DiMarco watched her with glittering eyes, a snake toying with a mouse he was about to devour. "No matter how painful? How degrading?"

Every muscle in Aidan's body went taut with strain. "He won't let me go, Zoe. Don't play his sick game."

"If you guarantee that he'll live, yes." Zoe raised her chin. Aidan had a family who depended on him, cared for him. A family who would mourn him forever. She had no one. He'd see that her mother's needs were met. "I'm the one investigating you. Take me instead. Please, just spare him."

"No!" Aidan shouted, wrenching against his bonds. "For God's sake, Zoe, *don't!*"

DiMarco smiled his cold, lethal smile. "Your loyalty is admirable. I wonder if you'll feel the same after we talk?"

"You can talk until you're blue in the face, DiMarco. Nothing you say or do will ever change my mind about Aidan."

He held her gaze, his eyes blazing with intensity. "You don't remember me at all then, Francesca?"

"Why did you call me by my middle name? My name is Zoe." She shook her head. "We've never met face to face. Why should I remem—" She stared into the black, bottomless pit of his eyes, and the world tilted. Without warning, the memory hurtled back so vividly, she staggered under the assault.

"Francie, get in the hall closet, under these coats."

"No, Mommy, I'm scared."

"You have to stay in here, baby girl, and don't make a sound, you hear me? Not a sound, no matter what."

Doors slamming. Heavy, measured footsteps. "Where is she? Where's my little princess?"

"At the sitter's. I want to talk to you about something I found today." Rustling noises. "Where did this money come from, Thomas?"

"What are you doing with my money, bitch? It better all be there."

Angry voices. Shouting. Slaps.

Mommy's scream, then sobbing. "I told you, I won't live this way."

"Fine. Leave any time you want. But Francie is mine! I'll raise her my way. She'll inherit my empire."

"Over my dead body!"

"If you insist. I've gotten away with murder before."

Choking sounds. Glass breaking. "Go get your damn money, Thomas. It's all you ever loved, anyway."

A shaft of light in the darkness. The flowery scent of Mommy's perfume. The taste of terror, like sour milk on her tongue. "Come on, baby girl. We have to hurry!"

Outside, in the cold, black night. Mommy's hand clutching hers too tight. Her breathless panting. "Run, Francie!"

Ragged breaths tore at Zoe's throat. She'd been three years old. Mom had told her about tossing the money out the window, had changed their names immediately afterward, but trauma had buried the memory. No wonder she'd over-identified with the scared little girls at the hostage site and felt sick.

She couldn't stop trembling. Couldn't look away from Tony DiMarco's smug expression. "You knew my mother," she whispered. "Knew my father."

"I *know* him."

She swallowed so hard it hurt. Her battered psyche rejected the implication. "His name was Thomas."

"It was."

From behind her, Aidan murmured, "Don't listen to him, sweetheart. He's messing with your head."

DiMarco stepped toward her. "It's past time you knew the truth, Francie."

No! She refused to accept it. Her mother's voice echoed inside her mind. *Run, Francie!* "No!" she screamed as pain shattered her. Clutching her bag, she bolted toward the woods. "Don't say it!"

DiMarco caught her before she ran five yards. He turned her to face him. "Don't be afraid, Francie."

She was no longer afraid of DiMarco. She was terrified of the truth. "My name is *Zoe!*" she yelled. "I am Zoe Zagretti!"

"You can call yourself whatever you like, but it doesn't change who you are."

Gasping for air, screaming inside, she willed him not to continue. She did not want to hear this.

He touched her cheek with a rough hand, and she flinched away. "I sometimes used the name Thomas Delgado back then. You are my only child. My heir. I've been searching for you for years, but every time I got close, Rita took off again. After you finally settled in San Francisco, I arranged for your job in Riverside so we could meet. I was going to take you with me and retire to the Grand Caymans on one last, big score." His heavy brow wrinkled in a black scowl. "Then that whelp Conall O'Rourke shot me and ruined all my careful plans."

Tight pain coiled in her chest, crushing her heart. She couldn't breathe. Couldn't speak.

The monster who had murdered Aidan's father was *her* father.

DiMarco swept his arm around the clearing. "I have unlimited power. Millions. Acknowledge me as your father, swear your loyalty and you'll never lack for anything. I'll teach you to run my empire. I'll give you everything you've ever wanted."

Every movement an effort, she slowly turned her head and looked at Aidan. Emotions flashed across his face. Confusion. Anger. Horror. And finally, the worst of all…agony. The only thing she'd ever wanted was a future with Aidan. The man who was staring at her with disbelieving, haunted eyes.

The man who, after today, would hate her forever.

Tony DiMarco's evil blood flowed in her veins. Her father's legacy was pain and death.

Nothing could erase this truth. Every time Aidan looked at her, he would remember grief. Would know hatred. He would never be able to love her. Not now. A few fateful words had snatched away her life. Killed her hopes. Devastated her dreams. Nothing could make it all right.

She'd lived for the truth…never knowing the truth could hurt so much.

Overwhelmed by grief, she reeled. She couldn't run. Couldn't hide. Could never escape from it. With the hideous knowledge eating away inside her, she could never again make a fresh start. Her future was as dead as the young man Tony DiMarco had just murdered so cold-bloodedly.

Her life was over.

Unable to stand under the agony, she crumpled to her knees.

DiMarco bent over her. "I know, it's mind-blowing, isn't it? Get up, little girl. It's time for lesson three."

She knelt in the dirt and did not want to move. Did not want to think. Could not bear to feel.

Her hands curled into fists as she battled torment. How she felt wasn't a priority right now. Her future was dead, but she could still save Aidan.

She struggled to her feet and picked up her bag. "All right. I am your daughter." She clenched her teeth against a wave of nausea. "I belong to you. I'll swear my loyalty. And you'll give me everything I want."

"Zoe!" Aidan's hoarse cry pierced her heart. Anguish vibrated in his voice. The wrenching ache inside her was nothing compared to the bitter betrayal he must feel.

"Satisfaction." A corrupt, triumphant grin bled across DiMarco's square face. "The best man won, O'Rourke. Francie has always been sharp. I knew I'd win her over to my side. How does it feel to die knowing she will always belong to me?"

Aidan again called her name, but she couldn't look at him. She could not bear to see the suffering haunting his eyes. Suffering she'd caused. Instead, she stared at DiMarco. "I want Aidan taken safely to the mainland."

DiMarco shook his head. "Sorry, little girl. You can have anything *but* that."

The denial wrenched inside her. "I thought you were all-powerful. The king of the empire. Two minutes as…" The words strangled her, but she forced herself to say them. She would do anything to save Aidan. "Two minutes as my father, and you've already let me down?"

"You have so much to learn." He shook his head, his expression rueful. "Lesson three, Francie. Never leave an enemy at your back. If Brian had killed me after betraying me, he'd be alive today. When you're covered in diamonds and dancing on my yacht, you won't even remember what the cop looked like."

DiMarco stalked toward Aidan, and she clutched his forearm to find unyielding steel beneath the fatigues. "Wait!" She had to either talk him out of killing Aidan, or buy time to formulate a plan. "Tell me why the O'Rourkes are your enemies."

"*Our* enemies, little girl." He turned, his face a stone mask of hatred. "Back in the day, Maureen was my woman, and I thought Brian was my friend. The three of us were inseparable. Then Brian stole Maureen from me. I got sent to hell, while he mustered out. He married her, and she gave him four sons who should have been mine."

Aidan snarled. "In your warped dreams, psycho."

"Shut your mouth, O'Rourke. Or I'll inject the poison a few drops at a time. You'll beg for death. Just like daddy."

"Inventing fairy tales might make you feel like a real man, you sorry son of a bitch," Aidan gritted. "But we both know Pop went down fighting."

She shot a snide glance in Aidan's direction. "Pipe down, cop. I'm talking to my father here." Her torn heart wept. But she couldn't help him if he ticked off DiMarco.

DiMarco chuckled. "I'm happy to see you've got so much of your old man in you. Too bad I didn't find you sooner."

She fought the urge to throw up. Focus. Lead him where you want him to go, just like Aidan did with Eric. "Is that why you killed Brian? Because he married Maureen instead of you?"

"I didn't set out to kill him. I wanted him to know what it felt like to suffer. I waited years, until he had it good. Then I set him up to look like a dirty cop." DiMarco shrugged. "If it had gone down as planned, I would have had the satisfaction of seeing him lose it all. The hero's job. The devoted wife. The loyal sons. Everyone would have turned on him."

How could a human being be so vicious? So depraved? "What went wrong?"

He scowled. "Do-Right O'Rourke was always by-the-book. I figured he'd take his lumps like a man. Surprised the hell outta me when he went against regs and ran an investigation on the sly. The pig-headed Mick just wouldn't give up. I'd more than covered my tracks, but he got too friggin' close."

She had to make him say the words. "So you killed him."

"Yeah, I took him out. Beat him to death. He died on his knees, sobbing like a baby."

"Lying bastard," Aidan choked.

The agonized whisper ripped Zoe's heart out. If it pained her to relive his father's death, it had to hurt Aidan a thousand times more. However, she'd just obtained what nobody else ever had. She'd wrangled an uncontestable murder confession from Tony DiMarco. And she wasn't done. Zoe clamped down on her bleeding emotions. The only way to get through this was to tightly lock up her feelings. She'd have plenty of time to grieve later. Alone. "You're good at what you do. And obviously smart. Is that why nobody ever found his body?"

DiMarco's arrogantly arched brow made her want to wrap her hands around his throat and squeeze. "I hid it too damn well."

She hesitated, afraid of pushing her luck. She was too deep into it now to matter, anyway. And she was determined to do this for Aidan. He needed to know in order to heal. "Where?"

He cocked his head, and the first hint of wariness flitted over his expression. "Why do you want to know, Francie?"

"If I'm going to run our empire some day, I need to learn from the best." The lies came easier now. The ends justified the means.

"Yes, you do." His obscene smile widened. "We're merely a small community of poor fishermen, eking out a squalid living. Nobody bothers us. We have a graveyard here on the island for our dearly departed. Some of the burials aren't…obvious." He rested his hand on her shoulder, and she fought to keep from knocking it off. "And speaking of learning from the best, it's time for lesson three. How to handle your enemies. Lesson four will come later, when we take out his brothers."

I'll kill you myself to stop that from happening. She sucked in a deep breath as eerie calm enveloped her. The moment of truth. She'd hand-deliver her gift-wrapped soul to the devil before she'd let DiMarco execute her cop. As they'd talked, she'd studied her surroundings and devised a plan. She surreptitiously unzipped her bag. *Please let plan B work.*

"All right." Zoe squared her shoulders and wrapped herself in a cloak of fatalism. If Aidan died, he would die fighting, not bound and helpless. And she would die fighting beside him. She stepped away from DiMarco. "Just let me say goodbye."

DiMarco scowled. "Why?"

"He's never going to have me, now." She forced her stiff lips into a gleeful smile. How did these ugly thoughts and cruel words spring so easily to mind? Perhaps some of her father's coldness lurked inside her after all. "I want to rub it in."

DiMarco rubbed his hands together. "That's my daughter."

The viper was proud of her. Shame would not allow her to meet Aidan's eyes. Instead, Zoe kept her gaze on his wide chest. She slid her hand inside her bag as she wove through the silent men. Nine, counting DiMarco. Stinking odds. They might not win, but they would take some of the scumbags with them.

When she reached Aidan, she stared fixedly at his neck. "Guess it's your loss, SWAT."

His Adam's apple jerked as he swallowed. "I know." Sorrow weighted his soft murmur.

Stinging tears burned her eyes and clogged her throat. She'd forfeited any chance to be with him. Before her facade could crumble, she slid her arms around his waist. The last time she'd ever touch him.

One final hug would have to last a lifetime.

She wanted to linger, imprint his scent on her senses, memorize the feel of his smooth, hot skin. But she didn't dare.

"Have a taste of what you'll be missing." She tossed her head and rubbed against him as she felt for the rope binding his hands at the small of his back. Using his body to conceal her true purpose, she flicked open the Swiss Army knife hidden in her fist. The sharp blade bit through the rope. She laid the knife in his palm, and his fingers closed around the handle. She planted a soft kiss on his lips. "On three," she breathed, and then stepped back.

Chuckling, Tony strode to Aidan's side. "With a few more lessons, you'll be damn good at this, Francie."

Anger burned away some of her grief. You think so? Well, she had a few lessons for dear old dad.

The tall, thin guy rushed out of the house where they'd held Kent and delivered a second syringe.

She strolled several yards to Aidan's right and leaned against a trailered boat's hull. She locked her knees to hide their trembling. "Lesson one wasn't anything new. Many people believe money is power."

"Money *is* power." DiMarco nodded. "Don't ever forget it."

"Lesson two, command respect." She set her bag down behind her. "I'm working on that one."

He uncapped the syringe. "You'll pick it up in no time."

"I'm nothing if not a quick study." She rested her hand on the boat's stern. "I believe this will be the most interesting lesson of all. How to deal with your enemies." Her fingers gripped the boat hook hanging over the side. "I'm ready for lesson number *three*."

As the words left her mouth, Aidan lunged and slashed the knife across the tendons in DiMarco's right arm.

DiMarco dropped the syringe. He staggered to the other side

of the totem pole and bellowed, "You morons missed his knife! Get my daughter somewhere safe! And keep those weapons down! Anybody who hurts my little girl dies!"

Guns bristled in every hand, but with DiMarco so close to Aidan, his men couldn't open fire. DiMarco fumbled at his belt with his left hand and yanked out his gun.

Zoe snatched up the boat hook. Four feet of wooden shaft with a lethal metal hook at the end. "Aidan, catch!" She tossed it to him.

Aidan dropped the knife and caught the boat hook in both hands. Whirling, he knocked the gun from DiMarco's fist, then slammed the metal tip into the side of DiMarco's head.

"What the—" Cursing and bloodied, DiMarco crashed to the dirt.

DiMarco was on the ground, and without him as a shield, his men could shoot Aidan. Zoe zigzagged through men intent on seizing her, and scrambled to Aidan's side. She scooped up the knife and circled, blocking the armed assailants from a clear shot at him.

Several men rushed him. The boat hook spun in a graceful, deadly arc, just like the sword he'd used earlier in his Kata. Blows thudded into bodies. As his opponents scattered and fell, more stampeded forward.

Whirling in the center of the melee, Zoe concentrated on keeping her footing. She had to stay out of Aidan's way while still providing him with cover *and* dodging DiMarco's men.

A big blond Viking lunged at her. She lashed at him with the knife, but he grabbed her wrist and spun her into his body, capturing her against his rock-hard chest. She rammed her elbow into his solar plexus and did the instep stomp again, and he let go. She dropped to the ground. On all fours, she scurried between a forest of shifting pant legs, back to Aidan. Who knew three-inch heels were a better weapon than a knife?

Men sprawled in the dirt, some dazed, some unconscious. Aidan sidestepped an attacker and moved closer to DiMarco. DiMarco kicked the back of Aidan's calf, and he dropped to one knee. DiMarco leapt on his back and bulldozed him to the ground. Swearing, they rolled. Fists brutalized flesh.

Two bad guys crouched, preparing to spring to DiMarco's aid.

Zoe snatched up a pistol from beside a guy who moaned and clutched his ribs. She pointed it at the five men left standing. "Drop your guns!" Weapons thudded to the dirt, and she bared her teeth in victory. "Stay back!"

Fighting viciously, Aidan and DiMarco rolled toward the totem poles. Aidan gained the top position. DiMarco's legs scissored and knocked Aidan aside.

Aidan came up with the syringe fisted in his hand. He lowered the needle toward DiMarco's neck, and DiMarco froze.

Aidan snarled. "Satisfy *this,* you sadistic, murdering bastard!"

Zoe's heart stopped, and everything stuttered into slow motion. She couldn't move. Nobody deserved to die more than DiMarco. Nobody deserved the privilege of killing him more than Aidan. Yet she wanted to scream at him not to do it. Not for DiMarco's sake. For Aidan's. She opened her mouth to cry out. Only a dry croak emerged.

Aidan raised the syringe for the death blow. Zoe's breath jammed in her lungs as the needle hovered a millimeter above Di-Marco's skin. Aidan stared down at DiMarco. His hand trembled.

A hundred taut, heavy seconds ticked past.

Aidan threw back his head and released a howl of rage. Teeth clenched, he stabbed the syringe downward.

Zoe went ice-cold. Her vision blurred. "No!" she screamed, a second too late. Aidan's thumb depressed the plunger. Shaking and sick, a cold sweat broke over her skin.

She waited to watch DiMarco die.

Seconds passed. Nothing happened.

She blinked to clear the haze of pain and fear. Stared. Blinked again. Aidan had rammed the syringe into the dirt beside Di-Marco's shoulder.

Aidan's laser glare burned into DiMarco. "I can't kill you like this," he growled. "It would make me feel too damn good."

Tony turned his head and saw Zoe holding the gun. He must have heard her cry of protest, because his nauseating, superior smile flashed. "Help your father, Francie. You'll be rich and powerful beyond your wildest dreams. Have everything you ever wanted. Take our enemy down."

She stared into his black-as-midnight eyes. "Lesson number one. My name is Zoe, and I don't give a flying fig about money or power." She shifted her gaze to the men in front of her to make sure nobody moved, then back. "Lesson number two. The cop who just spared your life is ten times the man you are. He commands respect. You inspire fear and loathing." Her lip curled in disgust. "Lesson number three. Make no mistake. You are my enemy. If you were on fire, I wouldn't spit to help you."

DiMarco's face crumpled in stunned disbelief. "You'd choose an O'Rourke over me?"

Slow, steady applause jerked Zoe's attention forward.

Dorothy sauntered up, clapping her hands. Her sorrowful green gaze swept over the assembled men, and then the cabins, where every door and window was tightly shut. "This little gal has more courage than all of us put together." Her husky contralto rang in the clearing. "We've been too concerned about our own hides and our own livelihoods to care about anyone else. And I'm just as guilty as all of you, if not more. I let Tony conduct his reign of terror and never once had the guts to stand up to him." The redhead grimaced at DiMarco. "You think you have our respect? She's right...we're terrified of you." Her mouth trembled. "Well, never again." She nodded at Zoe. "Her, I respect."

DiMarco spat a foul epithet. "How is it that O'Rourke got four loyal sons and I got stuck with lying, traitorous bitches?" He scowled at Dorothy, and then turned his evil, black glare on Zoe. "You take after your mother, after all."

"Yeah." She jutted her chin. "Much to my undying relief."

"You would have liked being my daughter far more than being my enemy." He stared past Zoe at the men she held at bay, and his eyes glittered ice-cold—death personified. "Kill her. Kill them all."

Chapter 16

8:00 a.m.

Dorothy's scream of outraged disbelief echoed in the clearing as she threw herself behind the boat. A gasp burst out of Zoe, and a stinging rush of fear-laced adrenaline dissolved the heaviness weighting her limbs.

Everything segued into fast forward.

Aidan snatched up Tony's pistol and pressed it to Tony's temple. He yelled at the men, "You move, and your boss dies!"

DiMarco shouted, "Carry out your orders! Kill them!"

Obediently, DiMarco's men scooped up their guns from the ground.

Aidan swore, slammed DiMarco's head against the totem pole and knocked him out. "Zoe!" He surged to his feet, gun in hand. "Hit the dirt!"

Her heart stuttered. Even knowing who she was, her cop's integrity compelled him to protect her. Ignoring his hoarse demands to drop, Zoe backpedaled until she stood beside him. Her shaking hands pointed her pistol at the biggest target, the blond Viking, and her finger trembled on the trigger.

Two against five. She swallowed hard. This was where they died fighting side-by-side.

Savage barking erupted behind the men. They half turned as a snarling German Shepherd charged out of the woods. The thwack-thwack of helicopter blades thundered overhead, kicking up a violent wind. Dust, leaves and pine needles swirled in a choking cloud. Thick cables tumbled from the sky, dangled in the air. Six Kevlar-hooded, Kevlar-suited SWAT officers rappelled to the ground.

The knights in black body armor formed a solid wall between Zoe and Aidan and their assailants. Six assault rifles bristled outward. Eight more SWAT officers burst from the woods and flanked the bad guys from behind.

Zoe's knees wobbled in relief. They'd sent both teams. The bad guys were now facing impossible odds.

"Police! Drop your weapons!" deep, masculine voices shouted over the chopper's roar. Guns thudded to the ground.

"Eat dirt! Get on the ground or die!"

Lights flashing, sirens wailing, four police cars and an ambulance boiled into the clearing. They must have commandeered the ferry. The chopper landed in the middle of the street, and the pilot jumped out, armed and dressed in battle gear.

The SWAT officers who had emerged from the woods broke into teams of two. Searching house by house, they ordered the occupants outside and on the ground.

Out of the noisy melee, a tall, well-built officer strode toward Zoe. "Put down the weapon."

She glanced at her hand and realized she still clutched the pistol. Nerves jittered in her stomach. "I'm on your side." She splayed her fingers and carefully set the gun on the ground. "Don't shoot me."

The cop flipped up the faceplate on his helmet, and Liam O'Rourke's emerald eyes twinkled with reassurance. "I never shoot reporters unless they've given me really bad press." He held out a black-gloved hand. "It's okay, Zoe. You can stand down."

The ordeal was finally over. She and Aidan were safe! Dizziness assaulted her, and the sky spun overhead.

"Easy does it." Liam went down on one knee, and strong arms supported her. Quick, gentle hands skimmed her body. "Are you hurt?"

Beyond speech, she shook her head.

"Let's go somewhere quieter." He swept her into his arms and carried her away from the chaos.

Zoe looked over his broad shoulder, searching for Aidan. In the midst of the fracas, DiMarco had regained consciousness and bolted toward the woods. Aidan sprinted after him and tackled him from behind. Aidan's brother Con moved into position and stood over DiMarco with a gun pointed at his head.

Seeing Con sent a new wave of tormented guilt through her. Con must have searched for his brother around the clock, ruining his and Bailey's wedding night, an additional insult to the injuries her father had caused the O'Rourke family.

Aidan knelt on DiMarco, cuffed his hands behind his back, and then hoisted him to his feet. Scowling, he hustled him off.

"Way to go, SWAT," she whispered. After one final, lingering look, she resolutely faced forward. She choked back tears. The only thing she could do for Aidan now was avoid causing him more pain.

Liam's concerned gaze searched her face. "Sure you're all right, Geraldo? It's not like you to be so subdued."

She couldn't tell him her heart had been ripped out. Or why. She nodded.

His arms tightened around her. "DiMarco is tagged and bagged. Ancient history. You're safe with us, now."

If only that were true. Once the O'Rourkes learned how her history was entangled with DiMarco's, they wouldn't want anything to do with her.

Murphy trotted over and heeled at Liam's side. Liam glanced down and grinned. "Good boy, Murphy. You made the bad guys crap their chaps."

Liam carried her to the ambulance, and carefully placed her on a raised stretcher parked outside the vehicle. Murphy sat on his haunches and stared at Zoe, his big brown eyes somber. The dog's gaze seemed accusatory, as if he were watching to make sure she didn't hurt his master. She cast her eyes downward.

Liam motioned, and Grady, the youngest O'Rourke brother sprinted over. "Zoe! You okay?"

She nodded again. They were being so kind. How would they react when they discovered her father had brutally murdered theirs? Nausea churned inside her and she swayed.

Liam gently rubbed her back. "Grady will take good care of you." He murmured to his brother. "I think she's in shock." He patted her shoulder. "Hang in there, Geraldo. I'll see you later." He strode off with Murphy ambling behind him.

No, he wouldn't see her later. Or any time. She hung her head. She could never face the O'Rourke family. They would despise her, and she didn't blame them.

She despised herself.

"Let's get you comfortable." Grady draped a blanket around her shoulders. "Do you need to lie down?"

She shook her head.

He shone a light in her eyes and made her follow his finger with her gaze. Then he grabbed a stethoscope and a blood pressure cuff from inside the ambulance and checked her pulse and BP. His concerned gray-green eyes studied her skimpy clothing and the scrapes and bruises marring her body before flickering to her throat. He frowned. "Were you...assaulted?"

She again shook her head.

"Aidan wouldn't—" he muttered under his breath. "He's never—" He broke off and cupped her face in his hand, the tender gesture so reminiscent of Aidan's, her tears threatened to burst free. "Don't be afraid to tell me. I'm here to help you. Or I can find a female officer, if that would be easier."

"No," she whispered. "I wasn't hurt." Not physically, anyway.

"All right." He patted her shoulder. "Just relax. I'm going to make you feel better."

Nothing in the world could accomplish that feat, except maybe turning back the clock to yesterday. Before she'd found out vile, corrupted blood flowed in her veins.

Grady sent another officer to fetch her a hot cup of coffee and an energy bar. Speaking soothing nonsense, he gently cleaned and bandaged the cut on her leg, and dabbed antiseptic ointment on her scrapes and bruises. The more tenderly he treated her, the more she felt like the dirt stains on her clothing.

Wyatt Cain, the hostage negotiator, arrived to ask if she was able to give a statement. Grady insisted on accompanying her, but she resolutely refused. She was more than ready to escape the gut-wrenching guilt.

Wyatt led her into a house at the end of the street. The big man with black, wavy hair and cobalt-blue eyes also treated her with exceptional gentleness as he jotted down her statement.

Aidan didn't seek her out, nor did she expect him to. She was the last person he'd want to see.

Zoe delivered her version of events in a flat monotone. Answered numerous questions. Clarified details. When she was done, she signed the statement and rose from the overstuffed sofa. One final task awaited. Clinging to the bare threads of her ragged emotions more tightly than to the blanket draped around her shoulders, she stepped outside.

The red sunrise had surrendered to a cool, overcast morning. Heavy cloud cover had moved in, encompassing the clearing in gloom. Pandemonium still reigned. Uniformed cops mingled with SWAT teams, jogging from houses to squad cars and back. Male voices barked orders and shouted questions. Stunned groups of handcuffed townspeople clustered in the streets, guarded by armed officers. A huge van had arrived to transport the prisoners. Blue-and-red lights strobed the clearing. She searched the sea of masculine faces for Liam, Grady or Con.

For any O'Rourke except Aidan.

Finally, she spotted Grady sitting inside the chopper, scribbling on a clipboard. She hurried over and waited for him to finish.

He climbed out of the aircraft. "Hey, Zoe. How are you feeling?"

Like Typhoid Mary, spreading death, destruction and sorrow in my wake.

She hated to ask, but had no choice. "I need a favor."

"Sure." He smiled, flashing his dimples. "Anything for the girl who helped bring down that slime bag DiMarco."

Zoe winced. She carried that slime bag's DNA. She'd said and done things in the past twenty-four hours that made her realize just how strong those repulsive genes were. Terrible things that made her doubt herself and everything she stood for.

Her hand shook as she scooped Aidan's Swiss Army knife from her bag. Her fingers clenched painfully around the smooth red handle. Severing her last link to him was more wrenching than she'd ever imagined. "Please give this to Aidan for me, and tell him…" She swallowed the lump in her throat that threatened to strangle her. "Tell him I'm sorry for everything." Her voice dropped to a whisper. "And I hope that someday he can find it in his heart to forgive me."

"Zoe?" Grady's dark brows drew together in puzzlement as he accepted the knife. "I don't understand. Why—"

"You will," she choked out.

Then she did the only thing she knew how to do.

She fled.

Three hours later, Zoe rested her cheek against the cool glass window as the bus chugged down the I-5 corridor toward the California border. Dismal, battleship gray storm clouds seethed on the horizon, mirroring her turbulent feelings. Unshed tears pressed a hot, stinging weight behind her eyelids. No time to cry. After a fast shower, she'd changed into a turquoise peasant blouse and turquoise-and-black print broomstick skirt, one of her best Goodwill bargain outfits. Packing essentials and giving her landlord and employer notice had taken less than thirty minutes. She was a pro at running.

She was going back to Mom. Though Mom wouldn't recognize her, simply being with her would be comforting.

As if sensing her distress, Evander poked his head out of her bag and nosed her hand. "Stay down," she whispered, pushing him back inside. When the ticket agent had informed her the bus company didn't allow animals on board, she'd ditched Evander's carrier and hidden him in her bag. He was all she had left, and she wasn't about to leave him behind. So far, she didn't have a seatmate, and her secret was safe. If she got booted off the bus for smuggling a stowaway, she'd walk to San Francisco. There was no hurry. She had no family waiting for her. No job.

She had nothing.

She'd started over countless times, in countless places. But now, only dark days and lonely nights loomed ahead. She no longer had the heart to begin anew. Only an empty, aching shell remained where her heart used to beat.

Mere hours ago, happiness had danced inside her after the wonderful night she and Aidan had shared. The possibilities had made her giddy with hope. Then, just when she'd glimpsed a bright, glorious future with the man she loved, the ugly truth about her parentage had brought the universe crashing down around her. The contrast was too cruel.

She gazed at the heavy black clouds and tried to blank out her mind. Don't think about Aidan. His smoky brown eyes caressing her. His husky laughter curling around her heart. His strong, hard body gifting her with ultimate pleasure. Agony coiled tightly in her chest, making it hard to breathe. DiMarco's coup de grâce had killed their relationship. Strangled her happiness. Obliterated her future. The pain would never go away. But in time, the grief might fade.

In a hundred years or so.

The bus lumbered past towering pines, a poignant reminder of her night in the forest with Aidan, and choking anguish clogged her throat. She prayed his pain would fade. Perhaps finding his father's remains would finally bring him peace.

She owed him at least that much.

Uneasy murmurs and restless movements of passengers behind her made her turn around. Blue lights flashed and a siren screamed as a police cruiser appeared in the distance. A bloodred Corvette nosed into the left lane and sped past the bus. Slumping, Zoe again faced front. Only a trooper after another leadfoot.

Without warning, the rhythmic thud of helicopter blades echoed overhead, and a chopper swooped over the front of the bus. Dropping dangerously low, the aircraft zoomed down the freeway, and then spun three-hundred and sixty degrees to face the bus. Everyone gasped.

Zoe peered at the amazing sight over the seats, along with every other amazed passenger. The police must be conducting a high-speed chase.

The chopper floated down like a giant dragonfly and landed in the middle of the freeway, blades whirring. The bus driver swore and slammed on the brakes, and the bus skidded to a halt.

Zoe blinked. Whoa! Maybe they were filming a movie.

The chopper door flew open. A dark-haired, broad-shouldered police officer dressed in a black SWAT uniform leapt out of the passenger side, ducking beneath the deadly blades. No swaggering movie star, this cop was all business.

The heart she'd thought damaged beyond repair kicked against her ribs. *Surely not.* Besides, the last time she'd seen her cop, he was wearing tuxedo pants and not much else.

The officer stalked toward the bus, and Zoe's pulse thundered into triple time. The fluid, loose-limbed grace, the powerful predator's stride belonged to only one man.

Aidan O'Rourke.

The driver opened the door, and Aidan strode up the steps. His handsome face was stoic, but his taut muscles and rigid posture told her he was mad. Fury vibrated in every pore of his long, lean-muscled body. She gulped. Was he angry because she'd cheated him out of a final showdown? He flashed his badge at the driver and then prowled down the aisle.

Oily panic swelled, and she closed her eyes, bracing herself to face Aidan's wrath. His footsteps grew louder. Closer. Stopped. Thick, heavy silence descended. She gulped. Facing him was her obligation. He deserved reparation she could never give. She opened her eyes, but could not meet his gaze. The revulsion that had twisted his face, the horror-stricken disbelief that had darkened his eyes when DiMarco had dropped his bomb would haunt her forever. She couldn't bear to see the disgust, the betrayal he must feel every time he looked at her.

"We have unfinished business, Zoe."

Her name spoken in his deep, velvet tones sank a heavy boulder of misery in her stomach. "I would have apologized in person, but I knew it would only hurt you to see me." She inhaled a shuddering breath. "I'm sorry for the sick, cruel acts my father perpetrated on you and your family. I'm sorry for pursuing the investigation when you told me to stop. I'm sorry for the awful things I said to you." Another shaky breath. "I can't begin to express how awful I feel."

"Don't apologize." His low voice was implacable.

"You're right. I can never make it up to you. You have every right to be furious. But I promise, you'll never have to set eyes on me again. It's over."

"I'm not angry at you," he said softly. "And it's far from over. Come with me."

Dread whirled inside her. Of course he was angry with her. Who else did he have reason to be furious with? By leaving so quickly, she'd hoped to avoid this. Hashing it out would only cause more torment. He'd been hurt beyond bearing. No words could undo the truth of who and what she was. "It's better if it ends now."

He shrugged. "Fine by me. But do you really want to do this here?"

She glanced around at the curious faces riveted on them. By now, his family would know. Would be beginning the preparations to finally lay Brian to rest. Her presence would sting like acid in an open wound. Every time the O'Rourke brothers looked at her, they would remember the barbarian who had bludgeoned their father to death. Every time Maureen saw her face, she would be reminded of the evil butcher who had murdered her husband. Zoe refused to hurt them more. "Please understand, Aidan. I'm trying to spare you and your family. I don't think we should do this at all."

He leaned over and spoke so quietly she could barely hear. "Don't make me get out the handcuffs, Zoe."

Her jaw dropped. "You wouldn't."

"Feel free to try me." He squatted to her level, but she stared fixedly at the seat back. "I'll only ask once more. Come with me."

Leaving him the first time had been excruciating. Having to walk away a second time would be her undoing. "I can't. I just can't. I'll call you when I get to San Francisco, and you can tear a strip off my hide over the phone. I promise, I'll listen. You deserve the chance to speak your mind."

"Stubborn little gypsy. I knew you were trouble the first time I laid eyes on you." He sighed. "Don't say I didn't warn you." He moved too fast for her to react. Cold steel clamped around her right wrist. Before she could blink, he'd cuffed her wrist to his. He rose. "Let's go."

Dismay rocketed through her. Was she under arrest? She'd seen him like this at the hospital. Furious, but controlled. Because she didn't have any choice, she stood and moved into the aisle with him.

He slung her bag over his shoulder, grunting at the weight. "Very important protected witness," he told the bus at large as he led her out.

Why did he bother to defend her pride? He shouldn't care if her fellow passengers thought her a criminal. After all, she was the spawn of one.

Aidan had the bus driver unload her suitcase, and then towed her toward the helicopter. Halfway there, the dusky clouds began to spit raindrops. Evander popped his head out of the bag and me-owed. Aidan stopped dead in his tracks. "What the—" He looked down at the cat and chuckled. "I doubt you'd like a chopper ride, buddy. I don't have ear protection to fit you."

He reversed direction and sauntered behind the bus to the pa-trol car. Liam lowered the window and grinned at his brother. "I see you have our witness in protective custody."

Confusion muddied her thoughts. Apparently, the police *did* need her as a witness.

"I've got more than that." Aidan passed over her bag. "Meet Evander. Evander, Liam. I'll pick him up tomorrow."

"Murphy will be happy to have the company. The nutball loves cats." Liam scratched Evander behind the ears and arched a brow at Zoe. "Don't worry, as companions, not canapés."

Aidan towed her back into the mini-tornado created by the chopper blades. Grady waved from the pilot's seat. Aidan boosted her into the back and settled in beside her. He buckled her in and then gently fastened a pair of miked headphones over her ears. "Let's rock and roll."

Grady's amused, mellow voice floated into her ears. "Geez, bro. Dragging your women in cuffed, nowadays? A tad Neanderthal, even for you."

"Stick it on ice, baby brother," Aidan growled. "And drive."

"Yes, sir, Officer O'Rourke, sir." The helicopter zoomed skyward, making her stomach dip. "Welcome aboard Air O'Rourke," Grady intoned. "Hopefully, we'll be flying at an altitude high enough not to freak you into wetting your Depends, unless the A-man here demands that we buzz a bus and land on a freeway."

Aidan snorted. "You loved every minute of it."

"*Yee haw,* I live to mow grass with my chopper blades." Grady chuckled. "Next stop, Riverside PD."

The destination confirmed her theory. Though Officer Cain had said she could leave after giving her statement, they must need more information. No wonder Aidan was angry. His superiors had sent him after her—the last person he wanted to see. She'd be angry in his place, too. She would try to make it as easy on him as possible. On her part, she'd tough it out and get through it.

A sorrow-laden sigh escaped. Easier said than done. Walking away from Aidan again would devastate her. She shifted as far away from him as possible and concentrated on blocking out the aching sensory overload caused by his nearness. The warm strength radiating from him tempted her to rest her weary head on his chest. Dejected, she tipped her head back and closed her eyes. Though physically linked by the handcuffs, they were oceans apart emotionally. He'd only push her away. Not that she'd blame him. He had every right to reject her.

Twenty minutes later, Grady landed on the helipad atop the police station. She and Aidan exited, and Grady snapped her a jaunty goodbye salute from the pilot's seat. Instead of leading her inside, Aidan took the elevator to the parking garage.

He stopped beside a black Jeep and unlocked the cuffs. Puzzled, she hung back as he opened the car door. "Whose car is this and where are we going?"

"The Jeep is Grady's. He'll catch a ride with Liam, later." He gestured at her to get in. "We're going to my place."

Anxiety scraped over her raw nerve endings. "Why?"

"We need privacy to discuss everything that's happened."

Crushing apprehension overpowered her, and she reeled. Official statements she could deal with. Alone in Aidan's apartment, faced with his pain and rage, she might melt into a useless, sobbing puddle. Beg him not to hate her. Put him on the spot. And wouldn't that be a comfort to him?

Aidan helped her inside. As they left the parking garage, the raindrops picked up speed and momentum, turning into a downpour. Aidan focused on the unusually heavy traffic, and she spent the taut, silent fifteen minutes shoring up her courage. He needed closure, and she would give it to him. Even if it killed her.

Aidan toed the door to his apartment shut, and then led her into the living room.

Standing close to him, she breathed in his scent. He smelled so good. So masculine. So clean. She covertly studied his strong profile. "You shaved." A safe, innocuous topic.

"Yeah, I couldn't stand myself." She knew how that felt. "I grabbed a fast shower at the command post before I changed into an extra uniform. Didn't want anyone to mistake me for a perp." He reached out to touch her face, and she flinched. If he touched her, she would fall apart. He froze, and his brows snapped together in a frown. "Are you *afraid* of me?"

Their talk was going to shred her soul, and she wasn't sure she could handle any more pain today. However, if a discussion would help him, then she would find the strength. Somewhere. "No, of course not. I'm fine." She stiffened, braced for the blow. "Go ahead. Let me have it."

Chapter 17

Twelve noon

"Zoe." Aidan's voice went low and very gentle. "We're just going to talk. Nothing bad will happen, and we'll both feel better afterward."

Her stomach rolled. A conversation dredging up her relationship to DiMarco couldn't be good. Aidan might feel better, but she had no hope for herself. Nothing could change the fact that his father's legacy was courage and honor, while her father's legacy was cruelty and death.

He gestured at the rich brown leather sofa. "Make yourself comfortable. Are you hungry?"

"No, thank you."

"Well, I'm starving." He hesitated, and the weight of his gaze bore down on her. "Don't go anywhere. I'll be right back."

There was no running away this time. She was obligated to stay and face the music. No matter how discordant. Aidan hadn't turned on the lights when they'd entered the room, and the wan atmosphere was as murky as her spirits. She trudged to the rain-streaked window and stared out at the cityscape, washed in gloom. The river reflected steely clouds overhead, its gray water cold and unwelcoming. A solitary barge struggled through choppy waves, making slow headway against the storm.

The barge had battled its lonely way around the river bend by the time Aidan strode into the room carrying two platters. One brimmed with bite-size summer fruits, the other held assorted cheeses, crackers and miniature rounds of bread.

He'd also changed clothes. Snug, faded jeans showcased his muscular thighs and long legs to perfection, and a dark-plum cotton shirt hugged his broad shoulders. His shirtsleeves were rolled up on sinewy forearms; his long feet were bare. She hungered for him far more than the food.

She wrapped her arms around herself, but the defensive gesture couldn't ease the pain. He made her yearn for something she could never have. She now understood why he had closed himself off for so many years. Why he'd been afraid to hope. To want. To care.

Caring hurt way too much.

"I took a few seconds to change out of uniform." He set the platters on the glass-topped coffee table and smiled. "Don't want you to feel like you're being interrogated."

She didn't know if the smile reached his eyes. She still could not meet his gaze.

He left again, and returned balancing dark green plates topped with matching napkins, a steaming, fragrant casserole dish of gingered chicken wings and a bowl of deviled crab.

"I hope you didn't go to all that trouble for me. I really can't eat a thing."

"Wedding reception leftovers. Found 'em in my fridge with a note from Mom. She figured we'd be tired and hungry after our ordeal, and not up to cooking. There's wedding cake for dessert."

He made one more trip for a bottle of white wine and two stemmed goblets. He arranged dishes, poured wine and then held out his hand. "Come and sit down."

Rather than endure the torment of close contact with him on the sofa, she toed off her sandals, confiscated a suede floor pillow and sat in front of the low coffee table. Shivers crept over her as she stared at the icy, unforgiving glass tabletop and waited for him to speak his mind.

"Here." He gently draped a sand-colored chenille throw over her shoulders. "It's turned unseasonably chilly." He moved to the fireplace and touched a button. A steady red-gold flame instantly sprang to life. "The beauty of a gas fireplace. No wood to chop." He opened glass bi-fold doors and crackling warmth radiated toward her.

She clutched the downy throw like a lifeline. "Thank you."

"No problem." He tossed down a second floor pillow and sat beside her.

So much for evading his overwhelming presence.

He didn't waste any time. "Why did you run, Zoe?"

She stared at the fire as heavy silence thrummed between them. The eternal flames of hell could not hurt any worse than this discussion. She ached for him to hold her. To take away the pain. But the only person in the world who could comfort her was the one person she had no right to seek comfort from.

Finally, she steeled her nerves and dove in. Better to rip off the bandage in one screaming moment than drag out the agony millimeter by millimeter. "Because I couldn't do anything else." A furious gust of wind slammed rain against the window. "Why did you follow me?"

He took a drink. "Because I couldn't do anything else."

She nodded. She'd suspected as much. "Your superiors didn' give you a choice. I don't blame you for being angry."

He choked on his wine. "You thought I was mad because headquarters forced me to track you down?" He sounded incredulous "Look at me, Zoe."

"I can't."

Thunder rumbled in the distance, heralding the storm outside "Why not?" Thunder rumbled in his voice. It was going to storm inside, as well.

The truth stung, cold and bitter in her mouth. "Because I can' bear to see the disgust and horror in your eyes again. Because you've been betrayed and I can never make that up to you. Because of who I am—" Her chest tightened until she could barely breathe, and her voice broke. "I—I'm the daughter of the man who murdered your father. The child of the filth who caused you and your family so much pain."

"Zoe, I need you to look at me." His plea sounded strangled. "Please."

She closed her eyes. This was the one thing she'd dreaded the most. The one thing she didn't have the courage to face. The one thing that could finally break her beyond her ability to recover. She battled back tears. But he'd asked it of her, and she owed him at least that.

And so much more she could never, ever make right.

Her hands fisted, nails cutting into her palms. Mortal fear of what she would see made her eyelids slow to open. She stared at Aidan's square chin, firmed in stubborn determination. His full, sculpted lips, compacted so tightly they were white. His regal nose, nostrils flared with emotion. Fearing, dreading the moment of impact, she forced her gaze upward.

Lightning flashes of emotion raged in his eyes.

Pain. Stark anguish shadowed his irises, and arrowed into her chest.

Anger. Dark, hot fury smoldered, and made her stomach clench.

Sorrow. Tears glistened in the deep brown pools, clung to his long, thick eyelashes.

Her breath jammed, thick, painful cement in her lungs.

Tears?

Her tough cop didn't cry. He had declared tears were useless. She bit her lip so hard she tasted blood. She would rather have died at DiMarco's hands than cause Aidan pain. Would rather die, right here, right now, than see him cry. "I'm sorry," she choked out. "So sorry. Reliving your father's death at DiMarco's hands had to hurt so badly."

"No, baby." He cupped her face. His hands were shaking. "*I'm* sorry. The disgust and horror I felt wasn't about who you are. I lost it because I was trapped in my worst nightmare. I let you down. I let you die."

Confusion jumbled her thoughts. "Wh-what? What do you mean?"

"I had to stand there and let that monster rip out your heart, and I couldn't do anything. I had to listen to him slice your soul into bloody scraps, and I couldn't stop him. He hurt you beyond bearing, and I couldn't protect you." His voice wavered, and he swallowed hard. The storm crashed overhead, and the tears pooling in his eyes leaked over. "I watched you die, inch by inch. Your optimism. Your spirit. Worst of all, your hope."

Stunned, bewildered, her bruised, aching soul in turmoil, she gasped. He was upset because *she'd* been hurt? He was crying over *her* pain? Her throat closed up, and her eyes filled with hot tears. "Don't," she whispered. "Oh, God, please, don't." She gently touched the warm, wet streaks on his face as moisture streamed down her own. "None of it was your fault. *My* investigation got us kidnapped. *My* father tried to kill you. *I'm* contaminated. Dirty." She hung her head. "The blame is mine. The shame is mine."

He hissed through gritted teeth, and thunder boomed in the sky. "DiMarco might have contributed to your existence—the only good thing he ever did in his sorry life—but he was never your father. And never will be." His entire body was trembling. "As surely as if DiMarco held a gun to your head and pulled the trigger, he murdered you. I had to watch a shell of the woman I've grown to respect and admire and care about crumple to the dirt. I couldn't pick you up and hold you." His fingers slid into her hair, and tipped up her face. His tormented gaze held her captive. "You wouldn't look at me. I couldn't comfort you. I nearly exploded from helplessness and rage. If I'd had a chance then, I'd have strangled DiMarco without a qualm." His hands moved down, gripped her shoulders, and he shook her gently. "You are not to blame for his actions. The guilt belongs to *him.* The shame belongs to *him.*"

They were both trembling now. Her dazed mind could not process his meaning. She'd expected revulsion and scorn. Instead, he was showering her with care and compassion? "I th-thought you were f-furious with me when you got on the bus. You should despise me."

"No." His jaw tightened. "I was furious with myself for not being able to help you. I despised DiMarco for making you feel you had to run from me. But I was never angry at you, Zoe."

"I don't understand. Why don't you…" She sucked in a ragged, quivering breath and listened to the rain pummel the building. "…hate me?"

"Ah, sweetheart." He drew her tenderly into his embrace. "How could I ever hate you?" He chuckled raggedly. "When I need you more than my next breath? I love you, Zoe."

Lightning speared the sky in a bright, hard flash. Aidan had just spoken words she'd waited all her life to hear. And, oh, how they hurt. Her heart stopped beating. She couldn't draw in enough air. The floodgates collapsed, and sobs burst out on a tangled surge of bittersweet despair.

"Zoe?" Aidan's strong arms tightened around her, and he tugged her into his lap. "That was supposed to make you happy."

"It c-can't happen." She'd finally found the devotion, the closeness she'd craved all her life, and she couldn't accept it. She was a starving urchin, locked outside in the dark with her nose pressed to the bright window of a tempting banquet she could never taste. Everything had been torn away from her. She sobbed harder. "I 1-don't belong here. W-with you."

"Shh." He held her tight and rocked her. "You don't belong anywhere else."

"N-no, I can't." Didn't he understand that a relationship was impossible? Grief was as hot and jagged as the lightning splitting apart the sky. Aidan was right about one thing; her hopes had been strangled to slow, painful death in those woods.

She didn't cry often, but her unfettered emotions ran rampant. "My entire life has been a lie. I don't even know who I am anymore. I'm so scared," she sobbed into his shirt. "So lost."

"Your life stands on its own merit. Your work speaks for itself. And you're not lost, sweetheart." He stroked her hair, kissed the top of her head. "I have you."

She struggled for control, but hours of repression wouldn't be denied. The rain outside poured down, echoing her torrent of sorrow. As she sobbed out her pain, Aidan rocked her and hummed, his deep velvet voice low and soothing.

Eventually, her sobs tapered off, and then stopped. She rested her cheek against his warm, wide chest and listened to his heart, thumping strong and steady beneath the soft cotton. Suddenly, she realized what he was humming. "You Really Got a Hold On Me." Though her own heart was in shreds, her lips wobbled in a watery smile.

He gently blotted her tears with a napkin. "There's my girl." He held a goblet to her lips. "Drink."

She obediently sipped. Wine slid down her raw throat and warmed her chilled insides.

"Here, nice and ripe." He brought a strawberry to her mouth.

Tangy sweetness melted on her tongue. She swallowed the fruit along with another wave of sorrow. "I don't deserve you. Can't be with you."

He scowled down at her. "What brand of twisted female logic arrived at that conclusion?"

"What if…" Merely thinking it stabbed her with unspeakable pain. Saying it out aloud twisted the dagger gut-deep. "What happens down the road if…if DiMarco's genes win, and I turn out…badly? What if I end up hurting you?"

"What?" Shock sharpened his rugged features. "You're worried about becoming like *him?*" he growled. "Impossible. What you are in life isn't stamped on your birth certificate." He fed her a cube of tangy cheese, then a cracker. "C'mon, baby, I don't believe for a second you think people are born bad. Would you condemn Kylie and Emma because their father went on a rant and took them hostage?"

She jerked upright in his arms. "No." He was right. Those little girls were completely innocent. If they were innocent of their father's wrongdoing, surely she… She had always tried to see some good in everyone. Until recently. "I'm…so mixed up." The summer storm subsided into the rhythmic drumming of rain on the window. Held in Aidan's steadfast embrace, the gale raging inside her began to abate, as well. "But I *feel* responsible."

"So I see." He offered her a crisp grape. "We'll sort it all out. Talk to me, Zoe."

His calm strength gave her the courage to confess the terrifying worries that had tortured her since she'd learned the awful truth. "Back there in Satisfaction, I said and did such horrible cruel things to you. And they seemed…seemed to come naturally to me. I—I threatened a man's life to get you off the cliff, and I *meant* it. I always considered myself a decent, moral woman." She gulped another drink of wine, and let her worst fear tumble out. "But what kind of person does those things? What kind of person am I? Maybe…maybe I take after him more than I want. Maybe I can't help it. Maybe Tony DiMarco's daughter did those things."

"Did you enjoy it?"

"What?" It was her turn to express shock. "My God, *no!*"

"Of course you didn't. Because you *are* a decent, moral woman." His jaw clenched so tightly, she feared it might snap. "Listen to me." Again, his burning gaze would not release her. Willed her to believe. "*Zoe Zagretti* was with me in those woods. And I'm damn grateful, because otherwise, instead of Mom leaving leftovers in my fridge this morning, she would have been choosing my coffin." He shifted her closer to his hard warmth, and stroked gentle fingertips down her cheek. "I'll tell you what kind of person you are. Smart and creative. With a lightning-fast mind that comes through in the clutch." His mouth slanted in a rueful smile. "The kind of person who risks her life for someone else. Give me *some* credit. I knew you didn't mean those things you said. I knew you were scamming DiMarco to throw him off guard."

Suddenly weak, she leaned against his broad chest and stared into the fire. She trusted Aidan beyond measure. He dealt with the worst elements of society daily. He'd seen and heard everything she'd done. If he believed in her goodness, maybe she wasn't corrupted. A hidden ember of the hope she'd thought dead ignited a tiny glow in the cold ashes of her soul. "I'd feel less awful if you'd accept my apology."

He scooped crab dip onto a cracker, and she couldn't resist the tempting morsel. "Will you accept mine for making you jump out of a moving car, forcing you to crawl into a hole in the ground *and* a dark cave, robbing you of your clothes and towing you around in handcuffs?"

"No, because you were trying to keep us alive."

"Ditto." The afternoon had grown darker, and flickering flames washed light and shadows across the strong angles of his face. "You had the conviction to do what was necessary to survive. The courage to save us both. Just like I protected you, you protected *me*. You saved my life at incredible risk to your own. Twice."

"You did the same for me." The ember of hope flared, its golden heat dissipating the bone-deep chill as she stared into Aidan's eyes. She'd been viewing herself in a dirty, abandoned funhouse mirror, her image ugly and warped by the vile words and ruthless deeds of a killer. Aidan had wiped away the filth and turned the mirror upside down. She saw her true reflection in his clear gaze, undistorted by lies. "Also twice. In the woods…" Again on the verge of tears, of relief this time, she took another swallow of wine. "And just now."

He closed his eyes. When he opened them, the lingering shadows had fled. "Thank God. I was afraid…" His lips compressed in a hard line. "I was worried that I might not be able to bring you back from the brink." His tautness eased, and he smiled. "Don't ever doubt yourself. You're intelligent, strong and brave." His voice deepened with emotion. "You're like your mom all the way, Zoe. It took strong moral conviction and major guts to leave a man like DiMarco. And extreme intelligence to stay one step ahead of him."

She couldn't stop a few tears from escaping. "That's the greatest compliment I could ever receive."

"I didn't mean to restart the waterworks." He brushed away the wetness with his thumb. "Speaking of brave women, Dorothy came through for us after all. Inspired by your segment on battered women and your encouragement in the warehouse, she called nine-one-one after DiMarco killed Kent. Your integrity and dedication to the truth brought the cavalry to our rescue, Brenda Starr."

"Go, Dorothy." Zoe's throat tightened with gratitude at Aidan's continued faith in her, and she stared at the glittering trails of rain on the windowpanes until she regained control. "Thank you for not giving up on me. For coming after me."

"I figured you'd be okay with my brothers until I could reach you." He fed her a bite of cheese on bread. "I was really torqued at myself when Grady finally found me to deliver your message, and I discovered you'd left on a patrol boat."

"I left to protect you."

"From what, sweetheart?"

"From me."

He swore softly. "Liam said you were suffering battle shock, but seemed okay otherwise, and that Grady had you under his wing. If I'd realized what was going on in your head, nothing short of Armageddon would have kept me away."

"I thought you were avoiding me. Not that I blamed you."

He gritted his teeth, clearly frustrated. "I'm sorry I wasn't able to reach you right after the takedown. I knew Con would assign Liam or Grady to take care of you. Debriefing took longer than I wanted, but I couldn't afford to omit any details and take a chance DiMarco or his crew will walk on a technicality." He stroked her hair. "Because we're both material witnesses, I couldn't be present when you gave your statement. And after DiMarco tried to rabbit, I made damn sure he was securely in the Feds' custody before I left to find you."

"I…I thought for sure you were going to kill him with the syringe."

"That was gut-check time. I came too damn close." He exhaled fiercely. "But sticking that needle into him would have been revenge for my father under the pretense of 'saving' you. *DiMarco* kills helpless people…the weak, the unarmed, someone who is tied up." His hands balled into fists. "If I'd killed him, I would have lowered myself to his level, and I couldn't stand that."

His voice hoarse with raw emotion, he jerked his wineglass to his lips. "Ultimately, you would have suffered. My family would have suffered. And so would I." Calmer, he set the glass on the tabletop. "I'm not a killer. I'm a cop."

She touched his face, and the harsh lines of strain softened under her fingertips. "I'm so glad you didn't. The momentary, fleeting satisfaction of revenge wouldn't have justified the nightmares."

He offered her a succulent strawberry, dripping with aromatic wine. "Do you hear what you're saying, sweetheart? Though you have every reason to wish him dead, to want him permanently out of your life, you didn't want me to kill him."

Zoe's spirit lifted, her hopes revived. Aidan had forced her to see the truth. She was truly nothing like the monster who had haunted her childhood nightmares. Her fears scuttled away like cockroaches exposed to the light. All except for one lingering doubt. It was a biggie, and she needed time to prepare before asking. "*He* would have relished the 'satisfaction,' and it wouldn't have cost him a moment's sleep."

"There you go." He feathered a hand through her curls and rubbed the back of her neck, and she relaxed into the sensual massage. "The fact that it gives *us* nightmares is the difference between him and us. You would take a life if you *had* to. To truly protect your loved ones. So will I. DiMarco kills for power, money and because it gives him perverted pleasure."

Soothed by his quiet understanding, she nodded. "He'll suffer more in prison, anyway. He's lost his power, his precious money and what he perceived as people's respect. It will eat away at him every minute of every day."

"He made the choice, sweetheart." His fingertips traced the shell of her ear, and she shivered. "His moral compass veered off true north a long time ago, and he followed it into hell."

Loath to voice the doubt still tormenting her, she closed her eyes. "It's scary how drastically your life can change in just twenty-four hours. Yesterday morning, all I cared about was nailing the story and putting him away." Gathering her courage in both hands, she opened her eyes. "Today, I'm…I can't help but worry that whenever you look at me, you'll remember grief." She took a deep breath. "That whenever you see my face, you'll always be reminded of the man who murdered your father."

He brushed her lips with a cool, moist cube of watermelon, and then fed it to her. "Letty's quite the gardener. We used to help her plant, weed and water when we were kids, and her fruits and vegetables were always on our table." He fed her another delicious bite. "Did you know it takes a hundred sunny days to grow a watermelon? Without enough sun, their growth is stunted and they stay green and sour. Never mature. They end up on the compost heap, as useless as those piles of trash at the city landfill."

She blinked, puzzled. What on earth was he trying to tell her? "Um…all righty then."

He smiled at her bewildered expression. "Every time I look at you, I will remember that until I met you, I felt only murky shadows of emotions. Whenever I see your face, I will be reminded that my heart was cold and dead until you brought it back to life. You don't have any of DiMarco's darkness inside you, sweetheart. Your light conquered my shadows. Your love conquered my sorrow." He bent and tenderly touched his lips to hers. "No matter how long and dark the night, the sun always triumphs in the morning," he breathed. "I've been alone in the dark so long. Stunted. Useless. You're my sunshine, Zoe."

Joy soared on bright, shiny wings. She was struck speechless, but any reply she might have made drowned in a tsunami of tears.

"Hey, now! Crying?" He tapped the tip of her nose. "There's no crying in baseball," he teased her with the movie quote.

She giggled through her tears. "Happy tears this time."

"Yeah, I got that." He grinned. "You know what, Zoe? If we can let go of our hatred for DiMarco and be happy together—cast him out of our lives for good—that will be the sweetest revenge of all. He killed my dad, and he'll pay for it. But nothing he can do could ever kill my love for you."

And he hadn't killed her future, after all. She couldn't breathe. Could barely speak. "C-could you maybe just s-say that one more time? For the record?"

"This just in. Breaking news…" Aidan kissed her again, lingering over her mouth. She tasted juicy watermelon and warm, heady man. "I love you, Zoe. With all my heart. All my soul. Forever and always."

The glow spread, filled her from head to toe and spilled over. "I love you, too, Aidan. More than life itself."

His grin turned white and wicked, and the delighted sound of his deep laughter cruised along her skin. "Then I'm the luckiest man on the planet." He selected a chicken wing, stripped tender meat from the bones and fed her the spicy bite with his fingers. Holding her gaze, he licked the sauce from each of his fingertips slowly, thoroughly, savoring every drop.

She suddenly realized what he'd been doing with the food and wine, and tendrils of warmth unfurled inside her. "Are you seducing me, SWAT?"

He dipped a fingertip in his wine and moistened her bottom lip. "Damn, I hope so." His low, fervent murmur sent a giddy, swooping sensation through her.

She nipped his fingertip, then drew it into her mouth. He sucked in his breath, and she grinned. "It is *so* working."

He captured her mouth and kissed her. All her needs, wants and hopes poured from her into him. His soft, tender kiss restored her with absolution. Enticed her with anticipation. Then he took the kiss deeper and filled her with sweet promise.

Breaths ragged, they eased apart. She stared into his warm caramel eyes, and smiled. "And I thought I didn't have an appetite."

He held up a cube of bright green melon. "Honeydew?" Instead of feeding it to her, he trailed the cool morsel over her lips, down her chin, her throat, to the ruffled neckline of her blouse. He popped the fruit in his mouth and then followed the path he'd created on her skin with his hot, silky tongue.

Her nerve endings tingling with pleasure, she tipped her head back, and his lips cruised the sensitive spot where her neck joined her shoulder. "Honeydew that again."

He chuckled, and his warm breath feathered over her damp skin. "Anything you want. Everything you ever dreamed. And this time, we're gonna take it nice and slow."

She shivered as he eased down the loose elastic neckline of her peasant blouse and tasted her shoulder. "Mmm," she purred. "SWAT...slow, wanton and talented."

His gorgeous mouth curved into a grin a breath away from the swell of her left breast, and her nipples pebbled beneath the turquoise lace of her bra. "Do the wheels in your brain ever stop turning?"

"Once." She smiled at him. "And that was your fault."

"Soon to be twice." He drew her blouse over her head and tossed it aside. "Or a half dozen." He wiggled his eyebrows at her. "All of which will be my fault."

She started to giggle, but caught a glimpse of the predatory male glint in his eyes. Her heart stuttered. "You're serious!"

He nuzzled her ear. "Baby, let me show you just how serious I am."

Chapter 18

Since she was sitting on his lap, Zoe had a pretty darn good idea of how serious Aidan was. "You know what we need?" She walked her fingers up the placket of his shirt and opened it, button by button. She'd reported from enough SWAT team incident sites to pick up the jargon. "An eyes-on assessment."

His sexy laugh rumbled. He kneaded her bottom through the gauzy fabric of her skirt. "Good plan."

She slid his shirt over his broad shoulders and off his arms. His sculpted chest and ridged abs were more intoxicating than the wine. She skated her fingertips through the fine mat of crisp, dark hair, and his heart jumped under her palms. "Do you recommend a dynamic entry, officer?"

Carnal chuckles spilled out of him. "Definitely." He eased her down to the plush carpet in front of the fire, his hard, hot body on top of hers.

She rolled her hips, reveling in the amazing feeling of his blatant arousal rubbing against her. "You're packing heat, SWAT."

"Locked and loaded." He groaned and took her mouth in another breath-stealing kiss.

She tunneled her fingers into his thick, wavy hair and urged him closer. He kissed like a fallen angel. All dark passion and fiery sin, with the sweet taste of heaven on his tongue.

He pulled back, breaking the kiss, and shook his head. "Hold that thought."

"You're not getting all noble and backing off *now,* are you?" She scowled. "Don't make me get out the handcuffs, SWAT."

His chest shook in amusement. "I'm not that noble." His wicked grin flashed. "Though the cuffs idea has merit." He shoved to his feet. "We need protection."

"Ah. Right." Her cop would always protect her, in every way. Just one of the many things she loved about him. Propped on her elbows, she looked up at him. "Please make me the happiest woman on the planet and tell me you have some on the premises."

"An Eagle Scout is always prepared." He strode toward the hallway.

She watched him walk away, the powerful muscles in his back rippling with his graceful predator's stride, his taut, perfect backside hugged by snug denim. Desire streamed through her in a potent flood of liquid flame. "Hey, SWAT?"

He half turned. "Yeah?"

"Bring the whole box."

He tossed back his head, and laughter exploded out of him. "I love a woman with ambition."

"Oh, baby, do I have plans for you."

His lightning movements during the firefight paled in comparison to how quickly he completed his errand. True to her request, he brought the entire box.

"I love a man who takes direction well."

He knelt at her side, his body caressed by golden firelight. "Your wish is my command, sweetheart."

She rose to her knees, facing him. "Will you take off your jeans?"

"This will be rather difficult if I don't." His lips quirked in a naughty smile, and he indicated the snap at his waistband. "I'm all yours."

This had to be a dream. A wonderful, lovely fantasy that would disappear when she awoke, heartbroken and alone in her empty apartment. Her hands shook as she unsnapped his jeans, and she fumbled with the zipper covering the mind-boggling bulge beneath her fingers.

"Don't be nervous." Aidan's big, warm hands covered hers, and helped her ease down the zipper. "I'll be careful. I won't hurt you."

"I know you won't. I'm not nervous. I'm overwhelmed." She gulped as he stood and skimmed the denim down his powerful thighs, stepped out of his pants. "I can't believe this is actually happening. I've waited all my life for you."

Wearing only black briefs, he tugged her to her feet. "And I for you." He slipped his hands inside the elastic waist of her skirt, eased it over her hips and off.

She stood before him in her turquoise bra and matching bikini. His smoldering gaze roamed a meandering path down her body and snagged on the small silver ring in her navel. A sensual grin flirted with his mouth. "Big gambler, are you?"

She glanced at the two tiny pink dice on the ring and grinned back at him. "Lady Luck hasn't deserted me yet."

His fingers tunneled into her hair, and he drew her close. "I know this is my lucky day." He bent his head and kissed her.

Embraced in his heat, immersed in his clean, masculine scent, she swayed, sighed. She nestled into him and let him take her under. He whispered her name against her lips, then again feasted on her. The fervor and fire she'd felt from him in the cave raged beneath the surface, but remained leashed under his tight control. His lips were soft and patient. His hands tender. Savoring what before he'd devoured. Lingering where before he'd sped. Creating a slow, erotic swell of pleasure.

His fingertips traced the turquoise lace covering her breasts, and her nipples tightened to hard, aching peaks. "Very pretty." He released the catch and deftly removed her bra, and his eyes darkened in appreciation. "Even prettier."

He drew her down to the rug to sit beside him. One strong arm supported her back. Talking, laughing they fed each other. She conducted an intriguing exploration, learning what touches made his breath catch, which kisses made his eyes darken in arousal. His hands skimmed her body lightly, reverently, both soothing and inciting. He teased and tantalized, a leisurely seduction of body and mind.

The food contented her, the wine relaxed her and Aidan's lingering kisses and butterfly strokes simmered in her blood. He served a heady cocktail of comfort and desire, and her thirsty spirit drank every drop. He offered unconditional love and her hungry soul devoured its fill. His need, his desire for her humbled her. Awed her. She didn't have to earn his love. Or deserve it. It was hers for the asking.

Aidan reached over to the coffee table, dipped a strawberry in wine and offered her a bite. As she savored the succulent fruit, his gaze locked on hers, and he slipped the other half of the berry between his full lips. The sensual burn in his eyes glittered over her skin. "Mmm. Sweet." The fine roughness of his cheek gently rasped hers as he leaned close. His whisper was a brush of velvet against her ear. "But not as sweet as every inch of your body will taste."

The simmer in her blood erupted into an inferno, and her pulse leapt. He didn't even have to touch her. He could seduce her with his husky voice, his sultry words alone.

He eased her down to the carpet. Rain pattered on the windows, sparkled like diamonds on the panes. The fire snapped, and red and gold light danced on the walls. Aidan brushed a tousled curl off her forehead. "Starting right…" He bent and pressed a tender kiss to her brow. "Here."

He kissed her eyelids. Her cheeks. The tip of her nose. He loitered over her ears and neck until she was flushed and trembling before moving to her breasts. His moist breath tingled over her nipple. A shivery scrape of teeth. A silky swipe of tongue, then the long, lovely pull. Lava streamed along her nerve endings, a delicious flutter in her belly curled her toes. Her Dark Champion was thorough and dedicated in his quest, and she purred with pleasure.

His lips curved in a smile against her sensitized skin. "That little purr makes me crazy for you, sweetheart."

"Everything you do makes me crazy for you, Aidan."

He rose up to look at her and arched a brow. "Maybe later, you'll beg for mercy."

She glided her fingertips over his sculpted pecs and smiled when his flat nipples hardened and his muscles jumped under her touch. "Or maybe you will. Master."

His grin was lopsided. "Looking forward to it." His talented mouth roved to her navel. His tongue toyed with her belly ring as he removed her panties, and her smile dissolved in a moan. He kissed a sensual path down her thigh. A lazy detour to the back of her knee sent shock waves of electric need through her system. Her right instep and each toe received lavish attention before he moved to the left foot and forged the trail of delight in reverse. "Oh, SWAT," she panted. "You are definitely a detail man."

He parted her legs and settled between them. "Every sweet inch, baby." Then his mouth took her in the most intimate kiss. Her body jerked in shock, in response. She quivered under the gentle, erotic caress of teeth, the sensual glide of tongue.

Seeking an anchor, her hands found Aidan's hair, clung as his finger slid inside her, stroking slow and deep. Intimately connected, there were no longer any secrets between them, no lies. She was fully open to him. Trusted him with her body. With her heart. She gave herself over to the sweet bliss and let him spin her up the long, slow climb.

Thousands of bright pinpoints of pleasure awoke under his seeking mouth and clever hands. Need thrummed in her blood, her pulse pounded in her ears. Her body arched taut, poised and quivering on the mountaintop. Then Aidan slid a second finger inside her and sent her flying.

He drew out the shining pleasure until her muscles went limp, and her breaths came in ragged gasps. Instead of abating, need began to build again.

Gradually, he took her back up. But her body knew him now, craved what only he could give, and demanded more. When he again had her quaking on the edge, he crawled up her vibrating body, his expression an arousing mix of fierce tenderness and untamed hunger. He cupped her face in his hands, and his dark eyes smoldered with promise.

She hadn't been aware of him removing his briefs, but he was naked, warm and solid on top of her. She instinctively drew up her knees, cradling him, and his thick heat pressed gently into her. She stared into his eyes in wonder as slowly, patiently, he filled her body. Filled her heart and her soul. Filled the aching, lonely emptiness with himself.

Holding her gaze, he kept his weight on his elbows and went still. "Okay?"

No longer fearing the past, no longer dreading the future, for the first time in her life, she was safe. "Better than okay." She would never be alone again. Shaking with awe, she slid her arms around his neck, and swallowed the lump in her throat. "Now I'm whole. Finally complete."

"Zoe." Her name was a fervent prayer. "Damn, you're gonna make me tear up again." He gave her a crooked smile. "Twice in one day would unman me."

Her heart stuttered. "That tender side of you touches me to the core." He tilted his hips, and she moaned at the exquisite sensation of fullness. "And for the record, there's no doubt whatsoever about your manhood, SWAT."

His grin snagged on a sharp inhale. "I love you, Zoe Zagretti."

She feathered a kiss over his gorgeous mouth. "I love you, too."

He rocked in a leisurely rhythm, and heat curled through her in sweet ribbons of pleasure. His thumbs caressed her cheeks, traced her bottom lip. "I saved your life. That means you belong to me, now."

Her breath caught. "I saved your life, too. So you belong to me."

"Yes." He kissed her as if he could spend the rest of his life doing nothing else, and she drowned in the rush of love that streamed through her.

He glided above her in long, lush strokes and she rose to meet him. He touched her, watched her with fierce longing, as if she were his most precious treasure, and he could never get enough. The possessive, masculine intensity in his eyes made her heart turn over.

Heartbeat thundered against heartbeat, warm skin sliding over warm skin. Breathy moans floated in air gone moist and hazy.

Locked in the primal rhythm that grew in urgency and intensity, she surrounded him, he possessed her.

And shimmering over it all in a shiny silver cloud was the feeling of belonging.

This time when she hovered on the mountaintop, her arms outstretched to the sun, Aidan hovered there with her.

Emotion stormed in his eyes. "You're mine, Zoe," he growled fiercely against her mouth. "Forever."

"Forever," she whispered, and soared off the edge of the world with him.

Joy. Her heart danced with it. Her soul shone with it. Fiery hot and exquisitely bright, her body sang with it. Liquid lightning pulsed and exploded in her veins. It was a shared moment of completion that transcended the merely physical.

Above her, Aidan shuddered, shouted her name, and she sank into the warm waves of pleasure.

Aidan jerked awake with a start, Zoe's name on his lips. He hadn't awakened from a nightmare this time, but a beautiful dream. He glanced over at Zoe, dozing beside him in his bed. Her pale, creamy skin was luminous against his navy sheets, her sleeping smile a sunbeam.

No, not a dream. Awesome reality.

Their lovemaking in front of the fire had been followed by dessert. Brenda Starr could now write an editorial on a hundred and one creative uses for buttercream frosting. He grinned. None of which would be featured in his mother's home living magazines. *Dessert* had necessitated a shower, which had become a steamy interlude with his shower gel and massaging showerhead. His grin widened at the sight of the half-empty box on his nightstand. His initial assessment had hit dead-center. Life with Zoe would never be dull.

Careful not to disturb her, he eased out of bed and cat-footed to the living room. He stared out at the rainy afternoon, remembering DiMarco's vicious attack on the woman he loved. His jaw clenched. His nightmare had come crashing back on him during those horrifying moments. He hadn't been able to protect her...but

she hadn't died, after all. Thank God, Zoe had had the guts and for-
titude to rebound from DiMarco's cruel blow to the heart. He rolled
his shoulders, and his tension dissolved. His girl was a survivor.

He picked up the depleted platter of leftovers and grimaced in
realization. He'd underestimated every woman around him. Letty,
Mom, Bailey and Zoe had all stood up to circumstances and events
that might have crushed lesser people…and come out swinging.
They had prevailed over life's hardships with their spirits intact.
O'Rourke women weren't weak, helpless females to be coddled
and protected. They stood side-by-side with their men and fought
the good fight. Zoe would be okay, no matter what life threw at
the pair of them.

Hell, she'd probably haul his butt out of the fire more than once.

He dumped the platter's contents and set it in the sink. He *was*
the luckiest man on the planet. Zoe had given him contentment
he'd never thought he could have. She had made him experience
emotions he'd never thought he could feel. Before Zoe, sex had
merely satisfied a physical need. Making love to her had been more
intense, more heart-shaking, more amazing than he'd ever imagined. Their physical bond had tied him to her, body and soul.
Whatever DNA she'd inherited didn't matter—their life together
would be what they made of it. His girl was funny, mischievous,
irreverent, warm-hearted and generous to a fault.

Zoe was his heart. His light. His life.

Aidan headed for the phone. He would never forget what it was
like to live without love. Would always be grateful for her. After
years of sleepwalking through a cold, barren existence like a
damned zombie, her dauntless resolution and unconquerable optimism had yanked him kicking and screaming back into the land
of the living. He owed her a debt he could never repay.

But he was willing to spend the rest of his life trying. He picked
up the receiver and dialed.

Starting right now.

Floating in a warm bubble of contentment, Zoe stretched lan-
guid limbs and let her eyelids drift open. She turned her head, and
her heart stuttered. Aidan was gone. But on his pillow beside her

rested a sock monkey. A small tag dangled from a red bow around its neck. With trembling hands, she reached over and cradled the toy. Aidan's bold scrawl on the tag read George II. Tears brimmed in her eyes at his sweet thoughtfulness.

She sat up, but before she could climb out of bed, the door swung open. Aidan slipped inside, carrying a tray and wearing only jeans unbuttoned at the waist. "I thought I heard you stirring in here." He crossed to the bed, and set the tray on the foot. His eyes glowed with warm regard. "How you doing, sweetheart?"

"Mmm. Wonderful. You?"

"Pretty damn fine." He wiggled his eyebrows at her. "Although, I think I sprained something I might need later in life."

She held up the monkey, her throat tight. "Thank you. Where did you find it?"

"You're welcome. Letty knows someone who makes them." He cocked his head. "Hungry?"

Zoe gazed longingly at his hard-muscled body clad only in snug denim. She now knew the unbelievable stamina that body possessed, and the staggering pleasure it could give her. She flashed him a suggestive grin. "Starving."

Sensual fire smoldered in his gaze, but he shook his head. "Sustenance first." He glanced at the stuffed animal. "Cover your ears, George." She propped the monkey on the pillow and covered his little sock ears, and Aidan's lusty laugh tumbled out. "Wild monkey sex afterward." He swung the tray around and rested it on her knees. "Room service, milady. Appropriate for the occasion."

She giggled at the Cracker Jack and bottled water. "From now on, this will be our special celebration meal."

"You got it." The mattress dipped beneath his weight as he settled in beside her. "Liam called while you were asleep. He has a buddy in the FBI. They extracted enough evidence off those hard drives you found to convict DiMarco on racketeering charges. Combined with the confession you finessed from him for Pop's murder, Tony will die in prison a very old man."

"Good. I'm so relieved that he'll finally pay for his crimes."

Cocooned in the cozy intimacy known only to sated lovers, they shared conversation and laughter, sipped from the same water bottle and fed each other candied peanuts and popcorn.

When the Cracker Jack was nearly gone, Zoe scooped the tiny envelope from the bottom of the box. "Sometimes you get the same prize twice." She tore open the paper. "I wonder if I'll get another monk—"

She stared, stunned by the heavy ring that fell into her palm. "How did you do…?" Made of white gold, the band formed a pair of hands supporting a heart. An emerald gleamed green fire in the heart's center, and an intricate crown sat atop the heart. She gulped. "Oh, my gosh! This is real!"

"It is." Aidan dropped to one knee beside the bed. "As real as my love for you." He clasped her free hand. "I want to spend the rest of my life with you. Have children with you. Grow old with you. Zoe, will you marry me?"

Astonished and dismayed, she bit her lip. "I don't know what to say."

"*Yes* works for me."

Dark doubt beat against the edges of her happiness. "What about…your family? You were able to get past the fact that DiMarco is my father, but—" She swallowed, tasted bitter despair. "I can't answer until I'm sure I won't cause a rift between you and your family, Aidan."

He frowned. "Honey, my brothers were fully informed at the incident site. When I found out you'd left, they threatened to collectively kick my keister six ways to sundown if I didn't go after you." He rose and sat on the bed beside her. "Not that there was ever any doubt. I would have followed you to the ends of the earth." He stroked a fingertip down her nose. "Liam and Grady helped track you down, remember? Con wasn't there only because he bolted for his honeymoon before the ink on the paperwork dried."

She clutched the ring so hard the edges cut into her palm. "But how will your mother feel? DiMarco hurt her worst of all."

"The ring was in safekeeping at her house for…a while. Who do you think rushed it—and the sock monkey—over while you were asleep, in response to my phone call? And in record time, I might add. I'll bet she broke fourteen speeding regulations." He handed Zoe a folded sheet of lavender, violet-scented stationary. "She also brought this."

Her hands shook so badly she could hardly unfold the note. "My Dear Zoe," she read.

I'm sorry for the trauma you've suffered at Tony DiMarco's hands. Please don't worry that anyone will think badly of you because of his actions. You gave my son back his smile. If nothing else, I could love you for that.

Zoe's eyes misted, and she blinked the blurry words into focus.

I've heard the entire story. Because of your courage, Aidan is alive today. And I will finally be able to lay my husband to rest. You shine with both truth and beauty, Zoe. I've always wanted daughters, and now I'm delighted to have two. I'll talk to you in a few days, Maureen.

Tears rushed out in a hot river of relief. "You and your mom think alike."

"In the most important ways, yeah." He wiped her damp cheeks with gentle fingers. "She'd be the last person to hold what DiMarco did against you. Sheesh, Con and Bailey just tied the knot and Mom and Letty are already salivating over *our* wedding plans." He held her gaze, and she saw the vulnerability shadowing his eyes. "That is, if you accept my proposal."

Black despair fled in the brilliant shine of happiness. She flung her arms around him. *"I do! I will! I accept!"*

The apprehension warmed out of his eyes. His joyous laugh cascaded over her, and he hugged her tight. "Whew! You had me worried."

She drew back and studied the ring. "This is so uniquely beautiful. I've never seen anything like it."

"It's a Claddagh ring, Irish in design. There's a story."

She bounced on the bed. "Ooh! Tell!"

"How did I know you'd love the fact that there's a story behind it?" He grinned. "In the seventeenth century, an Irishman named Richard Joyce left Claddagh, a small fishing village in Galway, on a ship en route to the West Indies. He was supposed to return and be married, but his ship was captured by Algerian pirates and the crew were sold as slaves."

"Oh, how awful! What happened to him?"

"He was sold to a Moorish goldsmith who trained him in his craft. He became a master in his trade and hand-crafted a special ring for the woman at home he couldn't forget. Years later, King William III bartered for the release of his captive subjects. The Moorish goldsmith offered Richard his only daughter in marriage and half his wealth if he would stay. He declined and returned to Claddagh to find the woman who owned his heart."

Zoe held her breath. "Please don't tell me she had married someone else while he was gone?"

He chuckled. "No. She had waited for him all those years, hoping he would some day return to her. He gave her the ring and they were married. He set up a goldsmith shop in the town of Claddagh, where I presume, they lived happily ever after."

She sighed. "That is the most romantic story."

"The ring symbolizes a trinity." He extended his hand. She placed the ring on his palm and he pointed to the elements. "The hands signify friendship, the crown is for loyalty and the heart for love." His face was earnest, his gaze intense. "This particular ring is an O'Rourke family heirloom. It's over two hundred years old, and is always bequeathed to the eldest grandson. My family…I…would be honored if you'd wear it."

Zoe studied the ring sparkling on Aidan's palm, and then looked up at the love gleaming in his eyes. Her breath caught. She had always been alone. Never had anyone. Yet, now she shared in a noble heritage. She belonged to a family who extended back generations. She belonged to Aidan. Happiness overflowed, spilled out of her heart. Someday, she would give the ring to her and Aidan's grandson.

Aidan. Her own special miracle.

"May I?" He offered the ring, and her left hand trembled as she held it out to him. He slipped the Claddagh over her fingertip. "

pledge you my friendship. My loyalty. And my love." He gave her a tender kiss and slid the ring down her finger. "Forever."

The heirloom was warm and solid on her hand. It fit as if it had been made for her. Indeed, maybe it had.

Aidan wrapped his arms around her and took her down to the bed. His tender smile embraced her in the shelter of his love. "Welcome home, Zoe."

* * * * *

RAMIREZ'S WOMAN by Beverly Barton

The Protectors

Mocorito's presidential candidate Miguel Ramirez wanted a female bodyguard to pose as his fiancée and Dundee agent JJ Blair steps in. Though neither one of them welcomed their instant attraction, they both seemed helpless to resist. With political threats placing their lives on the line, would they be strong enough to risk their hearts too?

STOLEN MEMORY by Virginia Kantra

Trouble in Eden

Reclusive millionaire inventor Simon Ford woke up on the floor of his lab with a case of amnesia, a missing fortune in rubies and a lot of questions. Could he trust by-the-book cop Laura Baker to pose as his girlfriend and help him solve the mystery? Even when her father becomes their number one suspect...?

WARRIOR WITHOUT A CAUSE
by Nancy Gideon

Aloof mercenary trainer Jack Chaney was the last person straight-arrow legal assistant Tessa D'Angelo would turn to for help...that is if her life wasn't in danger. She knew her father was innocent of the crimes he'd been accused of, but if she wanted to live long enough to clear his name, she would need to put herself in Jack's hands.

On sale from 17th March 2006

*Available at WHSmith, Tesco, ASDA, Borders, Eason,
Sainsbury's and most bookshops*

www.silhouette.co.uk

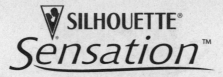

SILHOUETTE®
Sensation™

GET BLONDIE by Carla Cassidy

Bombshell

Blonde or not, Cassandra Newton is one gutsy cop. So when a top secret crime-fighting organisation wants to take down a drug lord with a weakness for leggy blonde dancers, Cassandra is the obvious choice for the case. And naturally, they send her former partner and love to persuade her.

DANGER CALLS by Caridad Piñeiro

The Calling

Ever since Melissa Danvers became a vampire's personal physician, she'd had no time for a normal life, much less love. But when her experiments promised the key to eternal life, she knew her enemies would stop at nothing to steal her knowledge. Only the expertise of former lover Sebastian Reyes can keep her safe now...

CHECKMATE by Doranna Durgin

Bombshell: An Athena Force Adventure

Her marriage on the rocks, FBI legal attaché Serena Jones took refuge in an assignment to a foreign land only to be caught when rebels took over the capitol. Trapped in the building but free to move inside, Serena tries to lay a trap for the rebel leader using the weapons at hand – her dying cell phone, her wits and an unexpected ally, her estranged husband...

On sale from 17th March 2006

Available at WHSmith, Tesco, ASDA, Borders, Eason, Sainsbury's and most bookshops

www.silhouette.co.uk

▼ SILHOUETTE®
INTRIGUE™

PARTNER-PROTECTOR by Julie Miller

The Precinct

Detective T Merle Banning prided himself on concluding his investigations based on hard evidence. So he was incensed when he had to team up with the department psychic on an unsolved serial killer case. But when Kelsey Ryan's unsettling visions turned out to be true, he couldn't discount the truth—or his fierce desire to watch over her 24/7.

BEHIND THE SHIELD by Sheryl Lynn

Cowboy Cops

Police chief Carson Cody wasn't happy that artist Madeline Shay was in town. She was a reminder of all that he had lost, but he found it impossible to turn away when her life was threatened. Madeline hoped Carson felt more than just obligation, but was their smouldering passion powerful enough to heal his painful wounds?

STRAIGHT SILVER by Darlene Scalera

Lipstick Ltd.

Silver LeGrande had plenty of street smarts. So when three of her friends turned up dead, she decided to use all her skills to find the killer. She teamed up with cop Alexi Serras, who saw through her tough-girl façade. Silver knew Alexi would help her find the murderer, but could she trust him with her heart?

SUDDEN RECALL by Jean Barrett

Dead Bolt

PI Eden Hawke may have just been given the hardest case of her life—pretending to be the wife of an amnesiac man who thought they were married. She'd put herself in this charismatic stranger's life to find out why he carried a picture of her missing son. But soon, playing pretend may have more consequences than Eden expected…

On sale from 17th March 2006

www.silhouette.co.uk

FREE!

4 Books
and a surprise gift!

We would like to take this opportunity to thank you for reading this Silhouette® book by offering you the chance to take FOUR more specially selected titles from the Sensation™ series absolutely FREE! We're also making this offer to introduce you to the benefits of the Reader Service™—

- ★ **FREE home delivery**
- ★ **FREE gifts and competitions**
- ★ **FREE monthly Newsletter**
- ★ **Exclusive Reader Service offers**
- ★ **Books available before they're in the shops**

Accepting these FREE books and gift places you under no obligation to buy. you may cancel at any time. even after receiving your free shipment. Simply complete your details below and return the entire page to the address below. You don't even need a stamp!

YES! Please send me 4 free Sensation books and a surprise gift. I understand that unless you hear from me. I will receive 6 superb new titles every month for just £3.10 each. postage and packing free. I am under no obligation to purchase any books and may cancel my subscription at any time. The free books and gift will be mine to keep in any case.

S6ZEF

Ms/Mrs/Miss/Mr ....Initials ....

BLOCK CAPITALS PLEASE

Surname ....

Address ....

....

....Postcode ....

Send this whole page to:
UK: FREEPOST CN81, Croydon, CR9 3WZ

Offer valid in UK only and is not available to current Reader service subscribers to this series. Overseas and Eire please write for details. We reserve the right to refuse an application and applicants must be aged 18 years or over. Only one application per household. Terms and prices subject to change without notice. Offer expires 30th June 2006. As a result of this application. you may receive offers from Harlequin Mills & Boon and other carefully selected companies. If you would prefer not to share in this opportunity please write to The Data Manager, PO Box 676, Richmond. TW9 1WU.

Silhouette® is a registered trademark owned and used under licence.
Sensation™ is being used as a trademark. The Reader Service™ is being used as a trademark.